Praise for Mary McNear
and her **BUTTERNUT LAKE** series!

"*Butternut Lake* is so beautifully rendered, you'll wish it was real. McNear takes the reader on an emotional journey with this story of second chances, starting over, and the healing power of love. A book to relax with, enjoy, and savor any time of year, but especially during the long, lazy days of summer."

—#1 *New York Times* Bestselling Author
Susan Wiggs

"A delicious setting and a heroine to cheer for, *Moonlight on Butternut Lake* is my favorite kind of book, one that treads that pleasurable line between romance and women's fiction. Enjoy!"

—*New York Times* Bestselling Author
Susan Elizabeth Phillips

"*The Space Between Sisters* explores the complex relationship between sisters, their differences, their mirrored history, their love and support of one another. This triumphant story had me reading until the wee hours of the morning."

—#1 *New York Times* Bestselling Author
Debbie Macomber

"*Up at Butternut Lake* is a great, emotional read for every woman who must face the past before moving forward."

—#1 *New York Times* Bestselling Author
Sherryl Woods

By Mary McNear

The LIGHT in SUMMER

A Butternut Lake Novel

MARY McNEAR

wm

WILLIAM MORROW

An Imprint of HarperCollinsPublishers

THE LIGHT IN SUMMER. Copyright © 2017 by Mary McNear. All rights reserved. Printed in the United States of America. No part of this book may be used or reproduced in any manner whatsoever without written permission except in the case of brief quotations embodied in critical articles and reviews. For information, address HarperCollins Publishers, 195 Broadway, New York, NY 10007.

First William Morrow mass market printing: July 2020
First William Morrow paperback printing: June 2017
First William Morrow hardcover printing: June 2017

Print Edition ISBN: 978-0-06-299341-0
Digital Edition ISBN: 978-0-06-239938-0

Cover design by Lex Maudlin
Cover photographs: © AZarubaika/Getty Images;
© Nicolas Russell/Getty Images (dog)

William Morrow and HarperCollins are registered trademarks of HarperCollins Publishers in the United States of America and other countries.

20 21 22 23 24   CWM   10 9 8 7 6 5 4 3 2 1

For Irving and Thelma Bialer,
with love and gratitude.

The LIGHT in SUMMER

CHAPTER 1

Mr. Finch?" Billy Harper said, placing a hand on his shoulder. "Mr. Finch? We're closing now." She shook him gently. Nothing. She sighed. "I can't wake him up," she said to Rae, who was standing at the public library's front windows and looking out onto Butternut's Main Street.

"Are you sure he's still . . . with us?" Rae asked over her shoulder.

"*Yes*," Billy said, scowling at her, though, in truth, she'd already checked to see if Mr. Finch's concave chest was rising and falling under his habitual cardigan sweater.

"Well, don't say I didn't warn you about those armchairs," Rae said. "They're too comfortable. Now people are just coming in here to sleep."

"Maybe," Billy murmured, lifting up the *Minneapolis Star Tribune* draped over the arm of an overstuffed chair and hanging it on a nearby rack. She didn't mind. The library's new furniture *was* comfortable—she'd seen to that herself. It was all part of her "library as your living room" campaign. And for the main reading room, she'd chosen a sofa and chairs that were deep and soft in an acorn-colored suede. If someone decided to take a nap in one of them, as Mr. Finch occasionally did, that was all right with her. Especially when it was so pleasant here now, with the late afternoon sunshine slanting in through the windows and burnishing the rows of books in a million jewel tones. She loved this library. It was small, but not too small. It had been built in 1929, and while on the outside it was a serviceable red brick, on the inside it had an old-world elegance that included high ceilings, large multipaned windows, and the original walnut paneling.

Mr. Finch stirred now, and Billy waited hopefully to see if he'd wake up. He didn't. She wished, just this once, he'd taken his nap a little earlier in the day. It was closing time now, and she had a sulky teenager to get home to. She left Mr. Finch and started to gather up the books and magazines that had been left on the long pine table running down the center of the library's reading room. One of the books, *Pride and Prejudice*, made Billy smile. She was always recommending this novel, though not everyone took her up on it.

"What are you looking at?" Billy asked, glancing over at Rae, who was still standing at the library's front windows.

"Officer Sawyer pulled someone over," Rae said, gesturing out onto Main Street.

"And this passes for entertainment now?" Billy chuckled, thinking that even Butternut, Minnesota, population 1,200, had more to offer than watching someone get a ticket.

"It does when the man getting the ticket is driving a Porsche 911 GT2 RS."

"Oh," Billy said, barely glancing at the windows as she turned off the green-shaded lamps on the reading table. Unlike Rae, she had no interest in cars, unless it was in her own 2005 Ford Focus, which was sitting in the shop right now, waiting to do more damage to her credit card.

"The guy driving the Porsche isn't bad either," Rae added. "Come take a look at him."

"No, thanks," Billy said, sliding some books onto the reshelving cart. "I've got to get home."

Rae appeared not to hear her. "I'd love to get a better look at that car," she said. "I wonder if this guy will be sticking around."

"A good-looking man driving an expensive car? I doubt it," Billy said, only half joking. "If he's in Butternut at all, it's only because his GPS malfunctioned."

"That's probably true," Rae said. She left the windows and started straightening up the checkout desk, and Billy went to shut down the computers. There were five of them available to the public, housed in a quiet corner behind the stacks.

"Why don't you go home," Rae said as Billy returned to the checkout area. "I can finish up here."

"But Mr. Finch . . ."

"I'll wake him up," Rae growled. "Just not as politely as you would have."

Billy, who really *did* need to get home, stopped and

lingered at the display she'd set up that morning, "In Celebration of Midwestern Authors: From Theodore Dreiser to Jonathan Franzen." Should she have chosen *My Ántonia* for Willa Cather? she wondered now, straightening this book a little. It was her best-known novel, of course, but Billy herself had always been partial to *O Pioneers!*

"You don't want to go home, do you?" Rae asked her. She'd sat herself down on a swivel chair and was extracting her enormous handbag from the checkout desk's bottom drawer. "You're stalling."

"No, I'm not," Billy said automatically.

"Yes, you are," Rae said shrewdly. "You'd sort paper clips by size now if you thought it would buy you another five minutes here."

"Not true," Billy said, going to gather up her own things.

"Honey," Rae said, "you can lie to yourself, but you can't lie to me."

"Oh, all right," Billy said, pulling another chair over to the checkout desk and sinking down onto it. She slipped off her flats—she'd been standing up most of the day—and wiggled her bare toes with pleasure, then tucked her feet underneath her. "I *don't* want to go home. I *can't* go home. You should see him, Rae," she said of her thirteen-year-old son, Luke. "When I checked up on him at lunchtime . . ." She shook her head.

"Why? What was he doing?"

"He wasn't *doing* anything. That's the point. He's lost all his privileges. The computer, the cell phone, the Xbox," Billy said, ticking off the terms of Luke's confinement on her fingers. "All of his favorite electronics have been either disabled or confiscated. So he was just . . . *sulking*." It wasn't the sulking she was worried about, though. That, she hoped, would pass. What worried her was something more amorphous, harder to pinpoint. She couldn't explain it to Rae. She couldn't even explain it to herself.

"Oh, *please*," Rae said. "Tell him enough with the sulking. What I don't understand is why they suspended him on the last day of school. I mean, what's the point? Everyone knows that day's a complete waste of time anyway." Billy started to answer, but Rae, indignant, was just getting started. "And another thing. Why are they still busting kids for smoking under the bleachers? They've been smoking under them since they put them up, and they'll be smoking under them when they tear them down." She smiled, a little wistfully. "Did I ever tell you that's where I had my first cigarette?"

"Nope," Billy said.

"Well, it was. I was right around Luke's age," she said, "but I remember it like it was yesterday. Those were good times," she added, practically glowing with the memory. "Good times."

Billy rolled her eyes. Rae's nostalgia was definitely misplaced, she thought, especially considering it had taken her twenty-five years to quit the smoking habit she'd acquired under those bleachers. Even today, Rae, who was in her midforties, had the gravelly voice of a heavy ex-smoker.

"What, you never smoked under the bleachers?" Rae asked.

"Definitely not," Billy said. "Not with a mom who was the vice principal at my high school."

"Oh, right. I forgot about that," Rae said. "Probably not worth the risk, then." And she laughed the deep, rumbling laugh that, unbeknownst to her, had gotten her the job of library assistant. During her interview with Billy three years ago, she'd laughed that laugh, and Billy had decided she liked listening to it. After all, it was like Rae herself: full-bodied and warm, with an almost contagious sense of fun. No, Rae didn't do anything halfway, and that included laughing, Billy thought affectionately. Her colorful appearance was another example. Her red hair came compliments of L'Oréal and ranged anywhere from Blowout Burgundy to Cherry Crush, depending on the time of year and her mood. Her plum eye shadow and pink lipstick, on the other hand, were perennial fixtures. And when it came to her wardrobe, she favored snug jeans and bright blouses that showed off a little cleavage.

"I'm willing to overlook Luke sneaking one cigarette," she said to Billy now, "but his attitude, that's another matter. The last time I saw him, he wouldn't even look at me, and he barely grunted when I spoke to him. What exactly is he so angry about?"

"He's a teenager," Billy said. "Does he really need an excuse to be angry?" But the truth, she knew, was more complicated than this.

"Oh, he can be angry," Rae grumbled, "as long as he keeps it to himself. If he'd grown up in my family, his attitude would have gotten some adjusting, I can tell you that right now. But, you know, I could ask Big Moe to have a talk with him," she added. Big Moe was Rae's boyfriend, and he came by his name honestly.

"No, thanks," Billy said. "I don't think that would go over too well with Luke."

"Maybe not. But in my family"—Rae was one of seven children—"one whipping from my dad, and us kids would think hard about copping an attitude. That's what they used to call discipline."

"Mmm," Billy said skeptically. "Now I'm pretty sure they call that assault."

Here Rae shrugged blithely, dismissing the whole subject. She wasn't done with Billy yet, though. "Honey," she said, "we both know Luke isn't your only problem right now."

"Do we?" Billy said casually, standing. She knew which topic was coming up now, and she fully intended to get herself out the library's front door before Rae got started on it.

"Hey, hey, hey, not so fast," Rae said as Billy slipped on her flats.

"I've got to get going," Billy said, edging away. "You know, juvenile delinquent son and all."

"Fine, I'll let you go. Just answer me one question."

Billy, almost at the door, held up her finger. "*One,*" she said.

"When was the last time you were with a man?" Rae asked.

"I'm with men *all* the time."

"I don't mean men Mr. Finch's age. I mean men of a pre-Viagra age."

"You know what, let's talk about this on Monday," Billy said, her hand on the doorknob.

"Oh no, I'm not letting you off that easily," Rae said,

waving her back over. "And since you won't answer my question, I'll answer it for you. It's been at least a year since you went on a date, and it was another year before that you were romantically involved with someone. By the way, being a single mom is *not* an excuse. I'm telling you, Billy, two years of celibacy at your age is not normal."

What is normal? Billy wanted to ask, coming back and leaning against the checkout desk, but Rae didn't give her time. "Here you are," she continued, "thirty-two years old, a woman in her sexual prime, who still turns heads wherever she goes . . . and what do you have to show for it? Nada. Nothing. Not a damn thing. Honestly, I'm fifteen years older than you, and I couldn't live the way you live. Big Moe and I can't go twenty-four hours without—"

"Stop, please," Billy said, holding up her hands. She knew from experience that she did not want to get Rae started on her and Moe's sex life. After all, Billy had been raised in a family in which people did not discuss sex in polite company. "Look, Rae. I get it. You're worried about me. You think I need to date more—"

"*Date?*" Rae hooted. "Honey, at this point I'd settle for you just *getting laid*. Really, haven't you ever heard of meaningless sex? Because in my opinion, it is *way, way* underrated."

"That may be, but where is this man I'm supposed to have all of this meaningless sex with, and when, exactly, would I find the time to have it? In a free minute between meeting with the guidance counselor about Luke and wrangling with the library board about next year's budget?" She would have continued had she not caught sight of something out of the corner of her eye. "Mr. Finch," she said, turning to him and flushing instantly. *How much had he heard?*

Mr. Finch, though, seemed unfazed.

"I'm sorry," he said. "I guess I drifted off. I hope I haven't kept you two here past closing."

"Not at all," Billy said, smiling. She liked Mr. Finch, and she knew, the way you knew everything about everyone when you live in a small town, that he was eighty-five, lived alone, and had never quite come to terms with his wife's death several years earlier. "Come on," Billy said, "I'll leave with you." She held her arm out to him, and he took it companionably.

"I'll finish up here," Rae called. "Say hi to Luke for me. And tell him that if he doesn't shape up—"

"I know, I know," Billy said as she was closing the door behind her and Mr. Finch. "You're sending Big Moe over."

CHAPTER 2

Everything took longer in Butternut, Cal Cooper reflected, glancing at the patrol car in his rearview mirror. Even getting a speeding ticket. He checked the dashboard clock of his Porsche 911. He was already fifteen minutes late meeting his sister, Allie, at their family's cabin on Butternut Lake. He reached for his cell phone and started to text her, then changed his mind and called her instead. He needed to hear her voice.

"Cal? Where are you?"

"In town. I'm getting ticketed, I think."

"For what?"

"For going thirty-five in a twenty-five-mile zone. Figures, right? I've sped through five states since I left Seattle, and it wasn't until I was on Main Street in Butternut that I got pulled over. It's the out-of-state plates, isn't it?" he asked.

"No, Cal. It's the car," Allie said. "Seriously, you're just *asking* for a ticket when you drive something that expensive."

"That's class warfare," he objected.

"Maybe. But if it is, your class is winning," Allie teased.

Cal smiled. He missed her. And the events of the last several weeks had only made him miss her more. "I'll be there soon," he said, though another glance in the rearview mirror told him that the policeman—Officer Sawyer, according to his name tag—was still checking his license and registration.

"I'll be waiting," Allie said.

Cal hung up. It would be good to get to the cabin, he thought, good to get out of this car. The last three days of his life were already a blur best summed up by numbers: nine cups of coffee, seventeen hundred miles of highway, twenty-seven hours of driving, and twenty-six of those hours spent trying *not* to think about why he'd left Seattle. He wouldn't think about it now, either. He'd concentrate instead on Butternut's Main Street, which on this June afternoon looked like a movie set of small-town America. Children with ice cream cones, a black Lab lazing on the sidewalk outside the hardware store, a woman pulling a little boy in a red wagon, some teenage girls clumped on a bench in front of Pearl's coffee shop, and an older couple stopping to look at a display in the window of the variety store. But Cal saw Butternut's charm without really feeling it. Feeling wasn't something he was that eager to do right now.

"Mr. Cooper?" Officer Sawyer said, appearing at his car window. He handed Cal his license, registration, and a $145 speeding ticket. "Are you just passing through Butternut?"

"No," Cal said. "I'll be here for a couple weeks, maybe more."

"Well, slow down, then," the officer said gruffly. "This is a small town."

I know, Cal thought. He'd spent the first eighteen summers of his life at his family's cabin on nearby Butternut Lake. But to Officer Sawyer he said, "I'll drive at the speed limit, Officer." And he would. After all, he'd sped halfway across the country, and he still hadn't outrun his life.

The rest of Cal's drive was uneventful. A half hour later, he and Allie were sitting on the front porch steps of the cabin their grandparents had built in the 1950s. The cabin itself was modest. The *view* from it was not. It overlooked Otter Bay, one of the largest bays on Butternut Lake, a twelve-mile-long spring-fed lake that was over a hundred feet deep in places and that, on a sunny day like today, was apt to be a dazzling blue. The water was made to seem even bluer, of course, by its contrast to the green of the pine, balsam, and spruce trees that bordered the lake, the granite boulders that dotted its shores, and the occasional crescents of golden beach etched into its sides. The term *pretty as a postcard* didn't apply here, Cal thought. He'd seen the postcards of Butternut Lake on sale at the drugstore in town. The real thing was prettier by far.

"Are you going to tell me what's going on?" Allie asked finally.

"What do you mean?" Cal said, turning to her.

"Well, for one thing, you look . . ."

"Like hell?" he suggested.

"I was going to say 'tired.'"

He shrugged. "I didn't have the best luck with mo-tels." He'd checked into the first one, outside Gold Creek, Montana, late at night. After he was asked to pay up front for his room—never a good sign—he'd discovered the door to it had already been kicked in. The surly management hadn't seemed overly con-cerned by this. Neither, for that matter, had the Hells Angels drinking in the motel's parking lot. Cal had a fitful night's sleep and left early the next morning. The second night of his drive, he'd found a motel outside Bismarck, North Dakota, that had seemed promising, but that was before he'd realized it was hosting the Dakota conference of Seventh-day Adventists. They'd been nice people, but after he'd found himself on the receiving end of their proselytizing, he'd again cut his stay short and gotten back on the road.

"Now that you're here, you'll sleep well," Allie said confidently. "I swear this air is like . . . breathable Am-bien or something. So I won't worry about your being tired. I'd be lying, though, if I said I wasn't worried about the other stuff."

"What other stuff?"

"You've been impossible to reach."

"I've been busy."

"You've *always* been busy, Cal. But you've *always* stayed in touch."

"I'm here now," he pointed out.

"And that's *another* thing. Since when do you come up here?"

"I can't take a vacation?" he chided her.

"You *can*. I just don't remember you ever taking one before."

He couldn't argue this point. He hadn't built a successful architectural firm by taking vacations. But Cal, who'd already found plenty of excuses to stall, found another one now. "Oh, I forgot," he said, turning to the suitcase he'd set down on the porch and unzipping one of its compartments. He took out a plastic bag from a souvenir shop he'd stopped at in Big Horn County, Montana. "I got some presents for the kids." He reached into the bag. "This is for Wyatt," he said, extracting a fur hat with side flaps. "It's coyote fur, apparently. Made in Canada, I noticed, but still, I think it's supposed to evoke the American Frontier." He handed the hat to Allie and reached back into the bag. "This is for Brooke. It's a bobcat tail keychain."

Allie chuckled. "Cal, she's *two*. She doesn't have any keys yet."

"Oh, right. Maybe I can get her a set, then. You know, just for show."

Allie smiled. "But *this*," she said, holding up the hat with its furry top and fluffy side flaps. "*This* could definitely come in handy in the depths of a northern Minnesota winter."

"Oh, God, it's hideous," Cal said, reaching for it. He wondered now what had possessed him to buy it for his nephew, Wyatt, when no self-respecting eleven-year-old would ever be caught dead in it. "I'll burn it later," he told Allie. "Or maybe I should just . . ." He pantomimed throwing it, Frisbee style, into the nearby woods.

"Are you kidding?" Allie said, taking it away from him. "Wyatt will love it. Anything from his cool uncle," she added, twirling it around on one finger. "And who knows? I may even wear it myself." She tried it on, and Cal had to smile. She was thirty-six, a mother of two, and the owner of a successful gallery in town, but she looked like a kid. Or at least a teenager, with her long honey-colored hair streaming out from under the hat and her complexion already sporting an early summer tan. She wore a uniform he remembered well from their family's summers at the lake: a faded T-shirt, cut-off blue jeans, and a pair of flip-flops.

"Do you ever get older?" Cal asked, tugging affectionately on one of the hat's earflaps. Allie brushed this question aside, though. She pulled the offending hat off and stuffed it back into the bag.

"Do you want some lemonade?" she asked. "I made a pitcher before you got here."

"I'd love some. Thank you," he said. As Allie went into the cabin, he was grateful for another reprieve from the conversation he knew they were going to have. He rubbed his bleary eyes. He felt jittery and weary at the same time. Too much coffee, too little sleep. How to talk about this thing, though? he wondered. How to talk about it when he still didn't even want to *think* about it? So he tried not to think about it and tried instead to take comfort in the familiarity of this place, the scent of sun-warmed pine needles, and the play of light on the water.

"This is my favorite time of day here," Allie said when she came back with two glasses of lemonade. She handed Cal one, and, sitting down again, sipped from the other one, looking thoughtful. "When was the last time you were here?" she asked.

"Ten years ago, maybe?" Cal said. "I brought Adam

and Danny and Josh"—friends from college—"up for some fishing."

"Some *fishing* or some *drinking*?" Allie asked.

"I don't think the two were ever mutually exclusive," Cal said.

"No, I guess not," Allie said, amused. "Did you ever think it would take you this long to come back, though?"

"Never," Cal said honestly. When he was growing up, he didn't even consider summer to have begun until his family had loaded up their station wagon, and, with him and Allie squabbling in the backseat before they'd even pulled out of the driveway, made the five-hour drive from suburban Minneapolis to Butternut. "I never thought I'd be away this long," he said now. "But I never stopped thinking about it, either. The thing is, though, I can't really tell any of those summers apart now. At a certain point, they all just started to . . . run together."

"That's because they were all the same. Or they *felt* that way, anyway. That's called boredom, Cal. That's what children used to feel before they had Facebook and Instagram and Snapchat."

"No, it wasn't boredom, exactly," Cal said. "It was more like . . ."

"More like we did the same things over and over again?" Allie said. "Like catching those little crayfish—God, those used to pinch—or taking the motorboat over to Birch Tree Bait for ice cream, or building those blanket forts in the bunkroom? But you know, Cal," she added mischievously, "not every summer was the same. There was the summer of your first kiss, remember? What was her name? That girl whose parents owned the campground?"

"Shannon."

"That's right. Shannon. Shannon with the buck-teeth."

"She did *not* have buckteeth."

"*Yes*, she did. I don't know why you've always denied it."

"Because it's not true. She was perfect," Cal said.

But Allie had already moved on. "And what about the first time you ever got drunk? That was up here, too. You and Matty filched a bottle of Kahlúa from the liquor cabinet. And you drank it *straight*. I swear, Cal, you looked *so* ill afterward."

"That was the last time I had Kahlúa," he said, shaking his head. "Just the *thought* of it now—"

"Wait, wasn't that around the same time you and James ran the motorboat up on the sandbar and Mom and Dad grounded you for two weeks?"

"Same time," Cal agreed. "But those two incidents—the Kahlúa and the sandbar—were totally unrelated."

They continued in this nostalgic vein for a little while—Allie remembering things and Cal wondering, again, what had kept him away from here for so long. But he knew. Of course he knew. *Life* had kept him away. Or he had *let* it keep him away. And he wasn't the only one, either. According to Allie, the other "summer people" he'd grown up with here—Matty and James and Tyler—had long since stopped coming. And right around the time he and Allie left for college, his parents, tired of the long Minnesota winters and the constant upkeep of owning two homes, had downsized to a condominium in Florida and deeded the cabin over to their children, who, by some unspoken agreement, had allowed it to fall into a state of gentle decay.

All that had changed six years ago when Allie decided to buy Cal out of his half of the cabin and move up here with Wyatt, who was then five years old. At the time, Allie was recovering from the death of her husband, Gregg, whose National Guard unit had been deployed to Afghanistan. Meeting another man had been the last thing on her mind, but that's exactly what had happened. She'd fallen in love with Walker Ford, her neighbor across the bay, who owned the boatyard in Butternut. A year later, they'd gotten married, Allie and Wyatt had moved into Walker's larger and more modern cabin, and Walker had adopted Wyatt. Since then, their daughter, Brooke, had been born. Their family, Allie had told Cal, was just the right size.

Cal had wondered at first why Allie kept this cabin after she and Walker had gotten married. But she'd told him a few years ago that she was simply too attached to sell it, and that she'd find a use for it one day. In the meantime, she'd continued to improve it, and Cal could see that she'd restored the property to its former rustic charm and then some. She'd shored up the dock, replaced the boathouse roof, rebuilt the cabin's wrap-around porch, and even added a few homey touches, painting the window trim and window boxes a balsam green, and paving the dirt trail that led down the mossy, sloping lawn to the lake with hand-cut stone.

"You've done a nice job with the place, Allie," Cal said.

"I think so," she said, looking genuinely pleased. "I've enjoyed it. Really, I have. It's been a labor of love. And I want to show you what I've done inside, too. But before I do, you have to answer one question for me."

"Which is . . . ?"

"Why aren't you wearing your wedding ring?" she asked, leveling her hazel eyes at him.

"When did you notice?"

"About *ten seconds* after you got here. I wasn't going to say anything about it, but then I realized *you* weren't going to say anything about it, either. And I'm guessing you didn't just accidentally leave it at home."

"No," he said, suddenly cheered by a thought. "I left it on the counter of a diner in Fargo, North Dakota, this morning."

Allie frowned.

"*What?*" Cal asked defensively. "It was a good tip. That band is platinum. Not that my waitress didn't deserve it. She was *very* quick on the coffee refill."

"So you and Meghan . . . ?" she asked, astonished.

"Are over," Cal said. In his own way, he was as surprised as she was.

"When did this happen?"

"Six weeks ago."

"Cal, why didn't you tell me?"

"I haven't really talked to anyone about it. Except my lawyer."

"This is why you've been so hard to reach?" She shook her head. "But, I mean, a lawyer? Already? Isn't is possible you'll still . . . work things out?"

"No," he said. And he meant it.

"What happened?"

He looked away. Not yet, he thought. He wasn't ready to tell anyone yet. Not even Allie.

"There wasn't . . . anyone else involved, was there?" she asked quietly.

"No, no one else," he said.

"Well, I'd be lying if I said I wasn't surprised. When we saw you in April, you and Meghan seemed so . . . *compatible*," she said. It occurred to Cal that she hadn't said *happy*. There was a silence now, longer than it needed to be.

"So . . . where do you go from here?" Allie asked finally.

"I've moved out," he said. "Filed for divorce. The rest of it, though, I don't know." He ran his fingers through his hair. "We were married for five years and now . . . I have to rethink everything I knew. The problem is, I don't want to think about it, much less talk about it."

"Then you don't have to," she said, putting an arm around his shoulders. "But when you are ready to talk about it, I'll be here."

As she said this, something occurred to him. "There's at least one positive thing to come out of all this, though," he said.

"What's that?"

He smiled bleakly. "You don't have to work so hard to like Meghan anymore."

"*Cal*." When he met Allie's protest with a skeptical look, she added, "Do you really think I don't like her? Because that's not . . . completely true. I mean, I've never *disliked* her." This statement made Cal laugh.

Even Allie must have realized what faint praise this was for her sister-in-law, because she added, "Okay, look, I think she's a little intense, a little . . . *perfectionistic*, maybe. But that's important in her line of work, isn't it?" Meghan was an interior designer. That was how Cal had originally met her. They'd both been working with the same client.

Cal didn't answer her question. He was thinking about last spring, when Allie and her family had visited Seattle. Cal had loved showing them the city, but the time they'd spent at his and Meghan's apartment had been strained. After all, as Meghan had explained to Cal many times before, their duplex was more than a home to her; it was also a showcase. The entire apartment was white—or, as Cal used to tease her, "fifty shades of white." Meghan had looked practically ill when Brooke drank grape juice out of a sippy cup on their white couch, and it was all she could do not to follow Wyatt around with a MiniVac when he ate pretzels in their gleaming white-tiled kitchen. He wondered if Allie was remembering this, too, and he thought maybe she was when she said, "Well, if you're getting divorced, at least there are no children involved. There's that, anyway."

There *was* that, Cal thought bitterly. But he couldn't meet Allie's eyes. They were silent again until Cal's anger at Meghan subsided a little and was replaced by something else: gratitude. Gratitude for Allie. She'd always been there for him before, and she was there for him now. "Thank you," he said.

"What for?"

"For today," he said with a tired smile. "For the lemonade. For letting me stay, even though I didn't give you much notice."

"Cal, of course you can stay. You know that. Stay as long as you want. What about your firm, though? Can they survive without you?" And here was another thing that Cal couldn't talk to Allie about. This, too, it seemed, would have to wait.

"I can work from here," he said. "There is an Internet connection, isn't there?"

"Yes, Cal. There are plumbing and electricity, too," she said, nudging him playfully with her knee. "And there are groceries. I went shopping this morning for the basics, but we're expecting you for dinner tonight. Walker is grilling steaks, and Wyatt is going to make you watch about twelve hours of GoPro video of him waterskiing."

"I wouldn't want to miss that," Cal said, the prospect of an early night slipping away from him.

"And don't forget, tomorrow is Daisy Keegan's wedding."

"Oh, right. I *did* forget." When he'd told Allie he was coming three days ago, she'd mentioned he'd be arriving in time for Daisy's wedding and she could wrangle an invitation for him if he'd like. Daisy was the daughter of Caroline Keegan, Allie's best friend, and she was marrying Will Hughes after a three-year engagement. Cal wished now he'd told Allie he didn't want to go. The thought of attending someone else's wedding when his own marriage had fallen apart depressed him.

Allie seemed to sense this. "I know the timing's not great, Cal. If you want to sit it out, that's fine with me."

"No, Caroline has probably given the caterer a head count already," Cal said.

"The caterer?" Allie laughed. "Caroline *is* the caterer, Cal." Her friend owned Pearl's, the coffee shop in town that was justifiably famous for, among other things, its excellent blueberry pancakes.

"There's still the matter of a suit, though," he pointed out. "I didn't pack one."

"That's all right. You don't need a suit. This is Butternut. I mean, you have pants that aren't blue jeans, don't you?" she asked.

He nodded.

"And a shirt with a collar?"

He nodded again.

"Then you're good to go. And trust me, you'll be glad you did. Everyone in Butternut will be there. It's the social event of the season. No, it's the social event of *the decade*, at least in this town."

He smiled but didn't say anything. It was quiet, except for the waves from a powerboat slapping rhythmically against the dock's pilings, and the tinkling of the wind chimes that hung off the porch eaves.

"I'm so glad you're here," Allie said suddenly, giving him a hug. "We'll figure this out, Cal. This whole thing." And in that moment, she was the older sister of his childhood—the occasionally bossy but always loving older sister. (She was only two years older than him, but it was a role, Cal knew, she took to heart.)

"Thanks," he said for the second time that day.

CHAPTER 3

ello? Luke! A little help here, please," Billy called out, fumbling as she opened the front door to their house that evening. She was carrying a handbag and a grocery bag with one hand and balancing a pizza box with the other. There was no answer from her son, but from the opposite end of the house came an ominous sound: the clicking of nails against the hardwood floor. Her eighty-pound yellow Lab, Murphy, was starting his run down the hallway, and by the time he reached Billy, he would have attained his maximum speed. She closed the front door behind her and braced herself against it just in time for him to fling himself at her.

"Whoa, boy," Billy said, laughing. She set everything on the side table and knelt down. "Somebody's glad to see me." She nuzzled his face, then glanced down the hallway, where the sounds of an action movie were coming from the television set in the den. "How's Luke?" she asked Murphy, girding herself for the series of skirmishes that had become her relationship with her son. But Murphy didn't answer. He was too busy trying to rake his tongue over her face. "Oh, Murph, you sure know how to welcome a girl home," Billy said, giving him a final pat.

She hurried to the kitchen then, arms full. Murphy trotted along beside her, hoping that some of that pizza was destined for him. As she walked past the living room and dining room, she did a mental inventory of the state of the house. It was only moderately messy right now, which, on a day like today, could feel like a victory. Yes, there were pillows to be plumped, rugs to be vacuumed, floors to be mopped and almost immediately *re*mopped (thanks to the pale yellow balls of Murphy's fur that were apt to drift, tumbleweed-style, down the hallway) but to the untrained eye, it looked acceptable, and Billy had learned to be satisfied with that.

Was this her dream house? No, probably not! Certainly it was a far cry from the home Billy had grown up in, a two-story red brick colonial on a leafy street in St. Paul. This was a single-story clapboard house on a block of other single-story clapboard houses, each with a neat square of green lawn in front, each guilty of only minor transgressions of originality—a gazebo nobody ever sat in here, a slightly sinister garden gnome there. This neighborhood—only a few blocks from Butternut's Main Street—was what Billy could afford when she and Luke had moved here five years ago, and as a single mom, she liked to think she specialized in the possible, the practical, and most important, the achievable.

Besides, if it had felt like a compromise at the time

she'd bought it, it had revealed some pleasant surprises since then. After she'd had its peeling beige exterior repainted a Lake Tahoe blue, for instance, with a crisp white trim, the house had looked positively spiffy, and when she'd pulled up its wall-to-wall carpeting—again, beige—she'd been delighted to discover the original oak floors underneath. There'd been a few perks for Luke, too: a basketball hoop for the driveway, a tire swing for the backyard, and a long hallway he could slide down in his socks. Billy had furnished the house with Danish modern furniture she'd bought at an estate sale in St. Paul and added bright geometric area rugs, midcentury light fixtures she'd scavenged online, framed abstract art posters, and of course, books—lots and lots and lots of books. Overall, she was pleased with the effect, and if she hadn't quite succeeded in indulging all of her *Mad Men* fantasies here (teak boomerang coffee table notwithstanding), she at least liked to think of it as a place where the partners at Sterling Cooper would have felt comfortable.

But as she entered the kitchen, she had to admit this was one room in the house that had defeated her. The only signs anyone had even been in it were her unwashed coffee cup from that morning standing in the sink and the faint whiff of microwaved popcorn in the air. She sighed. After leaving the library, she'd briefly entertained the idea of cooking a well-balanced meal for Luke's dinner, but she knew all too well her efforts there would be spurned. These days, he seemed to find fault with almost everything she did. And truthfully, despite thirteen years of parenting, she still wasn't much of a cook. Partly it was because the timing always seemed to elude her—her vegetables underdone, her meat and fish overdone, her rice gummy. And partly it was because she and Luke had lived with her parents until he was eight, and Billy's mom, who was as gifted in the kitchen as Billy was inept, had been happy to do all the cooking for them. So tonight, for the second time this week, she'd stopped off at Spoon River Pizza in Butternut—a favorite haunt of Luke's—and picked up a cheese pizza for dinner. That was all right, though, wasn't it? she thought, putting the groceries in the fridge and refilling Murphy's water bowl. The cheese in pizza had protein in it, right?

She left the kitchen, pausing in the hallway outside the den. Converting this third, rarely used bedroom into a quasi-office/entertainment center had been Billy's idea, an attempt to transfer the sounds of Netflix movies, Xbox games, and cable sports out of the common areas and into a room where the door could be closed. This house felt small enough without the sounds of intergalactic battles and martial arts skirmishes issuing from the living room.

Billy listened now to the screeching sounds of a car chase mixed with the staccato of a gunfight, this on a day when Luke was supposed to be unplugged. *Fast & Furious*, she decided. Billy, a lover of serious drama *and* fluffy romantic comedy, had never imagined she'd become adept at knowing which action movie franchise was playing simply by the ratio of chaotic sound to terse dialogue.

The sound of the car chase continued unabated from the other side of the door, and Billy braced herself for Luke's moodiness, which she imagined would be worse now than usual, given that he'd had a whole day at home to brood. *Come on, Billy, get it over with,* she thought, and she cracked open the door far enough to see Luke, wearing a pair of jeans torn at the knee and a Reel Legends T-shirt, sprawled out on the couch. One of his feet was up on the coffee table, his sneakers half-off, their laces untied. He was wearing his baseball cap backward. He had one earbud in so he could listen to his iPod and one earbud out so he could listen to the movie. She shook her head. She'd never understand how Luke's generation could divide their attention in this way.

She opened the door a little further and, angling into the room, nudged him on the shoulder. "Luke," she said.

"*Mom,*" he yelped with surprise, yanking out his earbud and sitting up on the couch. Billy found the remote on the coffee table and pointed it at the TV. Yes, she'd been right—*Fast Five.* She clicked it off, but the subsequent silence seemed to overwhelm the small room, and when she spoke, her voice sounded unnaturally loud. "I thought we agreed on no electronics today," she said, putting down the remote.

"No, you said no cell phone, no computer, and no Xbox. You didn't say anything about the TV or my iPod. Besides, what else was I supposed to do?"

Gee, I don't know. Read a book, maybe? The house is full of them, you know, she wanted to say, but she stopped herself. This was a sore point with her. Sometime over the past year, Luke, who'd once consumed books the same way he'd consumed Oreos, had stopped reading everything but his skateboarding magazines. It was galling to Billy, first as a parent and only second as a librarian. But what could she do? She couldn't force him to read, could she? (Though honestly, the thought *had* occurred to her.) But now, because she didn't want tonight to be a replay of last night—Billy furious over Luke's suspension, Luke defiant but not yet entirely convincing in his defiance—she tried to find the line between caring and firm as she said, "All right. Next time, though, no electronics means no electronics. Are you hungry? I brought a pizza home. Let's have it while it's still hot, okay? Oh, and there are no pesky vegetables tonight, either," she added, referring to an old joke of theirs about how annoying it was to have vegetables every night with their dinner. She left before he could answer her or, more likely, not answer her, stopping only to pick up a few stray kernels of popcorn from the rug.

In the kitchen, she set plates and napkins on the table. She was filling two glasses with ice and water when Luke came in, flipped open the pizza box, and slid a piece of pizza onto his plate. He was on his way out of the room when Billy said, "*Whoa*. Where are you going?"

"To my room?" he said, stopping but not turning around.

"I don't think so. We're having dinner together, Luke. Remember?" Billy had once been more casual about this, but a mandatory sit-down dinner—even if it consisted only of a few slices of pizza—was one of many rules she'd put into place recently to improve parent-child communication. Luke sighed audibly, turned around, and came back to slump down at the table. This was new, too; he no longer sat on furniture so much as draped himself over it. Billy was tempted to tell him to sit up straight but restrained herself. She'd been frequenting the parenting section of the library lately, and all of the books said the same thing. *Choose your battles.* She wouldn't fight this one. Or about a hundred other battles over things he did that she found equally irritating.

She brought their water glasses to the table and sat down across from him, studying him under the kitchen lights and puzzling over his recent transformation. He'd grown taller. He'd lost more of his baby fat and found in its place a new angularity in his build, a new sharpness in his features. But for the most part, he still looked very much like himself, a self that happened to look very much like *her*self. Dark hair, fair skin, blue eyes heavily fringed with lashes, and a spray of freckles over his cheeks and across the bridge of his nose. No, the real changes in Luke were subtler, less direct, and harder to pin down. It was like looking at a snapshot of a Luke she knew well only to find it inexplicably blurred around the edges.

She served herself a slice of pizza and smiled as she watched Luke fold his slice in half lengthwise and take a bite. He'd eaten his pizza like this since his grandfather had taken him on a vacation to New York City for his tenth birthday, and when he'd come back, he'd informed Billy proudly that this was the way real New Yorkers ate their pizza. Billy almost reminded him of this now, but Billy's father, Pop-Pop to Luke, who'd died a year ago, was now on a long list of subjects Luke refused to discuss. Instead she said casually, "Margot came into the library today." Margot Hoffman was the educator/naturalist at the Butternut Nature Museum, and the director of its wildly popular Nature Camp. Wildly popular with local parents for being conveniently located and affordably priced, and *reasonably* popular with their children, ages five to twelve, whom Margot labeled "junior naturalists."

"She asked about you, Luke," Billy added.

He looked at her sharply.

"No, not about your suspension," she said quickly. "Just about how you're doing. She told me she's really excited about you being a counselor's helper this year."

Luke actually groaned. "You're not still going to make me do that, are you?"

"Luke, you *wanted* to do it. You practically begged Margot when you were a camper there last summer."

"That was before I realized how dumb it is. It's, like, so lame. I mean, the museum isn't even a real museum. It has, like, two little rooms, and they don't even have stuff in them that's interesting. Who cares about some old birds' nests, anyway?"

"Well, Margot, for one," Billy said. "I think she's done a lot with the space she has. And it's not just 'some old birds' nests,' either. There are some interesting dioramas, too, of the Northwoods."

"With gross dead animals in them."

"With *taxidermy* animals in them," Billy corrected him. "And you'd be amazed what an art form many people consider taxidermy to be. There's a long waiting list at the library for a book called *The Complete Guide to Small Game Taxidermy: How to Work with Squirrels, Varmints, and Predators*. Really, Luke, we *cannot* keep that book on the shelf," she said, trying and failing to coax a smile out of him. He looked, instead, disgusted by the whole topic, though not so disgusted by it as to lose his appetite. He slid another piece of pizza onto his plate, and Billy bit into her piece, conscious that Murphy was under the table, hoping like hell that one of them would drop something on the floor.

"Look, it's not like you spend that much time inside the museum, anyway," she said, changing tack. "Margot has tons of field trips planned. And you like helping out with the little kids, don't you? Giving them piggyback rides? Remember that little boy last year? What was his name? The one who—"

"And another thing," Luke said. "What kind of summer job doesn't even *pay* you? Like, what's the point?"

"Well, the point is the experience you'll get, which, hopefully, *will* lead to a paying job one day soon."

Luke had been avoiding eye contact, but now he stole a look at her. "This summer, though, I can't just . . . ?"

"Hang out?" Billy supplied, since they'd already had this conversation. She met his gaze, challenging him. *Hang out with the same friend you got suspended with? Hang out on your skateboard, which you ride obsessively? Hang out in your room, where you already spend way too much time?* "No, Luke. You can't just hang out. You're working at Nature Camp. Period. End of discussion. In a few more years, when you're sixteen, you'll have more options. Caroline's already said she'd give you a summer job busing tables at Pearl's as soon as you're old enough." Luke had always loved Caroline and Pearl's but this got no response from him.

"And *speaking* of Pearl's," Billy continued, undaunted, "don't forget tomorrow is Daisy's wedding. It starts at five, but I think we should leave here by four thirty at the latest. Since the car's in the shop, we'll have to walk over to the Johnsons'." The wedding was being held on their property. She started to reach for another slice of pizza, then stopped herself. She knew for a fact the navy-blue sleeveless linen dress she was planning on wearing tomorrow was just a *teensy* bit snug on her right now. She took another sip of water instead.

"Yeah . . . about that," Luke said, shifting in his chair.

Billy waited.

"I might not, like, actually go to the wedding."

"Luke, I already told Caroline both of us are coming."

He shrugged. And Billy, suddenly exhausted, lifted another piece of pizza out of the box and took a big bite. Calories be damned, she decided. She'd just layer on another pair of Spanx tomorrow. Spanx upon Spanx. "Luke," she said, keeping her tone deliberately light, "you know as well as I do that if it hadn't been for Pearl's, you and I would have starved to death. Seriously, how many times do you think we've eaten there since we moved here? Just a rough estimate?"

He didn't answer. But Billy was getting used to having these one-sided conversations with him. "Hmm. Let's see. I would say that, conservatively, over the last five years we have eaten there seven hundred and fifty times. I mean, come on, you've practically *grown up* there. And remember the crush you had on Daisy? You couldn't even look her in the eye when she'd come to take our order." This at least got a reaction from him. A scowl. He dropped an uneaten crust of pizza back in the box.

"What's the point of having a wedding, anyway?" he groused. "They're just going to get divorced."

"Daisy and Will?" Billy frowned. "Why would you say that?"

"Because most people get divorced."

"No, most people do *not* get divorced. Look at Pop-Pop and Grandma. They were married for thirty-five years. And they had a wonderful marriage. You know that, Luke. You saw it for yourself."

He wouldn't argue this point, but he wouldn't concede it, either. He met Billy's gaze. "If you think marriage is so great," he said, "then why didn't you get married?"

Billy's face flushed hot. "Because under the circumstances, it wasn't . . . possible," she said, feeling suddenly defensive. "But I didn't *need* to get married to have a family. You *are* my family, Luke. You and Grandma and, when he was still alive, Pop-Pop. You were the only family I needed. But that doesn't mean I don't believe in marriage. I do. I believe in it very much. And if I somehow gave you the impression I didn't, then I'm sorry. I didn't mean to."

She was surprised to feel tears gathering behind her eyes. *This is ridiculous,* she thought. *I'm not going to cry. Especially since I'm not even sure what I would be crying about.* To distract herself, she took Luke's pizza crust out of the box and fed it to Murphy under the table. He scarfed it down, then bumped his wet nose appreciatively against her knee. When she lifted her eyes again, the danger, and the tears, had subsided. She thought Luke wasn't looking at her anymore, though it was hard to tell; his too-long hair was covering his eyes. She wished he would sit up straight *and* get a haircut. But that was another battle she didn't want to fight right now.

"The wedding is nonnegotiable," she said quietly.

He glared at her, stood up, and pushed his chair back. He was leaving the kitchen when she called out to him. "Your plate, Luke."

He came back to the table, picked up his plate, and put it in the sink. Billy sighed, helping herself to a third slice of pizza. As Luke was on his way out of the room again, though, she suddenly said, "I miss him, too, Luke. I miss Pop-Pop all the time."

"God, Mom, why do you have to keep bringing that up?" he mumbled, and then he was gone. She heard the door to his room slam. So much for parent-child communication, she thought, tossing Murphy another pizza crust.

CHAPTER 4

After Billy had fed and walked Murphy, run the dishwasher, put in a load of laundry, answered her personal e-mails, and called her mother, she finally laid claim to the only time in each day that belonged, completely and unequivocally, to her. How did she spend this time? First she poured herself a glass of chardonnay. Then she took her Oxford Illustrated Jane Austen six-volume set from its place of honor on the bookshelf in her bedroom, and, with Murphy padding along beside her, she went out onto the back porch. Over the last couple of years, this had become her summertime nighttime ritual—back porch, chardonnay, Jane Austen, Murphy—and only occasionally did she deviate from it. The back porch, of course, was weather-dependent, but unless it was pouring rain, unseasonably cold, too buggy, or too muggy, she sat out there. And, as for the glass of chardonnay, every once in a while she might substitute a light beer, a gin and tonic, or even, if she was feeling especially adventurous, a frozen margarita

she'd made in the blender. But the Jane Austen part—
that was a constant. You couldn't improve on perfec-
tion. And that went double, of course, for Murphy.

Tonight, though, as Billy nudged open the screen
door and walked onto the porch, she knew the enjoy-
ment she usually took in this ritual would elude her.
It wasn't that the back porch was uninviting. It was
as cheerful and as comfortable as she'd known how
to make it. Someone who'd lived here before her had
slapped it, somewhat haphazardly, onto the back of the
house, and it showed, but it helped that Billy's parents
had given her a very pretty set of wicker furniture as a
housewarming present, and that, through trial and er-
ror, Billy had been able to get cornflowers, marigolds,
and even poppies to grow in galvanized metal planters.
But as she set her wine and books down on the little
side table and plucked a dead blossom off one of the
marigolds, she couldn't shake a pensive feeling. It was
her dinner with Luke, of course. Since then, he'd been
holed up in his room, his door vibrating with the thud
of music. Even Murphy seemed slightly offended by
the volume; instead of coming up to the porch to sit beside her, he stayed out in the backyard, nosing around
in the shrubbery.

Billy settled into her favorite reading chair. The
night was beautiful. It was dark, finally—in another ten
days it would be the longest day of the year—but the
darkness beyond the yellow porch light felt comforting
to her, as if it were somehow protecting the house, the
yard, the whole town. And it was warm outside—warm
enough for her to be out here without a sweater, but
not so warm that she wanted to take refuge in her air-

conditioned bedroom. Helping matters was the breeze. It moved through the leaves of the enormous northern red oak tree in the backyard, making a pleasant swishing sound, and bringing with it the scent—always appealing to Billy—of a charcoal grill burning somewhere nearby.

Billy had just taken a sip of wine when she saw her neighbor, Pastor Hanson, come out into his backyard. "I thought you might be here," he called, opening the fence gate and crossing over to her porch. "We got this in our mailbox by mistake," he added, holding up an envelope as he climbed the steps. "Sorry to say, it looks like a utility bill."

"Well, I wouldn't want to miss that." Billy smiled, reaching for it. Was it her imagination or did he frown, ever so slightly, at the glass of wine in her hand? *One glass, Pastor Hanson,* Billy wanted to say, *just one, never two.* He was, she knew, a famous teetotaler, and the one time she'd attended a service at his church, she'd half expected him to rail against the evils of alcohol. But while he might not have made a good drinking buddy, he *was* a good neighbor, he and his wife and their three children. More times than Billy could count, he'd helped her out: jump-starting her car, fixing her sprinkler, leaving a stack of wood on her back porch when he got his fall delivery.

"'Night," he said, starting back down the stairs.

"Thank you, Pastor Hanson," she said, setting the bill down on the table. She'd been tempted to ask him how his daughter was. She hadn't seen Annabelle recently. Annabelle was Luke's age, and she and Luke and another neighborhood boy, Toby Halsey, had been best friends until . . . until when? Until sometime last winter. Luke said they'd just drifted apart, but Billy wondered what had really happened. She could never get a straight answer out of Luke. Annabelle and Toby were good kids, the kind of kids you wanted your child to be friends with, and the absence of them in Luke's life made her uneasy. Contributing to this feeling was the fact that Luke had a new friend, Van, the boy he'd gotten caught smoking with.

There were other things about Luke that were worrying her, too. He'd gone from being a good student to being an indifferent one. This spring, he'd still done his homework at Billy's urging, but more often than not it was slapdash, something he did hurriedly between bites of cereal at the breakfast table. This alone hadn't bothered her that much. Neither had the many hours he spent skateboarding or holed up in his bedroom, listening to music. She knew some kind of separation was normal, even necessary, for kids Luke's age. What bothered her was that Luke's once sunny talkativeness had morphed into a brooding silence.

Billy slid *Persuasion* out of the box set now and set it down on her lap. It was the novel she read when she was feeling melancholy. The Jane Austen set had been a rare splurge for her, but it had been worth it. All of the Austen novels she had owned in the past had eventually disintegrated. Starting in the sixth grade, she'd worked her way through several copies of each one until they'd simply fallen apart. This set, she hoped, would stand the test of time.

Though Billy loved Jane Austen, she didn't consider herself a "Jane-ite" or belong to the Jane Austen Society or participate in any kind of Jane Austen fandom. She considered her relationship with Jane Austen's work to be a private one, and while she'd read biographies of her before, she was much more interested in the novels than she was in the woman who'd written them. Unlike most Austen lovers, she didn't have a favorite. She chose which one to read based on what kind of mood she was in. Sometimes she read one from beginning to end; sometimes she just read *in* one, a favorite scene or piece of dialogue. Sometimes, like tonight, she didn't read anything at all—just the proximity of the books made her feel better.

She smiled now as Murphy came up the porch steps and nudged her knee with his wet nose. She scratched him behind his ears. She'd read once that this released endorphins in a dog's brain, and she believed it. Thirty seconds of this and Murphy looked so blissed-out, she thought his eyeballs might roll back in his head. She stopped, rumpled his ears, and left him in peace to enjoy his endorphin rush. He liked this part of his day, she thought, taking another sip of wine, though in truth he liked *every* part of his day. All he needed most of the time was a bowl of water, a comfortable place to lie, and her proximity, or the promise of her proximity, and he was content. Add to that two meals a day, two walks a day, the occasional meaty bone from the butcher's, and the thrice-weekly trip out to the town beach at dusk, where he chased tennis balls until it was too dark, and his life was complete.

Billy, on the other hand, needed more. Still, she savored his companionship, especially during this nightly cocktail hour. This was when they talked to each other.

Or rather, *Billy* talked and Murphy listened. She didn't talk to him out loud. She wasn't completely crazy. She talked to him silently, but fortunately for her, Murphy, in addition to his many other exceptional qualities, was a mind reader. He was sensitive, thoughtful, and patient. He never passed judgment on her. Never reminded her of past mistakes. Never did anything, really, but listen and let her scratch him behind his ears.

In her imagination, Murphy had a drink, too. It wasn't a chilled white wine like hers. His tastes were more . . . masculine. Less refined. She'd wondered, once, about what his invisible drink might be. A scotch and soda, maybe? No, too complicated. He was more a fly-by-the-seat-of-his-pants kind of guy. How about an aged whiskey, straight up? No, that would be too expensive. Murphy, she was pretty sure, liked to watch his bottom line. No, Murphy's drink of choice would be a beer. A Pabst Blue Ribbon tallboy. Ice-cold. And he'd drink it straight from the can, the way a beer like that should be drunk. That was just the kind of guy Murphy was.

How are you doing, Murphy? she asked him now.

His liquid brown eyes seemed to consider this. *I'm good,* he said finally. (Billy could read Murphy's mind, too.) *I have no complaints. I mean, I've got a little arthritis in my hip, but that's just life, isn't it? You can't get to fifty-six without a few complaints. What about you, Billy? How are you doing?*

I've been better, she admitted, sipping her wine. Murphy, resting his head on his paws, blinked patiently. *I'm sorry, Murphy. I wish I were in a better mood tonight. I'll make it up to you at the beach tomor-*

row. And Murphy, in his own inimitable way, seemed satisfied with this.

Billy heard the sprinkler go on with a little hiss and noticed the flickering lights of fireflies in the tall grass at the edge of the yard. Luke had loved fireflies when he'd first discovered them. He was convinced they'd been put on this earth for his entertainment. He'd caught one once, but he'd worried that it would miss its mother, and he'd quickly let it go. That was Luke at five, sweetness personified. The sweetness was still there, she hoped, buried under all those layers of adolescent angst.

And she felt suddenly nostalgic for a simpler time in their life together. She wished she could flip through the photo album on the coffee table of her mother's living room in St. Paul. Her mom was a meticulous chronicler of their lives. Unlike so many people today, her photos weren't stored in a cellphone or on a computer. She still took them with her trusty Minolta, had them developed, and carefully arranged them in chronological order.

In her mind's eye, Billy saw an album labeled "Billy and Luke" that opened with a photograph of her at eighteen years old, looking equal parts anxious and thrilled, holding the tiny bundle that was a newborn Luke on the steps of the house she had grown up in. It was late December; snow covered the boxwood hedges, and the lights of a Christmas tree were visible through the living room window. Not pictured were Billy's parents, who, already in their early sixties, had been planning their retirement when Billy had surprised them—no, shocked them—with the news that she was pregnant. At first they were upset, especially since the father-to-be was nowhere to be found, but ultimately they rose to the challenge with energy and enthusiasm. Billy's father had painted Luke's room and assembled his crib. Her mother had shopped for onesies and blankets and a pale blue snowsuit with unrestrained delight. They were even busier after he was born. Her mother helped Billy with all the chores—big and little—that came with an infant, and her father spent hours walking his colicky grandson up and down the hallway until Billy's mother teased him that he'd wear out the rug.

There was another photograph of Billy taken in September of the next year, standing in front of the bookstore at St. Catherine University in St. Paul on her first day of classes. She'd begun a year later than expected. She was thinner here than in the last photo and, though she looked happy, there was a new maturity about her that belied her age. Most college freshmen were preoccupied with studying and parties. Billy was preoccupied with the wriggling baby her mother was taking care of at home. In yet another photograph, a smiling three-year-old Luke stood at the gate to his new preschool, holding a Star Wars lunchbox. Next came a photo of Billy and Luke cutting the ribbon across the doorway to their cozy new apartment. They weren't moving far; her parents had had it built for them over their garage. And now, time sped up. Billy graduated from college, Billy and Luke adopted a puppy—a golden ball of fluff they named Murphy—Luke started kindergarten, and Billy started a master's program in library and information sciences at St. Catherine.

Finally there was an eight-year old Luke on the front

steps of a house, only this time it was their *own* house in Butternut. They might have continued living near her parents, but Billy knew that no matter how comfortable they had all grown with the arrangement, it was probably time for her and Luke to be on their own. After almost two years as an assistant librarian at a branch library in St. Paul, she'd interviewed for, and been offered, the position of head librarian at the Butternut Library. After they'd moved, though, her parents continued to be a constant in their lives. An easy back-and-forth developed between the two households. Billy and Luke played host at Christmastime, decorating the house before her parents arrived with a car full of presents. And in the summer, Billy's parents would often come for the weekend. Billy's dad would take Luke fishing, and afterward the four of them would go to the Corner Bar for dinner and feed Luke a constant supply of quarters for the pinball machine. Then, of course, there were Billy and Luke's trips to St. Paul to go to see a baseball game, visit with old friends, and eat Billy's mom's fabulous cooking.

But photographs, Billy knew, told only part of the story; they left out many things she wanted to remember, and a few things, too, she would have preferred to forget. In the latter category was Luke's bout with croup when he was one year old. Billy and her mother had taken turns holding him in a steamy bathroom, and, when Billy wasn't holding him, she was studying for her statistics exam the next day, her eyes already bleary from lack of sleep. In that same category was a spate of epic temper tantrums Luke had when he was two, one of which took place at another child's birthday party during which Billy had felt sure the other parents were judging her and finding her wanting. And finally, there was their first night in their new house. Boxes still unpacked, Luke lonely for his grandparents and his best friend, Charlie, in St. Paul, and Billy worrying about whether she'd made the right decision.

Fortunately, the good memories far outnumbered the bad. She would always remember the winter morning when Luke was three and she'd taken him to the window to see that his whole world had turned white overnight. While they were sleeping, the first snowstorm of the season had blanketed the city; there would be no classes for Billy and no preschool for Luke. They spent the afternoon sledding down the hill behind their house. When Luke was in the second grade, Billy had spent every night of a rainy spring reading the first half of the Harry Potter series to him. Sometimes Luke would fall asleep in his wizarding costume. And the first summer they lived in Butternut, they'd spent almost every Saturday and Sunday at the town beach, Luke running around with a pack of kids, Billy reading under the shade of an umbrella and trying to keep her freckles to a minimum. When they got home in the evenings, sand between their toes, they'd be starving. After hosing themselves off, Billy would grill hot dogs they'd wolf down on the back porch, and later Luke would choose a movie for them to watch. Through it all, Billy had thought of Luke and herself as a team; they were best friends, they were buddies, they were partners in crime. All of which made her feel their recent estrangement so acutely.

Lately Billy had wondered if she should have made

getting married a priority. There had been men other than Luke's father: a classmate she'd dated in college, a fellow graduate student she'd seen when she was getting her master's degree, even a few men she'd met in Butternut. But there had never been anyone she was serious about. Sometimes, she'd explain to friends, like Rae, that being a mother and having a full-time job were all she could manage. Yes, she knew that boys of single mothers needed a father figure. But until last spring, Luke had had one. *Her* father had filled that role in Luke's life. Besides, she hadn't wanted to disrupt her own relationship with Luke. Another single mother she'd known had finally married, only to find herself struggling to reconcile her two sons to their new stepfather; as far as Billy knew, things were still tense between them.

Yes, those might have been good excuses for not getting seriously involved with anyone, and Billy had gotten used to hauling them out when the occasion required. Still, there was a more complicated reason, she knew, one she preferred to keep between herself and Murphy, and it had to do with Jane Austen. Billy was a romantic. Her lifelong love of novels had nurtured and sustained her through good times and bad. It had done more, though. It had convinced her that when it came to love, *romantic* love, her experience with it was bound to be disappointing. Life, after all, was not a novel. Love, after all, was not perfect. She knew this, but it didn't stop her from wanting a man like Mr. Darcy, witty dialogue, amusing plot twists, surprising new characters, and neatly tied-up endings in which hero and heroine were left with nothing more to do than contemplate their own happiness together.

Billy sighed now, and this served as Murphy's cue to stand up. It was late; he was probably wondering why they were still out here when he had a dog bed he was especially fond of in the corner of her room. Even Luke, it appeared, was ready for sleep; he'd turned off his music.

"All right, Murphy, let's call it a night," Billy said. "We have a wedding to go to tomorrow. Oh, sorry," she corrected herself. "You weren't invited. I'll try to smuggle out a piece of Caroline's fried chicken for you, though." And Murphy, who always understood her, wagged his tail in acknowledgment.

CHAPTER 5

Luke waited until the sounds of sleep overtook the house. Then he rolled his skateboard from under his bed, popped the screen out of his window, and dropped his skateboard onto the ground. He climbed out after it and stood there for a minute outside his bedroom window, listening to see if he'd woken up his mom or Murphy. But he didn't hear a sound. His mom was a deep sleeper, and at night, Murphy rarely budged from his dog bed. Luke started walking gingerly over grass still wet from the sprinkler, stopping to give the tire swing in the backyard a push. Its chain creaked in the quiet night, and there was something so lonely about it swinging like that, without anyone on it, that he looked away and kept walking. He cut through the Hansons' backyard and looked reflexively at the window he knew was Annabelle's. Her lights were off. No surprise there. She'd probably been asleep for hours.

He continued on to the next backyard, and the one

after that, and the one after that, using the moonlight to navigate an entire block of backyards, edging along shrubbery, swerving around children's toys—a bicycle, a Hula-Hoop, a wading pool—and slowing down outside the houses where he knew dogs lived. At the last house, the Kimballs', he skirted around the side yard to the front and then, still carrying his skateboard with him—its wheels were too loud for a residential street—headed down the sidewalk. This part would be trickier. The other two times he'd done this, he hadn't seen any cars. But you never knew. Still, he figured if he listened carefully, he'd be able to hear one in time to hide behind a tree before it drove by.

As it turned out, there were no cars, and no lights on in any of the houses, either, except occasionally a faint light in an upstairs bedroom, or a TV on in an otherwise dark living room. When he came to the end of that block, he turned onto the first of two commercial streets that anchored the town. "Downtown Butternut," his mom had heard someone call it after they'd moved here; at the time they'd both thought that was funny. First he walked down Main Street with its painted wooden benches, striped awnings, and window boxes filled with flowers. His mom had once described Butternut's Main Street as "circa 1950," but he'd forgotten what "circa" meant. Then he turned down Glover Street, staying close to the buildings as he passed a series of businesses: a pet groomer's, a chiropractic clinic, a knitting store. Another block of this and the buildings grew farther apart, the businesses bigger. He passed a plant nursery, an electric co-op, and an auto body garage. Finally he turned onto Northern Lights Road, dropped his skateboard, stepped onto it and, pushing off the concrete, cruised down the sidewalk.

The sky seemed to open up above him, black and starry, with a big yellow moon hanging low and looking like the rubber ball he'd seen lying in the wet grass of someone's backyard tonight. He pulled a deep breath into his lungs and felt the wind on his face, the board humming beneath his feet. It felt good to be out here after being inside all day, grounded because of his suspension. And he could have kept going, too, all the way out of town, but he knew the longer he stayed out the more likely he was to get caught. So when he reached the recreation center, which took up a whole block on one side of the street, he stopped, tried the gate and, when he realized it was locked, tossed his skateboard over the fence and went clambering after it. So much for keeping people out, he thought, getting back on his skateboard and cutting through the parking lot to the back of the building, where there was a playground, a grassy lawn with some picnic tables on it, and a sand volleyball court.

The volleyball court was the stupidest thing ever. Back when he was in sixth grade, his mom had been one of the parents who'd wanted the town to build a skate park here, but in the end, the town council had decided it was too dangerous and put in a sand volleyball court instead. Nobody ever used it. It wasn't even near an actual beach. But that was a small town for you, he guessed. You had to make your own fun. It was why he liked hanging out with his friend Van. He knew how to have fun. And plan stuff. They were always talking about things they were going to do. Places they were going to go. Like tomorrow, for instance, Luke and Van and Van's friend J.P. were going to do something cool. Something big. Thinking about it, though, made Luke feel kind of nervous, so he thought about what it was like being out here alone at night instead. He liked it, he decided. It was weird, but it was weird in a good way.

He reached the end of the parking lot and, picking up his skateboard, walked across the lawn to one of the picnic tables. He stowed his board under it, climbed up on it and, after hesitating for a second, lay down on it, and looked up at the sky. It made him feel small, just for a second. He remembered that when they'd moved here from the city, he'd been surprised at how much bigger the sky seemed, how easy it was to see the stars. He tried to pick out some of the constellations now, but he could find only the Big Dipper. Pop-Pop had known all the constellations: their names, where they were, the stories behind them. How had he known so much? Luke wondered. How had he had time to learn it all? And he didn't know just about stars, either. He'd been a structural engineer; he'd known about building things, too, big things like bridges and tunnels and roads.

Luke had that feeling now. That feeling like something was swelling up in his chest. He got that feeling, sometimes, when he thought about Pop-Pop. His mom was always trying to make him talk about him, like that would make him feel better or something. And it wasn't like he'd *forgotten* about him, anyway. He hadn't. Like now, he wished he were here. Not right this second, but the last couple of days, when he'd gotten suspended and his mom had made such a big deal out of it. Pop-Pop had understood how to calm his mom down, how to make her laugh at stuff, even stuff she was upset about. Who cared about him smoking under the bleachers, anyway, other than the principal, Mr. Gilmore? Even the PE teacher, Mr. Barry, who'd found them smoking, didn't really seem that shocked. It was more like he was pretending to be, because he knew he should be. And here was the thing that was so unfair: Mr. Gilmore smoked! It was like this big secret that everyone already knew. Once when he'd given Annabelle and two of her friends from the volleyball team a ride to one of their games, Annabelle had said his car positively reeked of cigarette smoke, and that his Christmas tree air freshener thingy had only made the smell worse.

Luke took a deep breath, then another one. He was mad now, and that bubble in his chest was still there. He knew if it got hard enough, it would start to hurt, and worse, it would make him cry, which he hated doing. Because what exactly was the point of crying? For a little while he lay there and breathed, and didn't think about anything, and then he thought about his dad. It was hard to think about someone when you didn't know that much about him. He didn't even know what his dad looked like, except what his mom had told him, and it hadn't been enough, except the part about him having one blue eye and one brown eye. That was cool, and sometimes Luke imagined that when he did find him, in Alaska, which was where his mom had met him, that was how he would know him, because how many people had two different-colored eyes?

Luke yawned. For the first time tonight, he felt tired.

He took another deep breath. The bubble was almost gone now. It wasn't going to hurt, after all. He'd think about his dad and Alaska on the way home, he decided, rolling off the table and grabbing his skateboard out from under it. And he'd have the whole town to himself while he was doing it.

CHAPTER 6

At five P.M. the next day, Cal sat on a folding chair in the Johnsons' backyard, waiting for the wedding to begin. There had been a summer shower an hour before, and Cal had arrived with his sister and her family in its aftermath to find Jax and Jeremy's four daughters furiously wiping down the chairs with dish towels and gently shaking out the taffeta bows tied to each row. Since then the sun had come out, and though the day had been hot before, it was pleasant now, with a breeze that smelled of wet grass and shook the leaves on the aspen trees, occasionally sending leftover raindrops down onto unsuspecting guests.

Cal heard a murmur of appreciation, and he turned with everyone else to see Daisy Keegan standing at the end of the aisle. She was wearing a simple silk wedding dress with a scoop neck, cap sleeves, and a white satin sash around her waist. A crown of tiny white roses was entwined in her strawberry-blond hair, and she was holding a bouquet of fresh white peonies. Her mother, Caroline, who looked like an older version of Daisy, stood on one side of her in a pale yellow skirt and jacket; and her father, Jack, wearing a navy-blue suit, stood on the other side. So they were both going to give her away, Cal thought. That was nice. It had always seemed unfair to him that mothers, who did so much of the work, had to cede this honor to fathers. The three of them started up the aisle now, and as they drew closer, Cal saw that Daisy, tremulous with emotion, was already crying; a tear ran unchecked down her cheek. Cal turned to look at the groom. He was handsome, standing tall and erect in his army dress blues. Once Daisy reached him, he smiled down at her and brushed her tear away with his thumb. It was such an intimate gesture, and there was so much tenderness there, that Cal looked away and fixed his gaze on a low-hanging tree branch instead.

His sister, as if knowing what he was feeling, gave his arm a reassuring pat. Cal mustered a smile for her. When he'd arrived at her cabin before the wedding, he'd found her, and her family, in total disarray. "Here, take her," Allie had said, opening the front door and handing him a wailing Brooke. He took her from Allie and held her a little awkwardly; his experience comforting toddlers was limited. In between gasps, Brooke kept repeating the same two unintelligible words.

"What's she saying?" he asked Allie.

"'Special sock,'" Allie said, gesturing at Brooke's feet. One had a little ruffled sock on it that matched her dress, and the other was bare. "She took her special sock off and now she can't find it."

"Well, maybe I can find it," Cal said, looking down

at Brooke and smiling uncertainly. And perhaps it was the novelty of Cal holding her, but Brooke's crying started to shift into a whimper. She looked at him now with wide, teary eyes.

"I've already tried finding it," Allie said. "But I've got to do something with my hair." She was wearing a silk print dress, her hair pinned up haphazardly. "Check in the living room. That's the last place I saw her wearing it." She gave Cal a quick kiss on the cheek. "And don't worry about Brooke," she added, patting her on the back. "She'll be fine. She just falls apart when she misses her nap."

"Right," Cal said, heading into the living room. "Let's find this special sock." After a brief search he found it sticking out from under the couch. "Look, here it is," he said to Brooke, who had stopped crying and was now hiccupping. She smiled shyly at him, and he slipped it onto her foot using his one free hand. Disaster averted, he thought.

He shifted Brooke into his other arm and went in search of the rest of the family. He found Walker and Wyatt in the kitchen.

"Dad, you're strangling me," Wyatt complained as Walker tried to knot his tie.

"Hey, can I help out?" Cal asked, jiggling Brooke, who was now rubbing her eyes sleepily. "I'm pretty good at that."

"Sure, that'd be great," Walker said, reaching for Brooke, who snuggled into his arms.

Cal set to work on the tie, strangely happy to be useful to both his niece and nephew in so short a time.

"There," he said, tightening the tie's knot and standing back to inspect his handiwork. "That looks good."

"Except that I can't breathe." Wyatt gasped dramatically. He put his hands around his neck and made a choking sound.

Cal looked at Walker in amusement, but Walker only smiled wryly. "Thank God he has to wear one only once in a blue moon," he said.

In the end, everything had come together. Brooke had fallen asleep in the car on the drive to the wedding and was still sleeping now in Allie's arms, a thumb tucked contentedly into her mouth. Wyatt, sitting beside Allie, had forgotten he was being choked by his tie, and instead had a stoic expression on his face that Cal imagined he reserved for occasions like this. Walker's hand was resting on Wyatt's shoulder. As Cal looked at the two of them in profile, he saw that there was something about them so utterly similar—the way they held themselves, their posture, or the tilt of their heads—that Cal knew that even a biological connection could not have made them more of a father and son than they already were.

And again, Cal felt compelled to look away. The bride and groom were now standing under a white wicker archway braided with white roses and ribbons, and the late afternoon sun lit up the gold in Daisy's hair. The judge, a gray-haired man in his sixties, was saying something about how love is what makes us human. Then he asked Daisy and Will to read their vows, and Cal's mind went automatically to his own wedding ceremony. What he remembered most about it, he realized, was not the wedding itself but the months of preparation leading up to it. He had wanted a small wedding; Meghan had wanted a big wedding. He'd suggested a vineyard for the reception; Meghan had her heart set on her parents' country club. In the end, Cal had given in. He didn't really care that much about the details, whereas Meghan seemed to care about them *so* much.

For him, the point was to get married. For Meghan, the point was to have the perfect wedding. And it *was* perfect, or at least, it had *looked* perfect. There were the bridesmaid's shoes that Meghan had dyed three times before she was satisfied they were an exact match to the blush-colored bridesmaid's dresses. There was the bridal bouquet, which featured the rare chocolate cosmos flower that Meghan had the florist fly in the morning of the wedding for optimum freshness. And there were the hors d'oeuvres that Meghan and the caterer designed to be completely unique, including the tuna sashimi on kaffir lime–scented rice with hibiscus "caviar" that looked more like tiny jeweled packages than something you could actually eat. But by the day of the ceremony, Cal couldn't help wishing that they'd eloped. By then, they hadn't had a conversation in months that didn't revolve around the wedding, and Meghan was starting to seem more like an event planner than a fiancée.

He watched now as Daisy and Will exchanged rings and kissed. The guests around him stood up and started to clap, and Cal, a beat behind, joined them. The two youngest Johnson daughters, giggling excitedly, threw pale pink rose petals at the couple as they walked down the aisle. "See, that wasn't so bad, was it?" Allie whispered in his ear, and even Brooke, who was awake now, looked pleased as she clapped her chubby hands.

"Come on," Allie said to him during the reception that followed. "I'll introduce you to Daisy and Will."

"They look busy," he said, but Allie had him firmly in tow and was working her way over to them.

"It's nice to meet you," Cal said a moment later as he shook hands with both of them. "And congratulations." Neither bride nor groom seemed surprised to have a guest at their wedding they'd never met before, but then again, neither seemed completely aware of what was happening around them. They were going through the motions, Cal understood, doing the right things, saying the right things, but the only other person who existed for them right now was the person they had just married. They were in their own private bubble of happiness. Nothing could puncture it for them, least of all a last-minute wedding guest. And Cal was reminded of something Allie had told him before the ceremony. Daisy's father, Jack, who'd built a successful business here buying, remodeling, and reselling old cabins, was giving Daisy and Will one of them as a wedding present, and was surprising them with the keys to it that evening. Allie and Caroline had been over at the cabin that morning, filling its refrigerator with groceries and its rooms with flowers. Cal watched as, hands entwined, Daisy and Will stole a smile at each other. He turned away from them abruptly. "I'm going to get something to eat," he told Allie, and he left before she could introduce him to anyone else.

The buffet table was set up under the spreading

branches of an oak tree, and everything about it—from its blue-and-white-checked cloth, to its centerpiece of vintage milk cans filled with sunflowers, to its mason jar glasses and speckled tin plates for the guests—was in keeping with the country picnic theme of the wedding. Cal took a plate and started working his way down the table. There were mouth-watering platters heaped with fried chicken and spareribs, plates stacked with deviled eggs, biscuits, and corn on the cob, and bowls brimming over with potato salad, coleslaw, green salad, and fruit salad.

Still, as delicious as everything looked, Cal couldn't help but feel as if he were a visitor from another country. *Another universe.* In Seattle, the meals he and Meghan had prepared at home and the restaurants they'd frequented were dedicated to a completely different kind of culinary experience, one best described by adjectives like *organic*, *responsibly sourced*, *artisan*, *heirloom*, and *vegetable-centric*. Trends were constantly changing. Seaweed, for instance, was the new kale. Small plates had given way to shared plates. Fermented foods—pickles, sauerkraut, and kimchi—were suddenly everywhere. Artisanal ice cream with flavors like pomegranate-carob, blackberry-basil, and caramel-cilantro now made choosing a simple cone infinitely complicated.

But the sole mission of *this* food, Cal thought, putting an especially flaky-looking biscuit on his plate, was to taste good. That was it. He snuck a bite of the biscuit. Christ, it was even better than it looked. It didn't need any butter, either. It was already *full* of butter, which was obviously the only ingredient on this table more highly prized than mayonnaise.

Cal's mouth quirked up at one corner. Meghan *hated* mayonnaise. She thought it was disgusting. What would she do if she were here? Pick at the salad, he decided. He paused to pile some of it onto his plate. It was swimming in ranch dressing, which was another thing Meghan hated, probably because she feared mayonnaise was lurking somewhere within it. He, on the other hand, could very happily eat this food until his dying day if it weren't for one thing: he already missed sushi. He was addicted to it. "God, I'd kill for a spicy tuna roll right now," he said under his breath as he helped himself to some coleslaw.

"A spicy tuna roll?" a woman standing next to him in line said. Cal hadn't noticed her before, but he turned to her now. "You're not going to find one of those here," she said, amused, as she lifted a deviled egg off a platter and popped it onto her plate. "Sushi hasn't reached Butternut yet."

"Do you think it ever will?" he asked. Even through the fog of his gloom, he could see this woman was attractive.

"Anything's possible," she said. "When we moved to Butternut five years ago, the only coffee they served at Pearl's, the coffee shop here, was regular and decaf. Now they serve lattes, espressos, and cappuccinos, too."

"Really?" Cal said, hard-pressed to imagine this. He'd spent the better part of his childhood summers spinning on the red leather stools that lined the Formica counter at Pearl's, and even then, the place had felt like a time capsule.

"Oh, absolutely. We're a fully caffeinated town now," she said, putting a generous dollop of potato salad next to the spareribs on her plate. "Of course, there's a downside to that. I'm up to two lattes a day now. So, I'm basically trapped in a downward spiral of addiction and poverty."

"I know something about that," Cal chuckled. "I live in the city that gave us Starbucks."

"Seattle?" she asked. They'd both paused at the end of the buffet table to gather up napkins and utensils. "Oh, I'd love to go there," she said. "I've seen photographs of the new Central Library. It looks amazing."

Now she'd gotten his attention. The Central Library was one of his favorite buildings in Seattle. He looked at her, really looked at her, for the first time. She was in her late twenties or early thirties, and she had long, straight, shiny, dark hair, blue eyes, and long lashes. She wore a sleeveless navy dress. But what he found especially appealing about her for some reason were her freckles; there was a sprinkling of them across her nose and cheeks.

"It *is* amazing," he said of the Central Library. "Are you . . . interested in architecture?"

She shook her head. "I'm interested in *libraries*." Cal looked at her quizzically. "I'm a librarian," she explained.

"*Oh*. Here? At the Butternut Library?"

She nodded. "Have you been there before?"

"Many, *many* times. When I was a kid, my mom used to drop my sister and me off there whenever we were driving her crazy—which, now that I think of it, was pretty much all of the time—and then she'd pick us up a couple of hours later. I think she used it as kind of a drop-in child care center."

She smiled. "People are still doing that. Did you . . . grow up here?"

"Only in the summertime. My family had a cabin up here. My sister still does. My name is Cal," he said, holding out his hand. "Cal Cooper. My sister is Allie Ford."

"Oh, of course. I know Allie," she said, shifting her plate, napkin, and silverware into one hand so she could shake his hand with the other. "She loves Jodi Picoult novels," she continued. "I always set them aside for her as soon as they come in. And *Wyatt*. Wyatt is one of our best Bookworms. It's a club," she added. "I'm Billy Harper, by the way."

"Billy?" Cal repeated.

"Uh-huh. I was named after my maternal grandfather. I would have been William if I'd been a boy, but since I was a girl, I was Wilhelmina. It was a lot of name, though, so everyone ended up calling me Billy."

He nodded. It suited her, though she was undeniably feminine. He glanced around now. They were still standing near the buffet table, but other guests who'd come through the line after them were sitting down at the little tables scattered around on the lawn. He looked at Billy questioningly. Should they sit down, too? But she seemed preoccupied, her eyes searching the throng of wedding-goers around them. He surreptitiously checked her ring finger. There was nothing there. Had she come with a date, then?

"Sorry," she said apologetically, her eyes resting on Cal again. "I'm trying to find someone. I was supposed to meet him here."

"Can I . . . help you?" Cal asked. "I don't know that many people here, but . . . you could describe him to me."

She smiled distractedly. "Well, let's see. He's a boy. He's thirteen. He needs a haircut. He usually has a skateboard attached to him. And he's perfected the art of looking bored, whether he's bored or not. He's my son. I walked here to the wedding, and he was supposed to ride his skateboard here after me. I thought maybe he was sitting in the back during the ceremony, but I didn't see him after it, either."

"And you're worried?"

"Not *worried*," she said. "Concerned."

"Are those different?"

She sighed. "No. Probably not."

"Well, if he's anything like I was at his age, he should be showing up at the buffet table any second now. Should we wait here for him?" Cal asked, gesturing at an empty table nearby.

"Yeah, okay, let's do that," Billy said with a cheerful smile. Just as they were setting down their plates and pulling out their chairs, they heard someone trill, "*Hello, Billy.*" An older woman, fine-boned as a bird, alighted at the table. She was tiny, but she was wearing a plum-colored dress that seemed to involve several yards of material and on top of her head sat a plum-colored bird's nest hat. She placed an enormous embroidered handbag down on the table. It was the same disconcerting color as her dress. Cal wondered how such a small woman could carry around such a large bag.

"I think I'll sit here if that's okay with you two," she said, but she didn't seem interested in an answer.

"Hello, Mrs. Streeter," Billy said, smiling at her. "Please join us."

"I'm going to go get some of those *amazing* biscuits," she said. "I'll be right back." But when she returned, she didn't have a plate. She had several biscuits wrapped in napkins, and she proceeded to deposit them into her handbag.

"Those should come in handy later," she said, hurrying off again.

Cal looked at Billy, who rolled her eyes almost imperceptibly. "She likes free stuff. Free stuff and Cary Grant," she explained, taking a bite of her biscuit. "She rents all of his films from the library." Cal chuckled, but at that moment, a cell phone rang.

"That'll be Luke, my son," Billy said, reaching into her purse. When she took her cell phone out and looked at the screen, she frowned uncertainly. "Excuse me. I'm going to take this over there," she said, getting up from the table. She returned less than a minute later, seeming shocked, her freckles standing out against her suddenly pale skin.

"Hey," he said, "is everything okay?"

She shook her head. "That was the police. They're . . . they're holding my son."

"What for?"

"He was caught spray-painting graffiti on public property."

"*In Butternut?*"

She nodded.

"Is that, like, a thing here now?" he asked. "Graffiti?" He'd never seen any here, and it didn't jibe with his squeaky-clean image of this town.

"I don't know," she said. "But I have to go pick him up." She reached into her handbag again, and then she froze. "Oh, no," she murmured, bringing a hand to her temple.

"What's wrong?"

"My car. It's in the shop. I'll have to walk there."

"Where's 'there'?"

"The state police satellite office. It's right outside town, on Highway 169."

"Don't walk," Cal said. "It'll take too long. I'll drive you."

"That's . . . that's really nice of you to offer. But . . . you don't want to leave now, do you? You've haven't even finished eating yet," she said.

"No, it's fine," he said. "Let me just tell my sister I'm going, okay? I'll be right back."

She nodded gratefully. "Thank you. I'll ask Officer Sawyer to give us a ride home."

Cal got up from the table then and went to find Allie. He explained the situation to her, and she understood, but she wanted him to come back after he'd given Billy a ride to the station. He begged off, saying he was tired. In truth, though, he'd already had enough marital bliss for one day.

When he returned to Billy, she looked more pensive than ever. "Let's go," he said. They passed the now mobbed buffet table and headed toward the nearby field where the wedding guests' cars were parked. He had no trouble finding his Porsche; it stood out like a shiny buoy floating on a sea of dusty pickups, SUVs, and minivans.

"Can you answer a question for me?" he asked Billy, partly to distract her from her obvious anxiety and partly because he was genuinely curious.

"Sure," she said.

"Why do so many people up here drive a pickup truck? I mean, obviously there are people who need one for work. I get that. But does every other person in this town need one?"

She shrugged. "You never know . . ."

"Know what?"

"When you'll need to throw something in the back," she said.

"Like what?"

"A cord of wood. A buck."

"A buck?"

"During hunting season," she murmured. He looked to see if she was joking, but she seemed serious. He couldn't actually picture her hunting, but the practitioners of this sport, he knew, could surprise you. He started to ask her whether she was a hunter but then changed his mind. She obviously wasn't in the mood to talk.

"Here we are," he said as they approached his car. He unlocked it with his key fob and went to open the passenger side door for her.

"Wait, this is yours?" she asked, hesitating.

"Yeah. Is it okay?"

"It's fine. But . . . did you get a ticket yesterday? On Main Street?"

"Yep. That was me. Wow, word gets around fast here."

"You have no idea," she said with a sigh as she got into his car.

CHAPTER 7

When Billy walked into the state police office, the first thing she saw was Luke sitting hunched over on a bench in the waiting area. The sleeve of his T-shirt was torn, his sneakers were muddy, and his tangled hair was hanging in his eyes. He looked about as forlorn as she'd ever seen him, and her first impulse was to comfort him. Before she could make a move to do this, the door to an adjoining office opened and Officer Sawyer leaned out.

"Ms. Harper," he called. Luke, who hadn't looked up when Billy came in, looked up now. And for a moment—just a moment—Billy thought she saw fear in his face. But then it was gone, replaced by an expression she could only describe as contrite *and* defiant. It was an expression that was starting to look all too familiar to her.

Officer Sawyer stepped forward then and gestured for Billy to come into his office. "Luke, why don't you stay there while your mom and I talk," he said sternly.

Luke, now aiming for nonchalance, shrugged and resumed looking at his shoes.

"Have a seat," Officer Sawyer said to Billy. He shut the door behind them and adjusted the blinds on an internal window so that they could still see Luke.

"Can I get you a coffee or a soda?" he asked, turning to her.

She shook her head, though her mouth was so dry her tongue felt like sandpaper.

"All right, then," he said, lowering himself into his swivel chair. He looked at Billy sympathetically over the stacks of files on his gunmetal-gray desk. He was a large man, with a thick neck, light red hair shaved into a buzz cut, and pale blue eyes that he usually kept hidden behind aviator sunglasses. He had trouble with the sun, she knew; his skin was so fair that when he'd coached Luke's Little League team in the fourth and fifth grades, he'd never come onto the field without a stripe of zinc oxide on his nose and across each of his cheeks.

Billy tried to smile at him now. She'd always liked him. He was from Butternut—she'd seen his retired baseball jersey in a glass case at the high school—and his wife, Leslie, was also from up here. She was a first-grade teacher at the elementary school, and she often brought their two young children to the library's Bookworms reading events.

"So . . . graffiti?" Billy asked tentatively. "I have to say, I have no idea where this is coming from. That's never been a problem before." She glanced at Luke through the office window as if he might shed some light on this now, but his eyes were still fixed on his shoes. "Whatever damage there is, though," she said, turning her attention back to Officer Sawyer, "Luke will clean it off."

Office Sawyer stirred. "There was some damage to property, but honestly, that's not my main concern here. My main concern is *where* they were when they were spray-painting the graffiti."

They? Billy thought. This was her first indication that Luke had not been alone. "Where . . . where were they?"

"They were on the Kawashiwi River overpass off Route 10. A motorist saw them climbing over the bridge and onto the ledge, and by the time we got there they were all standing on the six-inch concrete lip, dangling twenty feet over the river. I don't know if you're familiar with that part of the Kawashiwi, but the water there's pretty shallow, and it's rocky, too."

"*Oh my God,*" Billy exclaimed. "He could have broken his neck." She glared at Luke through the window. Maybe she should have felt relief that he was okay, but all she could feel now was anger at him for doing something so dangerous. "That is *not* the kid I raised," she sputtered. "I don't even *know* that kid," she added, gesturing at Luke. "We've always been safety-conscious in our family. *Always.* Luke still doesn't go out on his skateboard without his helmet on." Even as she was saying this, though, Billy was wondering if it was true. He wasn't *supposed* to go out on his skateboard without his helmet on. But the boy who'd hung off the side of that bridge probably wasn't worried about falling off a skateboard.

Officer Sawyer shuffled some files around on his

desk, "Look, the important thing is that he wasn't hurt.
And I *know* Luke is a good kid. Really, I do. You don't
coach someone for two seasons without learning anything about him. But Ms. Harper, the kids he's hanging
out with . . ."

"Which kids?"

"Van Olsen. Do you know him?"

"I know *of* him," she said, thinking that he was the
boy who was with Luke when he got caught smoking beneath the bleachers at school. "But I think their
friendship is still very new. Luke has mentioned him
only a couple of times recently. He's said he thinks Van
is cool."

"He's not cool," Officer Sawyer said flatly. "He's already on our radar over here. And his dad . . ." Officer
Sawyer tapped on a stack of files. "His dad has had
some pretty serious run-ins with the law. I can personally vouch for those."

"I had no idea," Billy murmured. "When Luke was
younger, I knew all of his friends, and their parents,
too, but now . . ." Her voice trailed off. Now, increasingly, Luke was independent. She'd been delighted at
first when she'd realized he was old enough to stay at
home alone, and mature enough to ride his bicycle to
and from school alone, but she understood now that
Luke's freedom was a double-edged sword. She'd
thought her son would be safe in a small town. Trouble
wouldn't find him here, she'd reasoned. It had never occurred to her that he would go looking for it instead.

"Yeah, I know. As they grow older it gets harder to
keep track of them," Officer Sawyer was saying when
her mind returned to the conversation. "And the Olsen

kid, they're in the same grade, so Luke's going to see him at school every day whether you like it or not. But this *other* kid they were with, J.P. Meyer—"

"What grade is he in?" Billy interrupted. She knew for a fact Luke had never mentioned him before.

"No grade. He's a dropout."

"Already?"

"He's sixteen."

"And he's hanging out with thirteen-year-olds?" Billy asked, mystified. "Why would he do that?"

Officer Sawyer shrugged. "Maybe because they look up to him."

"Is he . . . on your radar, too?"

He shrugged. "These two boys, Van and J.P., they don't have much parental supervision. Van's mother went AWOL years ago, and his dad is not around a lot. J.P. lives with his mom, but she works two shifts at the mill in Ely. Don't think she's around much, either. He already has a juvenile record. Which is why I think he might face charges for this incident today . . ."

"*Wait*," Billy said sharply. "There are going to be charges?"

"In Minnesota, graffiti falls under public nuisance laws," Officer Sawyer said, crossing his arms and leaning on his desk. "But since this is the first time Luke's been caught doing anything like this, I think there's a very good possibility he won't get charged. Especially since he's still really young. Just turned thirteen, right?"

Billy nodded, distracted. So there most likely wouldn't be any charges. *This time.*

As if reading her mind, Officer Sawyer continued. "Of course, if this kind of thing keeps happening, you're going to end up with legal fees, fees for cleaning up property, community service . . ." These images left Billy feeling something close to panic.

"Luke got suspended on the last day of school," she said, her words coming out in a rush. "And now this. He seems so angry and moody all the time. I don't—"

Officer Sawyer interrupted her here. "Leslie told me his granddad died last year. I remember him from the Little League games. They were obviously very close. That's got to be hard on the kid. Has he talked to any of the counselors at school?"

"No, he said he didn't want to." Billy felt suddenly overwhelmed and uncertain. And she felt the loss of her dad more than ever right now. He'd always seemed to know how to handle even the most complex problems with his own idiosyncratic blend of honesty and humor. He knew, too, how to nudge Luke subtly in the right direction without lecturing him or hectoring him. Billy wondered if she was capable of that kind of finesse. She turned again to look at Luke. His shoulders were still hunched, his eyes still hidden behind tangled hair. Where was the good, cheerful kid he'd been just a year ago?

Officer Sawyer was rummaging around in his desk drawers. "I think I might have something here," he mumbled. "I don't know if it's completely up-to-date, but . . . here it is." He pulled out a pamphlet and handed it to Billy. It was a little wrinkled and an ink stain covered its upper corner, but she could clearly read "North Woods Adventures for Teens: Teaching teamwork, building decision-making skills, and improving self-esteem." She smiled faintly in spite of herself.

She knew about North Woods Adventures. She and Amanda, her best friend in high school, had taken a Boundary Waters Canoeing course the summer before their senior year. It was much more rugged than either of them had realized it would be—the word *portaging* still struck fear in her heart—but it had been challenging and exhilarating, too, and she couldn't remember ever having slept as deeply as she had during the two weeks the trip had lasted.

"I've been on a North Woods Adventures trip before," she told Officer Sawyer.

"It's worth a thought, then. Leslie's nephew went on one of them and . . ." But Billy wasn't listening. She was thinking about how expensive something like that might be. Expensive enough, she decided, to put a crimp in their budget. Still, she might spread it over a couple of credit cards, or raid their rainy day fund.

"I think the point is, he needs some additional guidance," Officer Sawyer said. "In this day and age, it can be hard sometimes to know how to help your kid. Especially when you're doing it all alone." He looked a little embarrassed suddenly, as though he thought he might be trespassing. "I could give you some information on a program in Duluth," he added tentatively. "It's for parents who . . . need help with challenging kids."

Billy's face burned. Surely she was capable of parenting her own child. *Wasn't she?*

Her eyes went to a photograph on Officer Sawyer's desk. It was of him and his wife and their son and daughter on a vacation at Disneyland. They looked like the all-American family, emphasis on *family*. She'd never been ashamed to be a single mother before. She'd never felt defensive about it, either. But then she'd known she was doing a good job, and she'd assumed everyone else had known it, too. All they'd needed to do was look at her son—her bright, sweet, talkative son. And now? What now? She stole another glance at Luke. He looked as recalcitrant as ever. She sighed. North Woods Adventures for him; parenting classes for her.

"It's a lot to think about," Officer Sawyer said, pushing back his chair. "But for now, the best thing you can do is keep Luke busy."

"I will. *I am.* He's working as a counselor's assistant at the museum's Nature Camp this summer. His hours there, and my hours at work, are almost exactly the same."

"Good," Officer Sawyer said, standing up. "The busier the better. And, uh, if you can, keep him away from those boys . . ." He held out his hand to Billy, and she shook it. "You let me know if there's anything I can do."

"Absolutely. Do you mind if I . . . ?" She held up the pamphlet.

"Of course. You hold on to that." She tucked it into her purse and steeled herself to face Luke. Officer Sawyer opened the door for her. Luke looked up, then stood. Despite all his bravado, and the fact that he was now almost as tall as Billy, he was still very much a kid, she realized. She mustn't forget that.

"Let's go, Luke," she said in an even voice, marveling at how calm she sounded. They would have *the talk* when they got home, Billy decided. Right now, she would let Luke think about what he'd done.

CHAPTER 8

That night, when Billy went out on the back porch, she didn't take a glass of chardonnay or the Jane Austen box set with her. She just sat out there, feeling completely numb, and it was only when Murphy nudged her hand with his head that she remembered his presence. "Hey buddy," she said with a tired smile, "I'm sorry. I've been neglecting you." She scratched him behind his ears then for an extralong time. After all, this was *his* nighttime ritual, too.

After Murphy had his fill of her attention and flopped down contentedly at her feet, Billy sat still, very still, and tried to understand what had happened between her and Luke tonight. Officer Sawyer had given them a ride back from the police station, and Billy had made small talk with him while rehearsing, mentally, what she would say to Luke—who was sitting stonily beside her—as soon as they got home. Things didn't go exactly as she'd planned, though. First, Luke didn't follow her willingly into the kitchen; she'd had to head him off at the door to his room and insist that he follow her there. Then, once she'd started speaking to him, the lecture that had come so easily to her in the police car was suddenly nowhere to be found. Billy loved words. Written and spoken. Where, she'd wondered, had all of them gone now?

Still, she'd stumbled along. She told Luke how disappointed she was in him. He'd missed Daisy's wedding, he'd damaged public property and, most important, he'd risked his life in the process. He never looked up as she spoke to him. He was gazing, as usual, at the floor, but he made a tiny gesture, an almost imperceptible lifting of his shoulders, that seemed to imply she was overreacting on this last point. Billy was furious. She'd sputtered, angrily, about broken necks and spinal cord injuries and a boy she'd known growing up who was paralyzed after diving into the shallow end of a swimming pool. Luke seemed unimpressed by all of this, though, and Billy's anger finally petered out. What was the point of it, really? She wasn't getting through to him, and besides, she'd remembered something she'd read about teenagers recently. Apparently one of the reasons they were more likely than adults to engage in risky behaviors was because their prefrontal cortexes had not finished developing yet. Still, she couldn't just hope for the best while she waited for his to mature, so she changed tack and instead listed the new rules she'd be instituting.

He'd have no Internet or cell phone use during the week, and he'd have restricted use of both of these on weekends. He wouldn't be seeing Van or J.P., either.

Monday through Friday, he'd go to Nature Camp from nine A.M. to three P.M., after which he'd come directly to the library, where he'd stay until they left together at five o'clock. On Saturday and Sunday, they'd see. Maybe he could spend time with Annabelle, Toby, or another preapproved friend. Maybe he could visit his grandmother in St. Paul. But Luke being on his own, or at large in Butternut, or just "hanging out" with Van—*that* was over.

Luke was appalled. "Mom, you can't stop me from seeing my friends," he said, his blue eyes flashing.

"Actually, I can." Leaning against the kitchen counter, she folded her arms and tried to project a confidence she didn't really feel. "I can if I think they're a bad influence on you. I mean, Luke, you've never been in trouble before—at least, not like this—and in the last week, you've been suspended from school and picked up by the police. Both times you were with Van. And as for J.P., honestly, what are you even *doing* with him? He doesn't go to your school. He doesn't go to *any* school. He does, however, have a juvenile record. Is that really the kind of person you want to spend your time with?"

"Maybe," Luke said with a nonchalance that infuriated her all over again.

"So, this is someone you look up to? Someone you admire?"

"Could be," he mumbled, but he didn't meet her gaze. He looked down at his perennially untied shoelaces.

"Oh, Luke," she sighed, her anger ebbing away. She

wasn't going to argue this point with him, either. How could she? He wasn't ready yet to see what she saw. There was no way to force him to, either. Besides, she was getting off track. The *how* of Luke's changing, she believed, was in some ways less important than the *why*. And it was the why she wanted to talk about. She took a deep breath.

"Luke, I know you don't like it when I bring up Pop-Pop's death, but I'm sorry, I feel like I need to. Because let's be honest, he was more than a grandfather to you. He was . . . like a father to you," she said. Luke didn't raise his head, but she saw his body tense up. "We all miss him," she continued gently. "You and me, and Grandma, and we're all having a difficult time. But the two of us"—she made a gesture that included both of them—"we are our own family, and as the head of that family, I'm telling you there are going to be changes. There are going to be rules. Whether you—"

"But we're *not* a family," Luke broke in. "Not a *real* family."

"Of course we are," Billy said, shocked.

"I don't live with a dad," he said defiantly.

"*A lot* of kids don't live with a dad. Look at your class at school."

"No, you don't get it," Luke said, raising his voice. "They *know* who their dad is, even if he isn't married to their mom. I don't know *anything* about my dad."

"That's not . . . completely true, Luke. You know . . ." But she stopped herself here. For the simple reason that, for the past year, she'd known more than she was telling Luke.

"I know . . . what? His name?" he said, challenging

her. "So what? That's nothing. I've never even met him. I don't know where he lives. Or what he even really looks like. And he doesn't even know I exist. *Like, at all,*" he yelled. He ran out of the room and slammed his bedroom door so hard it made Billy jump. She turned, a little unsteadily, to pour herself a glass of water, less because she was thirsty than because she needed something to do. Well, he'd finally told her what he was feeling, she thought, sipping the lukewarm tap water. She just had no idea that he was feeling *that*.

Now, sitting on the back porch, barely conscious of the dusky twilight falling around her, she tried to think calmly about what Luke had said. This wasn't the first time he'd brought up his father, of course. But it was the first time he'd brought him up with that kind of anger. Starting when Luke was around three, he'd asked Billy about his father many times, and she'd always tried to answer him as honestly, and as patiently, as she could. The answers didn't add up to much. But at the time, Billy hadn't known any more than what she was telling him.

When Luke was still quite small, she'd looked for Wesley on her own. She'd typed his name into her web browser many times. Wesley Fitzgerald. There'd been other Wesley Fitzgeralds, just not *her* Wesley Fitzgerald. Even in the age of Google, not everyone was a click away from revealing himself or herself. At some point, though, around the time she and Luke moved to Butternut, she'd stopped looking for him. And until a year ago, she was left with nothing more than her memory of him, and of the night they had spent together.

She thought back to that night with Wesley now. As so often happened in Billy's life, it had begun with a book. This time it was Emily Brontë's *Wuthering Heights*, and she was reading it in, of all places, the lobby of a fishing lodge in Alaska. Coming here had not been her idea. It was April, and spring had finally, tentatively, arrived back home in St. Paul. Yet here she was, an hour outside of Fairbanks, where the daytime temperatures were still barely edging into the fifties and the nighttime temperatures were hovering close to zero. But Billy's father, an avid fisherman, had given himself this trip for his sixtieth birthday—fly-fishing for arctic grayling on the Chena River was a longtime dream of his—and since Billy's mother refused to go anywhere near a fishing rod, he'd invited Billy to come along with him instead. So there she was, on their last night at the lodge, curled up in an oversized leather arm-chair in front of a crackling fire, and so deep into one of her favorite novels—she'd just gotten to the scene where Heathcliff sees Catherine for the last time—that she was only tangentially aware of someone saying her name.

"Billy?"

"Uh-huh," she murmured distractedly, not bothering to look up from the page.

"It's Billy, right?"

Finally she glanced up. It was the fishing guide from that morning. *Wesley.* She'd liked his name because it had struck her as romantic. And the man, she'd thought, had fit the name. In fact, if Heathcliff had been an Alaskan fishing guide instead of—

"Your name *is* Billy, isn't it?" he asked, smiling down at her.

"Yes, it is," she said, blushing. "And you're Wesley." She straightened up in the armchair and closed her book, though she was careful to turn down the corner of the page to mark her place in it first.

"That must be a *really* good book," Wesley said. "I've been walking by you all night, and you've never once looked up from it."

"It's *Wuthering Heights*," Billy said, holding it up. "Have you ever read it?"

"Nope."

"Really? Not even in school?"

"Especially not in school. I didn't particularly like school. There were . . . too many books," he said with a half grimace, half smile.

"Oh, right," Billy said. She was always forgetting that not everyone loved reading as much as she did. "Well, you might like this one," she said. "It's very . . ."

"Very what?" he asked, sitting in the armchair opposite her. She'd assumed he'd said hello to her out of politeness, but now she realized he seemed to be enjoying himself.

"It's very . . . you know, romantic," Billy said, blushing again.

"Ahh," he said. "Romance. Maybe I should give it a try, then." He smiled as he reached for it. "That was the part of high school I actually liked."

Billy gave him the book, but he didn't open it. He talked to her instead. He was good at talking to people, she realized. Good at making them feel comfortable, and drawing them out of themselves. It was part of being a guide, he explained to her later when she commented on this. You had to know a lot about fishing, yes. But you had to know a lot about people, too. There wasn't really any way to learn this, though. Not in any school, at least. You either understood people or you didn't.

Now, as the nearby fire hissed and popped, they talked about their fishing trip that day. Wesley had taken Billy, her father, and four other guests fly-fishing on an "iced-out" stretch of the Chena River. "You're pretty good with a rod," he said approvingly of the graylings she'd caught.

"My dad saw to that," Billy said. "I'm an only child, so either I was going to be his fishing buddy, or no one was."

"It's just you and your mom and dad?" Wesley asked, surprised.

Billy nodded. She didn't think she was *meant* to be an only child. Her parents, she knew, had struggled to have a child. They'd both been in their early forties when she was born. If they were disappointed by the size of their family, though, they'd never shown it. She was the center of their lives. And maybe because she was an only child of older parents who adored her, she was that paradoxical blend of precociousness and naïveté. She always had friends, but they tended to be like her; they were more likely to spend weekends studying than sneaking alcohol or cigarettes.

Wesley, it turned out, was one of eleven children. He'd left his family's home in South Dakota at sixteen.

Billy was shocked to discover he was only twenty now, just two years older than she was. He looked so much more mature than the boys she knew at home. Then again, the boys she knew at home were from the Catholic boys' high school that was the brother to Billy's school. She couldn't imagine any of those boys being out on their own at sixteen. Their mothers were still laundering their school uniforms and packing their lunches.

"Didn't your parents miss you when you left?" she asked Wesley.

"I'm not sure they even noticed," he said. When Billy shook her head in wonderment, he added, "No. They noticed. Of course they did. But, still. It was one fewer person to keep track of. My dad probably said something like, 'Don't let the door hit you on the way out.'"

He told her about his travels a little bit, about some adventures he'd had out West and then in Alaska. He'd been a cook at a logging camp—he'd scrambled a thousand eggs a day there, he told Billy—he'd worked on a commercial fishing boat, and he'd been a rafting guide. But he'd landed here last year and it had felt right; he'd been fly-fishing since he was a kid. The money was pretty good. The guests were all right, or more than all right—here Billy got another smile—and the fishing, the fishing was fantastic. He could do a lot worse, he figured.

Billy listened to all this with fascination. Maybe it was the novel she was reading, or the firelight, or Wesley's rugged good looks—dark hair that was just a little longer than regulation length at the boys' high school, one blue eye and one brown eye, which Billy had never seen before and thought was incredibly exotic, and a nose that might have been broken before, in a fight, she secretly hoped—but the whole night seemed suddenly charged with possibility.

"Uh-oh, it looks like they're shutting down for the night," Wesley said finally, glancing around.

"Are they?" Billy said. She'd lost all track of time. But it was eleven o'clock already, and here was a middle-aged woman, the front desk manager, moving through the lobby, turning off all but a few lights. She gave Billy and Wesley a pointed time-to-be-saying-good-night smile.

Wesley gave Billy her book and they stood up. There was an awkward pause—awkward for Billy, not for Wesley. "Well, your dad's probably wondering where you are," he said.

Billy shook her head. "We have separate rooms. He said he was going to turn in early, though. Knowing him, he's already asleep." She hesitated. She didn't want to stop talking to Wesley, but it seemed they were out of options.

He, apparently, thought differently. "Do you want to go to a party?" he asked.

"*Now?*"

He nodded. "It's in one of the employee cabins. It's a nightly thing. We take turns buying the beer and . . ." He shrugged.

Billy looked around the lobby. The desk manager was gone. *Everyone* was gone. She was excited to be alone with him, but at the same time, she was also a little nervous.

"If you're too tired, though, I understand. That was an early call this morning."

"No," Billy said suddenly. Decisively. "I'm not tired. I'd like to go to a party." After all, she thought, the only things waiting for her in her room were more books, and for once, they didn't seem like they were going to be enough. Besides, her parents were always encouraging her—their quiet, studious daughter—to get out in the world more. The fact that this probably wasn't what they had in mind wasn't lost on her. Still, she had to take her opportunities as they came. "Let's go," she said, smiling at Wesley.

"We're going to go out the back way," Wesley said, leading her through the lobby and then down a corridor she hadn't noticed before. "Technically it's against the rules for employees to fraternize with the guests after hours," he added. "But it happens. Usually the management looks the other way."

When they got to the back entrance, though, Billy stopped. "I don't have a coat," she said, turning to him.

"That's all right," Wesley said. "You can borrow mine." He left her there for a minute and came back with a big down jacket that he bundled her up in before they left the lodge. "It's not that far," he said as they hurried along a walkway that led to employee housing. Billy nodded but didn't say anything. She was too cold to talk. Her cheeks stung, and her breath left wispy clouds around her face as her boots squeaked on the hard-packed snow. "Here we are," Wesley said, steer-

ing her toward the first in a row of small cabins. He
banged loudly on the door, but when no one answered,
he opened it himself. They came into a bright, warm
living room filled with the sounds of music and talking. Billy was instantly self-conscious. What kind of
person brings a book to a party? she chided herself of
the novel she was still holding. And then there was her
outfit: an Irish knit sweater, blue jeans, and a pair of
UGGs. But as Wesley closed the door behind them and
helped her out of his coat, she looked around and saw
that the "party" was just a group of people—dressed,
like her, in jeans and sweaters and boots—hanging
out and drinking beer. Wesley introduced her to a few
people who looked around his age, and then he went
to get her a drink. She didn't like beer, she told him,
so he came back from the tiny kitchen with a rum and
Coke he'd mixed for her. Billy took a hesitant sip. It
was sweet and fizzy, and if not for the funny taste in
it, the taste that was the rum, she would have liked it.
She took one more sip and then set it down. He found
a seat for the two of them on a couch, and he talked
to his friends—who called him Wes—about fishing,
and different kinds of rods, and a road trip they'd taken
to Anchorage earlier that spring. Billy listened, relieved that he didn't seem to expect her to contribute
anything to the conversation. At one point he put his
arm loosely around her, and she leaned, only a little
self-consciously, against him, pressing her cheek to the
soft flannel of his shirt. He smelled good, she decided,
especially considering that he spent a good part of his
time with fish. One of his friends got up then to get
another beer but didn't come back, and Wesley talked

only to Billy now, talked to her in that easy way he had, asking her questions about St. Paul and high school, and even books besides *Wuthering Heights* that she'd read and liked.

"You have no idea how pretty you are, do you?" he asked her at one point. Billy shook her head, her face warm. "Well, trust me, you are." He leaned down and started to kiss her, but there was a commotion at one of the windows of the cabin and Wesley stopped, grabbed her hand, and dragged her over to it.

"What is it?" Billy asked, disappointed that the kiss was over almost before it had even begun.

"It's the northern lights," Wesley said, making room for Billy at the window. "You don't always see them at this time of year." She looked outside. Bands of green light were shimmering in the night sky.

"Have you seen them in Minnesota?"

"Yes, but not like this," Billy said as a red band now shot across the sky.

"Come on," he said. He bundled her back into his coat and took her outside to get a better look at them. The bands of light, now green and red mixed together, rippled and swayed against the night. "They're amazing," Billy breathed, tipping her chin up toward the sky.

"They're putting on this show for you," Wesley commented, and while this might have sounded corny coming from anyone else, it sounded just right coming from him. She smiled at him, and he pulled her into his arms and kissed her. She'd been kissed before, a couple of times, but not like this. Her first kiss, in the hallway outside the gymnasium at a high school dance, had been especially disappointing. The boy's tongue, heavy and damp, had lain on the bottom of her mouth like an old rug that Billy had longed to push out of the way. And another, more recent kiss, this one at a party, had been with a boy who'd thrashed his tongue around in her mouth so relentlessly that in the end it had felt more like an assault than a kiss. This kiss was different; this kiss was *perfect*.

"Do you want to come back to my room?" Wesley asked finally, looking down at her. Billy nodded. At this point, she probably would have agreed to go anywhere with him, including the waters of the icy river.

On the narrow bed in his cabin—his roommate was blessedly absent—he stopped kissing her long enough to ask, "You've had boyfriends before, right?"

"Right," Billy said. *Wrong.* She'd had crushes, flirtations, and a short relationship carried out almost entirely through text messages, but she'd never had an actual boyfriend before. She understood, though, that that wasn't the real question that Wesley was asking her. He was asking her if she was a virgin, and while in old-fashioned novels, a young woman's virginity was often a gift to be given away to the man she loved, Billy suspected this was one gift Wesley might not particularly want.

"I've had a couple of boyfriends," she said softly as he eased her bulky sweater off.

"Are you . . . on the pill or something?" he asked hopefully.

Billy nodded yes. *What?* She was most assuredly *not* on the pill. So why hadn't she told him this? And since *she* had no protection, why hadn't she asked *him* to use some? These were only a few of the questions she asked herself in the days and weeks and months that followed. Sometimes she blamed her pregnancy on her Catholic education. Thirteen years of school and not a sex ed class in sight. But she'd known better. Of course she'd known better. She just hadn't wanted him to know she was a virgin, hadn't wanted him to know she wasn't on the pill. If he'd understood the truth, the night's momentum would be interrupted, and this thing, *this amazing thing*, would never happen. After all, she'd read enough novels to know the night's narrative was moving forward; it had a logic and a momentum of its own. She shouldn't interfere with it or change it or, worst of all, end it. She was meant to lose her virginity tonight, and she was meant to lose it with Wesley.

Later, of course, when she told her parents, when she postponed college, when she went shopping for maternity clothes while her friends were going to fraternity parties, she felt more than a little overwhelmed and more than a little critical of her own judgment that night. She'd made her choice, though. And comforting to her, in those often lonely months after her friends had all started college, was the image she remembered seeing outside Wesley's window as they made love. Through the opening in the tacked-on red-and-white-checked curtains, the northern lights, magical and mysterious, were still visible. That *must* have been a good sign, she told herself. Her child was conceived under the northern lights.

In any case, after the night was over, Wesley walked

her back to the lodge and up to her floor. He'd kissed
her good-bye since she and her dad were leaving early
the next morning, and waited while she let herself into
her room. It wasn't until Billy was right on the edge
of sleep that she remembered her copy of *Wuthering
Heights*. She'd left it at the party.

She went home without the book, and her dad left
empty-handed, as well; the arctic graylings they'd
fished for were catch-and-release only. But he did have
an unexpected souvenir from this trip. Eight months,
two weeks, and three days later, he had a grandson who
weighed in at seven pounds, eleven ounces, and who
had a dramatic thatch of black hair that the maternity
nurses couldn't help but admire.

A mosquito buzzed in Billy's ear now, bringing her
back to the present. The mosquitoes were out in full
force. She considered going inside and making dinner.
She'd offered to do this earlier for Luke through his
closed bedroom door, but he'd called back to her that
he wasn't hungry. He should have been hungry, and so
should she. The last time she'd eaten was at the wedding, and even then she hadn't had more than a few
bites. *Oh, that food,* she thought now. That must be
the food they served in heaven. As delicious as it had
tasted, though, it hadn't been the best part of the wedding. That was the ceremony—so simple, but beautiful and heartfelt at the same time. Remembering it, she
allowed herself a moment of wistfulness, but only a
moment.

Now Murphy raised his head off his paws and, suddenly alert, growled low in his throat. It was probably
Mrs. Wheaton's orange tabby in the next yard over.

Billy petted Murphy again and tried to think of something pleasant and upbeat to talk to him about since she'd been such poor company tonight. *Oh, I know, Murph. I met someone at the wedding. Cal. Cal Cooper. He gave me a ride to the police station. He's from Seattle, though. He's just passing through. In a Porsche, no less.* She gave Murphy's ears a final rub.

CHAPTER 9

When Billy was a child, she wanted to be a librarian because she assumed she would spend her days reading. Experience had long since relieved her of this idea. But every once in a while, her job struck her as very nearly perfect. She was having one of those moments—or rather, she *should* have been having one of those moments—on Monday morning. During a lull in activity, she was sitting at the checkout desk, sipping her latte and perusing a copy of *Publishers Weekly* for ideas on new books to order for the library. Ordinarily this was one of her favorite things to do, but today she was having difficulty concentrating on the page in front of her. Instead she kept seeing a picture of Luke hanging off of the edge of that bridge, the river's boulder-strewn rapids rushing beneath him. She shook her head a little now to dislodge this image from her mind and tried to refocus her attention. But there was something else bothering her, something other than Luke's reck-lessness. She stood up and, coming out from behind the checkout desk, walked over to the windows that faced Main Street. There, three bicycles idled, unlocked, on the sidewalk in front of the library. The boys were still here. She'd forgotten about them. They'd been so quiet—*too* quiet, she realized now. She headed back to the computer area, passing Rae on the way.

"Everything all right?" Rae asked, looking up from the books she was reshelving. Billy had debriefed her that morning about the incident with Luke on the bridge, and Rae, who'd been thoroughly exasperated with him, seemed especially sensitive to Billy's mood now.

"It will be," Billy said under her breath, walking faster. She turned right after the last aisle of books and saw the boys grouped around a computer, their urgent whispers punctuated only by the occasional guffaw.

"Oh my God, she's so hot," Billy heard Joey Stengel say as he pointed at the screen. "I would *totally* go out with her."

"Yeah, right. Like she's going to go out with an eleven-year-old," his friend Clay Lewis said.

"Hello, boys," Billy said, coming up behind them. Joey and Clay and Clay's younger brother, Theo, all jumped. Joey hurried to close the page, but not before Billy had a chance to see what they were looking at: a suntanned and windblown woman in a lace-up pale pink teddy, a come-hither expression on her face. Billy recognized a Victoria's Secret model when she saw one.

"That's it. No more lingerie Web sites for the three of you. And Theo," Billy said, "you are *nine* years old. You are *way* too young for this."

"Sorry, Ms. Harper," the boys all mumbled more or less in unison.

"Now, outside, all three of you," she said, shooing them away. "Go get some sunshine and fresh air." And as they shuffled out she wished, not for the first time, that the library's Internet filter, which screened out pornography Web sites, would also screen out lingerie catalogs. She made a mental note to speak to Anton, the high school student who was their unofficial tech support, about this.

She started to push in the chairs the boys had been sitting on, then changed her mind and sat down on one herself. With a quick glance behind her to make sure no one was watching, she reopened the web browser and typed "Cal Cooper Seattle" into the search bar. Five minutes later she was still skimming over web pages, so absorbed in what she was doing that she didn't even notice Rae come up behind her.

"What are we looking at?" she asked Billy.

"Nothing," Billy said guiltily, closing the web browser. "Is anyone else here?"

Rae shook her head. "Just you, me, and the mice. And speaking of the mice, it might be time to call pest control again."

"Here, have a seat," Billy said, indicating the chair next to hers. "I want to show you something."

Rae sat obligingly. Billy relaunched the browser, opened the history, and clicked on a site. "What's 'Forty under Forty'?" Rae asked of the article Billy had pulled up.

"It's *Seattle Magazine*'s annual ranking of the most influential young people in the city," Billy said, clicking through the slideshow. She stopped on number seventeen, Cal Cooper. In the photograph, he was dressed in a crisp blue shirt and suit pants, and standing in a glassed-in corner office, a view of downtown Seattle behind him.

"Very nice," Rae said. "He's got a killer smile. I definitely approve of"—she leaned closer to read his bio—"Cal Cooper. But why are we looking at him?"

"Because he's the guy who was driving the Porsche. Remember? The one Officer Sawyer pulled over on Friday afternoon?"

"That's *him*?" Rae said. "Okay, yeah. I can see a resemblance. I mean, I didn't have a *great* view of him from across the street." She shook her head. "*Jeez*, he's even better looking than that car of his. How did you know who he was, though? You wouldn't even come to the window to see him."

"I met him on Saturday," Billy explained, "at Daisy's wedding. He's Allie Ford's brother. And . . ." She hesitated, but only for a second. "I've been in that car, too. He gave me a ride in it."

"And you're just mentioning this to me *now*?" Rae said accusingly. "After we've been here for *two* hours?"

"I know. But . . . nothing happened. We had a five-minute conversation at the reception, and then, when Officer Sawyer called about Luke, I told him—Cal—that my car was in the shop. He gave me a ride. That's it. End of story."

Rae raised an eyebrow. "If that's 'end of story,' why are you Googling him?"

"Because . . . I was curious, obviously," Billy admitted. "And because . . . he wasn't wearing a wedding ring," she added. "At least, not at the wedding."

Rae started to say something, but Billy held up a hand to silence her. "No, it's not what you think," she said, returning to the browsing history and opening another web page. "See?" she said, gesturing at the screen. "He's married. He's *very* married."

"'Beauty and the Builder,'" Rae murmured, reading the title of the feature in *Seattle Met Magazine*, and studying the photograph that accompanied it. In it, a barefoot Cal, wearing a crisp white shirt and impeccably faded blue jeans, was sitting on a white couch next to his wife, a petite blonde in a sleeveless white dress with an asymmetrical neckline. The apartment was also white—white rugs, white couches, white coffee tables—with only a few hints of subtle color in it, mainly grays and sea foam greens. What would it be like to live someplace like that? Billy wondered. Someplace that perfect? And her mind went, involuntarily, to the state of her own house when she'd left it that morning. Breakfast dishes in the kitchen sink with congealed egg yolk on them, a hamper in the laundry room overflowing with dirty clothes, a chewed-on bone of Murphy's that she'd almost tripped over in the hall on her way out the door.

"That's his apartment?" Rae asked in disbelief.

Billy nodded. "And that's his *wife*," she said. "Meghan Mills-Cooper. She's an interior designer. They work together sometimes, according to this article. The rest of the time, apparently, they're just wearing their perfect clothes, sitting on their perfect furniture, living their perfect lives."

"Any children?" Rae asked.

"No, or at least not when this article was written. But

he says somewhere that he wants them. I'm sure they'll be perfect, too."

"Hmm. I don't know about that apartment, though," Rae said doubtfully. "I mean, you couldn't drink a glass of red wine in that living room, much less have a child running around in it." Rae was very fond of red wine, less fond of children.

"Wait until you see this," Billy said, clicking on the browser history again and pulling up another photograph. This one had been taken at the American Institute of Architects Seattle Honor Awards reception in 2015. In it, Cal wore a suit and his killer smile. His wife, standing next to him, wore a silver cocktail dress that probably cost more than the twelve most expensive items in Billy's closet combined. "Look at her," she said, pointing to Meghan. "How is it even possible for someone to have a waist that small?"

"Photoshop?" Rae suggested.

"Then they've photoshopped *all* of her."

"Oh, please," Rae said dismissively. "She looks like a milk-fed calf. And don't think for one minute that men find that attractive, either. They don't. They like a woman with a little extra flesh on her," she added, poking at her own waist. "Really. It's because of evolution. They did a study on it."

"I'll have to remind myself of that the next time I get on the scale. Right now, though, we need to get back to work."

"Indeed, we do," Rae said, but when Billy started to get up, Rae stopped her.

"Billy?"

"Yes?"

"I'm proud of you."

"For what? Surfing the Internet during working hours?"

"No, for noticing Mr. Porsche. First you checked to see if he was wearing a wedding ring, and then you Googled him. Even if he *is* married, I'd say that's progress. You were interested. That's a good thing."

"I guess," Billy said noncommittally.

"*Of course* . . . he's no Beige Ted," Rae drawled.

Billy rolled her eyes, but as she went back to the checkout desk, she thought about Beige Ted. His real name was Ted Whitaker, and Billy had dated him, briefly, two years ago. She'd met him at the library. He was an accountant whose office was down the block, and whose hobby of growing bonsai trees made him a frequent visitor to the library's gardening section. (Who knew there were so many bonsai books? Certainly not Billy.) The two of them had struck up a casual friendship, and when he'd asked her out, she'd thought, why not? She hadn't dated much since she and Luke had moved to Butternut three years before, and given her public role in the community, she was determined to date only someone she considered a safe choice. Ted was safe. He was a respected, if forgettable, figure in town. He was attractive, too, although in such a bland way that when Billy wasn't with him, she could rarely hold a clear image of him in her mind.

They'd gone out on a few dates, and they might have gone out on more but for one thing: Billy introduced Ted to Luke. She'd been warned about how difficult it might be to introduce a prospective boyfriend to her son, but in this case, it had been anticlimactic. Ted had come to pick her up for dinner, and she'd brought him into the den, where the babysitter was reading a magazine and Luke was working on an elaborate Lego construction.

"Luke, this is Ted," Billy had said brightly. "Ted, this is Luke." Luke had looked up and, leaning back on his heels, given Ted a thorough once-over. What Billy had seen in Luke's expression was not anxiety or jealousy or any of the other things she'd thought she might see, but instead, a complete and total lack of interest.

"Hi, Ted," Luke had said dismissively, and he'd gone back to his Legos.

It was right around this time, too, that Rae had started referring to Ted as Beige Ted. Billy couldn't remember now if it was because he often wore beige clothing, or his sandy hair and light brown eyes could be construed as beige, or his personality was somewhat colorless. In any case, the nickname stuck, and after Billy heard Luke—who must have heard it from Rae—refer to him as Beige Ted, she knew it was time to break things off.

Billy was settling in again at the checkout desk when the front door opened, and Maggie Donahue, a pretty, blond mother in her early thirties, came in with her three children, all of whom were under the age of six. Maggie always seemed a little frazzled—and who could blame her?—but this morning she seemed exhausted. "Hey, what's going on?" Billy asked, coming to meet her.

"Nothing. We just had a bad night," Maggie said,

barely suppressing a yawn. "Bella's teething," she added of the eleven-month-old she was holding, "and she was up and down every few hours."

"Here, let me take her," Billy said, reaching for Bella and settling her on her hip. Elliot, Maggie's five-year-old, scampered off now. Billy knew where he was going: to the children's area, to pull out all the books on airplanes, and then to lie on his stomach and stare at the pictures in them. Ian, Maggie's three-year-old, was shier. He hid himself partially behind his mom and looked up at Billy with a gentle curiosity. "I remember when Luke was teething," Billy said now, looking down at Bella, whose fuzzy blond hair called to mind a dandelion in bloom. "My grandmother kept telling me to let Luke suck on a dishcloth dipped in bourbon, and I kept thinking, 'Thanks, but I'd rather not have a drunken baby on my hands.' Have you tried the teething necklaces, though? They can be helpful sometimes."

"I have a couple of those," Maggie said. "I just can't find them. I think the dog might have gotten to them." She yawned again, and Billy smiled sympathetically. She remembered how chaotic those days were, and that was with one child, not three. Of course, unlike her, Maggie was married, but married to a man who traveled at least two weeks out of every month. Maybe, in a way, that was harder, Billy mused. To have that help and then *not* to have that help. Billy's parents, at least, had always been there.

Bella babbled something now, and Billy, whose nose was inches from her wispy blond hair, said, "She smells wonderful, like . . . cinnamon toast."

"That's what she had for breakfast. I think she got some of it in her hair."

Billy nestled Bella against her and reached out for Ian's hand. He smiled cautiously and, coming out from behind his mother, put his little palm inside hers.

"Go," she said to Maggie, pointing her chin at the door. "Make a break for it. I can watch them while you get a coffee at Pearl's."

"Oh, God, I would love a cappuccino, Billy. Five minutes, I promise," she said, making the Scout's honor sign.

"Go," Billy said again, though when she was gone, Billy had Rae to contend with. Rae didn't say anything; she didn't need to. Her look said it all: *I don't know why you're always doing that for her, Billy. You are not a babysitting service.*

Billy's look back at her said, *I know, I know. But she looks so tired. And it's only for five minutes. And let's face it, her kids are so cute.* And Billy felt the little pang she got every once in a while when she held someone else's baby. A pang accompanied by the knowledge that while she'd always wanted another child, the opportunity to have one was very possibly slipping away. Billy smiled down now at Bella, and Bella smiled back at her, revealing a tiny front tooth just coming in. "There it is," Billy said, "the tooth that kept you and your mommy awake last night." She let go of Ian's hand long enough to smooth out Bella's cinnamon toast hair, then said to Rae, who was hovering disapprovingly nearby, "Do you want to smell her head?"

"Her head? No. Why?"

"Because it smells so good. It's like, you know, a thing. Smelling babies' heads."

"Not for me, it isn't," Rae said.

"Your loss," Billy said blithely. She took Bella and Ian over to the children's area where, as predicted, their older brother Elliot was already sprawled out on the rug, surrounded by books. Billy perched on one of the little chairs, at a little table, and balanced Bella on her lap. "Do you want to do a puzzle?" she asked Ian. A wooden puzzle with large, easy-to-grasp pieces was on the tabletop.

Ian shook his head. "No," he said, pointing to it, his blue eyes serious. "Missing piece."

"That's true. It does have a missing piece." Billy sighed. "No sooner do we buy a new puzzle and put it out than one of its pieces goes missing. I don't know what becomes of them, Ian. It's a mystery."

Ian's eyes widened. He liked the idea of a mystery, Billy saw. "Who do you think could be taking them?" she asked.

He considered this. "A monster?" he said finally. Softly. He didn't look afraid at this possibility, though. He looked fascinated.

"Maybe." Billy smiled. "But if it is, it's a friendly monster."

He had some ideas about this, and by the time his mom had come back with her cappuccino, they'd talked about the monster—a puzzle monster—at length, and even done the puzzle, despite the missing piece. Billy had also put Bella down on the rug and followed her around as she crawled, pulling books out of the bottom shelves with gleeful abandon. After their mom had collected them, Billy reshelved these books, and thought about what Luke had been like when he was Ian's age.

He was so sweet, so curious and, in a way, so much easier than he was now. Yes, he'd needed her more then, in more immediate and practical ways than he did today—needed her to run his bath, tie his shoes, and make his chicken fingers. Motherhood was physical then, and physically tiring. But at least she'd understood what he needed. He needed her to love him, take care of him, and keep him safe. She'd never doubted her ability to do these things. Not really. Not after the first new mother jitters had worn off. She'd thought that this would be enough, that this love would see them through.

When, she wondered, shelving a last book, had things gotten so complicated? Yes, Luke still needed her. She knew that. But she didn't always know *who* he needed her to be, the loving parent or the disciplinarian? And the rules . . . the rules were constantly changing. Be involved, but not *too* involved. Foster independence, but not *too* much independence. There was always some elusive medium she couldn't find.

It wasn't just the rules that were always changing. *Luke* seemed always to be changing, too. This, it turned out, was the most fascinating and exhausting and challenging part of raising a child. You, the parent, might feel as if you were an established person with specific characteristics, interests, and traits. But your child was always changing from one year to the next. Sometimes from one month, week, or day to the next. Whereas the young boy of ten might give you a hug when he got home from school, the eleven-year-old might suddenly one day not just stop hugging but also appear to be altogether appalled by the possibility. The boy who had loved drawing in middle school might one day put away his colored pencils and never use them again. She remembered picking Luke up after school about six months ago on a rainy day, and when she'd asked him how school had been, instead of giving her his usual commentary about everything from the funny stories his history teacher had told them to amusing tales of his table in the cafeteria, he'd simply said, "It was okay." And then he was silent for the rest of the ride home. She'd tried to cajole him with stories of *her* day at the library, but he'd seemed intensely preoccupied, and eventually she'd turned on the car radio. That general silence had prevailed since, undermining the confidence she used to feel parenting Luke. She would give anything to get their easy camaraderie back. Give anything to know the right thing to say and do again, when everything she said and did now felt tentative and uncertain, a test balloon she was sending up to see how Luke would respond.

Just as Billy finished straightening up the children's area, there was a flurry of activity at the checkout desk. The summer tourist season was under way in Butternut now, and everyone wanted the perfect book to take to the beach, or read on the dock at their cabin, or maybe just fall asleep with in a lakeside hammock. Along with choosing which books to order, recommending books to patrons was the best part of Billy's job, and she quite happily took it upon herself to find the right book for everyone. This took a lot of reading on Billy's part. The Jane Austen books were for the back porch only. On her bedside table there was always a stack of contemporary fiction and nonfiction.

The rest of the morning flew by, and after she'd eaten her brown bag lunch on the library's back porch and was settling back in to work at the checkout desk, she heard a familiar voice say, "Ms. Harper?"

"Hi, Mara," Billy said, looking up and smiling at Mara Shepard, who, at ten years old, read more than anyone else who patronized the Butternut Library. "Are you done with those already?" Billy asked her of the stack of Louisa May Alcott novels Mara was balancing in her arms.

Mara nodded and slid them across the desk to Billy.

"How many times does that make for this series?" Billy asked, opening the top book—*Little Women*—and sliding the wand over its bar code to check it back in.

"Three times," Mara said. And then she added shyly, "But I still cry every time I read the scene when Beth dies."

"I know," Billy said with a sigh. "Just *thinking* about it, even now, is enough to get my tear glands working. When I was your age, I used to reread it and think maybe this time it would end differently. But of course it never did. What are you going to read next?" she asked, checking the second book back in.

"I don't know. Do you have any suggestions?"

Billy smiled. She always had a suggestion for Mara. She had never *not* had a suggestion for Mara. And what was so satisfying about Mara was that, unlike some of the patrons who asked for a recommendation from Billy, Mara actually followed it. She read the book and then, more often than not, she read it again. Since Mara had started coming here five years ago—her family lived across the street from the library—Billy had overseen her reading list, starting with her personal favorites, the *Little House* books, and progressing through the *Betsy-Tacy* books and the *Chronicles of Narnia*, with many other books between. Mara showed no sign of slowing down.

"I do have a recommendation for you, Mara," Billy said, jumping up and coming out from behind the checkout desk. "I've been saving this for you to read next year, but I think you're ready for it now." She led Mara to the *L*s in the fiction section and ran her finger along the book spines until she found it. She pulled it out—it was a lovely leather-bound edition—and presented it to Mara.

Mara examined the title. "*A Wrinkle in Time*?"

"That's right."

"Is it good?"

"It's *really* good."

"All right. I'll read it." Mara smiled.

"Let me know what you think of it," Billy said. As they went to check it out, she envied Mara reading it for the first time.

Once Mara left, the afternoon dragged. Billy was rarely bored at work because she didn't have time to be bored, but occasionally the day could feel heavy on her hands. The new books that had come in recently needed to be processed, cataloged, and covered with a clear plastic film for protection before she could shelve them. When she was done with that, there were bookkeeping, budgeting, and preparing for the next board meeting. At one point, staring at her computer screen, she felt her eyelids droop. The library's ambient noises weren't helping—the drone of the air conditioner, the humming and clicking of the copy machine, even the rhythmic ticking of the antique grandfather clock that was a gift from one of the patrons. All of these made her feel it would be a miracle if she could keep herself awake. But she did. And by three o'clock, she got a second wind and decided to do some housekeeping, something that she enjoyed doing much more at the library than at home. "I don't think the new cleaning woman is dusting," she commented to Rae as she ran a feather duster over one of the shelves.

"Genevieve?" Rae said of the woman Billy had recently hired to clean the library after hours once a week. "Oh, Genevieve is as blind as a bat."

"Hmm." Billy frowned. "Well, she might have mentioned that." She watched as the dust motes she'd disturbed swirled in the sunlight slanting in through the west-facing windows. "Rae," she called as her friend started to wheel the book cart back to the book return bin.

"Yes?"

"I called my mother this morning. You know, about Luke." This conversation had taken place in the bathroom at home, with Billy running the shower so Luke could not hear her as she told her mom about Saturday's incident.

"What did she say?"

"Well, she said if I wanted to send him to North Woods Adventures for Teens—a program Officer Sawyer suggested—she'd split the cost with me."

"That was nice of her."

"It was. But . . . when I broached the subject with Luke at the breakfast table, he said, 'No. No way.' The thing is, though, I think he'd really like it. A year ago, he would have jumped at the chance to go. I mean, the program for his age is 'The Call of the Woods: Hiking, Canoeing, and Camping the Superior Hiking Trail.' It's two weeks with three counselors and twelve other boys. Shouldn't that sound like heaven to him?"

"It probably does. He just doesn't want to give you the satisfaction of admitting it," Rae said.

Billy, still dusting, frowned. "I was on their Web site last night. I think it would be good for him. I don't want it to feel like a punishment, though."

"It doesn't sound like a punishment," Rae said. "And even if it was"—she shrugged—"that's your call."

"You sound like my mother." During their phone call this morning, her mother had said, "You don't need to be his friend right now. You need to be his parent. And if, as his parent, you feel strongly about him going on this trip, then he should go. Stop doubting your own authority."

And Rae, as if privy to this conversation, gave Billy a reassuring pat on the shoulder and said, "You're a good mom, Billy. You just have to trust your instincts."

Billy was about to point out that her instincts seemed to be failing her lately, but Mr. Finch came in then for his late afternoon nap and stopped to chat with her on the way to his armchair.

CHAPTER 10

A couple of days later, Luke was hanging out with the same friends Billy had forbidden him to see.

"Do you want another beer?" Van asked.

Luke shook his head. "I haven't finished this one yet," he said, indicating the can of Miller High Life he was holding. He took another sip as if to prove he would finish it, eventually. He didn't see how he could, though. It tasted so bitter. Did all beer taste like this, he wondered, or just this kind? He had no idea. He'd never tried it before today. Never tried any kind of alcohol, but he wasn't about to tell Van and J.P. that. Maybe, he thought, this beer would have tasted better if it'd been cold, but J.P. had brought them in a grubby old paper bag. They were not only warm but also had a coating of dirt on them, like they'd just been sitting in a garage somewhere. Luke started to ask him where he'd gotten them, but he stopped himself. J.P. didn't like it when Luke asked him questions. He always seemed suspicious of Luke, like he was going to snitch on him or something. It didn't help that he thought Luke had gotten special treatment for the graffiti incident. He'd gotten off with a warning. Van and J.P. had to perform community service, and J.P. had to see a counselor since it wasn't the first time he'd gotten into trouble.

"You're a slow drinker," J.P. said to him now. He made it sound like an accusation. But Luke only shrugged. J.P. was sort of okay if you just kind of ignored him. Then he just kind of ignored you back. Luke didn't like him that much, but when you hung out with Van, outside school anyway, J.P. kind of came with the package. J.P. lived next door to Van, and since he was a dropout, he had a lot of free time.

Luke balanced on his skateboard now and tried to do a flip-kick with it. He couldn't, though. For one thing, he was holding the beer, and for another, the concrete they were on—the parking lot behind an abandoned service station—was all cracked and choked with weeds. He gave up and went back under the overhang of the building's roof, where Van and J.P. were drinking.

God, it was hot, he thought, wiping his forehead. It should have felt cooler here in the shade, but it didn't. The air was so hot and still that the silence felt loud. Almost like it was buzzing inside his head. Or was that the beer? He didn't know. Maybe it was possible to get drunk on one beer—on less than one beer, if it was your first one. He took another sip and tried not to flinch as he tasted it, especially since J.P. was watching him.

"You don't even like it," J.P. said.

"It's okay," Luke said. And then, surprising himself, he added, "Vodka's better."

J.P. finished his beer. He threw the can on the ground and stomped on it, hard, so that he crushed it almost flat. "You don't know anything about vodka," he scoffed, kicking the can away.

"Whatever," Luke said, looking down at his skate-board.

"He knows about it," Van offered, leaning against the wall. "His mom has a liquor cabinet, doesn't she?"

"Yeah, she does," Luke said casually. He'd told Van this, and it was true, sort of. It wasn't really a cabinet. It was more of a cupboard, and the liquor didn't take up the whole thing, just a little bit of it. It was a couple of bottles, really, that his mom kept mostly for guests. She preferred wine, though. "Actually, my mom mostly drinks wine," he said, shooting a look at J.P., who was opening another can of beer.

"What kind?" he asked, instantly alert. "Red or white?"

"White," Luke said. "She likes chardonnay," he added, proud that he'd remembered the kind of wine she drank.

"*Chardonnay,*" J.P. hooted. "That's a ladies' drink. Men don't drink that. They drink red wine."

Luke's face burned. Was that true? He didn't know what men drank. His Pop-Pop had hardly drunk at all, except on special occasions, and as for his dad . . . who knew what his dad drank? But J.P. had already moved on. "I can't believe your mom is a librarian," he said. "That's so lame. Does she just, like, yell at people all day? 'Can you be quiet, please?'" he said in a high voice. "'Please! You're being very disrespectful of all the books here. They need absolute silence,'" he sang in a voice bordering on the hysterical.

"Shut up," Luke muttered, truly angry with J.P. for the first time. He didn't always want to be around his mom, but he didn't want people making fun of her, either. "She doesn't sound like that," he added, glaring at J.P. "That's, like, a librarian on TV or something."

"Yeah, his mom's actually pretty cool," Van said, coming to his rescue. Luke felt grateful. Van and his mom had never actually met each other. He didn't want them to meet each other, either. Not after the trouble Luke had gotten into with Van, and not when he wasn't even supposed to be with him at all. But still, it was a nice thing to say.

"And being a librarian is dope," Van continued, sipping his beer. "You . . . what? Sit there all day and do, like, nothing. Just read at story time or whatever and then you get paid for it. That's cool."

This was wrong, too, Luke knew, but he didn't say anything. He wished they'd stop talking about his mom, though. He felt bad. She thought he was at Nature Camp. It was where he was supposed to be. But he hadn't gone this morning, even though camp had only started three days ago. He'd waited until his mom had left for work, and then he'd called Margot and told her he wasn't feeling well. She'd been nice about it. She hadn't asked to talk to his mom or anything. She'd just told him to hurry up and get better because the Black Bears—that was the seven- and eight-year-old group he helped out with—would miss him. After they'd hung up, Luke had left the house and, careful to avoid Main Street, skateboarded to the rec center, where he'd met Van, who often hung out there in the mornings. (He felt like he needed to tell Van he was grounded and had his cell phone taken away. Otherwise Van might think he was avoiding him.) After they'd left the rec center they'd come here, and J.P. had met them later with the beer.

The time before J.P. had shown up had been the best. Luke and Van actually talked about stuff. They didn't *just* talk—they skateboarded while they talked—but Van told him stuff, like how he was going to move to LA one day, after high school, maybe, and how he was going to be part of a skateboarding crew there that had a house on the beach and just chilled and skateboarded all day. He'd asked Luke if he wanted to go, too, once, and that was when Luke had told him about Alaska. About his dad. And about how he wanted to find him and maybe go visit him. Van thought that was cool. So now, when they hung out, they talked about LA and Alaska and how they were going to save up for airfare. Luke already had over a thousand dollars in a bank account, most of it from birthday money and Christmas money, but he didn't tell Van that. It might make him feel bad, because Luke didn't see how Van would ever get the money to go away. He didn't even have enough for a hot dog at the Quick and Convenient; when they went there, Luke had to buy one for him.

Still, for someone who seemed so broke, Van had *a lot* of video games at his house. Maybe that was because his dad played them, too. He didn't play them *with* Van and Luke. He was never home when Luke was there. And Van's mom had moved out. Maybe that was another reason Luke liked Van. He didn't think it was weird that Luke didn't know who his dad was. Unlike Luke, though, Van didn't seem curious about where his mom had gone. All he'd said about her was that she'd left one day when he was little, and she hadn't come back. He seemed okay with it, but Luke wondered sometimes how he could be. Maybe it was because his aunt came over sometimes. She did some cooking and cleaning for Van and his dad. Luke didn't think she did a very good job, though. Most of the time their place was a total wreck.

Luke watched now as Van took his skateboard out into the parking lot and practiced kicking the tail of his board down while he jumped so that it popped into the air. He made it look easy, even on this crummy surface. Van, who had hair so blond it was almost white and light blue eyes, was small for his age. He was kind of skinny, too, but he was stronger and faster than he looked. He'd gotten in a fight once at school with a guy who played middle school football and he'd won. The kid, Michael, was a total jerk, and Van only fought with him because he'd said Van and his dad were trashy.

Luke put down his can of beer—it was still only half-empty—and stepped on his skateboard. He started to push off from it, then stopped. His stomach felt weird, and he knew if he skated now, the beer would just slosh around and he'd feel worse. Plus, he was hungry. He thought about the lunch his mom had packed for him, still sitting on the kitchen counter, and wished he'd remembered to take it. Maybe they could go to the Quick and Convenient?

"You're not going to get sick, are you?" J.P. asked, already finishing another beer. God, how did he do it?

"I'm fine," Luke said, watching Van skate.

J.P. shook his head. "You should have gone to that day care center you work at," he said disgustedly.

Luke didn't answer him.

"Don't they need you to change diapers there?" he asked.

"I told you, there are no diapers," Luke said, too hot to work up any real anger. "It's a day camp. You have to be five to go there." He knew no matter what he said, though, J.P. would keep calling it a day care center. He was almost missing it, too, when Van skated over.

"Let's go back to my place," he said. "We can play Halo, and my aunt got pizza pockets yesterday."

"Cool," J.P. said, chugging the rest of his beer. He crushed the can when he was done and kicked it away, too. Luke tried not to worry about littering, and thought about how stupid J.P. and Van would say he was if they knew it bothered him.

"You coming, Luke?" Van asked him now.

"I gotta get back," he said, picking up his skateboard. He was thinking that he should go to Nature Camp now and tell Margot he felt better. Of course, he'd have to buy some gum on the way there; he couldn't show up smelling like beer. With any luck, though, he'd be in time for the afternoon activity, using solar ovens made out of pizza boxes and aluminum foil to make s'mores.

This was actually kind of lame—the younger kids couldn't care less about solar energy, and instead got covered in melted chocolate—but at least Luke could eat some of the graham crackers and get rid of the sloshy feeling in his stomach.

"What, are you going home to mommy?" J.P. asked in a baby voice.

Luke started walking away. "Later," he said to Van over his shoulder, ignoring J.P.

"Later," Van said with his funny smile that was only on one side of his face. And then Luke was on his skateboard, pushing off hard, feeling the breeze on his face. Somehow he got back to the Nature Museum without seeing anyone he knew, and he was at the library, as planned, by three o'clock that afternoon to meet his mom.

CHAPTER 11

One afternoon about a week after he'd arrived at the lake, Cal found himself at his sister's gallery in town, holding a paperweight in his hand. He had no idea why he'd picked it up other than the fact that he was bored; he'd been waiting for fifteen minutes while Allie spoke to a prospective artist who was hoping the gallery would show her work. The young woman in question was in her early twenties, Cal guessed, and her long blond hair was braided, dirndl-style, into a crown on the top of her head, her slender arms adorned with rows of clanking silver bracelets. Add to that her outfit—a flowy skirt, a Central American–style poncho, and UGG boots—and she lent an odd yet appealing note to an otherwise staid Butternut afternoon. Cal hadn't been listening to her pitch to Allie that carefully, but he gathered that her specialty was found object animal sculptures. It definitely was not his kind of thing, and judging from the expression of strained politeness on Allie's face, it didn't appear to be *her* kind of thing, either, but she hadn't yet been able to convince her visitor of this. Now Cal held the azure paperweight up to his eyes and looked at the two of them through its blue swirls, then tilted it kaleidoscopically, so that they tilted with it. When he put it back down, Allie was frowning at him slightly. He shrugged.

He lingered, though, in this same corner, where Allie displayed the gallery's hand-blown glass. There were some nice pieces here, and they had the added attraction, for him, of being the kind of thing Meghan hated. She would never have allowed any of them into their apartment. It was absolutely imperative to her that all lines be "clean lines," that all surfaces be free of clutter. *Clutter.* Meghan could never say this word without a little shudder; it was something she believed she must be continually on guard against. If she gave even an inch to it—by, say, placing a framed family photograph on an end table, or a ceramic bowl on a shelf, or a clock on a mantelpiece—then it seemed she'd begin a slow but irreversible slide into hoarding, only to be discovered one future day buried under stacks of old newspapers and takeout food containers.

"Thank you so much for showing me your portfolio, Holly," Cal heard Allie say. "Your sculptures are very intriguing, not to mention *highly* sustainable. Right now, though, I just don't have the space to show them."

"I understand," Holly said cheerfully, snapping her portfolio shut and tucking it into the folds of her poncho. "But if you change your mind, let me know. Because honestly, I think the bottle cap prehistoric bird sculptures would look *amazing* in here. I got a *ton* of compliments on them at a craft fair last weekend."

"I'm sure you did," Allie said, ushering her toward the door. And as they passed him, Cal looked over—he'd been pretending to study an oil painting of pheasants taking flight in an autumnal setting—in time for Holly to grace him with a fetching smile. He smiled back at her reflexively. She was a picture of Bohemian prettiness, and he waited for something, *anything*, to register with him, but it didn't, and then she was gone, out the door. With the exception of Meghan, he realized, he'd rarely thought about women lately. No, that wasn't true. He had thought, at odd moments, about Billy. Billy from the wedding. Billy with the freckles. He had no idea why she'd stayed in his mind, but she had. He wondered now what had happened to her son, and whether she was at the library today.

Allie, who'd walked Holly out to a beat-up light blue Chevy pickup, came back into the gallery. "Sorry about that," she said to Cal, walking over and giving him a hug. "I didn't know you were stopping by. What a nice surprise."

"I hope so," he said. "Are you sure, though, that you don't want just *one* of those bottle cap prehistoric bird sculptures?"

"Maybe one," Allie mused. "But I'm going to have to pass on the woolly mammoth made out of deflated footballs."

"Was there a picture of that in her portfolio?"

"Uh-huh."

"Now, *that* I would have liked to have seen," Cal said.

"No, she's sweet," Allie said. "I think she should stick to her current occupation, though."

"Which is?"

"Doggie day care."

"Ahh," Cal said. He watched as Allie went to straighten up the counter. "Do you have time to come to Pearl's with me?" he asked, gesturing across the street at its red-and-white-striped awning.

"I'd love to, but I can't close for more than five minutes. I can make us both a cup of herbal tea to have in back, though," she said. She had a cubbyhole-sized office tucked behind the gallery.

"Got anything stronger than herbal tea?"

"Like coffee?"

"No, stronger than that."

"At this time of day?" Allie frowned.

"Why not?"

"Cal, you're not a drinker," she reminded him, going to stick a "Back in Five Minutes" note on the outside of the gallery's front door.

"That's only because I haven't had *time* to be a drinker before. I'm seriously considering it now."

Allie came back over to him, her frown deepening.

"What?" Cal said.

"Nothing. But since when are you growing a beard?"

"I'm not," he said. "I'm just not shaving every day. I'm on vacation. Besides, stubble is very in right now, or haven't you noticed?"

"Oh, I've noticed," Allie said. "Caroline and Jax and I watch *The Bachelorette*. And trust me, there's not a single clean-shaven contestant in sight on that show. How do they do that, though? How do they get their stubble just the right length?"

"Beats me." Cal shrugged. Meghan had always preferred that he shave once a day. Otherwise, she said his face was scratchy when they kissed, and then there was something else, too, that she'd tried to impress upon him, something about the exfoliating benefits of shaving. He cringed inwardly and vowed to banish words like *exfoliate* from his vocabulary.

"No, the stubble's fine," Allie said, leading him back to her office. "You're just not looking like your usual crisp self."

"That's because I'm reveling in my bachelorhood," he said of his uncombed hair, faded T-shirt, and old jeans. "It's been very liberating. Dropping my clothes on the floor. Leaving my bed unmade. Not putting the cap on the toothpaste tube."

"Wow, things sound like they're really going to seed over there," Allie teased, turning on an electric kettle on the counter in her office. "No cap on the toothpaste. What's next? Hanging up a hand towel crookedly?"

"Laugh all you want," Cal said, sitting down on a swivel chair. "You don't know what I've escaped from."

"Escaped from?" Allie raised an eyebrow. Cal knew she thought he was being uncharacteristically dramatic.

"No, it's true. You have no idea what it was like, living with Meghan. She had all of these rules. You couldn't wear shoes in our apartment because the carpeting was white. You couldn't read the newspaper on our couch—also white. You couldn't put a glass down on any surface without a coaster underneath it. I didn't complain about the rules, for the most part. And I didn't have any real trouble following them, either. I'm already pretty neat without someone constantly reminding me. But still, if I even slipped up a little . . ." He sighed. "Once I forgot the 'absolutely no dirty dishes left in the sink' rule. I'd made a cup of coffee, and I left the teaspoon in the sink. A few minutes later, I'm sitting at my desk, working on my computer, and Meghan comes in and waves a teaspoon in my face and says, in this weird little singsong voice, 'Are you *trying* to drive me crazy?'"

"*Jeez,*" Allie said. "What if you'd left the coffee cup in the sink, too?"

Cal drew a finger across his neck.

Allie laughed, but then she turned serious. "Cal, can I ask you a question?" He nodded. "Do you . . . do you miss her, though? Ever?"

Cal shrugged. "Her, specifically? And not just our life together?"

"*Yes*, her, specifically."

"I don't know. Sometimes I do, I think."

"You *think*?"

He lifted his shoulders. No, he didn't miss Meghan. Not after what she had done. But he hadn't told Allie about that yet. His hurt was still too new, his anger at her dishonesty still too raw. As far as Allie knew, the reason for their divorce was "irreconcilable differences," and if she wanted more information than that, she'd been careful not to press Cal for it. She was waiting for an answer, though, and since Cal knew it would seem wrong to her that there was nothing he missed about someone he'd been married to for five years, he told her something he thought was at least partly true.

"I miss . . . I miss the *idea* of her. The person I thought she was when I met her. I thought I knew how everything was going to turn out for us. And now, it's like . . . when you read the book with the big twist at the end. You should have seen it coming, but you didn't."

"*Cal*," Allie said. She'd been putting tea bags into teacups, but now she looked over at him, her face softened by a sadness that for some reason made her look even younger than usual. "I didn't know you felt that way."

"I'll survive."

"Of course you will," she said, pouring boiling water into the teacups. "I've never doubted that. In the meantime, though, if you need anything—anything at all—even just to talk, like now, please don't hesitate to ask me. Okay?"

There was a silence that lasted a beat too long. And Cal, unused to the serious turn their conversation had taken, said lightly, "You know what I need, Allie? A day without lawyers."

She handed him a cup of tea and sat down across from him. "*Lawyers*, as in, plural?"

He nodded and sipped his tea. "What is this?" he asked.

"It's called Tension Tamer."

He took another sip. He'd never liked herbal teas. "You wouldn't rather just be tense?" he asked.

She ignored him. "How many divorce lawyers do you need, Cal?"

"One. But I don't just need one for the divorce."

She looked at him, puzzled.

"I need one for the business, too."

"Are you . . . being sued?"

"No, although that is an occupational hazard. I need one because I'm selling my share of the firm."

"*What?*" Allie said, and he saw that she was only slightly less shocked by this news than she had been by the news of his divorce. She set her teacup down, hard, on the little desk between them. "What are you talking about, Cal? It's *your* firm. It has your *name* on it. It's Franklin & Cooper."

"*Was* Franklin & Cooper," he said. Franklin was Guy Franklin, a friend of Cal's from graduate school who was from a wealthy Seattle family. They'd started the firm together several years ago, and between Guy's family's money and connections, Cal's drive and talent and, frankly, luck, they'd made a name for their firm in a relatively short time. "Now it's going to be Franklin, Hoult & Washburn," Cal explained to Allie.

"You're just . . . quitting?"

"I'm not quitting. I'm selling my shares in it. It's not the same thing."

This distinction, though, was lost on Allie. "Did you and Guy have some kind of falling out, too? Is this like . . . another kind of divorce for you?"

"No," Cal said, taking offense. "Guy and I are still friends. Personally. *Professionally*, though, there have been some . . . philosophical disagreements between us." When he and Guy had started out, they'd found their niche converting warehouses into office spaces for start-up companies, but for the last couple of years the firm had designed large office buildings in downtown Seattle, which was much more lucrative than lofts, but also much less interesting to Cal. But Guy was determined to keep designing them, and for the last year, especially, they'd had some conflicts over the direction the firm was taking. "This kind of thing happens all the time in this field, Allie. Architectural firms can be very fluid. One partner leaves. Another comes in. It's not a big deal."

"It *is* a big deal, Cal. You *loved* it. That building you designed . . ."

"It's still there. I just don't want to design any more of them. You should see the building the firm is putting up next. It looks like an electric razor. I mean, how many more ugly buildings does the world need?"

"No one's saying you have to design ugly buildings. But there must be other things you want to design."

He didn't answer.

"Well, obviously, there was a reason you got into this field," Allie prompted.

"Yes. There was. I wanted to build houses, I think. Places where people actually live."

"So do that."

"Maybe I will. Right now, though, I don't want to do anything."

"Uh-huh," she said skeptically. "And how long do you think this will last? Your doing nothing?"

"A summer. Maybe longer." Granted, this would be a new experience for him. He'd been working for as long as he could remember, through high school and college for his dad's construction company, and in graduate school interning at architectural firms. Then, before he'd known it, he and Guy had been out on their own. The work, far from letting up, had only intensified.

"Cal," Allie said, shaking her head. "You're *incapable* of doing nothing."

"Maybe in the past. But this time is different. I've made *plans* to do nothing. I'm developing a *system* for doing nothing. Starting tomorrow, I'm going to take that rubber raft I saw in the boathouse, tie it up to the end of the dock, get in it and just . . . lie there. All day. If I get hot, I'll jump in the water. Thirsty? I'll grab a beer. Bored? I'll read a book."

Allie rolled her eyes. "Cal, it's not going to happen. You have the strongest work ethic of anyone I've ever known. Mom likes to tell people you started your first business at three. Your pet turtle feeding business."

"That was not a success, as I recall."

"No, but everything else you've done has been." This was not technically true. His was not a perfect record. There'd been bids he'd lost, clients who'd left for other firms, projects that had come in behind schedule or overbudget. Overall, though, he had to admit his career had followed a steady upward trajectory. And no one, he knew, had been prouder of this than Allie, who was looking at him now with a gently quizzical expression on her face, as if he were a much-loved puzzle whose pieces had suddenly been scrambled in a newly bewildering way. And then she sighed, sipped her tea, tried to put an escaped strand of her hair back into the loose bun she favored while working, and finally smiled, a little wearily, at him.

"I just realized something, Cal," she said. "You're having a midlife crisis. A full-blown one. A divorce, a sports car, a job change, you name it. Only you're having this crisis about ten years early. I've got to hand it to you, though. You really are precocious, aren't you? Mom always said so. By the way, have you told her about this, Cal? Her and Dad?"

"No."

"Not any of it?" She meant the divorce, too.

"Nope. They think I'm here just to get some rest. I'm not that worried, though. I think they can handle my getting divorced. They never liked Meghan, did they?"

Allie raised her shoulders noncommittally. She was loyal to the core, Cal thought. If her parents had told her this in confidence, she would never repeat it. "I don't know about that," she said. "They won't like the part about you leaving the firm, though. They're so proud of you, Cal. They had that feature from *Seattle Magazine* blown up and framed. It's hanging on their living room wall. What was it called? 'Forty under Forty'?"

"Those lists don't mean anything," Cal said. "Except that you have a good publicist or you're photogenic, or, preferably, both."

"What about that award you got?" Allie pressed, but Cal didn't want to talk about that, either. "You're going back to it, though, aren't you?" she asked. "Architecture? I mean, you can work for another firm, right? Or start your own?"

"Sure," he said, more to end the conversation than because he actually believed it.

Allie chewed her lip, something she did when she was worried, and stopped only because someone knocked on the gallery's door. "I've got to reopen," she said, standing up. "You're welcome to stick around, though."

"No, thanks. I've got to get going." He checked his watch. "I've got a phone conference soon."

"Lawyers?" Allie asked.

"Lawyers," Cal agreed.

CHAPTER 12

"Hi, Ms. Harper. Are you here for dinner?" Joy John-son, the Corner Bar's hostess, asked Billy when she came in on a Saturday night during the last week of June. Whenever Billy saw Joy—she was the eighteen-year-old daughter of Jax and Jeremy Johnson, the own-ers of the local hardware store—she immediately saw the covers of the novels in the *Divergent* series. When, she wondered, would she be able to meet people in town without automatically identifying them with the books they checked out of the library? Probably never, she decided, looking around the crowded room.

"I know," Joy said apologetically, seeing the expres-sion on Billy's face. She'd hoped to have a quiet dinner here tonight, but with the garrulous patrons filling the tables and booths, the clatter of dishes from the kitchen, and the strains of "Brown Eyed Girl" blaring from the jukebox, there was nothing quiet about the Corner Bar tonight. "It's the tourists," Joy said, lowering her voice.

"Are they driving you crazy?" Billy asked.

"Yes and no," Joy said. "They complain about the service more than the locals, but they leave bigger tips, too, so it's a toss-up. There's one table left, though," she said, selecting a menu for Billy and pointing to a table for two against a wall and wedged between an arcade video game and the swinging doors that led to the restrooms. "Do you want it?"

"No, thanks. I think I'll just get something to go."

Joy took a check pad out of her apron pocket. "The Cobb salad?" she asked of Billy's usual order. It was one of the only entrées on the menu with a "heart-healthy" symbol beside it.

"Actually, tonight, I think I'll get the cheeseburger, medium rare, and fries."

"You got it," Joy said, scribbling on the check pad. "I have to warn you, though, the kitchen staff is short-handed. It could be half an hour or more. Do you want to come back?"

"No, that's okay. I'll wait at the bar," Billy said, thinking that since it was drizzling outside, she could have a glass of wine here tonight instead of on her back porch.

"Great. You can pay Marty when you're ready," Joy said, grabbing a couple of menus and greeting the couple who'd come in behind Billy. Billy scanned the bar and took the only unoccupied stool, at the far end. She tried to catch the eye of Marty, the bartender, but he was busy, so she decided to engage in some people-watching instead. She looked, discreetly, at the man on the stool next to hers. "*Cal?*" she said a little louder than she'd intended.

He turned to her. Yes, it was definitely Cal Cooper.

He looked the same, only . . . only *better*. He was minus the jacket he'd worn to the wedding, but the casualness suited him. He wore a light blue button-down shirt and jeans—the same jeans he'd worn in the *Seattle Met Magazine* spread? she wondered—and his curly hair looked a little less tamed, his complexion a little tanner. She'd expected him to meet her with a blank stare, but he smiled and said, "Billy. Billy with the freckles."

"That's me," she said, blushing. Without knowing it, he'd zeroed in on the one feature she was most self-conscious about.

"I didn't . . . know you were still in town," she said.

"Apparently I am," he said with a trace of a smile. "I'm coming up on two weeks in Butternut." He raised a glass of what looked like whiskey to his mouth and took a sip. "I decided to make my vacation open-ended."

She smiled politely, but there was something disorienting about seeing him here tonight. He didn't belong at the Corner Bar, she decided, remembering the articles she'd skimmed on the Internet.

"Is there anything wrong?" he asked her now, over the noise of the bar.

"What? No," she said, shaking her head. "You just . . . you just seem a little out of place here." As soon as she said this, she blushed again. She hadn't meant it to sound rude, but it was hard to imagine it sounding any other way.

"I do?" he said. He didn't look offended, though. "Is there . . . a dress code I don't know about?"

"No," she said, smiling. "No, there's nothing wrong with what you're wearing," she told him, raising her voice to be heard over the room's noise. "You just seem like you're probably used to a different kind of establishment. You know, someplace that doesn't have snowshoes mounted on the wall above the bar, and macaroni and cheese curds on the menu."

"Oh, I see," he said, leaning closer, probably so he didn't have to shout at her. "It's funny you should say that, though. Because I was just thinking how nice it was to be somewhere they don't have a mixologist on staff. When I ordered a scotch from Marty over there, he didn't ask me which one of seventeen different brands I wanted. He just said, 'Dewar's?' and poured me one. And speaking of Dewar's," he said, draining the last of the scotch from his glass, "I'm going to ask Marty for another one. Can I, uh, get you something, Billy?"

"Oh, I'm just waiting for my dinner."

"Well, can I buy you a drink while you wait?"

She hesitated. "I can pay for my own drink," she said, thinking of the woman she'd seen in the pictures with him.

"I'm sure you can," he said, amused again. He seemed incapable of being offended. But he also seemed, Billy thought, like a nice guy. And this didn't feel like a pickup. Not when *she* was the one who'd sat down next to *him*. Still, why wasn't his wife with him? And since when did an award-winning architect take an open-ended vacation in the Northwoods? And, while she was at it, what the hell was he doing sitting here in this bar when he had that amazing life waiting for him back in Seattle?

Billy wanted to ask him all of these things, but what came out of her mouth first was, "Aren't you married?"

He seemed surprised.

"Small town," she lied quickly.

"Right," he said. "Technically, yes. I'm still married. But I've filed for divorce. And I've moved out of our apartment."

"I'm sorry to hear that," she said. What she was thinking, though, was, *You moved out of* that *apartment? That* gorgeous *apartment? Are you crazy?*

It was at this moment that Marty materialized in front of them. "Hello, Billy," he said. And then, including Cal in his look, "What can I get you two?"

"I'd like another Dewar's," Cal said. "And Billy would like . . . ?"

"A chardonnay," she said.

Marty nodded and moved off down the bar.

"How's your son?" Cal asked.

"My son is visiting his grandmother in St. Paul for the weekend," Billy said. She'd driven him down there after work yesterday and spent the night, then had driven back this morning. Tonight he and her mom were at a Minnesota Twins game. This break from each other had seemed necessary to Billy; it was becoming increasingly clear to her, and to Luke, presumably, that weekends under Billy's vigilant watch were a strain on both of them. She'd joked to Rae at the beginning of the summer about Luke being under house arrest, but in truth, that was what it was starting to feel like. And sometimes she wondered whom this was harder on— the jailer or the jailed?

"His grandmother, huh?" Cal said now. "That sounds . . . very wholesome."

"That's the idea," Billy said. "And next month,

he'll be on a longer but equally wholesome trip with North Woods Adventures." After having done her due diligence—she'd spoken to the program director, one of the counselors, and a couple of parents whose children had gone on past trips—she'd sat down with Luke a few days ago and shown him their Web site. She'd focused on all the "cool" aspects of the program, especially those activities she already knew he liked. And she pointed out that one of the counselors—whose nickname was Mad Dog, according to his bio—was an avid skateboarder *and* a BMX competitor. She'd mustered all of her parental charm and persuasion. And Luke had finally agreed, albeit grudgingly, to go on the trip.

Marty brought their drinks over now, along with a little bowl of pretzels he set down between them. Billy immediately popped one into her mouth—she was starving, as usual—but Cal ignored them and took a drink from his new scotch. Was he drunk? Billy wondered at the slight wobble she saw in his hand as he put his glass back down. She couldn't tell, though. She didn't know him well enough. But when he spoke to her again, he seemed perfectly sober.

"The day of the wedding, your son didn't get in any real trouble, did he?"

"No, he got off with a warning."

"I thought so. I got one of those, too, when I was around his age. Some of my friends and I used to try to blow things up in a field near my house. Finally someone complained about it, and the police brought us down to the station and gave us a little talking-to. You know, tried to put the fear of God in us."

"Did it work?" Billy asked, sipping her chardonnay. It was delicious. Sad to say that the Corner Bar, with its limited selection, was still serving better wine than Billy served at home.

"More or less." Cal smiled. "I don't know how much of it was the talk, though. Not long after that, we discovered girls. They were a lot more interesting, it turned out, than blowing things up."

"I'll bet," Billy said. "I don't know if Luke is there yet," she added, selecting another pretzel. She'd wondered once if he liked Annabelle that way, but that was before they'd stopped talking to each other.

She watched while Cal downed almost half his drink at once. Yikes, she thought, he was drinking fast. Was that why his marriage had ended? Somehow she didn't think so. He didn't look like a drinker. Then again, he did seem awfully comfortable with Marty.

"Have you, uh, been coming here often?" Billy asked, gesturing around the bar. *Like, every night?*

"Nope, first time here."

So, you prefer to drink alone? she almost asked. Instead she said, "So, what have you been doing in Butternut?"

"I've been spending time with my sister and her family," he said. "But mainly, I've been trying to relax. And you know what I've discovered about myself?"

"What?"

"I'm really bad at relaxing. Like, terrible at it."

"Not everyone can do it. What have you tried?"

"To relax?" he asked. She nodded. "Well, yesterday, I tied a raft to the end of the dock, got into it, and just lay there in the sun, bobbing up and down on the water.

I left my iPhone and my laptop in the cabin. I had my watch on, but I told myself I wouldn't look at it. What was the point? I was going to stay out there all afternoon. So I waited, and when I thought I'd been relaxing for at least an hour, I looked at my watch."

"How long were you there?"

"Fifteen minutes. A little less, actually."

Billy laughed. "I get it. I do. Relaxing is hard work. Have you tried reading? That helps."

"I have," Cal said. "The selection at the cabin, though . . ." He shook his head. "It's heavy on Hardy Boys mysteries, light on just about everything else."

"Come to the library, then," Billy said without thinking. "Making book recommendations is my favorite part of the job. Oh, and we also have a section on architecture. It's pretty small, but I can get you almost any book through interlibrary loan." She stopped, suddenly conscious that Cal had never actually mentioned to her that he was an architect.

Cal only smiled. "Thank you," he said. "I'll come in sometime. Reading would help. But I did find this TV show I like. It's called *Forensic Files*. Have you ever seen it?"

"Of course. Haven't you?"

"No. Not before I came up here."

"Really? You can't even turn on the television without stumbling across it. I think it's on at least sixteen hours a day."

"I've never watched much TV. But this show . . . it's totally addictive."

Billy smiled. "It is, except it's always the same, isn't it? If the wife was murdered, it turns out to be the husband who murdered her, and if the husband was murdered, it turns out to be the wife." As soon as she said this, though, she regretted it; he'd just told her about his own presumably unhappy marriage ending. "I mean," she added, quickly, "that's obviously an extreme response to a marriage that isn't working."

"Obviously," he said, his mouth quirking up in a half smile. He took another drink of his scotch.

"What about you?" he asked, his hazel eyes resting on her.

"Me?"

"Do you have a husband stashed in a freezer somewhere?"

Billy laughed in spite of herself. "No husband," she said. "Murdered or otherwise," she joked. "It's just me and Luke."

"His dad . . ." Cal paused. "He's not in the picture?"

"Nope."

"I'm sorry," he said, looking back down into his drink, or what was left of it. "It's none of my business."

"No, it's fine," Billy said. "I asked you about your marital status. Luke's dad has never been in the picture," she explained. "In fact, Luke's dad doesn't even *know* he's Luke's dad, as far as I can tell."

"Ah, the plot thickens."

"It's pretty thick," Billy agreed. "But, you know, it's an old story."

"Tell it to me," Cal said, leaning closer, and Billy had the strangest feeling, crowded bar aside, that the two of them were alone.

She took another sip of her wine, formulating her response. "Well, you know the story where the teenage girl goes on a fishing trip with her dad, and one night at this lodge where they're staying in Alaska, she tells him she's going to be reading *Wuthering Heights* in the lobby, but in fact she ends up having a fling with one of the guides who took them out on the river that morning?"

"Actually, I've never heard this one before," Cal said. "What happens next?"

"Hmm. Let's see. Fast-forward a month. The girl tells her parents that she's pregnant. Her mom cries. Her dad . . . her dad is *livid*. This part was not in the fine print when he booked their vacation package. He goes back to the lodge—unannounced—and demands to see the guide."

"Ouch," Cal winced. "Does it get violent here?"

"No. The girl's dad is not a violent man. And besides, the guide is nowhere to be found. He's gone. Poof," Billy said, mimicking him disappearing with her hands. "He left a few weeks before. No forwarding address. No nothing. The manager at the lodge tells the girl's dad the guides are always moving on. And this one's no different. But he does make some phone calls for the dad. He gets in touch with other lodges in the area. He puts the word out."

"And?"

"And nothing. The guide's gone."

"And that's the end of the story?"

"No. That's only the end of that *chapter* of the story. Because the girl has the baby, and despite the fact that her parents were upset, they come around, and help her out, and for a long time, everyone's happy."

"Aren't they happy anymore?"

"They . . ." Billy stopped. "They're fine," she said. And to deflect attention from herself, she asked lightly, "What about you? Do you have a story to tell?"

"I do. It's very different from yours, though. Let's see . . . Boy meets girl. They fall in love and get married. Girl said she wanted to have children . . . Girl lied. It took the boy five years to figure it out."

"So . . . she changed her mind about wanting children?"

"No," Cal said flatly. "She lied from the start. She never wanted children. She just hid the truth from him until he finally found out."

"And did he want kids?" Billy asked.

"Very much," Cal said.

Billy didn't know how to respond. She wanted to ask him more about this, but she felt the subject was somehow closed. Then something occurred to her: Cal's wife had lied. She'd hidden the truth from him. Wasn't Billy doing that very same thing to Luke? But Cal swirled the ice cubes in his glass, bringing her back to the present. "I'm sorry," she said finally.

"Did you ever want to have more kids?" he asked her.

"Yes, I did," she said, surprised at her own directness. But at that moment, Dawn, the waitress, signaled to her from the other end of the bar. She'd just put a plastic to-go bag at the register. "Oh, look, there's my order," Billy said, relieved to be changing the subject. Wanting another child was something she'd never discussed with anyone before, not even her mother. "I'll be right back."

"How's Mr. Cooper?" Marty asked as he rang up her dinner.

"Cal? He seems to be enjoying the Dewar's here," Billy said, handing him a twenty-dollar bill.

"You're damn right he's enjoying it," Marty said as he gave her the change. "That's his fifth one."

"His fifth? Marty, what were you thinking?"

"I was thinking, Billy, that sometimes a man needs to get drunk."

What kind of dime-store philosophy is that? she almost asked. But of course, it was *Marty's* dime-store philosophy.

"Oh, relax," he said. "I already asked for his car keys." He gestured at the wall behind the bar, where a set of car keys was indeed hanging from a hook.

"How's he going to get back to his cabin?" Billy asked.

"He said he'd call his brother-in-law to pick him up."

"He doesn't need to do that," she said, looking down the bar at Cal as she put her change back in her wallet. He was finishing off the last of his scotch. "Here, give me his keys. I'll give them back to him after I drive him home."

Marty handed her the keys, and with a philosophic air, dime-store or not, he went back to polishing glasses.

Billy walked over to Cal, amazed that he was still sitting upright on his stool. "Listen," she said, "Marty told me he took your keys away. I know you were going to call Walker, but I'll give you a ride home. I'm leaving anyway."

"You didn't finish your wine," he pointed out, and for the first time, Billy thought she detected a slight slur in his speech.

"That's all right. I can have a glass at home," she said.

She half expected him to want to stay, but he looked at his empty glass, shrugged, and said with a smile that was more charming than it needed to be, "If it's not too much trouble . . . ?"

"It's not."

"Thank you, then. I appreciate it. Let me just . . . settle up my tab here."

He took his wallet out of his pocket, extracted a bill from it, and left it on the bar.

Billy leaned closer. It was a hundred-dollar bill. "Are you . . . sure you want to leave that much?" she asked.

"Why not?" he said, getting off the barstool. "I like overtipping if the service is good."

Oh, it's a great hobby, Billy thought. *If you can afford it.* They left the bar together, and Billy tried to ignore the significant smile Joy gave her as she and Cal said good-night. It would take twelve hours to get all the way around Butternut that she'd left with him, she reflected—eighteen hours at the most.

She was parked only a block away, which turned out to be a good thing, since it was still drizzling outside. She and Cal walked quickly, Cal comporting himself like a man who could easily pass a field sobriety test, and Billy trying to stay dry under Main Street's awnings.

"Here we go," she said when they got to her car. "Don't mind about the dog hair," she added under her breath. She'd just vacuumed it up the other day, but Murphy's yellow fur still clung stubbornly to the front passenger seat. It was where Murphy sat when he and

Billy went anywhere without Luke, as they had today. She'd taken him to the beach to chase tennis balls in the rain. Oh, great, the car wasn't just covered in blond fur; it would also smell like wet dog.

When she got into the car, though, there was only a faint Murphy-ish smell. Still, she left her window cracked open for good measure. They were quiet as she drove out of town, the only sound in the car the not unpleasant squeak of windshield wipers.

"Do you know where the cabin is?" he asked once Billy had turned onto Butternut Lake Drive.

"It's the driveway after Allie and Walker's, right?"

"Right."

"Small town," she said for the second time that night. She glanced over at him and saw him smile faintly.

"It's nice," he said.

"No sushi," she reminded him.

"No. But have you had the Butternut Burger at Pearl's?"

"Have I had it? Only about a million times. If Pearl's were open for dinner, I'd never eat anywhere else. And speaking of dinner," she said, navigating carefully on the rain-slicked, twisty road, "have you had any?"

"Not really."

"You can have mine," she said of the to-go bag on the backseat. Its cheeseburger odor was countering the car's doggie odor, she hoped.

"I'm fine. Thank you for the offer, though."

They were quiet again, and though the view outside the car's windows was a wet, gloomy one as gray evening shaded into gray night, inside the car it felt warm and almost . . . cozy.

"Right up here," Cal said before they got to his driveway. She saw the cabin's lighted windows—bright squares of yellow—through the darkening pine trees.

"This looks cheerful," she said, more to herself than to him. She stopped in front of it and let the engine idle. It was raining harder now, and in between the wiper's strokes, water sheeted over the windshield.

"Do you want to come in for a nightcap?" Cal asked quietly.

Billy hesitated for only a second. "No, I've got to be getting back," she said, holding his car keys out to him.

"Thank you for the ride, Billy," he said, gracing her with another of his smiles.

"You're welcome," she said, smiling back. He got out, and she watched him climb the porch steps and let himself in. He never stumbled on the steps, never fumbled with the keys; he was a model of self-control. Before he disappeared inside, he waved at her, and she waved back. "Good night, Cal Cooper," she said softly before she turned around in his driveway and pulled out onto Butternut Lake Drive.

CHAPTER 13

When she got home, Billy took her dinner out on the back porch and split her cheeseburger with Murphy. It was still raining, but where Billy perched in her wicker reading chair under the roof's overhang, it was more or less dry. She thought about taking a bath and going to bed early, but she felt strangely restless. She'd poured herself another glass of wine when she'd gotten back, though it sat untouched on the side table now, and she'd taken *Pride and Prejudice* out of the box set. She wanted to read the scene—one of her favorites—where Elizabeth Bennet and Mr. Darcy have a conversation on the dance floor. Still, the book sat opened but unread on her lap. She was looking at Murphy curled up at her feet. Was it her imagination, or was there something faintly critical in his expression as he watched her now?

What, Murph? I gave you half my cheeseburger. The rest is gone. I was so hungry I could have eaten this chair. And it's only fair that I had the french fries, isn't it?

Murphy, usually so forthcoming in their conversations, said nothing. Billy frowned. This wasn't about the cheeseburger. This was about Cal.

Look, I gave the guy a ride home. Which was the only responsible thing to do, Billy explained to him now. *And I did not go in for a nightcap, even though there was a part of me that wanted to. I mean can you blame me, Murph? The guy is ridiculously good-looking, not to mention charming, and rich enough to throw one-hundred-dollar bills around like confetti. Of course I was tempted. The important thing is that I didn't give in.*

At this, Murphy actually sighed, a long though still patient sigh.

I know. I get it, Murph. I shouldn't even have been tempted. He is the definition of a poor risk. Still technically married, and planning, for all I know, to head back to Seattle tomorrow. I should put Cal Cooper right out of my head, shouldn't I, Murph? The whole thing is a bad idea, isn't it?

Murphy looked at her, and his liquid brown eyes confirmed this. *It is a bad idea,* he told Billy. *A very bad idea.*

Yes, still technically married isn't very promising, is it? she asked herself. But then she remembered something Cal had said about his wife. He'd spoken—somewhat bitterly, it seemed to Billy—about how his wife had kept from him, for years, her disinterest in having children. There it was again—the lie of omission. And Billy knew, sitting there on the porch with the rain dripping down, that she was doing the same thing to Luke; she was lying to him. Albeit for a different reason than Cal's wife had lied to Cal, and maybe Billy's reasons for lying, as a mother, were more defensible . . . but she was lying nonetheless. After all, she had the manila envelope her father had given her a year ago last spring, only months before he'd died, as evidence of this. She remembered now the afternoon her dad had summoned her into his study.

"Dad?" she said, standing in the doorway to this little-used room. "Mom said you wanted to see me."

"I do," he said, looking up from some papers on his desk. "Come on in, and close the door behind you, would you?"

"Of course," Billy said, closing it. "Why the secrecy, though?" she teased. The last time they'd had a discussion in this room behind a closed door had been . . . well, *never*. Even Billy's teenage pregnancy, as she recalled, had been discussed with both of her parents in the living room.

"No secrecy," he said, "just privacy. Your mother and I, by the way, have already discussed this." In the next moment, though, he took a key out of his trouser pocket, unlocked his top desk drawer, and removed a manila envelope from it. Her name was printed on it in her father's neat block lettering, and the flap was sealed and reinforced with clear tape.

"Okay, Dad. Now I *am* curious," Billy said, pulling a chair over to his desk. She felt a little tremor of anxiety then. The year before, her father had been diagnosed with Hodgkin's disease, and while it was in remission now, it was never far from any of their thoughts. "This . . . this isn't about your health, is it?" she asked.

"No, it's not. Let's sit on the couch, though," he said, gesturing at the nearby leather chesterfield. Billy sat down on it, but she was still apprehensive. "Are you feeling all right, Dad?" she asked as he joined her. "You look a little pale."

"I'm fine," he said. She would later learn that he was not fine. He'd found out a few days earlier that his cancer had returned. But he would wait until the following week to tell the rest of his family since, as he explained to them, Billy and Luke were down from Butternut for the Easter holiday and he hadn't wanted to spoil it for them. This was typical of her father's stoicism and unselfishness. The worst thing about his illness, he'd once remarked to Billy, was that it was so damned inconvenient for everyone else.

"If I look pale," he said to Billy, balancing the envelope on his knees, "it's probably because of this sweater your mother insisted on knitting for me."

Billy smiled. The sweater in question was bright yellow, or "baby chick yellow," as her father had pointed out light-heartedly at the breakfast table that morning. "Dad, why don't you just tell her you don't like it?" Billy said. "She'll get over it."

"I can't tell her because, if I'm going to be honest, I'd have to tell her that I've never liked any of the sweaters she's knit for me. I don't like wearing sweaters. Period."

"*Dad*, you've been wearing her sweaters for thirty-five years."

"Oh, longer," he said. "We've been *married* for thirty-five. She's been knitting them for me since we started dating."

"And you've never asked her to stop knitting them?"

"I have not."

Billy, who'd been amused, turned serious. "I'm not sure I understand marriage," she said, shaking her head.

"Well, every marriage is different. But I like to think ours has been a pretty good one."

"Are you kidding? Dad, it's been a *great* one. From my perspective, anyway."

He smiled, and she thought again how tired he looked. He studied the envelope, started to say something, and then stopped and started again. "I've been thinking about how to broach this subject with you," he said. "I don't know that there's any graceful way to do it, though. It's about Wesley. Wesley Fitzgerald."

Billy's eyes widened. It had been years since they'd discussed Luke's father, even in passing. "What . . . about him?"

"I found him," he said simply. "I mean, *I* didn't find him, not personally. The private investigator I hired found him."

Billy said the first thing that came to her mind. "Where was he?"

"Canada. Vancouver Island, actually."

Canada. Is that why her own feeble efforts to find him had been unsuccessful? Because she was looking for him in the wrong country?

Her father, as if reading her mind, said, "I know. I

tried to find him, too. Not in any methodical way, only the occasional late-night Google search. It didn't seem possible to me that in this day and age, someone could fly so completely under the radar."

Billy nodded. She'd felt the same way.

"I think I understand now why he was so hard to find," her father continued. "He hasn't left that much of a mark on the world. And I don't necessarily mean that in a negative way, either," he added quickly. "What I mean is, he has no criminal record. Not in this country or Canada. He has no record in civil court, either. Never sued anyone or been sued by anyone. He never graduated from college. Never served in the military. He's not on any social networking sites. Even his business—he owns a fishing boat that's available for charters—doesn't have a Web site. Apparently he relies on word of mouth for clients."

Billy nodded, distracted. She had another question for her father, but she was unsure about whether she really wanted to know the answer.

Again her father seemed to understand. "He's married. With two children," he said. "Both daughters. One is nine and one is five. It's all in here," he added, holding the envelope out to her. But when she didn't take it, he withdrew it.

"Look," he said quietly. "Take your time with this. It's a lot to absorb. I know that. And while I do want you to take this with you today," he said, indicating the envelope, "I don't want you to feel like you have to *do* anything with it yet. You don't even have to open it. Just put it away someplace private, and leave it there. Until . . ." He shrugged. "Until whenever."

Billy looked at it distrustfully. "Dad, how long have you . . . ?"

"I've had this for about six weeks," he said. "I contacted the detective a few weeks before that. For all of our amateur sleuthing," he said with a half smile at Billy, "it didn't take this man very long to put a file together on him."

"Did the private investigator . . . go there? To Canada?"

He nodded, a little sheepishly. "I okayed the trip only for records collection. I didn't say anything about taking . . . photographs. But he had some extra time while he was waiting for a flight to leave, so he followed him for a couple of hours and snapped a few photos. Not of his family. Just of him. They're in here, too."

"Does he—Wesley, I mean—does he seem like a, you know . . ."

"A nice guy?"

Billy nodded.

"There's nothing to suggest he *isn't* a nice guy. During the time the PI trailed him, he did what can only be described as some pretty . . . unremarkable things. He worked on his boat, picked up one of his kids at school, went to some kind of social function with his family at a church. I don't know if it's possible to get the measure of a man from the contents of a manila envelope, but . . ." He shrugged. "The PI said he seemed like an average joe. That was the phrase he used. He said he would be glad to dig a little deeper, talk to his ex-girlfriends, business partners, those kinds of things. I didn't want a whole dossier on the man, though. Really, what I wanted was his contact information. And I wanted to rule out, you know, a worst-case scenario kind of thing, in case he was someone we wouldn't want Luke to have any contact with, under any circumstances."

Neither of them said anything for a little while. And then Billy asked quietly, "Why hire someone to find him now? You could have done this years ago, Dad. After you found out I was pregnant, even." She wasn't angry at him, just curious about the timing.

"I could have done this sooner. The truth is, I didn't know if I *wanted* to. Honestly, at the time, and since then, too, I've often thought it might be simpler *not* to have him in your or Luke's lives. Remember, after we got home from that vacation, I didn't know anything about him, really. Except that he was young, rootless, and irresponsible."

"Hmm. Well, he wasn't the only one who was irresponsible," Billy felt compelled to say.

"Maybe," her dad allowed. "Still, he was older than you. And he was in a position of responsibility. It didn't say much about his judgment . . . impregnating a teenage guest at the lodge where he worked."

"Dad, we've talked about this," Billy said, feeling a little bit like eighteen again. "You know, the part about it taking two people to make a baby."

"So it does," he said with a ghost of a smile. "Anyway, if I had mixed thoughts about finding him then, I didn't now. I did it for you, Billy, to some extent. But mainly, I did it for Luke."

"So . . . you want me to show this to Luke?" she asked, glancing at the envelope. "Or do you think I should contact Wesley?" Billy asked, apprehensive again.

He sighed and rubbed his eyes. He looked exhausted, and Billy realized suddenly how much all of this must have taken out of him. "No, I'm not suggesting that you do either of those things. Not now. Not when Luke is doing so well. And when, frankly, he hasn't expressed that much interest in his father yet."

Billy nodded. That was true enough. Lately his curiosity about his dad had been on the wane. It had been a couple of years since Billy had fielded a question about him.

"And there's another thing we need to consider," her dad said. "We don't know what's going to happen if and when you get in touch with Wesley. He might be angry or resentful. He might not want to have anything to do with you or Luke. Or he might feel very differently. You know, want to have some kind of custody of Luke. If you and Luke aren't comfortable with that, and if it goes to court, it could be . . . it could be expensive and traumatic for both of you.

"But here's the thing, Billy," he said, leaning forward, and there was a new urgency in his voice. "Luke is growing up; he'll be a teenager soon. And if he starts asking questions about his dad, or he wants to start trying to find him, I think you'll have to make a decision. Before Luke is an adult, you can make that decision for him. By the time he turns eighteen, though, I think he'll have a right to this information, don't you?"

"I do," Billy said, though her voice sounded uncertain, even to her. "It's just . . . so complicated." And there was a part of her, then, that wished there was no envelope, and therefore no eventual decision to make.

"It *is* complicated, Billy. Most things outside Jane

Austen novels are," he said gently. "So take your time with it. Don't make any snap decisions. You'll do the right thing. You always do."

"Not always," Billy said. "Trust me. I've made plenty of mistakes."

"Well, Luke wasn't one of them. Your mother, you, and Luke," he said, counting off his fingers, "are the three best things that ever happened to me." He brushed something out of one of his eyes, and Billy was amazed to see that it was a tear.

"*Dad,*" she said, giving him a hug. "You're crying." She didn't know if she'd ever seen him cry before.

"No, I'm not," he said. "I'm probably just allergic to all of the dyes in the Easter candy I've been eating."

"That's got to be it," Billy said, and now she was crying, too. "I mean, those bright pink marshmallow chicks have *got* to be toxic." She hugged him harder. "I love you," she said, and for a moment, she put aside the thought of what was in that envelope and concentrated on her dad instead. Did she know then, on some level, that he was sick again? Probably. Had she hugged him hard enough? Told him she loved him often enough? She hoped so. She'd had the opportunity to do both, many times, in the weeks ahead. But it was always that afternoon she remembered when she thought of the time she'd spent with him before he died. Here he was, an engineer who helped to build things, big things, and yet he was the gentlest of souls. He already knew how little time he had left in the world, and he'd spent it thinking about the ones he'd loved, whether that meant hiring a private investigator to track down his grandson's father or wearing a yellow sweater he would have been very glad never to lay eyes on again.

Billy watched now, on the porch, as an errant raindrop plopped onto the little glass-topped table beside her. Truth be told, she'd never opened that envelope. God knew she'd been curious about its contents—how could she not be? But in the end, she'd taken her dad's advice and put it away unopened. Even now it was sitting in a safe deposit box at her bank, along with some savings bonds her father had bought for Luke when he was born and several pieces of jewelry that Billy's grandmother had left to her in her will. The key to the safe deposit box was in the bottom drawer of her file cabinet. She'd thought at the time that this had been the right thing to do; she and Luke had both been doing well, and she hadn't wanted to upset the balance of their lives.

But that was over a year ago. And though she'd been unwilling, in that last year, to admit to herself that what she was actually doing was lying to Luke, she had to be honest with herself now. It was possible to have a secret that didn't entail being untruthful to anyone. Yet most secrets required a degree of dishonesty. This one most certainly did. She would have to admit it to *herself*, at least, even if she wasn't sure she was ready to admit it to Luke.

Still, hadn't she lied to protect Luke? After all, there was no telling what, *exactly*, Wesley might do if he was informed that he had a son. He might try to gain custody of Luke, thereby creating a disruptive and disturbing court battle that could be damaging to her son. And imagining this, a nightmare odyssey through the family court system, Billy was shaken. It was *possible*, wasn't it? And wasn't it also possible that, with the assistance of a good lawyer, he could win at least partial custody of Luke? *That* was unthinkable, though she thought about it anyway as she popped one of the last, and now soggy, french fries into her mouth. On the one hand, she reasoned, determined to be rational, it didn't seem likely that a judge would grant Wesley custody. After all, she and Wesley had never been married. And she didn't think that unmarried fathers, particularly if they were not named on the child's birth certificate, were automatically entitled to custody rights. Plus, Wesley already had a wife and two daughters. Under those circumstances would he really want to wrestle custody of Luke away from her? Besides, Wesley had disappeared before she could tell him she was pregnant, and she had been irreproachable in her parenting and care of Luke. *Hadn't she?* She'd worked hard at her job, but she'd been Luke's mother first and foremost. And he'd been a happy, thriving kid . . . until recently, she realized. *Until recently*.

And this reminded her of something: a woman, a co-worker from St. Paul's Main Library, whom Billy had been friendly with. She'd been a single mom, older than Billy by fifteen years, and her teenage son was getting into trouble with the law. The boy's father, who lived an hour away, had sued, successfully, for full custody, arguing that she was unable to supervise their son. It was more complicated than that, and Billy hadn't been privy to all the details, but her coworker had been dev-

astated. Billy shook her head. There were countless unknowns involved in contacting Wesley.

There was, of course, a flip side to this whole line
of thought. It was possible that the opposite would be
true, that Wesley wouldn't want to have anything to do
with his son. And if Luke were aware of this . . . well,
he'd be crushed. What child wouldn't be if they understood one of their parents had no interest in getting
to know them? And she thought about how Luke was
changing now, faster than she'd anticipated. He was not
only acting troubled but also getting *into* trouble. If he
was floundering as a thirteen-year-old, how might his
father's rejection play out over his high school years?
Might what was now a single skirmish with Officer
Sawyer turn into a criminal record?

And what if . . . what if Billy contacted Wesley on
her own, without first telling Luke, and Wesley refused
to meet Luke? Would she then have to keep this knowledge of Wesley's whereabouts from Luke even when
he was eighteen? Would it be incumbent upon her to
keep it from him so that he wouldn't have to suffer the
pain of being rejected by his own father? And if she
kept this rejection from Luke and *he* located his father
through his own sleuthing later in life, and he found out
that long ago she'd contacted Wesley, Luke would feel
betrayed. It was a mess. All of it.

Billy put her head in her hands. She wouldn't—
couldn't—make any decisions tonight. "Come on,
Murphy," she said wearily, reaching down to pat him.
"Let's go to bed." She stood up and collected *Pride
and Prejudice* and the remnants of her dinner. The rain

had stopped now, except for an occasional drip, and the smell of wet earth permeated the night. As she shouldered open the screen door, she reached her first resolution of the night. She would let Luke be her guide. And in the days and weeks and months ahead, she would listen to him very carefully.

CHAPTER 14

The next morning, a very hungover Cal turned into the driveway of the White Pines, a rustic Alpine-style resort built in the 1930s on twenty-five acres of waterfront property on one of the lake's most scenic bays. Cal had been here before in summers past. It was the only place on Butternut Lake that was even remotely formal, and when he was growing up, his family had celebrated special occasions in its clubby dining room overlooking the water. Now, though, as he followed a winding gravel drive past the beachfront, the main lodge, and the guest cottages, he didn't feel any nostalgia. He felt only the throbbing pain in his head that was the result of the five scotches he'd drunk the night before.

Allie had given him a ride into town this morning to pick up his car, and during the drive, she'd asked him to stop by the White Pines. Her friend Caroline's husband, Jack, had a contract to renovate the cottages there, and he'd told Allie that he'd like to hear Cal's thoughts on the project. (According to Allie, Cal already had a measure of celebrity in Jack's eyes. He wasn't only Allie's brother; he was also an award-winning architect.) Cal hadn't really wanted to come, but it was better than sitting around the cabin all day feeling terrible.

When he reached the resort's last cottage, which was on a sandy point of land that jutted out into the bay, he parked next to a red pickup truck coated with dust. This was pretty, he thought of the wood-and-stone chalet-style cottage with water on three sides and northern pines towering above it. He followed the sound of hammering onto the front porch and called through the open door. "Hello?"

The hammering stopped, and a moment later, Jack Keegan appeared. "Hey," he said, pulling off a work glove and extending a hand for Cal to shake. "Thanks for coming over."

"Sure," Cal said.

"Do you have time for me to show you around?" Jack asked.

Nothing but time, Cal thought. But to Jack he nodded and said, "Yeah, I'd love to see what you're doing here."

Jack gestured for him to follow. Cal walked into the cottage, remembering now what he'd heard about Jack from Allie. Apparently at one time he'd been a drinker and a womanizer. When his daughter, Daisy, was three, he'd left her and Caroline and hadn't returned to Butternut until Daisy was in college. Now, though, he was a changed man: clean and sober, and devoted to the wife he'd remarried two and a half years ago and the daughter he'd given away at her recent wedding. Cal had liked him when he'd met him at the reception. He liked him now, too, as he talked animatedly about the improvements he planned to make to the cottage.

"Don't get me wrong. This place is rock solid," Jack said, reaching up and thumping on one of its rafters. "They *literally* don't build them like this anymore. The foundation is still in perfect condition, and the framing is premium Douglas fir. The trouble is, we need to open the floor plan up. Otherwise it's too dark, too claustrophobic. These non-load-bearing walls need to come down," he said, tapping on a wall. "These windows"— here he stopped in front of a modest window that looked out on a slice of lake—"these windows have got to go. This whole wall should be glass," he added of a wall facing the lake. "I mean, what's the point of having a view if you can't see it?"

Cal agreed. Jack's plans were solid. And, once executed, should improve on the natural beauty of the cottages. Cal noticed, though, that Jack didn't seem to have anyone working with him. There was no way he could do this job alone.

When Cal brought this up, Jack explained that he'd recently had to fire his full-time employee. "I met him at an AA meeting," he said. "He's a good guy. But after he showed up drunk, I had to let him go. Now he's working with my sponsor, Walt. So we'll see. I've got some new leads, though. Hopefully I won't have to keep working weekends."

He and Jack talked for a little while about the project. Finally Jack said he had to get back to work. Cal asked if he could take another look around. He went out on the back porch. The cottage and the view of the lake could hardly have been prettier. They reminded him of the first construction site he'd ever worked on. He had just turned sixteen, and his dad, a builder, was renovating a cottage on Cedar Lake. The year before that summer, Cal and his dad hadn't been getting along very well. Cal, who'd always excelled in math and science, stopped working hard in school. His real interests were girls and sports. He and his dad had numerous skirmishes about his grades, his drinking and going to parties, his running around with girls, and what his dad referred to as his "general lack of seriousness." Adding to the tension between them was the fact that Cal showed virtually no interest in his dad's business.

That summer he turned sixteen, Cal was crazy about a girl named Victoria. They'd been going out for six months, and he wanted to buy her a piece of expensive jewelry for her birthday in August. She'd dropped more than a few hints about a bracelet on sale at the mall; Cal could still remember the three tiny rubies set in a braided gold band. Victoria was what Cal's mom referred to as "high-maintenance." He didn't dare tell her that he was saving up to buy a ruby bracelet for Victoria. His mom would have thought it a frivolous expense. Besides, she already disapproved of Victoria's focus on money and status.

In June, Cal had gotten a summer job lifeguarding at a country club in St. Paul. And though the view from his lifeguard stand was great, the pay was not. So when he overheard his dad telling his mom that one of his workers had quit, Cal said half-jokingly that he'd be interested in the job. His dad, not one for joking, had leveled a stern look at him. "If you're really interested, I'll hire you. The pay is much better than you're making at the country club. But it's hard work. And you won't get any preferential treatment just because you're my son."

If it hadn't been for Victoria, Cal probably wouldn't have taken the job. He knew his dad was serious about making him work hard. And he wondered what the point was of sweating on a construction site if he could spend the summer watching girls in bikinis. But he took the job; he had that bracelet to think about. As it turned out, Cal was right—his dad *was* demanding—but he was also surprisingly patient, and he took the time to teach him how to do the work correctly. Cal discovered something about himself he hadn't known. He loved the whole process of building—putting up a wall, laying a new floor, installing a window. More than that, he was fascinated by the possibility of designing spaces for people to live in. Of course, he was still years away from being able to do that. But the idea of it began to take shape that summer.

By early August, Cal had saved enough money to buy the bracelet and then some. The problem was, he was so tired by the time he got home from the construction site that he'd canceled more than a few dates with Victoria. When he tried to tell her about the work he was doing, she looked hopelessly bored. Or worse, sulky. In retrospect, maybe it was asking too much of her to care about the challenges of installing an eyebrow dormer, or creating an interior archway, or building bookshelves under a stairwell. These things fascinated Cal. They were what had transformed a small, dark cottage into a charming summer retreat.

In any case, the day before Cal was planning to buy

the bracelet, Victoria called and told him she wanted to break up. Peter Marshall, a senior at their high school, was going to be her new boyfriend. Peter's family had plenty of money, she explained. He didn't need a summer job.

The summer was a turning point for Cal. Though he'd lost the girl, he'd gained a sense of direction. That fall he worked hard and pulled his grades up. He spent hours looking at buildings online. He continued working with his father, and by his senior year, he'd applied to colleges that offered undergraduate architectural courses. His dad, with whom he'd had an antagonistic relationship before, gained a new respect for Cal's work ethic and drive.

Now Cal looked out over the lake and prodded the porch railing, which was wobbly. That would have to be replaced, he thought. And for some reason, an image of Billy last night flashed into his mind. She'd been flustered after she'd asked him if he was married. Was Billy interested in him? He'd thought so, but then again, the large quantity of scotch he'd drunk at the Corner Bar had probably clouded his judgment. He'd need to see her again, this time sober, if he wanted to find out.

He returned to the living room to say good-bye to Jack, who was taking down one of the interior walls. Cal remembered doing this on that first cottage so many summers ago. Almost without realizing it, he picked up a pry bar and started to help Jack tear the wood panels down to the studs. "Do you have an extra pair of gloves?" he asked Jack.

Jack told him where he could find them in his truck. And then the two of them spent a couple of hours working. It was harder than it looked. These weren't the laminate, adhesive wood panels Cal had seen so often in midcentury houses. These were made of old-growth hardwood, and each panel was individually nailed into the studs. They worked in silence, and by the time they were done, Cal had broken a sweat and could feel the ache of muscles he hadn't worked out at the gym in Seattle.

After they'd carried all of the old panels out and loaded them into a Dumpster, Jack wanted to know what he thought of the cabin now. "It's much lighter," Cal said approvingly as he took off the work gloves and left them on a tool tray.

"Thanks for helping out," Jack said, shaking hands. "You probably didn't expect to be using a pry bar on your vacation."

"It turns out I'm not very good at being on vacation," Cal said.

"No? Well, stop by anytime you want to," Jack said, heading back into the cottage. "I'm going to need someone next week. On Wednesday I start putting in the windows."

"What are you doing tomorrow?" Cal called after him.

CHAPTER 15

Cal wasn't very good at waiting. He hadn't had a lot of practice at it. But that was exactly what he was doing now. He'd come into the library to see Billy, but he hadn't been prepared for how busy she would be. When he'd visited the library as a kid, it had been a sleepy backwater. Now it was buzzing with activity, and as far as he could tell, Billy was the only one working. She hadn't noticed him yet; she'd been sitting at the check-out desk helping other patrons, and he hadn't wanted to interrupt her. Instead he'd taken a *USA TODAY* off the newspaper rack and found a place to read it—an arm-chair that was not only comfortable but also gave him a view of Billy. God, she was pretty, he thought, and as he was watching her, a young girl carrying a wobbly tower of books staggered over to her desk.

"Mara, that's *a lot* to check out, even for you," Billy said to her when she'd finished helping another patron.

"I know," the girl said, setting the books down on the edge of the desk. "But I'm going on vacation."

"And they don't have any books where you're going?" Billy asked her, amused.

"No, they do. I'm going to Spokane, Washington," Mara explained, giving the books a little push so that they were more firmly on the desk. "I'm visiting my grandparents. I need a lot of books, though. I'm going to be flying on the airplane by myself."

"Oh, I see. An unaccompanied minor."

Mara nodded proudly.

"Well, you'll *definitely* want to take enough reading material for the flight," Billy said. "But"—and here she glanced at the books in the stack—"*seven* books? Do you really think you can read that many?"

"Probably not," Mara said. "Except, what if I don't like one of them? Or even *two* of them. Or what if I read them really fast?"

Billy smiled and, resting her elbows on the desk, leaned forward and asked confidentially, "Mara, do you have a fear of being without a book?"

Mara nodded her head vigorously.

Billy smiled. "I have that fear, too. It's why I keep at least three books in my shoulder bag at all times. In case I finish one and I don't like another. I also keep a book in the glove compartment of my car, and a couple more of them in the trunk. Just for good measure. Because you never know when you're going to need a book."

"That's exactly how I feel," Mara said, looking relieved. Cal smiled to himself. Had Billy been like Mara when she was her age? he wondered.

"All right," Billy said, standing up. "If you don't think those will be too heavy for you to carry on the plane, let's get you something to put them in. I think we still have some leftover 'Friends of the Library' totes from last year's book sale."

"Thank you," Mara said as Billy went over to a cupboard and started rummaging through it. She took a tote bag from the cupboard and stacked Mara's books inside it after she checked them out.

"How's this?" Billy asked, coming around to Mara's side of the checkout desk and handing her the tote bag. Mara hefted it up. It looked like it weighed more than she did.

"It's fine," she said cheerfully. "I'm even going to have enough to read at my grandparents'." She smiled her thanks at Billy and headed toward the door.

"Mara? Don't forget to spend some time with your grandparents, too," Billy called after her with a smile.

And Cal watched as this slight girl toting her heavy bag of books slipped out the door. Seeing an opening now, he put down his newspaper and approached Billy.

"Hey," he said.

"Cal." She blushed with surprise and, he hoped, pleasure. "How long have you been here?"

"Not long," he said, standing close enough now to see her delicate freckles.

"How are you doing?" she asked.

"Well, yesterday I was a little hungover. But today I have a job, so things must be looking up."

"You have a job . . . in Butternut?" she asked, her eyes traveling over his clothes.

He had on a T-shirt, jeans, and work boots, and while he'd been careful to wipe his feet on the doormat before coming into the library, his boots were still covered with dust from the remodel at the cottage. He'd spent the morning with Jack, helping him tear down another wall. Jack had offered to pay him, but Cal waved this off. The truth was that this was the first time in months he'd really enjoyed working.

"I *sort of* have a job," he explained. "I didn't need it and I wasn't looking for it, but it found me anyway." He smiled. "I'm helping Jack Keegan restore a cottage over at the White Pines, when he needs the help, and when I have the time. By the way," he said, moving closer because a patron was walking by, "I wanted to thank you for driving me home the other night."

"You don't need to thank me," she said. "I owed you a ride, remember?"

"I remember," he said, thinking that much of their brief relationship had played out in their cars. They stood for a moment in silence, Cal feeling a little bit like he was back in high school. The art of flirting, though, had come more naturally to him then.

"I love what you've done with this place," he said finally, gesturing around the library.

"What *I've* done with it?"

He nodded.

"You know"—it was her turn to lower her voice—"I don't actually own it. I just work here."

"No, I know," he smiled. "It's totally different, though, than I remember it. When I was a kid, it felt kind of gloomy. And threadbare."

"Oh, trust me. There are still a few bare threads around here."

"No, seriously. It looks great. And another thing, too—it smells good. Like . . . gardenias, I think."

"Oh. That's just my perfume," Billy said, blushing. "It's Chanel Gardénia."

Cal smiled. "Really? I thought it was the whole place. It used to have this kind of musty smell. This . . . old book smell."

"That's a real thing, you know. Old book smell. It's caused by the breakdown of cellulose in paper."

"Is it?"

"Yep. There was an article about it in *Smithsonian Magazine*. Some people love that smell, by the way. It reminds them of their childhood, or their grandparents' house, or . . . their old public library."

Cal nodded, distracted. Was it her perfume clouding his brain? Or was it just her? She was wearing a dress—she seemed to favor simple, classic dresses—this one sleeveless, blue and white striped. And while there was nothing immodest about it, the neckline was still incredibly flattering.

"Well," Cal said, trying to refocus his attention on what Billy was saying, "the place has real energy."

Billy smiled. "On most days it does. Not always in the dead of winter, though. Still, I'm really proud of our children's program. That *has* been a success. Thanks to parents like your sister. But you know, sometimes when I read an article about libraries that are offering Zumba classes or coding classes or things like that, I get jealous. We don't have the space for that here, or the resources. We make do, though. Recently I started . . ." She caught herself here, and broke off. "I'm sorry. You don't want to hear about this."

"I *do* want to hear about it," Cal corrected her. He

liked that she was so animated when she talked about her work.

"I was just going to say that recently, I started a program here called 'Community Conversations.' I mean, we're not a large community, obviously, but for a town of our size, we have a lot of interesting people. So I thought, why not get some of them to share their interests and expertise with the rest of us? We have two presentations coming up." She took a leaflet from the checkout desk and handed it to him. "One is called 'Contemporary Fur Trapping,' and the other is 'Planting for Native Pollinators.'"

Cal studied the leaflet. "Fur trapping? Are people still . . . ?"

"Well, I don't know about *people*, but a *person*, anyway. Mr. Jalowitz."

At that moment, a young woman approached them, and Cal found himself praying that she wouldn't need Billy's help. She didn't. She passed right by them, took a cooking magazine off one of the racks, and settled in at the reading table to peruse it.

"We have to watch the cooking magazines," Billy said softly. "Believe it or not, people still cut the recipes out of them."

"Huh. I had no idea you attracted such a rough crowd," Cal said teasingly. "Clipping recipes? That's some antisocial behavior."

"I know." Billy laughed. "This place is pretty quaint, at least compared to the library I worked at in St. Paul. There was a homeless problem there," she said, turning serious. "We don't have anything like that here."

"There is poverty, though," Cal pointed out. It wasn't as visible in the Northwoods as it was in a city, but it was there.

"Of course," Billy said. "And we see some of it at the library, especially in the winter. We have people who come for the day—mainly elderly, mainly living on fixed incomes—so they can keep their thermostat turned down at home and save on their heating bills. I like to think, though, that there are worse places to stay warm."

There are much worse places, Cal was about to say, but in that moment a rather shrill voice called out, "Billy," and a tiny but formidable person came sailing up to them.

"Oh, hi, Mrs. Streeter," Billy said with an enthusiasm that Cal thought had cost her some effort. "You remember Cal Cooper, don't you? He was at Daisy's wedding."

Cal *certainly* remembered Mrs. Streeter. Only now, instead of being wrapped in acres of plum material as she had been at the wedding, she was swathed in a blue-and-white-gingham dress that seemed nearly to swamp her small frame, and where the plum-colored bird's nest hat had been before, there was now a straw hat with a rather aggressive assortment of plastic flowers on top. The effect was slightly startling on someone so old, and so small, but Cal wondered if perhaps that was the purpose behind it.

"I remember him," Mrs. Streeter said, and though she was well over a foot shorter than Cal, she somehow managed to give the effect of looking down on him. "But I didn't come in here to socialize."

"No? What can I help you with?" Billy asked, her bright blue eyes resting patiently on her.

"I would like to check out a movie," Mrs. Streeter said.

"Let me guess," Billy said. "Cary Grant?"

"That's right. Today I'd like *Only Angels Have Wings.*"

"Oh, I'm sorry, Mrs. Streeter. We haven't gotten that in yet. It's at the top of our list, though. We'll be putting in another DVD order next month."

"Next month?"

"Uh-huh. If you can't wait that long, you could always . . . consider subscribing to Netflix," Billy said gently. Cal guessed this was not the first time Billy had suggested this.

"But that would cost money!" Mrs. Streeter said, clearly appalled. "And another thing—I don't understand why you can't have *all* of Mr. Cary Grant's movies. He's a *major* motion picture star."

Was, Cal thought.

"I know, Mrs. Streeter," Billy said. "He has a large body of work, though. And we consider other people's tastes, too. Most people who check out DVDs here want to see more . . . current movies."

"Then they don't know what they're missing."

"Probably not."

"Furthermore, you could order *more* movies. You know, expand your collection."

"We could. If we didn't have limited shelf space for it."

"Then allot more space."

"You mean take away the space that we're already using for books?"

"Of course," Mrs. Streeter said, as if Billy were being deliberately slow. "More movies. Fewer books."

Cal thought for a moment that Billy's politeness was going to falter, but he saw her draw in a steadying breath. "You know what, Mrs. Streeter? We will take that under advisement."

"Good," Mrs. Streeter said, seemingly satisfied. "For today, I suppose I'll take *Suspicion*. It was Cary's first collaboration, you know, with Mr. Alfred Hitchcock," she told Cal, speaking of each man as if she knew him personally.

Billy went to get the DVD, though there was nothing to prevent Mrs. Streeter from getting it herself, Cal thought. He watched as Billy checked it out and said good-bye to the fierce little woman.

Afterward Billy came back to Cal. "I, uh, should probably get going," he said reluctantly. "I told Jack I'd pick up some burgers from Pearl's."

"Okay. Was there . . . anything you needed here?" she asked. "Any books? *The Art of Doing Nothing*, maybe?"

"I probably should check that out. It might be too late for me, though. There are a couple of architectural books I was thinking of ordering online."

"Get them here," Billy said. "If you decide you want to buy them after you read them, you can always do that." She went behind the checkout desk, and Cal gave her the titles. They were both books on contemporary American homes, but when Billy typed them into the computer, she discovered the library didn't carry them. "I'll get them through interlibrary loan."

"Do I need a card?"

"I'll just use your sister's account. They should be here by the end of the week. Will you still be around?" She frowned, tapping on keys.

"Oh, yeah, I'll be here for at least a couple more weeks. Thank you for ordering them. I'll see you soon," he said, not wanting to leave. And maybe she didn't want him to leave, either, because he hadn't even gotten halfway to the door when she caught up with him.

"Cal?"

"Yes?"

"Do you want to . . . come over for dinner sometime? Maybe this Friday?"

"I'd love to," he said. They exchanged cell phone numbers.

"I'll . . . call you," Billy said smiling, before she turned to help someone who was waiting at the checkout desk.

Cal went over to Pearl's. There was a long line there, but that didn't stop his new friend, Mrs. Streeter, from pushing right to the front of it. Cal didn't mind, though. He was in too good a mood to care. In fact, he was even considering renting a Cary Grant movie on his computer tonight.

CHAPTER 16

On Thursday, the last day of June, Luke pushed
open the door to Pearl's coffee shop and made
a beeline for the counter. He was starving. At Nature
Camp today, he'd barely had time to eat his lunch. He
was supposed to eat it at the same time as the campers, but good luck with that. Some of the littlest kids
couldn't even open a juice box by themselves. And
then there was this kid in the seven- and eight-year-old
group—the Black Bears—whose mom had forgotten
he liked only smooth peanut butter and had made his
PB&J with chunky peanut butter instead. He'd actually
started to cry! By the time Luke had gone to the staff
room and dug up a granola bar for him, lunch was ending and he didn't have enough time to finish his turkey
sandwich.

Now, as he approached the counter and heard french
fries sizzling in the fryer and smelled that sweet ketch-
upy smell he always associated with Pearl's, he thought
he'd die of hunger. And then he saw Annabelle. He

hadn't run into her since school ended three weeks ago. She was sitting on one of the red leather stools, her long, dark blond hair tumbling down her back, and the charm bracelet she always wore clinking against the glass she was sipping a chocolate milkshake out of. Luke stopped. They weren't talking to each other right now, at least not technically. He looked around. Should he sit at a table? No, that would look weird. If he'd come in here with friends, they could have sat at one of the booths in back, but no one their age sat at a table alone. Still, if he sat at the counter, should he sit next to Annabelle or a few stools away from her? He was thinking about this when Annabelle turned and saw him.

"Hi, Luke," she said in a way that wasn't friendly or unfriendly.

"Hey," he said, making up his mind. He walked over to the counter and slid onto a stool, being careful to leave an empty one between them. He saw then that she had a pencil and an artist's pad on the counter in front of her. She loved to draw. She used to show him the things she'd drawn, too. Mostly she drew people, but sometimes she drew other things, like animals or trees. She was good at it. But now she closed her pad so he couldn't see what she'd been drawing. Things were still weird between them, Luke thought. They'd been that way since the day they'd walked home from school together last spring.

Luke grabbed a menu off the holder on the counter. He pretended to read it, which was dumb; everyone who lived in Butternut knew the menu by heart, and besides, he ordered the same thing every time he came in here. "I'm working at the Nature Camp now," he said to her, still looking at the menu. "I'm not getting paid or anything, but you know, it's a lot of responsibility." He realized as he said this that he was trying to impress her with a fact that he would have done anything to hide from J.P., who couldn't believe how stupid Luke's "job" was.

"I heard you were doing that," Annabelle said, twirling her straw in the parfait glass in front of her. "Do you like it?"

"It's okay." He was almost whispering. And then he looked around to make sure no one else he knew had come into Pearl's.

"That's cool," Annabelle said. "I'm taking an art class in Duluth. Like, a *real* class. It's in figure drawing. It has adults in it and everything. But my mom has to drive me, so"—she shrugged—"it's a lot of time for us to spend in the car together."

Luke nodded sympathetically. He liked looking at her. She seemed the same but different. Her hair was longer, and a lighter shade of blond. It always got that way over summer vacation. When it did it matched her eyes, which were a brownish gold. She already had a tan, too, probably from the town beach, where he used to go with her in the summertime when they were younger. He wondered briefly what kind of bathing suit she wore now. She'd had an orange-and-white polka-dot one-piece last summer and a green one-piece with a little skirt attached to it the summer before.

"Hey, Luke. What can I get you?" asked the waitress, Jessica, standing in front of him. She was so pregnant that her belly touched the counter. *"Twins,"* she'd already told everyone. *"God help her,"* Luke's mom had said. Jessica was married to Frankie, the cook at Pearl's, and Frankie was a big guy, big as in *huge*. Most people thought the babies would be gargantuan.

"I'll have the burger with fries and a Coke," Luke said nonchalantly.

Jessica smiled and said, "Coming right up." She came back to place a glass of ice water, a napkin, and silverware in front of him, and then went back to the grill to talk to Frankie.

"The Nature Museum's going to have a picnic at the town beach next week, on the Fourth of July," Luke said, the words spilling out unexpectedly. But after he'd said them, he felt a little surge of confidence. "I have to work there—I'm going to grill hot dogs or something—but if you come I could probably still hang out with you."

"My dad has something planned for the Fourth," Annabelle said, playing with her straw.

"You could come over to my house sometime, then," he said, like he didn't really care if she did or not. "We have Hulu now."

Annabelle shook her head just a tiny bit. "No. My dad won't let me. He doesn't want me hanging around with you anymore," she added quietly into her milk-shake glass.

"Why not?" Luke asked with surprise. Her dad had always liked him before. Annabelle was the first friend he'd made when he and his mom had moved to Butter-nut, and Toby Halsey, who was in their grade and lived down the block, was the second. Up until last year, the three of them were always together, running in and out of each other's houses. Pastor Hansen used to call them "The Three Musketeers." And he was always nice to them when they were over at his house. It was different from Luke's house—there were a lot of rules, and Annabelle and her two younger brothers had to do chores, like raking leaves and stuff. But it was still fun. And except for when he had to write a sermon and he'd tell them they needed to be quiet, Pastor Hansen was actually pretty cool. "Why won't your dad let you hang out with me?" Luke pressed her.

"He heard about your suspension," Annabelle said. She'd finished her milkshake, and now she was using her pencil to doodle on her napkin.

"That's not a big deal," Luke said, but he felt the heat rise in his face. He couldn't believe Annabelle's dad wouldn't want her to hang out with him just because he'd been suspended once.

"It is to my dad," she said. She was quiet for a moment, and then she said, "But I know a way we could see each other."

"You mean, like, in secret?" he asked, thinking about what it would be like to have her come with him when he snuck out at night.

"No. I mean there's a way I could see you with my parents knowing."

He raised his eyebrows.

"You could join the youth group at church."

"No. No way," Luke said automatically. He'd been to church before, of course. He and his mom went every Sunday when they'd lived with his grandparents, and they still went whenever they visited his grandmother in St. Paul. But once they'd moved to Butternut, his mom said he didn't have to go anymore if he didn't want to, and he didn't want to. It was okay, his mom said. You could still be close to God without going to church.

"What's wrong with the youth group?" Annabelle asked, her cheeks flushing.

"Nothing. I just don't want to sit around and, like, talk about Jesus all the time."

"That's not what we do. I mean *sometimes*, maybe, we do that, but most of the time we just have fun."

"Like what?" he asked skeptically.

"Like . . . like two weeks ago we went on a day trip to Lake Superior, to the Apostle Islands Sea Caves."

"Yeah?" That actually sounded pretty cool, but he wasn't going to say so. "I'm already doing something on Lake Superior," he said, fiddling with the saltshaker. "You know that program, North Woods Adventures? I'm going to be hiking the Lake Superior Trail. I'm leaving in the middle of July."

Annabelle looked interested. He hoped he hadn't seemed too excited about it.

"What other kinds of stuff do you do with your youth group?" he asked.

"Next month we're hosting a spaghetti dinner and talent show at church. You could . . . you could do that with us."

"No, thanks. I mean, no offense, but that sounds really . . . lame."

"I should probably get going," she said suddenly, reaching into her backpack and pulling out her wallet.

"Hey, don't," he said, wanting her to stay. "I'm sorry. That spaghetti dinner thing will probably be fun. I just don't do stuff like that anymore unless I have to. I mean, like the talent show thing, who wants to stand up there and act like an idiot in front of all those people? What are you guys going to do? Sing some Christian rock song or something?"

He'd made things worse, he saw. "Bye, Luke," she said, putting some money on the counter and sliding off her stool.

"Hey," he said.

"What? I'm not going to stay here so you can make fun of me."

"I'm not making fun of you," he said, suddenly confused. "God, Annabelle," he blurted. "When did you get so serious about everything? You used to be different."

"No, Luke. *You* used to be different. You used to be . . . nicer." She mumbled that last word, putting her backpack on.

"I'm still nice," Luke said, looking around him to make sure no one was listening.

"Why didn't you go to Toby's birthday party, then?" she asked, challenging. "He was your best friend, Luke, and he told me you didn't even answer his text when he invited you."

"That's why you're so mad at me?"

"He only invited the two of us, Luke. It was just me when you didn't come. We went to Soak City."

"I can't help it if he didn't invite more people," Luke said. But he felt strangely guilty. Would he have gone if he'd known this? He didn't know. But when he'd gotten the text, he hadn't even told his mom. She would have made him go. She liked Toby. She didn't understand how . . . how *not* cool he was now.

"Well, it was really rude," Annabelle said, turning to leave. Was that what this was about? he wondered, watching her retreating back. Toby? But it was about other stuff, too. He knew that. Because he hadn't just stopped being friends with Toby. He'd started being friends with Van. And Annabelle *hated* Van. She said he was mean. Van didn't hate Annabelle, though. He thought she was hot, "in a preacher's daughter kind of way."

He watched now as the door swung shut behind her, its little bells hopping and jingling. He was so mad that when Jessica put his plate in front of him a few minutes later, he didn't even feel that hungry anymore.

"Hey, where'd your girlfriend go?" Jessica teased, looking at Annabelle's empty stool.

"She's not my girlfriend," Luke snapped. And then he was sorry. Because what kind of person was rude to a pregnant lady? "I mean, she doesn't even like me," he said by way of explanation.

"I think you're wrong about that," Jessica said with a little smile. And then she picked up Annabelle's money and cleared her parfait glass away.

As Luke started to eat his burger—he was wrong about not being hungry anymore—he was reminded of another time he'd been with Annabelle. It was last summer, and they were swinging on the tire swing in his backyard, just the two of them. He didn't know how many times they'd done this over the years, probably about a million. And this time didn't seem any different at first. They were just talking, he couldn't even remember what about, and he was watching her. She'd swing up, and she'd have the sky behind her. She'd swing down, and she'd have the lawn behind her. She was wearing a pale blue T-shirt and denim shorts, and she was really tan—an end-of-summer tan—and her dark blond hair was flying around her face. Luke said something that made her laugh, and he remembered thinking, *She's beautiful. She's really beautiful.* He'd never thought that before. It surprised him, and he didn't know why but it scared him a little, too. That was when things started to change. After that, he couldn't forget she was beautiful, and he couldn't remember she was his best friend, either. All the things that had been easy between them suddenly felt harder.

Then a lot of other stuff had happened. Pop-Pop had died. He'd started hanging out with Van. He'd stopped hanging out with Toby . . . and the thing with Annabelle had just gotten more uncomfortable, so that he was actually trying to avoid her most of the time. Then he thought about one day last spring, after school, when he walked home with her, kind of by accident. It was one of those gray, slushy days in late March that made you feel like winter would never end. Van hadn't been at school that day—he missed a lot of school—so Luke hadn't really had anyone to hang out with at lunchtime. Now, with school over, he couldn't go back to Van's house and play Call of Duty: Modern Warfare 2 with him, which was too bad because he wasn't allowed to play any games "rated M for Mature" at home.

Luke was coming down the steps of the school, and he'd seen Annabelle cutting through the parking lot. She was alone, which was different. She usually had other girls around her. When Luke realized that they were both going home, he ran to catch up with her. He didn't even really know why he did this, because when he got to her he couldn't think of anything to say. She let him walk beside her, but she didn't help him out with the whole talking thing. It was strange to think they'd walked home from school together a thousand times since third grade without even thinking about it, and now walking the six blocks from school to the center of town felt like it took forever. He was thinking, in fact, of inventing an errand he needed to run in town, and just ditching her there, when it started to rain. It wasn't a normal rain, though. It was like this hard, icy rain. After they both started to run down Main Street, he took her arm and, without thinking, pulled her into the doorway of the building where Beige Ted had his accounting office.

"What are you doing?" Annabelle asked.

"Getting you out of the rain," he said, looking down at her. Her red down jacket was already streaked with water, and her hair was kind of wet, but she looked so pretty standing there that he bent down and kissed her. She was surprised, but he was more surprised. He'd had no idea he was going to do this until he'd actually done it. When he stopped, she didn't say anything, so he kissed her again.

"Someone's going to see us," she said after that kiss.

"No, they're not," he said, looking over his shoulder onto Main Street and then kissing her some more. He hoped he was doing it the right way. He tried to remember how Vin Diesel had kissed Michelle Rodriguez in *Furious 7*, but he hadn't really studied that scene. He didn't know he'd need to. Still, he put his arms around Annabelle and kind of squeezed her, and she did the same thing back to him. And it was nice. It was really nice. Except he wished he could feel her more through the puffy layers of her down jacket. It was like she was wearing a sleeping bag. But that was okay. He knew she was under there. They kissed a little more, and they might have kissed for a while, except the door behind them opened, and they had to pull themselves apart.

"What are you two doing?" Beige Ted asked as he came out of his office. He was wrapping a scarf around his neck and looking at them like they'd been doing something wrong.

"Nothing," Luke said, innocently. "We were just trying to get out of the rain." Annabelle had already left, though, and when Luke caught up with her, he couldn't tell if she was angry with him or not. She trudged down the slushy sidewalk, studying the storefronts as if she'd never seen them before though she'd walked by them every day of her life.

They were quiet until they reached the sidewalk in front of her house, and then she said, "Good-bye, Luke," reached up, and kissed him quickly on the lips. After that, she ran down the walkway to her house without looking back. He stood there, surprised as hell, wondering what had happened and what was going to happen.

What happened was this. The next day after school, Annabelle was waiting for him. He knew this because even though she was talking to a couple of friends as he came down the steps, she broke away from them, and she looked, kind of shyly, up at him. He waved at her, feeling nervous, but feeling something else, too. Before he got down the steps, though, Van rode up to the school on his bicycle through the still slushy parking lot.

"Hey, Luke, let's go," he said impatiently. "I got to get out of here before someone sees me." By someone he meant Mr. Niles, the school counselor. Once again, Van had skipped school that day. "Come on, let's go," Van said, jumping the curb on his bike and slamming on the brakes at the bottom of the steps. Luke shrugged, and, not looking at Annabelle, went with him. That was the last time she waited for him to walk home with her . . .

"Can I get you anything else?" Jessica asked now, standing in front of him. Luke had finished everything on his plate, even the lettuce and tomato that came with his burger.

"No, thanks," he said.

"All right then." She put the check on the counter and started to take his plate.

"Jessica?"

"Yeah?"

"I'm sorry I was rude before."

She smiled. "You were fine," she said.

When she left, he counted out his money. He had to go to the library now and stay there until closing time with his mom. That was the deal. Nature Camp. Library. Home. He could stop at Pearl's if he called his mom from the phone at the Nature Museum. No Van. No J.P. And no Annabelle, either. Not that his mom would mind if he saw Annabelle. But he had to face it: Annabelle didn't want to see him.

He was still thinking about this when he left Pearl's a few minutes later, but if he'd felt sorry before, he was feeling something else now . . . a little irritated, actually. Like, why did Annabelle have to make such a big deal out of everything? When he saw her the next time, he thought, he might not even really talk to her. He might just say hi or wave or whatever, but he wouldn't, like, *try* so hard. He wouldn't say he was sorry. Because what was it, exactly, that he was sorry for, unless it was for not being perfect? And nobody, not even the kids in the youth group at her church, was perfect.

He would have crossed the street then, on his way to the library, if he hadn't noticed one of the cars parked right up the block. *Whoa.* Even Luke, who didn't know a lot about cars, knew it was a Porsche. You almost never saw cars that cool in Butternut, unless you counted Rae's boyfriend Moe's tricked-out Chevy Tahoe, and even that didn't come close to this. He stopped to take a closer look at it and then realized there was a man leaning against it, typing on an iPhone.

"Hey," he said, noticing Luke.

"Hey," Luke said, and he started to move away, but something about the guy seemed friendly, so he stopped and asked, "Is this yours?"

"Yep," the man said. "It's mine." He stopped typing. "Are you interested in cars?" he asked.

"Not, like, in general," Luke said. "I can't even get my learner's permit for another year and a half. But *this* car . . ." he said, wanting to run a hand over its shiny silver surface. "One of the skateboarders I follow," he said, "his name's Theotis Beasley, bought a Porsche Cayenne when he went pro."

"I thought about getting a Cayenne," the guy said. "And now, actually, I kind of wish I had. It'd be a lot more practical to have an SUV on some of these back roads up here."

Luke nodded. He was right about that. Plus, if you drove a car like this up here in the wintertime, you'd probably end up in a snowbank or something. In fact, Luke and his mom were one of the few families he knew of in Butternut who didn't own a truck or an SUV. Instead, every winter his mom put snow tires on their Ford Focus. He'd asked her before if they could get a new car, a *cooler* car, but she said there was nothing wrong with the one they had, even if it was ten years old. And Luke knew she was right. Still, he couldn't help wondering what it would be like to ride in *this* car.

"How . . . how fast does this go?" Luke asked. "Isn't it, like, two hundred miles an hour?"

The guy had started typing on his iPhone again, but he looked up now and flashed a smile at Luke. "It's 197 miles an hour. But just between you and me, I've never even gotten close to that before. And I'm not going to now, either. Not with Officer Sawyer setting speed traps for me."

"You know Officer Sawyer?"

"Well . . . I wouldn't say we were the best of friends. He gave me a speeding ticket."

Luke, thinking about his own recent run-in with Officer Sawyer, studied this man more carefully. He didn't recognize him, so he didn't think he lived up here year round. That was the thing about this place. You saw everyone all the time, whether you wanted to or not. On the other hand, he didn't look exactly like a summer person, either. Summer people usually looked like they were dressed for . . . well, for fun, Luke supposed. This guy—with his T-shirt, blue jeans, and work boots—was dressed for work, and pretty dirty work, too.

"Where are you from?" Luke blurted out, interrupting the man's typing again. He didn't seem to mind, though.

"I'm from Seattle," he said, looking up. "Ever been there?"

Luke shook his head. He didn't know that much about Seattle, except for one thing. "Seattle has the Space Needle, right?" he said, wanting to lean against the car, too.

"Right," the man said, typing again. "And some great skate parks, too."

"Really?"

"Oh, yeah. By the time I moved there, though, my skating days were over," the man said, typing and talking at the same time.

"Why?" Luke asked, wondering how old this guy was. He was pretty sure some of his teachers—the younger ones—were around the same age, but this guy seemed different. More relaxed. And, well, *cooler*.

"Why?" he repeated, looking up from his iPhone. "Well, I was an architect by then. I think I was worried if I started skating again—I hadn't done it since high school—I might break a wrist or something."

Luke nodded. He'd sprained his wrist once in a fall off his board, but he'd only been in the sixth grade then, so it hadn't been that big a deal. It would be different for an architect, he guessed. This guy, though, he didn't really look like an architect, with his dusty boots. Then again, Luke didn't really know what an architect looked like. This one must make a lot of money. Otherwise, how could he afford a car like this? It must cost, what . . . ?

"Can I ask you something else?"

"Why not?" the man said, taking one hand off his phone and running it through his curly brown hair. He wasn't really giving Luke all of his attention, but the part he was giving him was friendly.

"How much does a car like this even cost?"

"It cost . . . it cost a lot," the man said seriously. "Too much, really. If you're ever a workaholic, though, with no family to support"—he shrugged—"you might be able to afford one." He typed something else on his phone, slid it into his back pocket, and pushed off the side of the car. "I've got to get going," he said to Luke. "But it was nice talking to you."

Could I get a ride sometime? Luke almost asked, but he knew better. You didn't ask strangers for a ride. "Nice talking to you," Luke agreed.

"I'll see you around," the man said, heading down the street. Luke, who knew he should be at the library already, started to cross the street. He wondered if Annabelle had seen the car when she came out of Pearl's. She probably wouldn't have been that excited about it, though. But Van would be. And so would Toby. Toby *loved* cars. And thinking about Toby, and the birthday party he'd had that only Annabelle had gone to, made Luke forget about the car and its owner. By the time he got to the library, in fact, he was in a bad mood all over again.

CHAPTER 17

"M*om?*"

"*Billy? Oh, my God. What's wrong? Is Luke okay?*"

"Luke is fine," Billy said, tucking the cordless phone between her shoulder and her ear and fanning herself with an oven mitt. "This isn't about him. It's about a roast."

"*A roast?*"

"Yes, Mom, a roast," Billy grumbled. It was July first, the hottest day of the summer so far, and her kitchen felt like a steam room. "You don't have to sound so surprised, either. I made a pork roast," she added, staring accusingly at it in its roasting pan on her stove top.

"*Oh, Billy. Why would you do that?*" her mother asked, her sympathy tinged with reproach. "*You know you should not, under any circumstances, cook. It's an invitation to disaster.*"

Billy didn't argue this point. Even *she* had no idea what had inspired her to try to cook dinner for Cal.

"Look, Mom, it's done. It's too late to rethink it now. My guest is arriving in"—she checked the oven clock— "in five minutes."

"Your guest?" her mother said, warming to the topic. "Who is he?"

"Why would you assume it's a *he*?"

"Because I doubt you'd risk life and limb to cook for a *she*."

That's true, Billy thought, fanning harder. But the fact was that she'd started this thing and she was going to finish it. "Look, Mom, you're right, it's a *he*, and, even though he's just a friend, I need your help. *Please.*"

"Of course, honey. What's the problem?" her mom asked, shifting into crisis mode.

"The problem is, I don't know if it's cooked all the way through or not."

"Use a meat thermometer. Pork should reach an internal temperature of 145 degrees."

Billy blinked. How did she *know* this? Billy knew it *now*, but only because she'd looked it up on the Internet. "I don't . . . I don't own a meat thermometer," she admitted.

There was a barely audible sigh on the other end of the line, and Billy knew her mother was asking herself how it was possible for anyone not to own a meat thermometer. Her mother, though, tended not to dwell on unanswerable questions. Not for nothing had she been a vice principal at a girls' school for twenty-five years. "All right. Why don't you start by telling me exactly how you cooked it?"

"In a roasting pan at 350 degrees for an hour."

"Then it should be done. Just to be sure, though, why

don't you cut into it? The inside should be *pinkish*, but not *pink*."

"Hold on," Billy said, putting down the phone. She got a fork and knife and, pushing past Murphy, who was *literally* drooling on the floor from the smell of cooking meat, sawed into the roast and examined it critically. It was definitely pink.

She picked up the phone again. "What's the difference between pink and pinkish?" she asked.

"Well, pinkish is just *slightly* pink."

"But still pink?"

"Well, of course still pink. Just not *very* pink."

"I can't tell which it is." Billy sighed. "It's one or the other."

"Then it's fine. I'm sure it'll be delicious."

Billy glared at the roast again. She was actually starting to hate it. "I don't know," she said, chewing on her lower lip. "It just doesn't look *done*. It's supposed to have this *glaze* on it, this maple and mustard glaze. But it doesn't look like the picture in the recipe. That roast"—she consulted the picture she'd printed from the Internet—"that roast has a nice browned look to it. You don't . . . you don't think I should put it back in the oven?"

"No. Now, what else did you make for dinner?"

"A tomato and red onion salad and a summer herb potato salad." Those, at least, had been a success. She'd made them ahead of time and had put them, proudly, on the already set kitchen table.

"Perfect," her mom said. "And don't worry about the roast."

"Easy for you to say. You've never served a piece

of meat in your life that wasn't perfectly cooked. I've got to go, though, Mom. My guest will be here any minute."

"All right, honey. I love you. And Billy, enjoy yourself tonight. I know that sometimes, between Luke and the library, you can forget to . . . focus on yourself. So have fun. *Promise?*"

"Promise," Billy echoed. "I love you, too. I'll call you tomorrow," she said, hanging up. She inspected the roast once more and made a snap decision. She turned the oven up from 350 degrees to 450 and popped the pan back inside it. There. The roast would cook a little more, to the right degree of pinkness, and with any luck, it would brown nicely in the process. She'd leave it in for only five minutes. She was about to set the oven timer when the doorbell rang.

Murphy, barking enthusiastically, bounded for the door, and Billy hurried after him, plagued by an unfamiliar nervousness. *For God's sake, relax,* she told herself. *This is not a date. This is a casual dinner.* This didn't stop her, though, from glancing into the hall mirror as she passed. She wasn't thrilled by what she saw. In the humidity, her cotton dress looked wilted, her hair was curling at the ends, and despite the pressed powder she'd applied so carefully to cover her freckles, her face looked a little shiny.

Great, she thought, opening the door with a grim determination. But she smiled as soon as she saw Cal standing there. "Hey," she said.

"Hi, there," he said, smiling back. While Billy might have felt hot and frazzled, Cal looked so cool and fresh in jeans and a button-down shirt that it was as if he were stepping into her house from another climate. "This is for you," he said, handing her a bottle of white wine. "Chardonnay, right?"

"Right," Billy said, trying to prevent a still barking Murphy from jumping up on him. Cal didn't seem to mind, though. He kneeled to pet him. "And who might this be?" he asked.

"This is Murphy," she said, closing the front door. "He's our wildly ineffective watchdog. If someone broke into our house in the middle of the night, he'd probably bring them a tennis ball to toss for him."

Cal laughed. "Is that true?" he asked Murphy seriously, scratching him behind his ears. "Are you a failure as a guard dog? Because I can see you have many other winning qualities. I miss having a dog," he said, straightening up. "We always had one when I was growing up, but the building I lived in in Seattle had a 'no pets' policy. Your son, Luke, must love him. Is he . . . around?"

She shook her head. "His friend Toby invited him to go out for pizza and minigolf with his family." Billy had taken this as a good sign. Had Luke reached out to Toby or had Toby reached out to Luke? she'd wondered. Either way, she'd been pleased. "He's one of Luke's old friends," she explained to Cal. "He's not . . . one of the friends he was with when he got picked up by the police."

"That's good, right?"

"That's very good. Toby and Luke were in Boy Scouts together. Toby's still in it. He's working toward his Eagle Scout badge."

"Ah, I see what you mean, then. Most parents would probably prefer their son be friends with a Boy Scout over a tagger."

Billy smiled. She watched as Cal looked around the small front hall, from which you could see the equally diminutive living room and dining room. "I like your house," he said. "Do you mind if I . . . ?" He gestured toward the living room.

"Not at all," Billy said, though in truth, when she compared it to the photographs of his living room— his *former* living room—in the *Seattle Met Magazine* spread, she felt self-conscious about it. Still, Cal was clearly interested in it, and not only that, he also looked at it differently than most people would have. Not critically, exactly, but carefully. He stopped to admire the teak boomerang coffee table and the midcentury starburst clock on the wall, both items that Billy was inordinately proud of. When he finally came to rest in front of one of the built-in floor-to-ceiling bookshelves on either side of the fireplace, he stood there for a long time. Then he selected a book from it, a biography of Frank Lloyd Wright. Billy smiled to herself. It was one of the few books she owned about architects or architecture, but there was no need to tell him that. He flipped through it, put it back, and looked around again. "Do you know what I like about this room?" he asked Billy finally.

"No," she said, though she expected him to say that it looked *lived-in*, or *comfortable*, or *quirky*.

"It looks like you," he said simply. "I mean . . . your personality comes through. You know, who you are, what's important to you, what makes you happy. That doesn't always happen in someone's home. In fact, most of the time, it doesn't."

"Thank you," she said, and as she smiled she felt suddenly shy. She was still holding the wine bottle, she realized, its chilly rivulets of condensation running over her hands. It felt nice. It was *so* hot in here, even with the windows open and the ceiling fan on. She started to apologize for this, but something in the dining room, which was connected to the living room, caught Cal's eyes.

"What's this?" he asked, heading over to the dining room table.

"Oh, that's a model town that Luke built. Well, Luke and my dad," she amended, following him. Shortly after they'd moved into this house, Billy had given Luke permission to use the dining room table for his myriad building projects. She'd known they wouldn't be using the table to *dine* on—the kitchen table worked just fine for that. So she'd covered this table with felt to protect it and let Luke take it over. What he'd done with it was build a miniature town, complete with its own courthouse, post office, bank, school, and, much to Billy's delight, library.

"This is *so* cool," Cal said. "Your dad must have had so much fun working on it with him." He bent over to get a better look. "How did Luke get started on it?"

Billy considered this. "When he was in preschool, he used to play with train sets. But my dad noticed he was more interested in the miniature towns the trains passed through than in the trains themselves. So we encouraged him to concentrate on the towns. He'd build and rebuild them over and over again. This was the first one that really stuck, though. *Literally* stuck. It's glued down."

"It's really good," Cal murmured. "A lot of it is built to scale, isn't it?"

"That was my dad. He was a structural engineer. He died a year ago," she added.

"I'm sorry to hear that," he said simply.

Billy had turned her attention back to the miniature town. "It's not Butternut, obviously," she pointed out.

"I noticed that. There's no comic book store in Butternut," he said of a corner grocery that Luke had repurposed as a comic book store.

"I think this town is what Luke thought Butternut *should* be."

"That explains the three playgrounds," Cal said. "And is this a skateboard park?"

"Yes." Billy smiled. "Most of the buildings are salvaged from old train sets or Christmas villages, but that skateboard park was built by hand. That's balsa wood."

Cal nodded, running a finger lightly over a ramp. "How long did it take to build this whole thing?"

"A year," she said. "Maybe more. He went through stages. Sometimes he'd work on it all the time, and sometimes he'd forget about it for a while. He always came back to it, though. And when he was really into it, you couldn't help but feel his excitement and share it. I know because I ended up doing some of the painting. That was all Luke trusted me with, apparently," she said with amusement, pointing to the white picket fences in front of the houses on Main Street that she had painted with a tiny paintbrush. "He's not quite finished with it, as you can see," she added, pointing to an undeveloped area of green felt. "He was thinking about putting a go-cart track over here, or maybe an outdoor ice-skating rink. That's the nice thing about model towns, I guess. No permits, no zoning, no planning commissions. But he stopped working on it"—she leaned over and straightened a traffic light—"a couple of years ago. Right around the time my dad first got sick. If I asked him about it now, he'd probably say, 'It's lame' or something like that. *Everything* is lame now, apparently." *And that includes me.*

"He can always come back to it," Cal said, using a finger to push a miniature working tire swing in the backyard of a house that looked a little like Billy and Luke's. Billy smiled. Luke and Annabelle had spent hours and hours and hours on the *real* tire swing when they were younger. Annabelle, come to think of it, had helped with this model town, too. Luke had let her glue individual leaves onto an oak tree on Main Street. It had been a thankless task, as Billy recalled, but Annabelle hadn't complained.

"Are you . . . cooking something?" Cal asked her then, straightening up. "I think it might be . . . burning," he added, almost apologetically.

"*Oh no,*" she said softly. She closed her eyes as if this might somehow postpone the inevitable. The inevitable, of course, was what happened next: Billy ran to the kitchen, Murphy hard on her heels, and Cal right behind them. She put down the wine bottle, found the oven mitts, and opened the oven door. As a cloud of smoke billowed out, she removed the roasting pan and slammed it onto the stove top. Then she turned off the oven and, making a flapping motion with the oven mitts, tried to disperse the smoke before it set off the smoke detector. Then, and only then, did she inspect the roast. It was completely charred, clearly neither pink nor pinkish inside anymore. Far from having a glaze on the outside, it now had a completely carbonized shell over it. What struck Billy, standing with Cal in the still smoky kitchen, was not simply that she'd forgotten about the roast but that she'd forgotten about it so *completely*. After the doorbell had rung, she hadn't given it another thought. And the reason for that, of course, was Cal, who so far had the decency not to say or do anything that would in any way increase her mortification. If she'd been trying to impress him, she thought, waving at the smoke that still hung over the shriveled meat, she'd failed. But since when, she wondered, did she try to impress anyone? Or, more accurately, try to pretend to be someone she wasn't? Which, in this case, was a cook. She picked up the pan and headed for the garbage can.

"What are you doing?" Cal asked.

"I'm throwing it away," Billy said, pausing. "Or would you like to take it back to your cabin to use as a doorstop?" Even Murphy, she noticed, had lost interest in what was left of the roast.

"Hold on a second," Cal said, taking an oven mitt from her and putting the pan back on the stove. He searched around, found a fork and knife, and tried to cut into its grizzled remains.

"What are *you* doing?" Billy asked.

"I'm tasting it," he said. Before she could stop him, he'd hacked a piece of it off and popped it into his mouth. She watched while he chewed it patiently. He looked like a man eating something with the consistency of a car tire, but he didn't give up. Eventually he swallowed. "I think . . . I think it's a little well done," he said.

Billy laughed. "Why did you do that?" she asked, still smiling.

"I thought it might make you laugh."

"You were right. But, Cal?"

"Yes?"

"I can't cook. I mean, *at all*. Even my scrambled eggs aren't great. And I've never understood why it's so difficult for me. How is it possible that someone who can read *Anna Karenina* for pleasure cannot follow a recipe?"

He smiled but didn't answer her. He leaned down and kissed her. She tasted, at first, the cindery traces of the roast he had so gallantly sampled. But the kiss—which was *not* a polite kiss, a "don't worry about burning our dinner" kiss, an "oh, cheer up, everything will be all right" kiss, but a full-blown seduction—soon made her forget about the roast. The only other time anyone had kissed her this way, she'd been a teenager, eighteen years old, and the next thing she'd known . . .

"Cal," she said, pulling away from him. "What are we doing?"

"Kissing?" he answered, a slightly quizzical expression on his face.

"No, I mean . . ." And for some reason, she remembered one of the posters that lined the hallways at Luke's school. *"Actions have consequences,"* it warned. Yeah, no kidding. Billy had a thirteen-year-old son to prove it. But it wasn't getting pregnant she was worried about. She and Cal weren't there yet, and even if they had been, she'd swallowed a birth control pill faithfully, as if it were a multivitamin, one a day, every day, since Luke was a year old. No, what she was concerned about was a different kind of consequence, a different kind of complication. She and Wesley had at least been unencumbered by other people when they met. She and Cal, on the other hand, not so much.

"Is everything okay?" he asked her now. "I mean, other than that roast?"

At that moment, though, there was a ping from her cell phone on the counter. "I'd better get that." She reached for it. "It's Luke," she said, scanning his text. "Toby's Dad is giving him a ride home now."

She frowned and texted him back.

> Billy: What about minigolf?
> Luke: I changed my mind.
> Billy: You told them you'd go with them.
> Luke: That was before I remembered how
> lame it is.

Billy put her cell phone back down on the counter. "He's coming home early," she said to Cal.

And something about the way she said it made him ask, "Do you want me to go?"

"No," she said. And then, almost immediately, "Yes. I'm sorry. I don't mean to be rude. I told him you were coming tonight. I just—I just assumed you'd be gone by the time he got home."

"No, I get it," Cal said. "Really. I do. It's fine."

It wasn't fine with Billy, who felt a sting of disappointment. She couldn't tell how much of it was from the knowledge that Luke's night with Toby had not been a success, and how much of it was from the knowledge that her night with Cal had been cut short. Either way, as she walked Cal to the front door, her sense of letdown was palpable.

"Thank you," Cal said.

"For what?" she joked.

"For the company."

She smiled, but then she turned serious. "Cal, things are complicated right now," she said. "With my son, but with . . . me, too."

He leaned down and kissed her on the forehead this time. "If things get less complicated, let me know. I can always burn you a dinner at my cabin." He gave her one last smile. Billy watched him walk to his car, his ridiculously beautiful car, and then she went back inside and closed the door.

She had meant to make a start of cleaning the kitchen, but as she was throwing the roast away, she was reminded of Cal tasting it. It was rare that people surprised her; Cal had surprised her. Why had she said that, about things being complicated? It was true, of course, but did that preclude her from having fun occasionally? She didn't want anything serious, but then, Cal probably didn't, either. He didn't even know how long he'd be here. So what was stopping her from having a little summer romance? Something discreet. Something light. Something *fun*. There was that word again. And she knew what Rae would say, and what her mom would say, too: she didn't have enough of it.

CHAPTER 18

At eleven o'clock that night, it was still hot—hot enough for Billy to put ice cubes in the glass of chardonnay she'd poured for herself. This was a crime, she knew. The bottle Cal had brought earlier was so much better than anything she typically bought herself; it deserved to be served properly. Chilled and aerated and whatever else it was you were supposed to do to a good wine before you drank it. But this was no time to stand on ceremony, she'd decided. Damn it, she *needed* a drink. What's more, she needed Jane Austen, needed her like never before. But when she'd finished the scene she'd been reading in *Emma*—for obvious reasons, she'd chosen the one in which Emma hosts the disastrous dinner party for Mr. and Mrs. Elton—she was disappointed. Usually Austen offered her some escapist relief from her life. Tonight it hadn't done the trick. Instead she'd ended up staying out on the porch, staring off into the backyard and, as she'd so often done recently, trying to fathom the unfathomable person Luke had become.

Why, she wondered, had he wanted to come home early tonight? Was it because he knew she'd invited a man over? Had he wanted to interrupt their time together or, at the very least, cut it short? It was possible, she supposed. Especially since he'd never met Cal before. He was an unknown entity to Luke. But when she'd told Luke about him earlier in the day, about how she was having Allie Ford's brother over for dinner, he'd seemed totally uninterested. *Cal*, on the other hand, had seemed completely captivated by Luke, or at least by his model town. In the past, the town had been something of a litmus test for Billy. If a newcomer to their house didn't show some kind of admiration for it, or interest in it, she figured it was because they lacked imagination. Cal had not disappointed her here. She smiled now, remembering his enthusiasm for it. He'd acted like a big kid, and she wondered how long he would have stayed there, exploring it, if he hadn't noticed that their dinner was burning.

Maybe . . . maybe Cal wasn't the reason Luke had come home early, she thought. Maybe it was because it was hard for Luke to see Toby and his dad together. Of course, Luke loved Toby's dad. Or *had* loved him. He was a nice guy, Billy thought, and the kind of father who slipped so easily into playing with his kids and their friends that Billy used to wonder who Luke had more fun with, Toby or Toby's dad. And that's why when Luke had made a disparaging comment when he got home tonight, something about how Toby and his dad were "acting like little kids," it had surprised her. Was Luke jealous of this father-and-son dynamic? And was that why his new "friends" Van and J.P. either didn't have fathers in their lives or had fathers who weren't very present? Were these boys easier to be friends with?

She stared at the windows to Luke's bedroom, which faced out onto the backyard, as if they might tell her something. But no, he was asleep; his room was dark and, except for the steady hum of the air conditioner, it was silent. The uneasiness she'd felt several weeks ago when Luke had mentioned not knowing his father returned to her now. With Pop-Pop gone, was Luke feeling the absence of his father more acutely? All of this made her think of a winter night fourteen years ago, when she was pregnant with Luke.

Billy hadn't been able to sleep. She couldn't get comfortable, for one thing—her pregnant body felt huge—*beyond* huge, really—and the baby, whom she'd decided to name Luke, was so active that every time she managed to find a more promising position, he'd unleash another little flurry of kicks, some of them powerful enough to dimple the fabric of her maternity nightgown. Finally she gave up and went downstairs to sit at the kitchen table. There was a stack of books on it, books about pregnancy, delivery, and parenthood, that she'd been working her way through. She was of half a mind to read one now, but she ended up just sitting there, staring out the kitchen window onto the frozen front lawn. It was a bitterly cold December, and despite the fact that the heat was on, the cold pressed up against the kitchen windowpanes and nipped at Billy's bare toes. Still she sat there. She was afraid. No, she was terrified. Who knew there were so many things that could go wrong being pregnant, giving birth, and raising a child? Not Billy, or at least not Billy before she'd read all of these books. Now, though, she had a whole catalog of things to be afraid of, some of which she might be able to anticipate, prevent, or remedy, and some of which, apparently, were completely beyond her control. She trembled a little—whether from the cold or the fear, she didn't know—and that was how her father found her a few minutes later.

"Do you know what time it is?" he asked mildly, from the kitchen door.

"Late?" she suggested.

"It's three A.M."

"Did I wake you up?" she asked guiltily.

"No." He sighed. "We seem to have an epidemic of sleeplessness in this house. Your mom is in bed, knitting, even as we speak." And then he frowned slightly. "It's cold in here." He left, presumably to turn up the thermostat, and Billy heard their furnace clanging noisily as it pumped more warm air up through the heating vents. Soon, she knew, her toes would be toasty. She reached for one of the books in the stack, fully intending to read it, but when her dad came back into the kitchen, he swept up the stack of books and toted them away with him.

"Dad, where are you taking those?" she called after him as he opened the kitchen door that led to the garage.

"I'm throwing them away."

"*Dad!*" Billy had a lifelong horror of books—any books—being thrown away.

He reappeared in the kitchen, closing the door behind him. "I didn't throw them away," he said. "I put them with the old paint cans. But you're not reading them anymore."

"*Dad.*"

"You know enough already," he said, opening the refrigerator door.

"I don't know *anything*," Billy objected.

Her father ignored her. He removed a carton of milk. Moving to the cupboard, he found bread, peanut butter, and Marshmallow Fluff.

She watched as he poured two glasses of milk, but when she saw that he was making not one but two fluffernutter sandwiches (these had once been her favorite), she said, "Dad, I don't eat those anymore. The Marshmallow Fluff, it's probably bad for the baby."

"He'll survive," he said, setting a glass of milk and a plate with a sandwich on it down in front of her. He sat across from her and bit into his own sandwich. "Not bad," he said.

Billy took a tiny bite of hers, then a bigger one. They ate in silence, and here were all the things they did *not* say to each other:

Dad, I'm scared.

I know you're scared. But you're going to be fine.

I can't do this.

Of course you can do this.

I feel so alone.

You're not alone. Your mother and I are with you.

What if I'm a bad mother?

You won't be. Just be yourself.
What if who I am isn't good enough?
Who you are is just fine.

The kitchen was quiet except for the thrum of the furnace and the occasional clink of a glass as one of them set milk back down on the table.

"How's the sandwich?" her dad asked as she bit into the second half of it.

She smiled. "It's pretty good, actually."

Billy shook herself out of this reverie. An almost imperceptible breeze stirred the thick, humid night air. It rustled—just barely—the leaves in the great red oak. *Oh, I miss him,* she thought. *I miss him so much.* And knowing how important her father had been to her, and how important he was still, it occurred to her now for the first time that in not telling Luke that she knew Wesley's whereabouts, she was denying him the opportunity to have his own relationship with his father. Of course, even if Luke knew Wesley, he might never be as close to him as she had been to her father. Luke, after all, hadn't grown up with Wesley. Then again, they would never know unless she told Luke about the unopened envelope. And here a thought crossed her mind that gave her no comfort. What if she told Luke that her father had given her Wesley's contact information over a year ago and Luke, instead of being excited, was furious, furious that she hadn't told him sooner? What if even telling him, at this point, entailed a loss of trust on his part? What if he couldn't forgive her for keeping this secret from him? The truth was that Pop-Pop, the person Luke believed was perfect, or pretty close to it, had been the one to suggest that she put the envelope away, that she not disturb the balance of her and Luke's life together. And she had agreed with him. Of course, a lot had changed since then . . .

And the person who she really wanted to talk to about all of this now was the one person she couldn't talk to. Yes, she missed her dad. She missed his companionship, his presence, his steadiness, his humor. But what she really missed at this moment was his counsel. He would know what she should do about Luke, and about Wesley. He *knew* what was right. He'd *always* known what was right. Except . . . except if he were here now, she suddenly understood, he wouldn't tell her what to do. He would trust her to decide instead. In her own way, and in her own time. She was Luke's mother, after all, and they were their own family. Their own fragile, imperfect, and yet still complete family.

Murphy shifted at her feet. He looked hot, Billy thought sympathetically, fishing an ice cube out of her wine, shaking it off, and holding it out to Murphy. He gave it a few cursory licks. "Are you ready to go in?" she asked him, reaching for her copy of *Emma* and her watery white wine. She moved through the house, locking the front door and turning off lights. In two weeks she'd take Luke to North Woods Adventures. If they could survive until then without any major conflicts, well, she would make a decision about contacting Wesley while Luke was away. Maybe she'd go down to St. Paul, spend a couple of days with her mom, and talk it over with her, too. But one thing was clear: it was unlikely she'd be able to put this off until Luke was eighteen.

CHAPTER 19

Luke stood up and threw the stone he was holding overhand into the Kawashiwi River. It was a good throw, he thought. The stone almost made it to the other side before it disappeared into the dark water with a little *plink*. He heard it from all the way over here. Neither Van nor J.P. said anything, though. Van was eating Cheetos; J.P. was smoking a Camel.

Luke sat back down on the riverbank. It was steep here, about a hundred yards from the Route 10 overpass where they'd spray-painted the graffiti. Their tagging was gone now; someone had cleaned it off. Van and J.P. were supposed to have done it for their community service, but Officer Sawyer had decided it was too dangerous; he'd told them they'd have to volunteer at a food bank sometime instead. It didn't sound that bad to Luke, but J.P. had still made a big deal out of it, like it would be so terrible to have to put cans of peas on a shelf or something.

Luke heard a rumble of thunder in the distance.

There was a storm coming; he'd seen the weather alert on Margot's iPhone. It was why she'd let him leave Nature Camp early today. Usually they did an outdoor activity before pickup—Margot liked to say she was doing the parents a favor by making their kids run around and tire themselves out—but today she'd been worried about lightning, and she'd had them all sit inside and watch a nature film called *Wings of Life* instead. Luke knew this movie. It was about butterflies, hummingbirds, and bees, and he'd seen it about five times when he was a camper there. Right as it was starting, though, Margot came over to him and whispered, "*Go. Now.* Before you die of boredom." And Luke had laughed. Because Margot was cool that way. He'd never tell Van or J.P. this, but he liked her. Liked hanging out with her. She was pretty old—in her midthirties, at least—and she wore socks with her sandals, which made Luke feel kind of embarrassed for her, but still, she could be fun.

After he'd left the Nature Museum, he'd gotten on his skateboard and headed over to the library, but then he'd changed his mind and went to the Quick and Convenient for a Sprite. That was where he'd seen Van and J.P. They were just kind of hanging out there. J.P. thought Jody, the girl who worked the register, liked him. But Luke doubted it. He'd seen them together, and he thought she was actually kind of rude to him. Luke didn't know, though. Maybe this was how some girls flirted. Anyway, Van and J.P. had already been there for a while, because when Luke paid for his Sprite and left, they left, too, and Van asked him if he wanted to go down to the river with them. Luke still had a while before he had to be at the library, so he'd said okay, and he'd skateboarded, and they'd ridden their bikes, and here they were. It had been a little weird at first. It had been three weeks since Luke had seen them, and J.P. kept making fun of Luke's "mommy," and saying how Luke had to report to her all the time and get her permission to do everything. Luke had stayed, though, because J.P. had said he was going to leave soon to see Jody after her shift ended, and Luke thought maybe then he could talk to Van about other stuff, like his dad and Alaska and the plans he'd been making to find him there.

Luke picked up another stone and started to throw it, but some kayakers were passing, so he waited. J.P. and Van talked about how cool their Fourth of July was; they'd set off a bunch of their own fireworks on the town beach and stayed out until two A.M. Luke, on the other hand, had to work yesterday at the Nature Museum picnic, and then he'd seen the official town fireworks with his mom and the rest of Butternut at the fairgrounds last night. He'd been sort of half listening to what Van and J.P. were talking about. But he heard them saying a name now, Michael Grey, and he paid attention. He was the kid Van had gotten into a fight with, and he and J.P. talked about him a lot, about how much they hated him, and about how they were going to steal his bike and everything. Luke didn't really like him, either. He was kind of a bully, and his family had a lot of money, so he was always bragging about all the things he had. Like, once he got a jet ski for his birthday. There weren't that many rich people in Butternut, so basically, Michael Grey's family was it.

"He's not even going to be at home," J.P. was saying. "My dad's cousin is, like, their cleaning lady, and she says all their kids go to camp in the summer. Like, away to camp, where you stay overnight. Can you believe people actually do that? It's like . . . what was that movie that was on the Disney Channel when I was, like, nine? What was that called?"

Camp Rock, Luke thought but didn't say. He didn't want to admit he'd ever heard of it before. Besides, he hadn't told Van or J.P. yet, but he was going away to camp in about ten days. Not that North Woods Adventures was an overnight camp, because it wasn't, not exactly. But it was sort of similar, and he knew they would think it sounded lame. Van and J.P. would never backpack or go hiking and canoeing or anything like that. The only thing they thought was cool was hanging out and playing video games. Still, his mom had been pushing this North Woods thing pretty hard, and even though he hadn't said it to her, it did look like it *might* be kind of cool.

Now Luke threw the stone he'd been holding, but it didn't go that far this time. Should he tell Van he was going away, he wondered, looking for another stone, or should he just leave and not say anything? Maybe Van wouldn't even notice he was gone. It was only for a couple of weeks.

"So, what are you saying?" Van asked J.P. then, stuffing more Cheetos into his mouth.

"I'm saying that no one is home there in the summer, not during the day," J.P. said. "The loser kids are at summer camp, the dad's at work, and the mom does stuff. She, like, volunteers or something."

"And you think we can just walk in there and take them?" Van asked.

"Yeah, pretty much. They keep them in the barn. And they leave the keys in them. I mean, who's that stupid? Who leaves keys in an ATV? You're, like, asking people to take them."

"I still don't get it, though," Van said. "How do we take them?"

"We just drive them out of the barn," J.P. explained. "Nobody sees us because nobody's *there* to see us. We drive it around on the ATV trails until it runs out of gas, and then we kind of, you know, wreck it and leave it. That's it. They'll get it back eventually."

Luke shook his head just a little bit. He didn't mean for J.P. to see it, but he did.

"What?" J.P. said to him. "What's your problem?"

"Nothing," Luke said, picking up another stone. "I just think . . ." He didn't throw the stone this time; he just kind of tossed it. He didn't want it to go far. He wanted to hear it land in the water. He liked that *plink* sound.

"You just think *what*?" J.P. challenged.

"I just think there's a lot of stuff that could go wrong," Luke said finally.

"Like . . . ?"

Like everything, he thought, but what he said was, "Like, how do you know the barn's not locked? Or doesn't have an alarm or, like, a security camera?"

"Who puts a security camera in a barn?" J.P. said scornfully.

"The same person who puts an ATV in there," Luke shot back. He didn't tell Van and J.P. this, but he'd been there before, to the Greys' place. Their Little League team used to go there for barbecues after games. And here was the thing: the Greys' barn wasn't really a barn. It only looked like one on the outside. On the inside, it was more like a garage. And there weren't just ATVs in there. There was tons of other stuff, too, like snowmobiles and jet skis.

Luke thought J.P. was going to try to get into an argument with him, but all he did was put his cigarette out in the dirt and say, "Then don't go with us, if you're so scared. Go have . . . Popsicle time at your little day care center." Then he turned away from Luke and slid his phone out of his pocket. "Do you want to see a picture of Jody where her boobs are kind of hanging out?" he asked Van.

"Sure," Van said cheerfully. He wiped his hands, which were covered with Cheetos dust, on his pants, and took the phone from J.P. "They look nice," he said, staring at the picture. "Do you want to . . . ?" he asked Luke, holding the phone out to him, but Luke shook his head. He didn't think Jody was that hot, and right now, he hated J.P. anyway.

Luke watched as Van handed the phone back and crumpled up the empty Cheetos bag. He ate a lot of junk food, but he was still always hungry. Luke wondered about him sometimes. He was so skinny, you could count his ribs, and so pale it looked like he didn't even go outdoors, even though he went outside sometimes when he wasn't playing video games. Still, did anyone worry about him? Worry about stuff like whether he ate vegetables or went to bed or did his homework during the school year? Luke didn't think so. Luke knew his mom didn't like Van. Or she didn't *think* she liked him. She didn't know him. But she'd decided he was a bad influence on Luke. The truth was, though, Van wasn't a *bad* person. He could be really nice. He just seemed like someone had . . . kind of forgotten about him.

Van and J.P. started talking again about stealing one of the Greys' ATVs, but Luke didn't say anything. He just kept throwing stones. He didn't think they were ever going to do it, anyway, but then, when they started talking about specific things, like days and times and what was the best route to take after they stole the ATV, he got kind of nervous. They were talking about it like it was definitely going to happen. He started to think about leaving. He was getting that weird feeling he got in his stomach sometimes, mostly when he was worried about stuff.

"What do you say, Luke?" Van asked him now, surprising him. "Like, are you coming with us?"

"You mean, if you really do it?" Luke was looking for another stone to throw.

"I'll do it if you do it," Van said.

Luke looked at him, surprised. Was he serious? He was, he decided. Van was staring at Luke, waiting to see what he was going to say. Which was weird, because Van didn't usually take things that seriously. It was one of the things Luke liked about him.

"Are you going to come or not?" Van asked in a real quiet way, like it was just the two of them talking and J.P. wasn't even there.

"I . . . I don't know. Do you, like, really want to?" Luke asked.

Van nodded. "I think it'd be cool."

"But the thing is . . ." Luke said, rubbing some dirt off the stone he'd found. "If you get caught . . . it's pretty serious. It's a felony, I think."

"What do you know about felonies?" J.P. interjected.

Luke shrugged. "Officer Sawyer. The day he picked us up, he told me about misdemeanors and felonies. Stealing an ATV, that would be a felony, probably. You could go to a juvenile detention center for that."

"It's called *juvie*," J.P. sneered. "And why do you always have to talk like that? Like you just go around reading books all the time?"

Luke ignored him, but his face felt hot. God, he hated J.P. He wished he'd leave already and go see Jody. But Van acted like he hadn't even heard J.P. He kept talking to Luke like it was just the two of them. "I don't think we'd get caught," he said. "And if we did, I don't think it'd be that big a deal. We'd just say we were messing around."

I don't think the police would see it that way, Luke thought, but he didn't say anything. He kept looking at the rock in his hand.

"Come on, let's do it," Van said, giving him a friendly push on the shoulder.

Still Luke said nothing. He was thinking about Pop-Pop. Most of the time he tried *not* to think about him. Most of the time he just kind of pushed him out of his head. Because what, really, did thinking about him do, other than make him feel worse? Now he let himself think about him, though. About a conversation they'd had. They'd had so many of these over the years, and the good thing about them was . . . they just happened. He and Pop-Pop just talked. Pop-Pop hadn't lectured him the way Officer Sawyer and his guidance counselor did. Pop-Pop hadn't told him what to do or what not to do. He let him figure it out for himself. Sometimes, when they were doing something, like fishing, or working on Luke's model town, or just walking someplace, Luke would ask him a question, and Pop-Pop would tell him what he thought. Like once, Luke had told him about a bully who was in his third-grade class. He wasn't bullying Luke—he was bullying another kid, and Luke felt bad for that kid. He'd told their teacher, but she hadn't really done anything about it, and the truth was, Luke didn't want to do anything about it, either, at least not if it meant getting in a fight with the bully. Plus, all of the other kids were going along with it. Anyway, he'd told Pop-Pop about this, and Pop-Pop had said something like, "Luke, I can't tell you what to do. You'll have to learn to listen to yourself. You already know what's right. It's who you are. It's how you're made. Sometimes, maybe, you'll get confused about it, but the more you listen to yourself, the more you'll hear that voice inside you, telling you what's right or wrong. When you really know what that voice is saying, what other people think about you won't matter as much."

Luke threw the stone he was holding. It *plink*ed into the water. The sky was getting darker. The water looked almost black. He heard thunder again. It didn't seem closer yet, but it was a long, slow roll this time.

"I'm not gonna do it," he said suddenly, turning to Van. "The other stuff we did"—he meant the smoking and the tagging—"that was different. We didn't, like, hurt anyone. But this . . . I don't want to steal things, even from people I don't like."

Van looked away from him and shrugged, but J.P. scowled at him.

"I told you we shouldn't tell him about it," he said to Van angrily. "I told you he's only going to snitch on us."

"I'm not going to snitch," Luke said, getting up. He saw the first raindrops on the water, and in the distance, he saw lightning. He started walking up the riverbank, but J.P. caught up to him, put his hand on his shoulder, and got his face really close to his, so close that Luke could smell cigarettes on his breath. "Remember, snitches get stitches," he said to Luke.

He pushed J.P.'s hand away and kept going. He thought J.P. would follow him and start a fight, but he didn't. When Luke got to the place where he'd left his skateboard and they'd left their bicycles, near the road but behind a tree, he stopped and turned back. They were still sitting there like nothing had happened. Like it wasn't even starting to rain.

"Van," he called down. "Are you coming?"

Van didn't turn around or say anything.

"Get lost, loser," J.P. called up.

Luke grabbed his skateboard and carried it over to the road. He got on it and pushed off, hard. And as he headed into town, he started shivering, even though the rain wasn't that cold.

CHAPTER 20

Billy knocked on the door of the little lakeside cottage, waited, and then knocked again. She knew someone was home. There was an unfamiliar car parked in the driveway beside Mrs. Streeter's old Volvo wagon, and she could hear something, a game show on TV inside.

Maybe she'd come at a bad time, she thought, and she was considering leaving her present in the mailbox when a middle-aged woman who, despite the noon hour, already looked weary opened the door. "Yes?"

"Hi, I'm a friend of Mrs. Streeter's," Billy explained. "I brought her a DVD from the library—"

"Billy? Is that you?" Mrs. Streeter called from inside the cottage. Billy had heard that she'd been released from the hospital only the day before—this was after a brief bout with pneumonia—but she sounded surprisingly vigorous now.

"Yes," Billy called back. "I brought you something, Mrs. Streeter."

"You can't come in, dear," Mrs. Streeter said.

"Oh, that's fine. I can give—"

The woman at the door, obviously a home health aide, leaned closer and said to Billy in an undertone, "She doesn't want anyone to see her in her bathrobe and slippers. She says unless she can wear an outfit with a matching hat . . ." The woman rolled her eyes. "She says she has a reputation to maintain."

"Of course," Billy said, reaching into her handbag and pulling out the DVD. "Why don't you just give this to her—"

"Billy! What have you brought me?" shouted Mrs. Streeter.

"*Only Angels Have Wings*," Billy called, feeling a little ridiculous about all of this yelling back and forth. "And you can keep it, Mrs. Streeter. You don't have to return it to the library." Billy, knowing that the library's DVD order wouldn't be in for a couple more weeks, had had Amazon overnight it to her personally.

"I don't want to pay for it, though," called Mrs. Streeter.

"You don't have to. It's a gift," Billy assured her.

"Oh, no. I'll return it to the library. But I don't know when I can get it back, and I don't want to be paying a late fee."

"No. No late fees," Billy called, giving the DVD to the home health worker. "I hope you feel better, Mrs. Streeter."

There was a long pause and then Mrs. Streeter yelled back, "Well, you'd better get going, dear."

Billy smiled wanly at the home health worker and turned away. Rae had been right. Mrs. Streeter would not thank her for this gift. As she started down the steps, a gust of wind caught her skirt, and she shivered in her short-sleeved cotton blouse. After it threatened to storm all day yesterday, there had finally been a torrential downpour last night. Now the day, while mostly sunny, had a crisp feel to it, despite the fact it was only the first week of July. Overhead the wind pushed scraps of clouds hurriedly along, and on the nearby lake, it churned up little waves, their foam white against the dark blue water.

Billy got into her car, glancing over at the two architectural books on the front passenger seat. They'd come in that morning from interlibrary loan, and she'd texted Cal to say she'd be "out his way," and would he like her to drop them off at his cabin? He would, he'd texted back, if it wouldn't be too much trouble. He was taking the day off from working on Jack's cottage, and some "non–Hardy Boys" reading material would be great.

Now, as she drove the several more miles to his cabin, she reflected on the last time she'd seen him, standing in her kitchen a week ago. She'd basically given him a polite but gentle push, not only out the door but also out of her life. Or at least, that's how she saw it in retrospect. She'd had misgivings ever since. He was the first man she'd been really attracted to in years, maybe even in fourteen years . . . There had been Beige Ted, but she'd never been *that* attracted to him. He'd just been a *really* nice, responsible man who lived in Butternut and had expressed an interest in her. And there had been a couple of guys she'd dated in Minneapolis-St. Paul when Luke was young and they were living with her parents. But none of them had stirred her the way Cal had. Her thoughts about him lately would make Jane Austen blush. Surely none of her female characters had such lustful fantasies. So she'd decided, over a recent glass of chardonnay on her back porch, served with a side of fireflies, to take him up on his kiss. She'd reminded herself, though, in the sternest possible terms, to not get too emotionally involved, to keep it light. After all, she had no idea how long he'd even be in Butternut.

Still, she was nervous as she pulled into his driveway. He made it easy for her, though. Even before she'd turned off the engine, he came out onto the front porch. He was wearing a T-shirt and blue jeans and he was barefoot. As Billy came up the steps to the cabin, she found herself staring at his feet. They were just like the rest of him, she thought. Tan. Tan and gorgeous. More gorgeous than feet had any right to be.

"Hey," he said when she handed the books to him. "Thank you for bringing these over. Is this, uh, a new service the library's offering? Home delivery?"

Billy blushed. "I thought since I was already going to be in the neighborhood . . . Mrs. Streeter—she's one of your neighbors—has pneumonia, so I brought her a DVD."

"Mrs. Streeter and I are neighbors?" Cal asked, surprised.

"If by *neighbors* you mean you live across the lake from each other, then yes."

Cal laughed. "Well, I'm glad you came. And I hope Mrs. Streeter is feeling better."

"I think she is," Billy said. Now his hazel eyes had her attention.

"Good. Can I offer you an iced tea? Or maybe something . . . hot?" Cal asked. Billy had shivered again.

She hesitated. "I'm on my lunch hour, so I need to be getting back, but . . . why not?"

Cal smiled. "I won't keep you long. Come on in."

She followed him into the cabin, the inside of which was as unlike his apartment in Seattle as it was possible for any place to be. There was *nothing* intimidating about it, Billy thought, glancing around at its knotty pine paneling, stone fireplace, and unintentionally retro decor. Rae could definitely have her glass of red wine here; she could even spill a few drops without someone having a nervous breakdown.

"What do you think?" Cal asked.

"I like it," Billy said honestly.

"It belongs to a very specific decorating school that hasn't gotten a lot of attention yet from museums and auction houses. It's called midtwentieth-century cabin."

She smiled. "But you've been comfortable here, haven't you?" she asked as Cal went into the kitchen, a cheerful room where open shelving revealed brightly colored Fiesta dishes.

"Very comfortable," Cal said, pouring them iced teas. "It's just an easy place to be. I keep hearing echoes of my childhood, though. My mother spent something like eighteen years telling my sister and me not to let the screen door slam."

"What about not sitting on the furniture in your wet bathing suit?" Billy asked, taking a glass from him.

"That, too," he said, and because they looked at each other now—just a beat too long, just long enough for Billy to shiver again—she moved away and went to look at the bookshelves in the living room.

"Wow, you weren't kidding about the Hardy Boys mysteries," she said, running her finger along a whole row of them. She pulled one out. *The Tower Treasure.* She checked the year of publication. 1958.

"My dad was raised on those," Cal said. "I imagine they've updated them by now."

Billy nodded. "They've tried to take out the racism and the sexism."

"Was there anything left?" Cal asked, standing closer to her.

"Not much. Now, I think, they work for a secret government organization. They battle terrorists and track down assassins. That kind of thing."

"Wow. Who knew the Hardy boys had it in them?" Cal took the book from her, opened it, and held it out to her. "Does it have that old book smell?" he asked.

She sniffed. "Definitely."

"You know what my sister says this cabin smells like?" he asked.

She shook her head.

"Mothballs and maple syrup. She says they're both just ingrained in this place."

"And wood smoke," Billy said. While there was no fire in the fireplace, this smell, too, seemed to have permeated the cabin. She took the book from him and put it back on the bookshelf. Because no matter how appropriate it might have been for him to seduce her over a book, she was the one planning on doing the seducing. Never mind that it meant stepping out of her comfort zone.

"Cal?" she asked, moving closer to him, so close that she could have kissed him.

"Yes?" he said with what she thought was the sexiest smile she'd ever seen.

"I'm glad you were home today," she said before she leaned in to kiss him.

Five minutes later, they were lying on one of the alcove-style beds in his room. It was a bedroom in keeping with the rest of the cabin's time capsule decor: checked window curtains, rag rug, and what looked like a paint-by-numbers sailboat scene hanging on the wall.

"Is this okay?" Cal asked. Now that they were on a bed, Billy found that some of her boldness had worn off.

"It's fine," Billy said.

"Sorry about the single bed," Cal said. "There are no double beds here. When my grandmother decorated this place, she was obviously thinking about a different kind of fun. You know, Parcheesi. Crossword puzzles. Gin rummy."

She smiled.

He kissed her gently and touched her cheek. Was he . . . touching her freckles? She knew he liked them.

"Those don't come off," she said.

"I hope not," he said, leaning down to kiss her. "You know what I just realized? I've wanted to do this since the first time I met you. Since we were both standing in line at the buffet at Daisy's wedding."

"You mean . . . with the biscuits?" she murmured doubtfully.

But now they started kissing again, this time in a way that precluded any more conversation. Talking was over. And as Cal ran a hand over her thin cotton blouse, Billy felt a tremor in her legs. Now the kiss deepened. He started to unbutton her blouse and it was as if he were unbuttoning all of her. She wanted him. She wanted him so badly it shocked her a little. He murmured her name—she loved the way it sounded— and he moved his lips down to her neck. *Yes, kiss me,* she thought. *Kiss me everywhere.*

As if he had heard her, his lips traveled down to the hollow at the bottom of her neck.

She felt her blouse fall open, and she moved her hands hungrily under his T-shirt and over the smooth skin of his back. This was going to be good. How did she know this? She knew it because of the way Cal was proceeding, taking his time, moving at a slow, un-hurried pace that suggested there was nothing else he would rather be doing right now than leaving this trail of kisses down her body. His lips were brushing over her navel when she heard something, something that hovered, for a moment, at the edge of her conscious-ness. The bedroom they were in faced the lake, and through its open window, she could hear little waves breaking against the shore, and the halyard of a moored sailboat clanging against the mast. Now, though, there was a new sound: a motorboat approaching, its engine getting louder and mingling with the sound of voices on board.

"Cal?" she asked softly.

He paused. His lips hovered above her navel. "Yes?"

"Do you hear that?"

"Hear what?" he asked, lowering his lips back to her skin.

"I think . . . I think someone's here," she said, rising up on her elbows, because whoever was driving the boat had cut the engine, and the two voices were now more distinct. "I think there's a boat at your dock."

Cal held perfectly still, listening. Then he pulled back the curtain a fraction of an inch and looked out the window. "Damn," he muttered.

"Who is it?"

"Walker and Wyatt. I forgot they were coming over. They just bought a new boat and . . ." He shook his head and smiled ruefully. "Want to go for a boat ride?" he asked her.

"I can't," Billy said, sitting up. Her legs were trembling, though.

"You okay?" he asked, watching wistfully as she buttoned her blouse.

"Of course," she said, smiling.

"Come on. I'll walk you out to your car."

As they came down the front steps of the cabin, Cal waved to Walker and Wyatt, who were tying up their boat at the dock. After Billy opened her car door, Cal leaned down and kissed her, chastely, on the cheek. "Thanks for the books," he said. "Are you free tomorrow?"

"I have work, Cal," she said teasingly.

"Maybe . . . I could stop by and take you to lunch one day?"

"Maybe," Billy said with a smile as she got into her car.

Driving back into town, her legs were finally still. But it was hours before she stopped feeling the sensation of Cal's lips against her skin.

CHAPTER 21

When Cal walked into the Butternut Library a couple of days later, he didn't see Billy. He did, however, see a redheaded woman sitting at the check-out desk, reading *Car and Driver* magazine. "Can I help you?" she asked without raising her eyes.

"Yes," he said. "Is Billy here?"

She looked up, suddenly animated, and Cal got the distinct impression she already knew who he was.

"Billy's in the computer area with our tech support," she said, pointing him in the right direction. "Go straight back and to the left."

"Thanks," Cal said. When he got to the computer area, he saw Billy talking to a boy who couldn't have been older than fourteen. He was sitting on a swivel chair and typing furiously on a laptop balanced on his knees.

"Is this really necessary?" Billy was asking him as Cal approached.

"*Yes.* I need to do a security update on the router's firmware."

"I thought . . . we already had a firewall for security."

"We do. But there's a vulnerability in it, and I need to apply a security patch to prevent DOS attacks."

Billy started to say something, but she stopped when she saw Cal. "Hi," she said, immediately flustered. "Are you . . . ordering more books?"

"Not today. I just wanted to . . ." *I just wanted to be with you,* he almost said, but her tech support had stopped typing on his laptop and had swiveled his chair around so that he was facing them. "I'm sorry," Cal said. "Were you two not done here?"

"No, we're done," she said. "I mean, *I'm* done. Anton won't rest until our computers are more secure than the Pentagon's."

"Actually, that's not possible," Anton said seriously. "The Pentagon has this program called 'Hack the Pentagon.' It actually invites select hackers to break into its computer system so it can find and fix weaknesses before they're exploited."

"All right, well, I think we can agree we don't need to do that here," Billy said, sounding faintly agitated. And then, as if remembering herself, she introduced them. "Anton, this is Cal. He's visiting here for the summer. And Cal, this is Anton. He knows more about computers than anyone within a sixty-mile radius."

"That *is* possible," Anton said without a flicker of a smile. He did, however, shake the hand that Cal had extended to him.

"Anton, I need to speak to Cal now," Billy said. "If there are more issues with our router, we can discuss them later," she added firmly, and she led Cal over to the sitting area, which was empty now.

"Your tech support looks like he's in high school," Cal said, keeping his voice low.

"Oh, he is. He'll be a junior this year," she said, starting to gather up a few newspapers and magazines that visitors had left lying around. "Are you sure I can't help you with something?" she asked, going to hang a newspaper up on a rack. "Or did you stop by just to . . . talk?" She smiled, a little shyly. God, she looked pretty today, Cal thought. She was wearing one of those summery print dresses she seemed to favor and a pair of flat sandals. Her long brunette hair was pinned up in a kind of bun, though a few strands had escaped from it and were floating appealingly around her face.

"No, actually I came by to see if you wanted to have lunch," Cal said.

"Lunch?" She glanced at her watch. "It's two thirty."

"Is it that late?"

She nodded. "I took my lunch hour at twelve thirty."

"So take another one," the redhead from the front desk said, bustling into the sitting area.

"Cal, have you met Rae?" Billy asked.

"I have now," Cal said as they shook hands.

But Rae was all business. "I'll take over here," she said. "I'll make sure Anton doesn't make our system so secure *we* can't even get into it. And *you*," she said to Billy. "You need to take a second lunch break. Right now."

Billy hesitated, but Rae took her arm and started

steering her toward the library's front door. "*All right,*" Billy said, obviously amused by Rae's pushiness. "I'll go. I just need to get my purse." Rae, satisfied, disappeared into the stacks, and Billy retrieved her purse from the checkout desk drawer. "It's hard to believe sometimes," she confided to Cal, "that Rae works for me."

"Still, she seems like an excellent employee," Cal said, eliciting a laugh from her.

"Do you want to go to Pearl's?" Billy asked once they were standing in the bright sunshine on the library's front steps.

"No. I already ate."

"I thought you said—"

"I wanted to be alone with you," Cal said, turning to her. "I was up all night last night thinking about you."

"You were?" she said, blushing.

"Yes, I was," he said. "Do you want to go for a drive?"

"That depends. Is Officer Sawyer going to pull us over?"

"No. I'll drive at the speed limit, I promise."

"All right, let's go," she said with a little shrug, and she let him take her hand and lead her over to the next block, where his car was parked. It wasn't until he'd reached the edge of town and, through sheer force of habit, found himself driving in the direction of the lake, that Billy asked with a trace of amusement, "Where are we going?"

"I haven't gotten that far yet," he said. "Any suggestions?"

"The town beach? That's close."

"Hmm." He looked at her, his eyes lingering on her legs. Her dress wasn't immodest in any way, but it still left plenty of bare leg exposed. He swallowed hard. "Isn't the town beach kind of crowded?"

"Only if you consider fifteen hundred sticky toddlers and their exhausted mothers crowded," she joked.

"Right," he said, glancing over at her again.

"You keep looking at my legs," she said.

"Do I?"

"Uh-huh."

"I'm sorry."

"Don't be sorry. I want you to look at them."

"Do you?" He looked at them again, and swerved his car slightly in the process.

"I mean, I want you to look at them if you can look at them *and* stay on the road at the same time."

He laughed. But before he could look at them again, she took one of his hands off the wheel and placed it on her knee. "Maybe that's safer," she said.

"You think so?" he asked, marveling at the softness of her skin beneath his hand. He caressed her knee and then gave it a little squeeze. They were on Butternut Lake Drive, the foliage so thick that it formed a green canopy over the road and only occasionally allowed a glimpse of the iridescent lake through the trees on their left. He moved his hand off her knee and began to slide it slowly up the velvety inside of her thigh.

"Here, take this right," she said, suddenly.

He slowed down, but there was nothing on his right but the entrance to an abandoned logging road. "Here?" he asked.

"Why not? No one uses these anymore."

He hesitated for less than a second before turning down it. Thankfully it hadn't rained in several days; a little mud, Cal thought, and he would have spent the rest of the afternoon digging his car out. Even as it was, though, the ride in his Porsche was a little bumpier than he would have liked. He was driving with two hands again, and Billy, he noticed, was bracing herself against the dashboard. When they'd driven a couple of hundred yards into the woods, she indicated a little clearing just off the trail. He turned into it, cut the engine, and looked around. "This is nice," he said of the dappled sunlight playing around them and the sweet-scented air coming in through the car's open windows.

"It *is* nice," she agreed, but he could see her shyness had returned. *God damn,* he thought, *who knew shyness could be so sexy?* He reached over and brushed a strand of hair off her cheek. Then, leaning over the console, he kissed her in a way that was meant to communicate what exactly he wanted the two of them to do together right now. He thought she understood, too, when a tiny moan escaped her.

"I wish this wasn't here," she said, indicating the gearshift.

"I wish I had a backseat," he said, still kissing her.

"I wish you had a Range Rover."

"Billy, if I'd known I was going to meet you this summer, I would have bought a Hummer." She laughed, but the fact remained that there was only so close they could get to each other in this car, which was ironic considering how little room it had. After some more kissing and touching, Cal failed to see any humor in the situation at all. "Do you think you could . . . come over here?" he said of his side of the car. "I could slide my seat back."

"I—I don't know," she said. "I can barely move in here. I can try, though." She tried. "Oh my God," she muttered when she got stuck at one point, "what would Lizzie Bennet say?"

"Who's she?" Cal asked, trying to help her.

"A friend of mine," she said, wriggling mightily. "Well, actually, she's a character in a Jane Austen novel. And she would definitely *not* approve of this."

Finally, with his help, she succeeded in climbing over the gearshift lever. Billy was straddling his lap—who knew it was possible for someone to straddle anything as demurely as she was straddling his lap?—and they were laughing and kissing at the same time. Cal couldn't get enough of her. Her mouth was cool and sweet, and her body pressed—no, *wedged*—against his managed to feel both firm and supple. He wanted to touch her everywhere at the same time. He brought a hand up to the front of her dress and started to unbutton it, which was no easy feat. He had so little room to maneuver that he was tempted to just rip the whole thing off her.

But no, he wanted to undress her with care. And besides, her dress was *way* too pretty to rip. So he unbuttoned another button and peeled open the top. He could see her bra now; it was buttercup yellow. He smiled. Of course she was wearing a buttercup-yellow bra. It was just the kind of thing he imagined Billy wearing. He ran his fingers over the outside of that bra, and when he felt her hardening nipple dimpling the fabric, he slipped his hand inside it and caressed her breast. Her skin here was soft, too, softer even than the inside of her thighs. His fingers settled on her nipple and stroked it, gently and then harder, until Billy squirmed in his lap in a way that made him groan. "I'm so glad you wore a dress," he said, reaching under it with his other hand. "Especially since I don't think we have enough room to take all our clothes off."

"Oh my God, Cal, are we really going to do this?" she whispered, her breath soft on his cheek. "In here?"

"I hope so," he said. "Why? Are you worried about what Lizzie will think?"

"It's *way* too late for that. I just didn't realize people actually . . . did this in cars. I mean, on TV or in the movies, but in real life . . . ?"

"Are you kidding? People do it in cars all the time. It's like . . . America's pastime," he said, nuzzling her neck with his lips.

"Isn't that baseball?" she asked absently. He already knew she loved it when he touched her neck.

"Then it's America's *other* pastime," he said, and he moved his lips to the extrasensitive hollow at the base of her neck.

After a few more minutes of him kissing and tonguing her there, she moaned a tiny moan. "Oh, all right, fine," she said. "What the hell." And when she kissed him now, he could feel her breasts through the thin, silky material of her bra. Her hands groped impatiently at his hardness through his blue jeans.

Cal wanted her so badly now he couldn't even think clearly. He tried to stay in the moment, though. And it was *such* a good moment. It was a lovely day, and there was a lovely woman straddling his lap. He breathed in the scent of her. It was delicious. Clean, like soap. But warm, too, and summery, as if she had the smell of the sun on her skin and the wind in her hair. He kissed her deeply and put his hands on her waist. She wriggled against him in a way that made him almost crazy with his desire for her. He was considering how best to remove her panties within the ridiculous confines of his front seat when he heard a noise. A faint humming noise like a mosquito, only from farther away. He tried to ignore it, but it got closer and louder. No, it was not like a mosquito, he decided. It was more like a lawnmower, a very large lawnmower.

He pulled his mouth reluctantly away from hers. "What's that noise?"

"What noise?" Billy asked, kissing him again.

"Listen," he said. She kept kissing him, though. "Do you hear it?" he asked, interrupting her. "It's getting closer now." She paused, and Cal saw the exact moment when Billy heard it. She bit her lip in consternation. "Oh no," she said, trying to scramble off his lap, and then giving up and reaching to open his car door.

"What?" he said, watching her practically tumble out of the car. "I thought you said this was just an old logging trail."

"It is. But it's an old logging trail that people ride ATVs on sometimes," she said, glancing back at the trail behind them.

"Oh, Christ," Cal groaned. As she straightened and pulled the bunched skirt of her dress down, he was treated to a last glimpse of her pale, smooth thighs. She looked so rumpled, so sexy, and so tempting standing there, buttoning the buttons on her dress, that he almost told her to stop, to get back into the car, and give the fast approaching off-roaders something to remember. But he knew she couldn't be persuaded to do this now, so he got out of the Porsche, closed the door, and leaned casually against it, as if the two of them had come out here just to have a conversation.

And no sooner had Billy finished buttoning up her dress than two boys on Motocross bikes came barreling down the logging road behind them. Billy waved to their occupants and their occupants waved back before disappearing down the trail.

Cal exhaled slowly and smiled at Billy, though his body was practically aching with disappointment. "I've got to get back. I'm sorry," she said, leaning over and giving him a conciliatory kiss on the lips.

"Don't be," he said, putting his arms around her waist. "Just come over to my cabin tonight."

"I can't. I have a library board meeting this evening, and they can last for hours. And then I have Luke . . . What about on Saturday?"

Cal shook his head. "I can't. I'm going to Minneapolis to see a friend of mine from graduate school."

"That sounds nice," Billy said.

"Well it's not just a social visit. He's got his own architectural firm, and he wants me to take a look at it. He might be expanding. I'm probably going to be there at least for a week, but I'd like to see you when I get back," he said seriously.

"All right," she said. "Except for next Friday. I'm driving Luke to camp." She sighed a little sigh. "Why do I feel like we're two ships in the night?"

Cal smiled. "I'm hoping eventually we'll collide."

CHAPTER 22

You know what I think?" Billy asked, glancing over at Luke, who was riding in the front passenger seat. "*I think,*" she said, not waiting for an answer she knew wasn't going to come, "that there are *more* than ten thousand lakes in Minnesota. Seriously, they are going to have to change the state slogan, or whatever it is you call that thingy on the bottom of the license plate. Because this is at least the five-hundredth lake we've passed since we left Butternut," she added, gesturing at the dazzlingly blue body of water sliding by on their left.

"See which lake that is," she said, picking up the map she'd set on the armrest and holding it out to Luke. To her surprise, he took it from her, albeit reluctantly, and with a sigh to indicate his exasperation at having to do this, he looked it over. Billy hid a smile. She loved maps; it was something she'd inherited from her father, and Luke had inherited it, too. Even after she'd bought a car with a navigational system, she'd always preferred to use paper maps, and more often than not, she'd made Luke her navigator. "It's Birch Lake," he said finally, without much interest, setting the map back down.

"Birch Lake, huh? Well, whoever named it that doesn't get any points for originality, do they?" she said. "But there are some wonderful names of lakes in this state, Luke. When I was little, and Pop-Pop and Grandma and I used to drive up north on vacation, I'd write down all my favorite ones. Let's see if I can remember some of them. There was . . . Lake Full of Fish. Fool Hen Lake. And . . . oh, I know, Little Too Much Lake. Swear to God on that last one," she said, stealing a look at him. She might—*might*—have seen a glimmer of a smile from him, but he didn't say anything.

For once, Billy didn't mind. It was one of those glorious Midwestern summer mornings she'd learned to expect but never to take for granted living up here. The flatness of the land had the effect of emphasizing the immensity of the sky, and of making the clouds that were drifting above it look fantastically puffy—like misshapen buffalo grazing in a field of blue. Billy had chosen the backroads route on their drive today, and every few miles they passed another lake, each of which was a variation on the same theme: cobalt water, granite shoreline, fringe of dark green pine trees. She turned off the radio now—the station was starting to break up—and rolled down her window, letting in the sounds of outside: the hum of insects and the swish of the wind in the trees. The morning air, warm and sweet, ruffled her hair, still damp from the shower. No, not even Luke, who had slumped down a little further in his seat and put his gloomy expression back in place, could stop Billy from taking pleasure in this day.

It wasn't just from the day, either. She was excited about Luke's North Woods Adventures trip; excited enough for both of them, she liked to think. But when she'd woken him up this morning to get up and ready for the drive to the meeting place, he'd buried his head under his pillow and mumbled something unintelligible, though definitely not positive, about the day ahead.

Billy, on the other hand, couldn't wait for it. She'd spent the last couple of weeks poring over Luke's itinerary and once again falling in love with place names. Were they *really* going to hike the Gitchi-Gami State Trail to Gooseberry Falls? They really were. She'd spent hours online, ordering Luke's equipment and debating the relative merits of flashlights versus headlights, hiking boots versus trail runners, down versus synthetic sleeping bags. Finally she'd agonized, pleasantly, over what book to pack for him. He hadn't asked her to do this, and she hadn't told him she was going to, but she'd be damned if her son left on a two-week trip without anything to read. After much debate, she'd slipped the underappreciated classic *Canoeing with the Cree* into his backpack. The rest, she figured, was up to him.

"How long before we get to Duluth?" Billy asked now, nudging the map over to him. He studied it.

"About an hour?" he said finally.

"We're making good time, then. I thought we'd have lunch at Canal Park," she said, knowing that Luke had once loved (and maybe, for all she knew, *still* loved) looking at the carrier ships that docked there. "And then, about an hour after that—maybe less if we're lucky—we'll be at the meet-up point, Split Rock Lighthouse. Remember your report?" When Luke was in fifth grade and at the peak of his "shipwrecks of the Great Lakes" obsession, he'd written a report about this lighthouse. (It had been built in the early twentieth century after a stormy November during which two ships had sunk off that particularly rocky stretch of coastline.) "Did you ever think you'd visit it?" Billy prodded.

Amazingly, this got his attention. He sat up straight and turned to her. "Mom?"

"Yes?"

"I don't really care about the lighthouse, but . . . do you know where I do want to go?"

"Where?"

"Alaska."

She looked at him, astonished, before looking back at the road. A logging truck was coming up behind them and she needed to concentrate.

"I tried to find him in Alaska, Mom," Luke said, the words spilling out. "I looked online. He's not there, though. There are other Wesley Fitzgeralds in other states, but they weren't him."

Billy said nothing. She was waiting for a turnout so she could let the logging truck pass.

"Mom, I can't do it by myself. You need to . . . help me find him. Maybe we could go back to the fishing lodge—the last place you saw him—and start from there."

"Just a second," Billy said in a controlled panic. They were approaching a roadside business, a general store. She put on her turn single, slowed, and pulled into its graveled parking lot. The logging truck rattled by. *Remember when you were fascinated by those, too?* she wanted, almost desperately, to ask Luke. *Remember when you used to count how many we would see on our drives between Butternut and St. Paul?* But when she glanced over at him, she realized he could not be distracted; he was staring intently at her. *So we're going to have this conversation now,* she thought, mentally bracing herself. She put the car in park and turned the engine off.

"Luke, I understand why you're curious about your father," she began with what she thought was an admirable calmness. The palms of her hands, though, still on the steering wheel, felt suddenly clammy with perspiration.

"So *do* something about it," he burst out. "Don't just *say* you understand. That doesn't do anything."

"Luke," she said, taking a hand off of the steering wheel and putting it on the dashboard, as if this would somehow steady her, "it's a little more complicated than that. This isn't just about contacting your father. It's about . . . what kind of a person your father is now. And how the person he is now would feel about all of this. It's been fourteen years since I saw him. And you have to understand, I *barely* knew him then. I was a *teenager*. I didn't . . . I didn't know as much about the world as I know now. He seemed like a nice guy, but I may not have been . . . the best judge of character."

"Okay. I get it. You didn't know him that well," Luke said impatiently. "You told me that already. I don't care. You act like he might be some kind of loser, Mom, but you wouldn't have *liked* him when you met him if he'd been like that. You just . . . wouldn't have."

"I'm not saying he's a loser, but what if, when you meet him, he's not what you expect? What if he's . . . different?"

Luke set his jaw stubbornly. "It doesn't matter. Pop-Pop told me once, 'Family is family. You take care of each other.' He said, 'It's that simple.' So even if my dad isn't, like, perfect, that doesn't mean I don't want to know him."

"Pop-Pop said that?" Billy asked. She'd never heard him say this, but she knew that Pop-Pop's own father, Douglas Harper, had been a famously difficult man. He'd had a serious gambling problem and had once lost Pop-Pop's boyhood home in a card game. But that hadn't stopped Pop-Pop from taking care of him before he died.

"You're right, Luke. Family is important," she said evenly. "But you're forgetting something. You don't know . . ." . . . *how your dad will feel about you. Or whether he'll even accept that you're his son or, if he does, whether he'll want to have anything to do with you.* But she couldn't say this. She looked over at Luke instead. His head was down, and he was unraveling a loose thread from the frayed edges of a hole in the knee of his blue jeans. This was the kind of thing she'd seen him do countless times before without feeling anything more than a mild annoyance—did he really have to make the hole *bigger*?—but now, for some reason, it made her throat tighten with emotion. She didn't want to hurt him. She'd *never* wanted to hurt him. But she had to broach this subject now, because if they were going to reach out to Wesley, Luke had to be prepared for the possibility of rejection.

"Luke," she started again.

He looked up. "I know what you're going to say, Mom."

"You do?"

"You're going to say he might not want to be my dad."

"If he knew you, he'd want to be your dad," Billy said quickly, the lump hardening in her throat. "He doesn't know you, though, Luke. He doesn't know anything about you." She whispered this last part because it seemed awful to her now to think that someone as amazing as Luke should be in this world without both of his parents knowing everything about him.

"Mom," he said. "We won't know until we find him. And if he doesn't want to know me, or know us, then we won't see him again." He said this with a resolve that surprised Billy. So he was willing to take that chance, the chance of being rejected by his own father? Billy wasn't sure it was a chance *she* was willing to take.

They sat there quietly for a moment while she wrestled with what to say. Should she tell him she would think about all this while he was at camp? Or should she tell him about Pop-Pop finding his father? Now that he was so adamant about tracking Wesley down, it seemed wrong to continue pretending she didn't know where he was. On the other hand, telling Luke now, a couple of hours before she was supposed to drop him off at camp, seemed like an inopportune moment to tell him something so . . . *so momentous.*

"You know what?" Luke said, interrupting her thinking. "I'm not going to camp."

"Of course you're going," Billy said automatically.

"No, I'm not," he said. "I *never* wanted to go. You just didn't listen to me. And now . . . you can't make me," he added, bracing himself against the front seat of the car as if, even now, Billy was going to try to remove him from it.

"Luke," she said incredulously. "You *have* to go. It's . . . *paid* for. It's nonrefundable. And it's *a lot* of money—for us, anyway, and for Grandma, too. She paid for half of it." But she could feel Luke's resistance hardening, and something occurred to her then. He was right. She couldn't *force* him to go on a two-week hiking trip. Couldn't even force him to get out of *the car* if he didn't want to. Even if she could, if he was that unwilling to go, the counselors probably wouldn't want him to come. It was a voluntary program, after all. Not one of those boot camps for troubled teens.

She inhaled a shaky breath and looked out the window while she tried to gather her thoughts. Luke had never defied her authority before, not so completely. Now that he had, she felt helpless. And, to be honest, a little afraid. She couldn't let him see this, though. She needed to treat this like just another negotiation. If there was anything she'd learned to do over the last six months, it was to negotiate with Luke.

She was considering her opening move when he said impatiently, "I know you think if I don't go on this trip I'm just going to hang out at home, but I'm not. I'm going to look for my dad. And if you won't help me, I'll do it myself. I have money saved up. I think it's enough to buy an airline ticket to Alaska."

"*Luke,*" she murmured, shaking her head, panic edg-

ing up on her again. And while her instincts might once
have told her to list all of the reasons this plan was un-
workable, the truth was, she was too afraid to do this.
He had tapped, unknowingly, into one of her greatest
fears: that he would run away from home. At her lowest
points this summer, after his suspension and his trip to
the police station, she'd asked herself if that was the direction he was heading in, the logical conclusion of his
rebelliousness and the breakdown of their relationship.
Now, as so often happened lately, she didn't know if she
was overreacting or not. The idea of a thirteen-year-old
Luke leaving home alone on some quixotic journey to
find his father seemed unlikely. Then again, even if
he didn't get far, he could still try, and that in and of
itself was terrifying. (She remembered a scene she'd
witnessed once from her car window: a bunch of what
looked like teenagers living in a homeless encampment
under a freeway overpass outside Minneapolis.)

And she knew then that she would have to tell him,
right now, about Wesley. She was not going to be able
to take two weeks while he was away to prepare for this
moment. The moment was now.

"Luke, look at me," she said, since he was once
again pulling at a loose thread in his jeans. "I need to
tell you something."

He turned to her, his expression alert.

There was no way to say this elegantly, she realized.
She pulled in a little breath. "I know where your father is."

Luke stared at her, dumbstruck.

She nodded vigorously. "Your Pop-Pop found him.
Or, rather, the private investigator Pop-Pop hired did.

I've never contacted him, Luke. But I have an address and a phone number."

"Where . . . where is he?" he sputtered.

"He's on Vancouver Island. That's in Canada."

"Canada?"

"He lives there . . . and works there," Billy explained, wishing she knew more. But she told him what little she did know while he stared wide-eyed back at her. She told him that his father owned a charter boat business, that he was married and had two daughters. This last piece of information seemed to stun Luke all over again.

"I have two sisters?"

"Actually, they're considered half sisters. But yes, you are related to them."

"I have two sisters," he repeated as though he were still familiarizing himself with this piece of information. "How old are they?"

"They're . . . around six and ten now, I think," she said. It seemed incredible to her now that she hadn't even *opened* the envelope. A year ago, though, she had felt as if it was a ticking time bomb that would be safer in a safe deposit box than at home. How wrong she had been.

"Wait. When did you find all this stuff out?" he asked.

"Before your Pop-Pop died," she began. And then she made herself go back to that Easter weekend and tell Luke about her conversation with Pop-Pop in his study, and the manila envelope he'd given to her, and the safe deposit box at the bank in Butternut.

"You knew about my dad this whole time?" he

asked. "Why didn't you tell me, like, right away? And what about Pop-Pop? Why didn't he tell me?"

"Your Pop-Pop let me make that decision. And I thought about it," she said. "Remember, though, Luke, you were twelve at the time, and you were doing so well. Your Pop-Pop and I, we thought . . . well, we didn't know what your dad was like, or how he'd feel if we contacted him. And it was . . . it was never a question of *if*," she added quickly. "It was only a question of *when* you were going to get the information about him." It struck Billy now that this reasoning seemed hollow.

He was quiet for a long time. "That's what I used to talk to Van about," he said when he spoke again. "About my dad. About how I'd find him and, you know, what it'd be like when I did."

"*Really?*" she said. "I didn't . . . I didn't know that." Why hadn't he told *her* this? she wondered, tears burning unexpectedly in her eyes. Unless . . . unless, of course, he *had* told her. Or *tried* to tell her. And she remembered his heated words after they'd come back from the police station. "No, you don't get it," Luke had shouted. "I don't know *anything* about my dad." And this whole time, Luke was now realizing, Billy could have enlightened him. She blinked back a tear. "I'm sorry," she said, but there was no answer from Luke.

Finally, though, he mumbled, "Okay, so, whatever." And then he said, "When can I meet him? Like, how soon?" And he looked reflexively at Billy's cell phone, which was propped in the cup holder.

"We're not going to call him, Luke," she said,

alarmed. "Not right this second. And we're not going to rush into things, either."

"But you are going to call him?"

"I am. Eventually."

"*Eventually?*" He looked incredulous.

"No, soon," Billy amended. "I'll get in touch with him when I get home."

"*You* get home. You're not still going to make me go to camp . . . ?"

"*Yes*, Luke. I am. You're going. We just went over this."

"Yeah, but that was *before* I knew—"

"This doesn't change that," she said firmly. "Especially since . . . I have to figure out how to do this. Try to see this from his perspective. We can't just . . . *drop* this on him. I mean, we can. We'll sort of . . . *have to*. But there's a right way and a wrong way." Even as she was saying this, though, Billy was wondering what the right way would be. They had definitely not covered this particular challenge in the parenting books she'd been reading recently.

"Look, I will contact him," she said. "But not right this minute. We need to get you to Split Rock Lighthouse." She glanced at her watch.

"I still don't get why I have to go."

"Because I think it'll be good for you. I think you'll love it. I know the timing's not great. The timing almost never is great for anything," she admitted with a rueful smile. "But, look. You've waited thirteen years to find out more about your dad. Do you think, maybe, you could wait another two weeks?"

"I guess," Luke said finally, though Billy could see how conflicted he still was. It was all there in his expression. Excitement. Nervousness. Impatience. And something else, too, something she couldn't quite name. Anger? Distrust? He turned to look out the window. She started the engine and pulled back onto the road.

By the time they'd reached the parking lot of the visitor center at Split Rock Lighthouse, where counselors, campers, and parents were already congregating, Luke had settled back inside himself—settled so far back, in fact, that when Billy said good-bye to him, she understood that she was not, under any circumstance, to hug him. She spoke instead to the head counselor, whose nickname was Mad Dog, and who had long blond hair, a BMX biking T-shirt on, and a quintessential coolness that she thought might have impressed Luke under ordinary circumstances.

"Luke," she said quietly as the campers started getting ready to leave. "You're going to be okay with all of this, aren't you? I need to know that before I leave here."

"I'll be fine," he said, glancing around to make sure none of the other boys had heard her.

"Good," she said. And she couldn't resist reaching out and pushing an errant lock of hair off his forehead.

"Mom," he said in warning, hoisting his backpack on.

"Okay," she said. "I'll go before I make a scene." She tried to smile. "I love you, though," she said in a voice no louder than a whisper. "I love you so much,

Luke." And then she turned and, without looking back, made her way across the parking lot to her car. She wasn't feeling particularly lucky, but she must have had *a little* luck on her side, because she was safely back inside the car by the time the tears *really* came.

CHAPTER 23

Once Billy was ready to start driving again, she made good time on the way back from Split Rock Lighthouse—so good, in fact, that she was at the bank in Butternut a full hour before it closed. She retrieved the manila envelope out of her safe deposit box and returned with it—still unopened—to the house. She took Murphy for a walk, an *extra*long walk, then drove out to the town beach for a swim. She was hoping some exercise would loosen the knot of tension that had formed between her shoulder blades and, more importantly, bring her some measure of calm, no matter how small. The relief she'd felt briefly after she'd told Luke about Wesley had been replaced by a tumult of other feelings, feelings that had been her relentless companions on the drive home. There was worry: how would Wesley respond when she contacted him? There was self-recrimination: why had she waited so long to tell Luke? There was defensiveness: she had made the decisions she thought best at the time. There was disbelief:

had she really dropped all this information about Wesley on Luke just before he left for a two-week hike? There was guilt: she had hurt Luke—she'd heard it in his voice—when he'd realized she'd known about Wesley for more than a year. And there was fear, of course: had she lost Luke's trust? Maybe forever?

Though the walk and the swim hadn't completely cleared her head, she did feel a not-unpleasant fatigue afterward. Now, as she sat on the back porch, an untouched glass of wine on the table beside her, an unfamiliar emptiness settled over the house. She already missed Luke. Other than a five-day trip with his grandfather to New York City several years ago, he'd never been away from her for more than a single night's sleepover or a weekend visiting his grandmother. Now he'd be gone for almost two weeks. Billy watched as Murphy nosed around in the darkening backyard and decided it was time—time to get to the matter at hand.

She reached for the manila envelope she'd put on the table beside her and a letter opener she'd set down next to it. Before she could lose her nerve, she sliced through the envelope and shook its contents out onto her lap. The first thing she saw was what she assumed was a recent photograph of Wesley. She picked it up and studied it. He was older now, obviously, and a little heavier than he'd been the last time she'd seen him, but she recognized him. Of course she did. He had more or less burned himself into her memory. Also in the file was a three-page report, which she read slowly. Wesley had left Alaska fourteen years ago after meeting a guest at the fishing lodge who'd hired him away to work for his fishing club in Vancouver. Wesley had worked there as a dock manager for three years, and then he'd met a Vancouver girl, Erin Wallace. They'd gotten married ten years ago, and they'd moved to the northeastern coast of Vancouver Island, not far from Port McNeil, where they owned and operated a charter fishing business. The couple had two daughters, Hannah and Eleanor. Among the papers the detective had gathered was a copy of a clipping from a local newspaper—an article about a fishing tournament in Port McNeil—and there was a photo of Wesley and Erin together. She was petite, her dark hair pulled back in a ponytail, a friendly smile on her face, and she and Wesley were standing on the end of a dock, their arms around each other, the water and towering pines behind them.

She looked at the grainy photograph closely, as though she might find the answer to some riddle in it. The picture evoked in her something she could describe only as a pain, a kind of heartache she had not allowed herself to feel before. She wondered, for the first time in years, what a life with Wesley might have been like. Might she have been happy with him? Might they—she and Luke and Wesley—have made a good family? This was not a productive line of questioning, though. She knew that.

When she'd decided to have Luke all those years ago, she'd been reconciled to not finding Wesley. She'd been reconciled, too, to not raising Luke in a traditional family. This was because, despite her romantic nature, she also had a strong dose of her dad's practicality, and he'd taught her not to dwell on what might have been. It was a fool's errand, he'd said, to imagine a past that hadn't taken place. The point was to move forward, count one's blessings, and appreciate what one did have. For the most part, that's what she'd done over the years. And so had her dad. She remembered him telling her once about his crushing disappointment after he'd been unable to go to Cornell University's engineering school. He'd been accepted there, but he couldn't afford the tuition. In fact, his family was in such debt that he had to attend a nearby college, live at home to save money, and work a full-time job to help his mom pay the bills. But sometime in his second year of college, he'd met Billy's mom and he'd fallen "madly, hopelessly" in love with her. "I never would have met her if I'd gone to Cornell," he'd explained to Billy one afternoon. "I learned then that you should work hard, have dreams, and set goals, but don't let the things you didn't attain prevent you from being grateful for the things right in front of your eyes." Yes, he was right. Now was not the time to imagine what *had not* happened. Not when she had Luke to show for all this.

She looked through the rest of the documents. There was a report showing that Wesley had no "criminal or negative financial" findings, a page showing his ownership of his house and a boat, and three newspaper announcements from his marriage and the births of his two daughters.

When Billy was done, she put everything back in the envelope and set it on the table. Murphy, satisfied with his nightly exploration of their yard, came up on the porch, and Billy petted him, deep in thought. It was true, as her father had said, that you couldn't find the measure of a man in the contents of an envelope, but of one thing she was now sure: Wesley was not a bad man. She'd known that the night she'd met him, and she'd known that tonight reading over the private investigator's report. The worst she could say about him, probably, was that he was unexceptional. But most of us are unexceptional she reminded herself. At the end of the day, most of us are just trying, the best we can, to make our way in the world. Wesley was one of those people. So was she. And if Luke could love her, which she knew he did, even during their worst moments together, he could love Wesley, too—provided, of course, that Wesley was open to having a relationship with him. That Wesley was open to loving him back.

And therein lay the problem. Wesley could be a perfectly good man but still not want to have a relationship with a son he didn't choose to have, especially when he already had a wife and two daughters. And would he even remember Billy? Billy and the night they'd spent together fourteen years ago? Most important, would he even *believe* that Luke was actually his child? Well, there was only one way to find out, Billy thought. She had Wesley's address and phone number. Calling him, she decided, might be too much of a shock for him, and Billy didn't know if she had the courage to do that, anyway. No, she would write him a letter, a carefully worded letter that he could read privately and then think about. She would try not to overwhelm him with information. The basics about her and Luke would do. She would stress the fact that she didn't want any financial support from him, and that her intention in writing this letter was not to disrupt his life or his relationship with his wife and children, but only to explore the possibility of him meeting his son. She'd include all her contact information, too, so he could decide the best way to respond.

Ideally he would respond to her before she went to pick up Luke in two weeks. Then she would know where the three of them stood. If Wesley didn't respond, or if he were averse to meeting Billy and Luke, well, then, she would cross that bridge when she came to it. Now, though, she would write the letter. Tomorrow she would mail it.

Her cell phone, sitting on the table beside her, pinged to life. Billy picked it up and read a text from Cal.

> Billy, I'll be back from Minneapolis on Wednesday. Are you free? I'd love to cook you dinner this time. Please don't say no! Cal

She smiled and pictured Cal standing barefoot on the porch of his cabin, smiling at her as she came up the steps. Did *everything* have to happen at once? she wondered, touching Cal's message with her fingers. But she wouldn't want this thing with him *not* to be happening, would she? She glanced over at Murphy, who'd settled near her feet, and his friendly brown eyes seemed to be saying to her, *Definitely not.*

CHAPTER 24

"Hey, Luke. Can I talk to you?" Mad Dog asked as they hiked into the Bear Lake campsite at the end of the third day of the trip.

"Yeah, okay." Luke sighed. Mad Dog seemed cool. He was still in college, but in his free time, he was a competitive BMX biker. He had shoulder-length blond hair that he sometimes wore down, sometimes in a ponytail, and he had a killer scar on his knee—big and jagged and still pink—that Luke suspected was from a BMX injury. Best of all, though, was the tattoo on his shoulder that spelled out *Lola*. Was she his girlfriend? Luke wondered. But Luke didn't want to ask him, because, well . . . he just wanted to be alone. He couldn't stop thinking about what his mom had told him before she'd dropped him off. Sometimes he felt excited and sometimes he felt angry. It was confusing. He needed to straighten it all out somehow.

"Why don't we set these packs down and check out

the lake," Mad Dog suggested, slipping off his back-pack and leaning it against a tree.

"Shouldn't I be helping to . . . set up?" Luke asked, watching as the other boys came trudging into camp. He was assigned to a four-man tent, and he and his tent mates were supposed to pitch it together.

"Oh, I think your friends can handle it," Mad Dog said easily.

Friends? He'd barely talked to the three boys in his tent. Two of them were okay, he guessed, but one of them, this kid named Oscar, was so homesick he cried in his sleeping bag at night when he thought everyone was asleep. Luke felt sorry for him, but what could he do? Mad Dog was waiting for him now, though, so he took his pack off, too. He immediately felt lighter—twenty pounds was heavier than he'd expected it to be—but they'd still done a fairly easy hike today. Mad Dog had warned it would get harder. By the end of the first week they'd be hiking full days over rough terrain. This was the warm-up, he'd said. "*Great*," Luke had mumbled, rolling his eyes.

Mad Dog started down the path to Bear Lake, and Luke followed him. "Not bad, huh?" Mad Dog asked when they reached the lake. It looked smaller than But-ternut Lake, but Luke had to admit it was pretty. Tall aspen and pine trees ringed the shore, and the water was so clear that the shallow, rocky bottom was visible even from several yards away.

"It's okay," Luke said of the lake, looking back toward the camp. He was wondering what Mad Dog wanted to talk to him about. He hadn't pulled any of the other kids aside yet.

"We're going swimming here after dinner," Mad Dog confided, sitting down on a nearby boulder. "Shoes on, though. Some of those rocks are pretty slippery."

Luke nodded. *More fun.*

"Have a seat," Mad Dog said, pointing to another boulder nearby. Luke sat down on it.

"So, Luke. What's up?" Mad Dog asked.

"What do you mean?"

"I mean, what's going on?"

"With me?" Luke asked.

Mad Dog nodded. "You're doing fine with the physical part of the trip. You're obviously in good shape. I can see you're a pretty good athlete."

"I skateboard," Luke said.

"I can tell," Mad Dog said. "You breezed right up that big hill today. So, *physically*, you've got this covered," he continued. "But Luke, you're not talking to any of the other campers or counselors. You're just keeping to yourself. That'd be okay if this was a *solo* hike. But it's a *group* hike."

Luke didn't say anything. He knew what Mad Dog was talking about, though. Yesterday after lunch, when everyone else went for a swim, Luke had said no, thanks, and sat on a rock instead. And last night, when everyone else was sitting around the campfire after dinner, he'd gone back into his tent.

Luke kicked at a rock on the ground. He didn't know what Mad Dog wanted him to say. That he'd try harder? Forget it, he thought. "This trip wasn't even my idea," he mumbled.

"What was that?" Mad Dog asked.

"My mom wanted me to go on this trip," he said louder, kicking the rock free.

"Okay." Mad Dog nodded. "So, hiking's not your thing?"

"No, I like it. I just didn't want to go now."

"What's wrong with now?"

"There's stuff going on."

"At home?"

"Yeah, I guess," Luke said, focusing on the lake's surface. It would be evening soon, and little clouds of gnats were starting to form above the water. He was hoping if he didn't say anything more, then Mad Dog might just drop it.

Instead he asked, "Luke, do you want to know what my worst grade in college has been so far?"

Luke shrugged again.

"It was a C minus. In psychology."

"That's . . . that's a pretty bad grade," Luke said honestly. His mom would not be happy if he got a grade like that.

"Yeah, well, the point I'm trying to make is if you think I'm trying to be some kind of . . . *therapist* here with you, you're wrong. And as for that class, it was at 8:10 A.M. I'm not a morning person."

"You are here," Luke pointed out. They had to get up at six thirty A.M. the past two mornings, and both times Mad Dog was in a really good mood.

"Well, that's because this isn't real life." Mad Dog grinned. He threw his arms up to indicate the lake, and the trees, and the sky. "This is *way* more fun."

Luke looked away. He wasn't having any fun.

Though he thought he probably would have had fun on this hike a couple of years ago. He kicked another rock near his shoe and watched it roll toward the water's edge.

"Look, like I said. I'm not going to try to analyze you here or anything, but do you want to talk about it? Just . . . talk? I'm a pretty good listener, I think," Mad Dog said. He produced an elastic band from a pocket and pulled his hair back in a ponytail.

Luke hesitated. "Why does everyone always want me to talk about everything?" His guidance counselor, Officer Sawyer, his mom . . . they all acted as if talking would make things better. How did they know it wouldn't make things worse?

Mad Dog smiled. "It's hard to explain. But it's like when you take your backpack off at the end of the hike. You feel lighter. Sometimes, I think, talking can give you the same feeling. Does that make sense?"

"Maybe," Luke said. He'd found another rock to kick at. "Can I ask you a question?"

"Sure."

"Did you, like, grow up with your dad?" Then he felt embarrassed. Why was he even asking Mad Dog that?

"I did. But I know people who didn't. What about you?"

"I've never met my dad. My mom couldn't find him when she . . . knew she was going to have me," Luke said. Mad Dog didn't say anything. It looked like he was waiting for Luke to tell him more. And here was the thing—he suddenly *did* want to tell him more. It was weird. He didn't even know why, but he told Mad Dog then, as fast as he could but also as best as he could, about his Pop-Pop finding his dad a year ago and telling his mom, and his mom not telling him anything about it until the drive to the meet-up place three days ago.

Mad Dog seemed a little confused then. "So . . . Pop-Pop's your granddad?" he asked Luke.

Luke nodded. "He died. But before that he told my mom about finding my dad. He didn't tell me, though. And she didn't, either, until a couple days ago. Why would they do that?" Luke asked.

Here Mad Dog took a deep breath. "You mean, not tell you right away?"

"*Yeah*. They should have," Luke said. "I'm not a little kid."

"I don't know," Mad Dog said. "I met your mom at the meet-up point, though, and she seemed like a nice lady. Parents have their reasons for doing things," he added, swatting at a mosquito.

Luke shrugged. "She's going to call my dad now, while I'm on this trip," he said, looking quickly over at him. "Maybe I'll meet him, or something. I don't know." He had a weird feeling in his stomach when he said that.

"That sounds cool."

Luke nodded. "Yeah. That part's . . . good." The *bad* part was that Luke didn't know what his dad would say when his mom talked to him.

They were quiet for a while. Through the trees, Luke could hear the sounds of the other counselors and campers talking and laughing. He caught a whiff of wood smoke, too. He was pretty sure he was on campfire duty tonight. "Do we need to go back?" he asked.

"In a while," Mad Dog said. "We'll give them enough time to get all the hard stuff done."

Luke laughed a little at this.

A few minutes later, Mad Dog stood up and dusted off the seat of his pants. "Luke, you've got a lot going on. These are all complicated things. And you probably aren't going to figure them all out on this trip. It might . . . take a little while. But I need you to be here. Okay? This trip doesn't work unless we're all part of it. And just between you and me, you're one of the best hikers here. Plus, you've picked up the basics really quickly. I'm counting on you to help out. And show these other kids how it's done."

"Yeah, okay," Luke said, kind of surprised that Mad Dog needed his help.

Mad Dog grinned. "Cool," he said. "Good to know you've got my back. You can hang out here for a little while if you want to. I'm going to head up."

Luke nodded. After Mad Dog left, he slid down the boulder and leaned his back against it. It felt cool through his T-shirt, and he just breathed for a little while, and tried to keep the mosquitoes away from his face. Talking to Mad Dog hadn't been bad, he realized, but there was only one person he *really* wanted to talk to now, and that was Pop-Pop. If he were here now, he could have explained everything to Luke, about why he and his mom had done what they did. He didn't lecture people, Pop-Pop, but he was good at talking. He didn't always say a lot, but what he did say he made count.

I miss him, Luke thought. He felt a lump in his throat, and he tried to swallow past it, but he couldn't. He was scared he was going to cry, and then his eyes blurred, and he was crying. It was too late to stop. He hunched over and put his face on his knees, and he tried to be quiet, but he made these snuffling noises he was worried they would hear in camp. It wasn't just Pop-Pop he missed. It was his mom, too. And he saw her the way she was when she said good-bye to him, all anxious and worried. He was still mad at her, but not as much, and he thought about something Rae had said to him about his mom once. "You got yourself a good mom, Luke. There is not a thing in the world that woman wouldn't do for you."

He cried some more and, after a little while, he looked up to make sure no one else had come down the path to the lake. No, he was still alone, but it was getting darker now; the sun had slid down behind the tops of the trees. He heard a burst of laughter coming from camp, and he thought he could smell something cooking, too. They were supposed to be having stew and soda bread tonight. He breathed in, sounding quivery and shaky, and then he breathed out. He pulled up his T-shirt and wiped his face with it. He'd stay for a few more minutes, he decided. By then the light would be too dim for anyone to notice he'd been crying.

CHAPTER 25

W ell?" Cal asked, watching Billy expectantly.
"Bliss," Billy said. "Sheer bliss. But where did you learn how to make it?" She was referring to the spaghetti carbonara Cal had prepared for dinner. She wrapped more of it around her fork and popped it into her mouth, and Cal smiled, pleased with her reaction. No need to tell her now that it was the only dish he knew how to cook *really* well. He'd gone grocery shopping in town and met her at her place after she'd gotten home from work. She'd perched on the kitchen counter, sipped the red wine he'd brought, and watched as he cooked the spaghetti, fried the pancetta, beat the eggs, and tossed it all together. She'd wanted to help him, but he'd refused. Not because she'd burned their dinner, but because he'd wanted to do something concrete and tangible for her. And she had let him. It was a simple thing, he knew. So why did it feel as if he had crossed into new territory—not only in their relationship but also in his life—tonight?

"My college roommate's mother taught me how to make it," he explained, only now picking up his fork and digging into it himself. "I used to spend Thanksgiving with them on the East Coast, and they pulled out all the stops. I mean, they made the whole traditional Thanksgiving Day dinner, but they also made a separate traditional Italian dinner, too. And some of those recipes had been in their family for generations."

"Mmm. Well, this one's a keeper." Billy sighed, reaching over to the bowl of grated Parmesan cheese he'd set on her kitchen table and sprinkling some more of it onto her pasta. "But since when does the Butternut IGA sell pancetta?"

"Oh. I bought that in Minneapolis. That and the . . . wine and the Parmesan. I didn't want to leave anything to chance."

She blushed then, a soft, lovely blush made even lovelier by the flickering light of the candles on the table. She was wearing an eyelet summer blouse and blue jeans, and her glossy, dark hair was loose on her shoulders. How was it possible, he wondered, that every single time he saw her, she was even prettier than she'd been the time before? Was she really changing? No, he thought. She wasn't. He was the one changing.

He caught site of Murphy now and smiled. While Cal had cooked the pasta and made the sauce, Murphy had lingered nearby, wagging his tail and looking hopeful. But after Billy had given him a treat and patted him, he'd wandered over to a corner of the kitchen and lay down on a small rag rug that was obviously there for that purpose. Now he seemed content, though he was keeping one soulful eye on the two of them in case they decided to toss any food his way.

Cal took a sip of his wine. The attraction was still there between them, he knew, but while it had been nearly out of control the last time he'd seen her—he pictured the two of them entangled together in the Porsche—it was different now, thrumming gently between them like an underground river. Maybe it was because she was so preoccupied; she'd been unfailingly pleasant tonight, as always, but Cal sensed that she was only half there with him.

"You must miss Luke," he said.

"I do miss him." She looked up from her plate. "It's more than that, though. I think . . ." She put her fork down, and her fingers came up to her temples in a gesture that combined both fatigue and stress. "I think I might have made a huge mistake with him. I mean, *huge* as in unforgivable."

"I can't imagine you doing anything unforgivable," Cal said. "Especially to your son." She had never struck him as anything other than an incredibly conscientious mother.

"No, I mean it. This time I might have."

"What happened? If you don't mind my asking."

She hesitated. "Do you remember the story I told you that night at the Corner Bar?"

"Every word of it."

She looked surprised.

"The one about the teenage girl who went on a fishing trip with her dad to Alaska?" he asked. "She had a fling with the guide, and later, when she told her parents she was pregnant, her dad went back to the lodge. But he couldn't find the guide."

"That's the one," Billy said, looking faintly amused. "I'm impressed you remembered it, given the amount of scotch you'd imbibed that night."

"It was an interesting story," Cal observed. "I thought it had a happy ending, though." Right now, Billy looked anything but happy.

"It did, for a while. But before the girl's dad died—wait, I'm going to stop telling this in the third person, if that's okay?"

He smiled. "That's fine."

"Before *my* dad died last year he hired a private investigator and found the fishing guide. And he gave me his contact information, too, in a sealed envelope. I put it away in a safe deposit box. I didn't tell Luke. But I opened the envelope on Friday night, after I got back from driving him to camp." She paused, considered Cal. "So you see . . . the guide didn't just disappear. He was living on Vancouver Island the whole time. He's got a boat charter business, a wife, two daughters, and . . . a son, of course."

"So he . . . knows about Luke?"

"That depends. I wrote to him that night. He—his name is Wesley, Wesley Fitzgerald—might have gotten the letter by now. Or not."

"And . . . Luke?"

"And Luke . . ." Here there was a sigh from Billy, and her fingers went to her temples again. "I told Luke about it for the first time on Friday on the drive to camp . . . It all came out." Something about the expression on Cal's face made her say, "I know. It wasn't the way I wanted it to happen. I think, in retrospect, I wanted to contact his dad first and make sure he was okay with all of this. But on the way to the meet-up place, Luke said he wasn't going on the hike, and I couldn't make him go. He said he was going to go to Alaska, alone, to find his dad. And I just panicked. When I first told him, he was excited. But then he was angry, too, and hurt, I think, that I kept it from him for so long."

She picked up her fork again, but now only to poke halfheartedly at the pasta on her plate. "And then, after I told him everything, I dropped him off at Split Rock Lighthouse and sent him off on this two-week trip. I feel terrible now. I'm worried about how he's doing, knowing all of this. I'm wondering, too, how he's feeling . . . about me." Her voice dropped on this last word, so that she practically whispered it. "I mean," she said, her voice still so soft that he needed to lean closer to hear her, "Luke knows I had his dad's contact information for a year, for more than a year, and I didn't do anything with it. Didn't get in touch with his dad. Didn't tell Luke. Just . . . decided to put it all off until sometime in the future when everything would suddenly be clear to me. I was trying to protect him from all the unknowns. But what I'm wondering now is whether or not Luke will be able to trust me again. Or, if not trust me, at least forgive me."

Her blue eyes were shiny with what might have been tears, but she didn't cry. She smiled, or tried to smile. "Sorry. I should have warned you. Not exactly bedtime story material, is it?"

Cal said nothing. His first impulse was to comfort

her. And he almost—*almost*—reached for one of her hands. They were both on the table now, smooth and graceful in the candlelight. But something stopped him. It was the understanding that Billy needed more from him than that now. The thing was, he wasn't a parent. He couldn't second-guess her decisions as a parent, even if he was inclined to. And he wasn't inclined to. He wasn't, by nature, a judgmental person. Furthermore, he knew intuitively that she was a good person and a caring mother. "I think," he said finally, "that at the time you made the decision not to tell Luke, you thought it was the right one. Whether it was or not—and there's no point in revisiting it—you've come forward now. You've told him. And as for him forgiving you"—he hesitated—"I'm remembering myself at thirteen. I think if there's one thing kids that age are good at doing, it's moving on. They're much better at letting go of the things we hold on to even when we shouldn't hold on to them. The trust thing—I don't know. It might take some time for you to regain it. Then again, it might not. Life at his age is so . . . so fluid. There's so much happening. Sports, and girls and, if he's like me when I was his age, more girls." He smiled. "And if he does have a relationship with his dad . . . well. That's all the more reason for him not to dwell on it."

Now he took one of her hands, which was soft. He held it and ran his thumb over her knuckles. She squeezed his hand back. "What if Wesley doesn't answer my letter, though? Or he does, and he says he wants nothing to do with Luke?"

"Then you'll . . . you'll deal with it. One step at a time, though, Billy. Just . . . one step."

"I think I can do that," she said, her fingers moving to caress his hand. And he noticed, for the first time, the faint bluish circles under her eyes. She was tired. Of course she was. She was exhausted. She probably hadn't been sleeping well. Should he ask her if she wanted him to leave? He didn't want to leave, though. He wanted to be there for her, even if all he could do was hold her hand.

"Cal?" she said, tightening her fingers around his. "That night I drove you home from the Corner Bar? That was a turning point for me, in a way. After I got back, I thought about what you'd said, about . . . your wife lying to you about wanting to have children. And I realized I was doing the same thing to Luke. I was lying to him."

Cal shook his head. "No, it's very different, Billy. You were trying to protect Luke. Meghan . . . I don't know who she was trying to protect, unless it was herself. She . . ." He stopped. "I've never told anyone this before. I mean, I told you and Allie she didn't want kids, but I didn't tell you how I found out." Billy looked at him questioningly. "Do you have time for another story?"

"*Always,*" she said, with the trace of a smile. She fingered the rim of her wineglass with the hand that wasn't holding his.

"All right, let's see. Where to start . . ." But there was only one place to start, and that was with him finding the file. Still, Billy needed a little backstory. "So . . . this was about three months ago, give or take a little. Meghan was at a spa weekend in wine country with two of her friends. It was something they did every year."

The point of these weekends was not to drink wine—which Meghan thought was too caloric—but to get various scrubs and wraps and treatments done. This was more detail than Billy needed, though, and he was determined to keep any bitterness out of this telling, if possible. He started again. "While she was away, I was paying our taxes, and I needed some information from her on her medical deductions. I didn't want to disturb one of her herbal wraps or whatever, so I went into her home office and looked in her file cabinet for the medical deductions folder. I didn't have any trouble finding it. Every one of her files was perfectly labeled. Except for one. It was blank. And damn it, I was curious," he admitted. "An unlabeled file?" That, of course, was the *antithesis* of Meghan's organizational style, which bordered on the fanatical. "Anyway, I took out the file and I flipped through it. At first I couldn't even understand what I was rea___ ___ Then, when I did finally understand it, I didn't believe it. I thought, 'Am I losing my mind? Or do these forms belong to someone else—a friend of Meghan's, maybe?' They were hers, though. They had her name, her personal information, everything. I made myself go through them again. All of them. The postoperative instructions, the hospital bill, the credit card receipt. Not surprisingly, she didn't submit any of this information to our insurance company."

He stopped again and reached for his wineglass. "Turns out she'd gotten a laparoscopic tubal ligation," he said. Billy frowned slightly. "She had her tubes tied," he clarified. "Which, as you probably know, is only recommended for someone who's looking for a permanent method of birth control. Someone who's sure she doesn't want to become pregnant in the future. Here's the thing, though. As far as I knew, we'd spent the last year *trying* to have a baby. She told me she'd gone off birth control pills—which, obviously, she *had*, but only because she'd found a more reliable form of birth control."

"When had she . . . ?"

"Gotten the procedure? Seven months earlier. I did the math. She'd done it while I was at a conference in Chicago. And when I got home from that, I remembered, she'd seemed fine. Of course, it was outpatient surgery, with a pretty quick recovery time." The other thing he'd remembered, which he didn't share with Billy now, was that she hadn't felt like sex for about a week after he'd gotten back. He'd been disappointed. Less about the sex than about the fact that he'd sat next to a couple with a baby on the flight back from Chicago, and the baby was so goddamned cute that he couldn't wait to get home and keep trying to have one with Meghan. "Anyway," he said, pushing on, "after I found the file, I spent the rest of that weekend in a fog. I kept dodging her texts and kind of wandering around our apartment, drinking scotch. By the time she got home—I'm not going to sugarcoat this—I was drunk. Dead drunk," he added flatly. "I'd finished a whole bottle of scotch by myself. That, and the one night here at the Corner Bar, are the only two times I've gotten drunk in recent memory. The night Meghan came home was a doozy, though."

"Oh, Cal," Billy murmured, a worried frown line appearing between her eyes.

"No, it was okay. I didn't lose it. Not completely, anyway. And when I confronted her, she was . . . she was so in control." That was Meghan, cool under pressure, right up until the end, he thought to himself. It was one of the things that had first attracted Cal to her, when he'd met her on a job right after he had moved to Seattle. That night, though, there was a part of him that had wished she would crack a little. She didn't. Instead, after he'd said he was leaving, she'd followed him upstairs and, being careful not to touch him—she'd understood, intuitively, that he wouldn't tolerate that— she'd tried to reason with him. Tried to minimize the damage she'd done and rationalize her reason for doing it. She wasn't parent material, she said, and she never would be. Her own parents had been cold and distant. Besides, she'd argued, her and Cal's life together was so good without children. Why would they want to risk disrupting that? And their careers would suffer, especially hers. Having children would interrupt the momentum they'd worked so hard to build. Cal had tried to shut out what she was saying, but in the time it took him to throw some clothes into a suitcase and let himself out of the apartment, he'd still heard enough of it.

"I don't understand something, though," Billy said. "If you hadn't found this out that weekend, how was she going to explain it when she didn't get pregnant?"

"I asked her that," Cal said. "Later, in a calmer moment. I asked her how far she was willing to carry the charade. She said she was hoping, over time, to convince me that we would be happier without children. The crazy thing, though, was that if she'd told me from the beginning she didn't want children, I would have understood. I don't know if I would have seen myself having *a future* with her, but I wouldn't have judged her. By keeping it from me, and then, of course, by outright lying about it, she undermined our whole relationship." What he didn't say to Billy was that somehow, over the last month, his bitterness toward Meghan had dissipated. Was Butternut or Billy responsible for that transformation? Then again, he couldn't really have had one without the other. He smiled at her, and she smiled back, a tentative though still lovely smile.

"The thing is, Billy," he said, stroking her fingers, "your not telling Luke is very different from Meghan's not telling me. You're a parent with a child you're responsible for. And there were, and still are, a lot of unknowns about contacting his dad. But more important, you've told him now. And you and Luke will work it out together."

She returned the pressure on his hand. She took a sip of her wine, but it looked to Cal like she'd lost her appetite. Most of the spaghetti carbonara sat untouched on her plate.

"It's good cold," Cal offered, indicating her plate.

"I'm sorry," she said. "It's delicious. I think I'm just too tired to eat. I didn't even know that was possible for me."

"You need a good night's sleep more than you need dinner," Cal said, releasing her hand. He stood up and reached for her plate and his. She tried to help him, but he waved her back down. She sat there contemplatively while he cleared the table and put the leftover spaghetti into the fridge.

"Don't do any more, Cal," Billy said when he started to load the dishwasher. "I'll finish up in the morning."

"You sure?"

"Absolutely. Come on. I'll walk you to the door." When they stood in the open doorway, facing each other, she swayed against him. "I'm sorry I wasn't very good company," she said.

"As far as I'm concerned, you're *always* good company," he said, kissing her on the forehead.

"I'm going to bed early," she said. "What about tomorrow, after I get home from the library? I don't expect you to cook for me again, but maybe we can get something at the Corner Bar."

"I'd love that," Cal said, running the back of his hand over her cheek. What he really wanted to do more than anything right now was take her in his arms, carry her into her bedroom, and tuck her into bed. But he thought it might be misinterpreted. So instead he said, "Good night. And Billy . . ."

"Yes?"

"You're a good mom. Don't forget that." After he gave a waiting Murphy a pat on the head, he left, closing the door softly behind him.

CHAPTER 26

That night, Billy slept deeply, and the next morning, she awoke feeling utterly refreshed. As she stretched out on her sun-stippled bed, with Murphy lolling on the hardwood floor nearby, she thought about her dinner with Cal. Talking to him last night had been a good thing. Was she still worried about Luke? Still feeling guilty about withholding information from him? Still anxious about how Wesley would fit into all of this? Yes, yes, and yes. But as she gave herself the customary five minutes between the time her alarm went off and the time she got out of bed, as she lounged against the pillows and watched a breeze lift and then lazily drop one of the sheer white window curtains, she remembered the way Cal's fingers had skated over her cheek before he'd said good-night to her. The way he'd smiled that sexy-as-hell smile at her before he'd closed the door behind him. And it came to her then with a fierceness that shocked her. She wanted him. *God damn it*, she wanted him. And the fact that a whole day now separated them from each other seemed to her as absurd as it did unfair.

Somehow she survived it. Although as she made polite conversation with patrons, checked books in and out, and generally tended to all of the other responsibilities her work demanded, Cal was never far from her mind, and neither, for that matter, was what she wanted to happen between them that night. She called him on her lunch hour, and somehow her tone of voice or her choice of words when she invited him to come over that evening must have conveyed her desire for him, because no sooner had she gotten home from work than the phone rang.

"Billy?" he said. "I'm on my way over. I'll be there in about five minutes."

"So soon?"

"Yes. I'm sorry. I know you said six, but I can't wait that long."

"Okay," she breathed, her heart pounding.

"And Billy?"

"Yes?" she said.

"Remember that dress you wore to the wedding?"

"I remember it. It's hanging in my closet."

"If it's not too much trouble . . . do you think you could put it on?"

"Now?"

"Yes, I love that dress. And one more thing? But only if you . . . don't mind. I don't want to be too demanding here."

"What?"

"Your freckles. I know you like to cover them up. But if you're wearing any makeup . . . could you take it off? I want to see them. Every single one of them. I love them, Billy."

She hesitated, puzzled, as always, by his fascination with something she'd spent a lifetime trying to hide. "All right, fine," she said. "I've got to go, though." She hung up and started racing around the house. She plumped the couch pillows, kicked one of Murphy's chew toys into a corner, and piled the soaking dishes and pots from the night before into the dishwasher. Then she headed for the bedroom, moving a little unsteadily since she was taking her clothes off on the way there. She kicked off her sandals, peeled off her blouse, and wiggled out of her skirt, flinging them willy-nilly as she went. No matter. She'd pick them up later. Right now, she was focused on one thing and one thing only: Cal. He'd be here soon. And she needed to bring her freckles out of hiding and put that dress on before he walked through the front door.

She arrived in the bathroom dressed only in her bra and underwear, her breath coming fast, her hands shaking slightly as she stood in front of the sink and turned on the faucet. But she picked up the soap and, staring into the mirror, scrubbed her face clean of any makeup. When she was satisfied that it was all washed away, and that each of her freckles was proudly on display, she turned off the water, patted her face dry with a hand towel, and rushed into the bedroom, stubbing her toe on the door frame in the process.

"*Ouch, ouch, ouch,*" she said, grabbing her injured foot in her hands and jumping up and down on the other foot. "*Damn it, damn it, damn it,*" she muttered, hopping over to the closet and riffling through its contents.

She'd hoped to find the dress neatly encased in the dry cleaner's plastic, but no, she must not have taken it in after the wedding. There it was, trapped between a frayed cardigan that had once belonged to her grandmother and a jean jacket she hadn't worn since college. She pulled it out and studied it critically. It looked . . . it looked fine. A little wrinkled, maybe, but there were no stains on it, though that wasn't that surprising given that she'd been at that wedding reception for less than fifteen minutes.

She slipped the dress off the hanger, unzipped it, and stepped into it. And as she hurriedly tugged it up over her body, she caught sight of herself in the mirror. Why did Cal like this dress so much? she wondered. It was so plain, so conservative. And then she remembered something her mother, bless her heart, had said to her once when she'd taken her shopping for a fancy dress. "Sometimes, Billy, less is more."

Maybe Cal believed that, too, she thought, reaching around behind her for the zipper. She struggled with it a little, her hands sweaty with nerves and excitement. But when she'd worked it halfway up, the zipper got stuck, and no amount of cajoling on her part could get it any further. Oh, what difference did it make? she decided finally, abandoning it. Cal was just going to take off the dress, anyway, wasn't he? And as if on cue, the doorbell rang. She heard Murphy bark and gallop excitedly to the door. She ran out of the bedroom, barefoot and half-zipped into her dress, only to stub her *other* toe on the bedroom doorjamb.

"You've *got* to be kidding me," she said to no one in particular, hopping down the hallway, this time on the other foot. But when she passed the mirror over the hall table, she stopped and looked at herself. *Big mistake.* Her hair was flying everywhere, and her freckles . . . She leaned closer to the mirror. Her freckles were not just on view; they appeared to have multiplied. Multiplied *and* expanded. They were colonizing her entire face. She was so horrified that, for a moment, she almost went back to her bureau for her pressed powder compact, but the doorbell rang again, startling her. She turned away from the mirror and, walking the few remaining steps to the door, yanked it open.

As soon as she saw Cal, she forgot about everything else. The unzipped dress, the flyaway hair, the mysterious reproducing freckles. Even the throbbing pain in her most recently stubbed toe. She forgot about all of that now because of the way Cal was smiling at her. It was a smile that could take off a woman's dress, and she half expected to feel the zipper sliding down the rest of the way of its own accord, powered by nothing more than the sheer sex appeal of the man standing on her doorstep.

"Are you going to invite me in?" he asked, still smiling as he bent to pat Murphy.

She nodded mutely and stepped aside. When he came in, he shut the door behind her, backed her up against it, and kissed her, a slow, simmering kiss that she never wanted to end. Just when it was starting to heat up even more, though, he pulled away from her and asked, "Do you have a bedroom?"

"I think so," she said, slightly dazed. She took his hand and pulled him down the hallway. But Cal kept stopping and kissing her, so that they ended up navigating the hallway blindly, feeling their way to her room. When they reached it, they stumbled to the bed. Then, before she knew it, he was lying beside her, still kissing her, and running a hand up her back, feeling for the zipper on her dress. He found it and fiddled with it. It was still stuck.

"Just break the damn thing," Billy said through their kiss.

"Really?"

"Positive." But instead, he reached back with both hands and, with astonishing deftness, worked the zipper slowly, miraculously unsticking it.

"Hurry," she whispered as he started to slide the dress off her. This was happening, she thought. This was really happening. After two false starts, they were actually going to do this. And she was ready, wasn't she? She mentally reviewed her readiness. She was wearing her favorite bra and underwear, navy blue with cream-colored lace edging. Plus she'd remembered this morning to put on the perfume Cal had told her he liked, the Chanel Gardénia. She'd touched it to her wrists and her throat. But Cal, running a hand up her thigh, reminded her of something. "Oh no," Billy said, sitting up on the bed.

"What?"

"I forgot to shave my legs in the shower this morning," she said, scrambling over to the edge of the bed. "I'll be right back. It'll take me five minutes. Ten tops."

But Cal reached over and ran a hand up one of her bare calves. "Your legs feel fine," he said. "Come here."

She held up two fingers. "Two minutes, I promise," she said in a placating tone.

Cal shook his head. "Billy, if you leave here now, this is never going to happen. Because in the time it takes you to shave your legs, a meteorite will crash into Butternut, or a tree will fall through your bedroom ceiling, or a swarm of locusts will descend on this house. I'm serious," he continued when she smiled. "I'm actually starting to believe that the universe does not want us to make love to each other."

And Billy, looking over at him, sighed. The man had a point. "Come on," he said, his hand encircling her ankle. "You can shave your legs later. Hell, *I'll* shave them for you later. But right now, you need to be here, with me, on this bed." He patted it with the hand that wasn't holding her ankle and smiled at her, a slow smile that made her insides quiver. Still, she wanted everything to be perfect. Or at least as perfect as possible. Having razor stubble on her legs would make it . . . well, *less* perfect. She tried to explain this to him now. He looked unconvinced, though.

"Billy, it doesn't need to be perfect. It just needs to be . . ." He searched for the right word. "Real," he decided. "And trust me, real, in this case, is going to be pretty goddamned amazing. I mean, I don't know about you, but I've never waited this long to be with someone I've wanted before. And I've never wanted anyone as much as I want you right now."

"Really?" she whispered, feeling an odd sensation, a simultaneous heat and chill sliding through her whole body.

"Now come over here," he said, tugging on her ankle. "And let's relax. When you're ready, we can make imperfect, but still amazing, love to each other."

"Oh, all right," she said, laughing. She came back over to him and lay down next to him, and when he kissed her, she kissed him back. It was going to be okay, she thought, settling into his arms. It was going to be *better* than okay. She liked him. She liked him a lot. She might even be in love with him, as improbable as that seemed given how short a time she had known him. Still, he was kind, and funny, and sweet, and sexy. *Oh God, he was sexy.* And the way he kissed . . . with a slow intensity that made her practically squirm with impatience in his arms. He caressed the skin on her shoulders, her arms, her back as, with infinite patience, he eased her dress down to her waist. She moved her hands to his hair and ran her fingers through it, tugging on his curls, which she knew he liked.

Now that she'd worked through all her layers of self-consciousness, she found herself possessed of a new fearlessness. "Let's take this off," she said, pulling his T-shirt up over his head and exposing his smooth, suntanned chest. She ran her hands over it eagerly, hungrily, and then followed her hands with her lips, kissing his neck, and collarbone, and shoulders, wanting to touch and taste all of him at the same time.

He let out a little groan as her lips brushed over his chest, but then he hesitated. She felt an indecision settle over him. "What's wrong?" she asked.

Cal used his chin to gesture behind her, and she turned around. "Oh, I forgot about him," she said of Murphy. He was sitting beside the bed, his head resting on it, his friendly eyes watching them.

"He's . . . staring at us," Cal said.

"Well, maybe. But he doesn't know what we're doing," Billy said. She started moving her hands and her lips over his chest again. But now it was Cal who couldn't relax.

"Is he just going to stay there, though, the whole time?" he wanted to know.

Billy sighed. This had never been an issue before. She'd never been interested enough in anyone to let it get this far right here in her own home. She looked at Murphy again. His front paws and his head were both up on the bed now, and he had an eager look in his eyes. The look he got before Billy threw the tennis ball for him. He wagged his tail and let out a little bark. "I think he thinks we're playing," she said to Cal.

"Well, we're *trying* to," he said. "Could he maybe . . . go in the other room?"

"Of course," Billy said. She got up, pulling her dress back on, and led Murphy out by his collar. She took him to the pantry and got a bone off a top shelf.

"Here you go," she said, giving him the bone. He took it between his teeth, flopped down on the floor, and commenced his gnawing. "Good boy," Billy said, patting him. She left him there, walked back to the bedroom, and closed and locked the door behind her. Cal was lying on the bed, waiting for her, his hair adorably tousled, his smile unmistakably carnal.

"I think I bought us a little time," she said, lying down next to him.

"Good," he said, taking her in his arms. "Now let's get this dress off you."

"I thought you liked this dress," she teased, her hands in his hair, her lips on his neck.

"I *love* this dress," he said as he shimmied it down over her hips. "But I'm going to love it even more in another ten seconds, when it's on the floor."

Afterward, they lay on their sides, facing each other, the top sheet tangled around them. It was so quiet in the room that, through her open windows, Billy could hear a screen door slapping shut in the house next door, and the drone of a baseball game coming from another neighbor's television set. A heavy black fly bumped lazily against one of her window screens. Neither of them said anything, though. Neither of them wanted to break the spell.

A breeze lifted the window curtains, and Cal, as if freed by this motion, smiled at Billy. She sighed, and something inside her stirred. She wanted him again. She wanted him *now*. Which seemed nothing short of amazing considering how long they'd just made love to each other. But there it was.

"I take it back," he said. "That was actually kind of perfect." He reached out a hand and rested his fingers lightly against her cheek.

She smiled, and taking his fingers, kissed them. She loved his hands, she decided. They were suntanned, like the rest of him, and pleasantly roughened from his work this summer, but there was nothing coarse or inelegant about them. They had moved over her with a confidence that was new to Billy, and with an intimacy she'd never experienced before. When she was done kissing his fingers, he pulled her closer, his bare skin touching hers, and her desire for him was like a warm tide washing over her, pulling her under, and pulling him under with her. He started kissing her again, and Billy was just arching her back, when she heard a familiar whining and scratching at the bedroom door.

"That would be Murphy," she said. "I think he's jealous."

"I don't blame him," Cal said, still kissing her. But when the whining continued, he said, "You should let him in. Otherwise he might start to resent me, and I want to stay on his good side, if possible."

"Anyone on my good side is already on his good side," she said. "But I think he's been patient enough for one evening." She gave Cal a conciliatory kiss and, sitting up, gathered the bedsheet around her.

"You don't have to do that," Cal said. "You can just . . ."

"Walk around naked?"

He nodded, his hazel eyes glinting mischievously.

"I don't think so," she said. It was hard for her to shake her natural modesty, no matter how intimate they had just been.

"Why?" he asked. "Would Lizzie Bennet disapprove?"

She laughed, delighted that he'd remembered her reference to her favorite Austen character. "Who knows?" she said. "There's no telling how she and Mr. Darcy behaved behind closed doors."

She climbed off the bed and, trailing part of the sheet on the floor behind her, went to open the door for Murphy. He came in, wagged his tail, and immediately plopped down on his dog bed in the corner.

"Look at him," Cal said, propped up on one elbow. "He's as happy as a clam."

"Or a dog," Billy said, coming back over to the bed.

"That's right. That's why I've never understood that expression 'It's a dog's life.' Murphy's life looks pretty great to me."

Billy looked down at Cal admiringly. Since she was covered with the sheet, he was covered with nothing at all, though, unlike Billy, he seemed to feel perfectly comfortable this way. Why shouldn't he be? He looked amazing. When Billy held a hand out to him, he took it and tugged on it a little, so that she fell back into bed with him.

"Mmm," he said, nuzzling her neck with his lips. "I *will* get this sheet off you. You know that, don't you?"

"I do," Billy said, enjoying the languorous sensation of being in bed with Cal, the daylight fading slowly in the room. When had she last done this? When had she *ever* done this? She laughed now as Cal's lips, which were moving over her neck, tickled her. She looked up at the ceiling, where the shadows from the oak tree's myriad branches quivered. She heard, as if on cue, the *shhh-tik-tik-tik* of her sprinkler coming to life.

"Billy?" Cal said, the word coming out against the hollow at the base of her neck.

"Yes?" she said, moving her hands up into his tousled brown curls.

"I have to talk to you."

"Right now?" she asked, amused.

"Yes. Right now," he said, looking up at her. "Just for a minute, okay?"

"Okay," she said, taking her fingers out of his hair. She reached for a pillow, tucked it under her head, and patted the other half of it. He put his head next to hers.

His eyes, usually hazel, looked greener, his tan darker, against the pillow's white case. "What's up?" she asked.

He hesitated. "It's just . . . I have to go back to Seattle."

Billy didn't say anything. She couldn't. She was too busy feeling the way she'd felt when, as a child, the roller-coaster car dropped suddenly. The bottom had fallen out of her stomach. She'd always hated that feeling.

"When are you going?" she heard herself say finally.

"Tomorrow. I've got a six thirty P.M. flight."

"That's . . . soon," she said, pulling the sheet around her.

"Yes. I was going to tell you, but the last couple times I saw you, we weren't really *trying* to talk," he said, smiling. "Last night we were talking about other things. Today I didn't really have time before, you know . . ."

"No, I get it," Billy said. She *didn't* get it, but she kept talking, more for her benefit, she thought, than for his. "You never said you were going to stay the whole summer." She paused. There was a hurt she was trying to hold at bay, a hurt whose sharpness surprised her, and there was something else, too. Self-recrimination? she wondered. She was the one who'd told herself to keep it light. Had she really believed she'd be capable of anything that casual?

Cal was looking at her carefully. "You're not . . . Are you thinking that I'm leaving? As in not coming back?"

"Isn't that what you're saying?"

"*No.* God, no. I'll be gone for a week. Ten days at the most. I should be back by the end of July. I don't want to go. I didn't think I'd have to go away again so soon. Meghan and I put our apartment on the market, though. It looks like we have a cash buyer. And we've decided we're going to try to get divorced without attorneys. You know, use a mediator. It's faster that way. We found one who can meet with us in a couple days."

"Okay," Billy said softly. She reached out to touch him, not with hunger, but with tenderness. She tousled his hair, which was already pretty tousled.

He smiled at her. "I'll call you while I'm in Seattle. And when I get back, I want to see you. And I want to . . . I want to do this thing right. You know. Go out to dinner with you. Walk Murphy with you. And . . . I'd like to meet Luke, too, if that's okay. You know, when you're ready for it, and he's ready for it."

She nodded, knowing that by being involved with Cal, her relationship with Luke could be even more complicated than it already was. But she couldn't help that; she would have to deal with it later. Right now she was happy, a light, sweet, summer evening happiness.

Cal started kissing her again, and this was not like the playful, ticklish kisses he had given her neck. "You don't have anywhere you need to be tonight, do you?" he asked.

"No," she said, watching him unwrap the sheet from her. For once it was true. The rest of this day, and the night, belonged to them.

CHAPTER 27

When the grandfather clock in the library struck the half hour that evening, Billy looked up from the computer at the checkout desk and eyed the clock skeptically. Was it *really* only six thirty? She could have sworn it had been *hours* since the library had closed, and Rae had left, and she had turned off her cell phone and sat down to do the budget she would present at the next board meeting in September. She blew a loose hair off her face and swiveled around in her chair. This was her absolutely least favorite part of being a librarian: wrangling money from taxpayers.

She clasped her hands behind her head and stretched her back. She'd take a short break and stretch her legs, and then it was back to work. She came out from behind the desk and padded softly past the rows of shelves. She liked *this* part of staying after hours. She liked the stillness, the subdued lighting and, most of all, the unfettered sense of possibility. After all, it was just her, the armchairs, and four thousand books, any one of which she was free to browse through now. Then again, at this moment, there was only one book she was interested in, and she found it in fiction, shelved under *A* for Austen. She pulled out *Sense and Sensibility* and carried it over to an armchair, which she sank down into, draping her legs over one side. She flipped through its pages until she found the quote she was looking for.

"It is not time or opportunity that is to determine intimacy; it is disposition alone. Seven years would be insufficient to make some people acquainted with each other, and seven days are more than enough for others."

She smiled and let the book fall closed. She knew there were those who thought *Sense and Sensibility* was Austen's weakest novel, but she didn't agree with them. Besides, those words perfectly captured how she was feeling about Cal Cooper right now. She'd known him *slightly* longer than seven days, and she felt a closeness to him and an intimacy with him that she'd never felt with anyone before.

Oddly enough, though, since Cal had left for Seattle five days ago, they'd drawn even closer. They'd spent hours talking on the phone at all different times of the day and night. Billy had talked to Cal while she was walking Murphy in the early mornings through a still-quiet Butternut, her flip-flop-clad feet wet from the dewy lawns she'd cut across. She'd talked to him on her lunch hour on the library's back porch, her turkey sandwich consigned to stay in its brown paper bag. She'd talked to him one night while she soaked in the bathtub and wondered if she was too old to sext. (She'd decided she wasn't too old, just too proper. She had Jane to thank for that.) And she'd talked to him another night while she lay in bed, propped up on pillows, a gentle rain falling outside the window. That conversation had lasted for hours, and when they'd finally, reluctantly, said good-night and Billy had hung up, she'd wished he were there to crawl into bed beside her.

What did they talk about? What *didn't* they talk about? They'd started, at their dinner at Billy's house, with the present, with Luke and Wesley and Meghan. Now they moved backward in time, to their childhoods, and what they'd had in common then, which was geography. They were both from the Twin Cities area, Cal from Eden Prairie, a suburb of Minneapolis, and Billy from the Cathedral Hill neighborhood of St. Paul. They discovered that, growing up, they'd had many of the same experiences. They'd gone on the same field trips with their grade school classes, the same outings with their families. They'd both visited the state capitol building on desultory school trips, and trailed through the Como Park Zoo and Conservatory with their parents, holding sticky cotton candy cones. In the summers, they'd cheered on the Minnesota Twins at the Metrodome, sat through concerts at Minnehaha Park, and wandered through livestock barns at the Minnesota State Fair. In the winters, they'd spent more subzero afternoons than they could count prowling through the Mall of America and trying, valiantly, to pry open their parents' wallets and get them to buy one thing or another. They also discovered that during high school and college, they'd both frequented many of the same restaurants and bars. And as it turned out, they'd known a couple of the same people, too. A girl from St. Paul who'd lived in Cal's dorm his freshman year in college, Janie McNiff, had once been Billy's neighbor. And both Billy and Cal had spent many high school afternoons with Brian O'Neil, a St. Paul man with a bad comb-over who ran excruciating dull workshops for students who wanted to improve their SAT scores.

Gradually, though, their conversational topics moved forward in time again. Cal asked Billy about her early years with Luke, about juggling college with parenthood, and about why she'd decided to become a librarian. He was endlessly interested in her job. This was a first for Billy. (The only other people who'd ever expressed this much interest in it were her parents, and even with them, she'd often wondered if they were just being polite.) It seemed as if Cal could not get enough information about her, though, and Billy, unused to talking so much about herself, still tried to satisfy his curiosity. Of course, she asked him about himself, too, especially about his work, which she found fascinating, though privately, she was appalled by how little she knew about architecture. Occasionally, when Cal talked about his old life, and work, in Seattle, she remembered the morning in the library when she'd Googled him like a smitten schoolgirl, and she felt more than a little self-conscious. But Cal had also told her he'd grown disillusioned with the firm where he'd been a partner, and he was in the process of selling his shares back to it. This was why, he explained, he'd gone to Minneapolis earlier in July to look into working with a graduate school friend who had an architectural firm there.

But then, the night before last, the night they'd talked into the early hours of the morning, something had happened, and the connection between them had deepened even more. He'd talked about the bitterness he'd felt at first toward Meghan because she had a tubal ligation. This summer, he thought, had helped him begin to move past it. And although he hadn't spent any time alone with Meghan in Seattle, she'd told him one morning in the mediator's office that she was sorry she'd lied to him. She said there was no excuse for what she'd done and she should have had the courage to tell him from the beginning about her aversion to having children.

Billy had talked to him in turn about Luke and Wesley. She was anxious to know how Luke was doing on his trip and how he was feeling about his new knowledge of his father, and she was worried, increasingly, about Wesley. He still had not responded to her letter. How would she tell Luke this when she picked him up the day after tomorrow? And should she try to reach out to Wesley again, or try instead to temper Luke's expectations about having a relationship with his father, at least in the near-term?

The best thing about their conversations, though, was that they were free from pat advice and easy platitudes. They simply listened to each other, and the only things they offered each other were encouragement and support. It was the act of unburdening themselves that was the point, Billy understood. Not the idea that the other person might magically have all the answers. *That* was why they felt so much closer to each other.

Would Jane Austen have understood that? Billy wondered. She reached for the book, but it had fallen to the floor. She didn't need to read it again, anyway.

Like most of Jane Austen's famous quotes, she already knew this one by heart. She thought about how disposition or character—to use a more modern word—not time or opportunity, determined intimacy. Marianne, one of the two main characters in *Sense and Sensibility*, first fell passionately in love with the caddish Mr. Willoughby, but after having her heart broken, ended up in a more practical—if still loving—union with the reliable Colonel Brandon. Practicality over passion, Jane was arguing. And in her day, it was a sensible strategy for a woman. But surely now, in the twenty-first century, it was possible to have both. Why must they be mutually exclusive? And practicality without passion—well, that was the sum of her relationship with Beige Ted. On the other hand, passion without practicality could bring heartache. She'd told herself the day she dropped in at Cal's cabin that she would need to keep things light, not to get emotionally involved. But it wasn't always possible to have control over one's feelings. And it wasn't always desirable, either. She felt things now for Cal that she wasn't sure she could, or even wanted, to control.

A noise in the library—was it a mouse? she hoped not—made her sit up and look around. She'd completely lost track of the time, and of her surroundings. Outside the windows the evening had turned a bluish, dusky color, and inside, in the reading room, the corners were shadowy and insubstantial. Billy picked up *Sense and Sensibility* and carried it back over to its shelf, slotting it neatly into place. Then she went back to the checkout desk and sat down at the computer. She needed to finish this budget; tomorrow was her last full day without

Luke, and she didn't want this hanging over her head once she picked him up. It was why she'd turned off her cell phone. As much as she loved talking to Cal, she'd promised herself that tonight she'd wait until her work was done. Now, though, she couldn't resist turning it on to check the caller history. Nothing from Cal, but she'd missed a call from someone else. She stared at the iPhone screen. She knew that number, though she'd never dialed it before. It was Wesley's, and he'd left a message. *"Oh my God,"* she said softly, but there was no one else there to hear her.

CHAPTER 28

On the last night of the trip, Luke stirred awake. Something was digging into his ribs. He groped around on the ground. It was a rock, or a tree root, or something. Where had that been when he'd put his sleeping pad and sleeping bag down earlier in the night? He had no idea. The place he'd chosen had seemed like a perfectly flat piece of ground. He'd told Mad Dog that he wanted to sleep outside tonight, and Mad Dog had said, "Go right ahead. It's a beautiful night to do it."

Should he go back in the tent now? he wondered. He could if he wanted. There was plenty of room for him in there. He was too tired, though. Too tired even to crawl the short distance over there. They'd spent the night before at a campsite on the Caribou River, then hiked almost nine miles today through birch forests with views of Lake Superior, past a pond with floating bogs in it, and past a northern hardwoods marsh before stopping to camp tonight at Dyer's Creek. Every few miles, it seemed, there'd been surprises. A covered bridge over a creek, an old mining site, a part of the trail lined by thousands of little white flowers called bunchberries. He thought about all the places they'd passed through over the last couple of weeks: Temperance River State Park, Tettegouche State Park, Beaver Bay, and Fredenberg Creek. And they'd spent two days canoeing on Gunflint Lake and Rose Lake. He'd learned a lot, too. How to purify water, start a fire from scratch, track wildlife, and identify native plants. Tomorrow they'd go back to where they started at Split Rock Lighthouse. Then they'd hike to Gooseberry Falls, where their parents would pick them up at the visitor center.

He rolled onto his back now and tried not to think about how lumpy the ground felt. After a few minutes, it stopped bothering him. Other things bothered him, though. A whole bunch of mosquito bites on his ankles that itched like crazy, and an ache in his shoulders from the backpack even though he'd taken it off hours ago, but pretty soon these stopped bothering him, too. The thing was, he felt good. Even with all the bites and stuff. Because what Mad Dog hadn't told them that first day, when he'd warned them how tired they were going to be on this hike, was that it would be a *good* kind of tiredness. The kind that made you feel empty, but empty in a good way. The kind that made you feel *light*. Like now, he felt like he could almost float away, though that might have been his sleepiness. Sleepiness, he decided, was different from tiredness.

Still, he didn't want to fall back asleep just yet. He lifted his head and looked around the campsite, at the silhouettes of the tents, the fire pit, and the benches. Everything was still. And the only sounds—the only *people* sounds—were the sounds of sleep coming from the tents. Someone was snoring softly; otherwise there was only the occasional cough, or mumble, or rustle of a sleeping bag. He put his head back down. He liked this feeling of being alone but at the same time not being alone. It was nice. *Cozy*, his mom would probably say. Or maybe she'd have a better word for it. She loved words. And she knew a lot of them. He missed her. He wondered if she'd talked to his dad. And if she had, what his dad had said. Would he and his dad go fishing together one day? And what about his sisters? That was the weirdest thing of all. To think it was just you, and then find out you had *sisters*? He'd tried to imagine what they were like, but he hadn't been able to. Would he meet them one day, too?

Mad Dog had told him to focus on the present, though. (Mad Dog was all about "the present.") Luke had tried to do that. And on most nights, he was so tired he didn't even have time before he fell asleep to think about all of these things. But now, even though his body felt tired, his mind felt awake.

He thought about how everyone, it seemed, the campers and the counselors, had changed since the first day. His tent mate, Oscar, had changed the most. He was so homesick at the beginning that it could make you feel kind of miserable just to be around him. Then one day, on, like, the fifth day of hiking, right after they'd stopped for lunch, Oscar had been kind of crying, and Luke had walked with him for a while and talked to him about stuff. Just little stuff, just to keep his mind off being homesick. Later, when Luke was walking alone, Mad Dog had come up to him and said,

"Hey, thanks for talking to Oscar. I think he's doing better now." And then Mad Dog kept walking with him and told him he'd noticed that Luke always helped other people, and that he didn't have to be asked to do stuff—he just did it. "You're a leader, Luke," Mad Dog had told him, and Luke hadn't even known what to say. He'd just nodded and looked away, like it wasn't even a big deal, but it was. Luke figured if Mad Dog said something like that, he meant it. He didn't just go around saying things to be nice, like a kindergarten teacher or something. He wasn't the kind of person who acted fake. He was real. He wasn't like J.P., who just said things to sound cool.

He wondered if Van and J.P. had really gone through with their plan to steal an ATV from the Greys' barn. He didn't think so. And then he thought about other things—what Annabelle had looked like the last time he'd seen her, at Pearl's, and the way her charm bracelet had clinked against the side of her milkshake glass. He thought about going into eighth grade in the fall and wondered if it would be as lame as seventh grade. And he thought about Pop-Pop, and about how ever since that day he'd talked to Mad Dog, he'd been able to think about him, think about missing him, without wanting to cry. Which was the reason he'd tried so hard for the past year *not* to think about Pop-Pop. Because he was afraid he might cry. Now that he had cried, though, down by the lake after Mad Dog left, he wasn't afraid. He'd even felt better afterward.

He yawned and looked up at the sky. There were about a million stars. More than he could see in Butternut, even. He listened to the frogs in the nearby creek.

Why were they so loud? What were they doing? It probably had something to do with mating, he thought. He'd ask Randall tomorrow. He was the counselor with the bushy beard who knew the most about nature. Luke blinked, and started to drift, and he was almost asleep when something made him open his eyes.

There was a milky white cloud in the sky that hadn't been there a minute ago. Was it . . . light from a flashlight? No. It was too high up. And then it was gone. Strange. He blinked again, sleepily, and it came back again, only this time it was greenish, and it was moving, moving almost like a wave, or a . . . a slinky? It was spooky, but he wasn't scared. He knew what it was. Not because he'd seen it before, but because he'd heard his mom talk about it. It was the northern lights. The light green cloud spread out again, and now there were even little threads of red in it. Should he tell somebody? Mad Dog? Or wake up the kids in his tent? No, he decided, sleepy again. He wouldn't tell anyone. It was cool that he was the only one seeing it. It was like the lights belonged to him, for right now, anyway. He watched them a little bit longer, feeling this kind of happy feeling. When they stopped after a few minutes, the feeling stayed with him until he fell asleep. He still felt it, in fact, when he woke up the next morning. But he didn't tell anyone what he had seen. He kept it inside, a good kind of secret.

CHAPTER 29

Billy arrived early to pick up Luke from camp that afternoon and ended up sitting in her car in the Gooseberry Falls visitor center parking lot, eating Cracker Jack and trying to keep her emotions in check, since excitement and anxiety were both vying for attention. To distract herself, she took a copy of Luke's itinerary out of her purse, unfolded it, and checked the schedule for today. It had begun with a "special breakfast" at the last campsite—Billy guessed that at this point, any breakfast without an errant pine needle in it would probably qualify as "special"—and was followed by hiking to the spectacular Gooseberry waterfalls. The campers were due at the visitor center by noon. Billy folded the itinerary and put it back in her purse, then reached into the box of Cracker Jack and searched for a peanut. (Where were the peanuts? This was an outrage. Her father, whose first stop on any long drive had always been at a gas station to buy a bag of Cracker Jack, would *not* have approved.)

She checked her cell phone. It was 12:05 now. And she was about to get out of the car when she saw a group—a couple of counselors and a handful of rag-tag boys—come around the corner of the visitor center. There was the soft, pasty-looking boy named Oscar who'd clung miserably to his parents at the drop-off point two weeks earlier. Luke had looked embarrassed for him, but Billy had been secretly jealous. A little part of her had wished her own son, who'd been sullen in his good-bye, would miss her as much as Oscar was obviously going to miss his parents. This Oscar, though, looked different. He was suntanned and cheerful as he chatted with one of the counselors. But where was Luke?

And then she saw him. He was walking between two other boys, toting his backpack and wearing a baseball cap she didn't recognize. It was obvious, from his animated gestures, that he was telling some kind of a story, and he and his friends were laughing and jostling each other as they walked along. In that second, Billy felt like crying. Then she realized something. She hadn't just missed Luke. She'd missed the Luke who got excited and laughed and told stories. He'd been absent for far too long.

As Billy got out of the car, Luke saw her and waved, a big wave. She wanted to run over to him and give him a hug, but recently hugging had seemed to be *out*, so she forced herself to walk calmly until he called out, "*Mom!*" and gestured for her to hurry. When she got to him, Luke gave her a look that seemed to say, *Well . . . ?* Billy smiled and nodded emphatically. But one of the boys with Luke—a sandy-haired kid in a snowboarding T-shirt—asked Luke for his contact information, and there ensued a search for something to write with and on. Billy provided them a scrap of paper—the back of a recent shopping list—and a stubby library pencil from her purse. As Luke's friend was scribbling away, Billy gave Luke a hug, which, miraculously, he didn't resist.

"Mom, this is Travis," he said then, indicating his friend. "He's from Minneapolis. He plays youth hockey with Charlie," he added. "Can you believe it?" Charlie had been Luke's best friend when they'd lived in St. Paul.

"What a coincidence!" Billy said, though she was staring at Luke's sunburned, peeling nose. What had happened to the sunscreen she'd so carefully labeled "Harper" before packing it in his backpack? And, for that matter, what had happened to the insect repellant? she wondered, noticing a collection of mosquito bites on one of his arms, a few of them scratched almost to the point of bleeding. Oh, well, nothing to be done for it now, she decided, smiling at Luke's new friend instead.

"Mom, Travis and I are going to get together the next time we visit Grandma, all right?"

"Absolutely," Billy said, and there was a bustle of activity now as more parents arrived, more introductions took place, and more cell phone numbers were exchanged. As families began to leave, Billy reached down and picked up Luke's backpack, which he'd let slide onto the ground.

"I'll get that, Mom," Luke said, taking it from her—whether out of protectiveness or politeness, she didn't know.

"Okay," she said. But as they headed for the car, they were stopped by Mad Dog, the head counselor Billy had met at drop-off. "Hey, Luke," he said, seeming incredibly relaxed for someone who'd just spent two weeks with a dozen adolescent boys. "I wanted to be sure to say good-bye before you left." He put his hand on Luke's shoulder. "You've got a great son here," he said to Billy. "If he wants a job with us in five years, we'd be happy to have him." Billy beamed, and Luke, she saw, tried to appear nonchalant.

"It sounds like the trip was a success," she said.

"It was the best group of boys we've ever had," Mad Dog said. He told Luke and Billy good-bye, and Luke started walking toward the car.

"What does *astute* mean?" Luke asked her after he'd tossed his pack onto the backseat.

"Astute? It means . . . being perceptive or insightful. Someone who's astute is someone who's good at assessing a person or a situation," Billy said as they got into the car.

"*Oh*. 'Cause, um, Mad Dog said I was astute," Luke said casually, not looking at her.

She hid a smile. "Well, it sounds like Mad Dog knows what he's talking about."

Once they were both in the car, though, with the doors closed, Luke turned toward her. "Mom, what'd he say?" he blurted. And she realized he'd used all his self-restraint to wait until they were alone to ask her.

"He said . . . he said he wants to meet you. He's going to try to come to Minneapolis sometime in the next couple of weeks, before school starts."

He stared at her, elation and fear mingling in his

face. She was tempted to put her hand on his arm, to offer reassurance, but something told her not to. Something told her he needed space to process this on his own.

"I can't believe it," he said finally, shaking his head.

"That makes two of us," she said.

"And, um, my sisters? Are they coming, too?"

She hesitated. "I don't think so," she said, though she hadn't asked Wesley about this. "I think you might have to wait for that," she added carefully. What she wouldn't—*couldn't*—tell Luke now was how uncertain Wesley had sounded on the phone. Not unfriendly, but uncertain. He'd told her that he'd thought about her letter for more than a week before calling her. She'd worried that he might not remember the night they'd spent together, but he'd told her he remembered it "very clearly." And then he'd asked her, with more than a little awkwardness, how she knew Luke was his. She'd told him that he was the first man she'd ever been with and that she'd lied about being on birth control pills. "I see," he'd said finally, and it was impossible for Billy to read in those two words what Wesley might be feeling. He'd asked her then about Luke—he wanted to know more than she'd put in her letter—and she'd told him, honestly, what an amazing kid she thought he was. And then she'd pressed, gently, for them to arrange a time and a place for him to meet his son.

"Did you tell him I'm a really good fisherman?" Luke asked, excitedly.

"I did not," she said, smiling. "I'll let you tell him that in person. He's going to confirm with me in the next couple of days."

"I'm really going to meet him," Luke said, more to himself than to her. "Holy shit," he breathed.

"No swearing," Billy said, though this so perfectly described the way she was feeling that she was tempted to laugh.

"Sorry, Mom," he muttered.

She started the car now and pulled out of the parking lot. "Are you hungry?" she asked. "Because we can go straight to lunch."

"No, I can wait," he said, reaching into the open box of Cracker Jack in the console. He put a handful in his mouth. "I can just eat this."

As they headed toward Butternut, she asked him questions about his trip, and he answered them, more or less, though she had the distinct impression now that he had to work hard to focus on anything other than meeting his dad. But he did tell her some funny stories about mystery dinners, tent mix-ups, and sleeping bag pranks.

"Oh, Luke," she said then, "your Pop-Pop would have loved to hear about all of this." She looked over at him quickly. She knew she wasn't supposed to bring up Pop-Pop. "I'm sorry," she said, but Luke was staring steadily out his window. She sighed. Apparently their conversation was over. As they drove on in silence, Billy was reminded how quickly his mood could change.

And then he surprised her. "I missed him on this trip," he said, not looking at her. "I miss him all the time, but especially when I was out there. It was all the stuff he liked to do, you know?"

"I know," she said. *Amazing,* she thought to herself.

This was the first time in the year since his grandfather died that Luke had admitted—to her, anyway—that he missed Pop-Pop. Just as she'd hoped, hiking the Superior Trail had offered him more than an adventure in the wilderness. "Do you want to get something to eat now?" she asked loudly as a logging truck thundered by.

"Sure," he said, fiddling with the radio.

"I thought you weren't that hungry," Billy said, watching him bite into a second cheeseburger a little while later. They'd gotten hamburgers and fries to go from a Dairy Queen and were parked in the parking lot, eating them in the car. Or, rather, *Luke* was eating them. All Billy could do was sip her Diet Coke. She was still recovering, tentatively, from the stresses of the last couple of days.

"I'm not *that* hungry," he said. "But . . . can I have your fries, too?"

"Knock yourself out," Billy said, retrieving them from the greasy paper bag and handing them to him. She watched him eat them ravenously.

CHAPTER 30

O h, good, it looks like we got here ahead of the crowd," Billy said to Luke as she tugged open the wooden door to the Corner Bar. It was evening, a couple of days after she'd brought Luke home, and they were meeting Cal for dinner. To say that Billy was nervous about this was an understatement. It would be the first time not only that Cal and Luke had met each other but also that Billy and Cal had seen each other since he'd left for Seattle nine days earlier. (He'd driven straight here from the airport in Minneapolis.)

Billy blinked in the room's dim light—she'd always found this place unnecessarily dark—and tried to make out Cal sitting at the bar. But he was waiting instead at the hostess station, and he waved to the two of them now. Billy waved back at him and then, impulsively, squeezed Luke's shoulder. "Hey, thanks," she said to him. She meant "thanks for agreeing to do this when we both know the only thing you can think about right now is meeting your dad in two weeks." Luke wasn't looking at her, though. He was looking at Cal.

"That's him?" he said. "That's the guy with the Porsche."

"That's right. Do you . . . know him?" Billy asked, mystified.

But Cal was already grinning at Luke. "Hey. I think we've met before?"

"Outside Pearl's," Luke agreed, shaking the hand Cal was holding out to him.

"Luke was, uh, admiring my car," Cal explained to Billy. *Of course,* she thought. She should have known that *everyone* in Butternut would have seen his car by now. "Small town and all," Cal said, as if reading her mind. At that moment, Joy, the hostess, descended on the three of them with menus.

And how had the rest of the evening gone? On the whole, Billy thought, pretty well. It was *a little bit* awkward, though that was, perhaps, to be expected. There were a couple of overlong pauses, a few unfinished sentences and, on Billy's part, some gratuitous conversation with the waitress, Dawn. (Anything, she'd decided, to keep the table from sinking into silence.) It was possible that she tried too hard, and possible, too, that Luke didn't try hard enough. Then again, maybe what Billy saw as a lack of effort on his part was really something else—watchfulness, or wariness. This was new for Luke. With the exception of Beige Ted, she'd never introduced anyone to Luke before, and even with Ted, Luke must have sensed the stakes weren't very high. The only person at the table who seemed relaxed, in fact, was Cal; he was low-key, self-effacing, and funny. More important, he was careful not to be too affectionate with Billy, or too chummy with Luke.

That wasn't so bad, Billy thought again later that night as she stood at her kitchen counter, twisting a corkscrew into a bottle of wine. (Luke was in his bedroom listening to music; Cal was out on the back porch with Murphy.) As she pulled the cork out and got two wineglasses from the cupboard, she considered how different Luke had been since she'd picked him up from camp. It wasn't a vast sea of change, but rather a dozen subtle changes, and a fractional shift in mood. He seemed less angry and gloomy than he'd been before, more thoughtful and mature. Before picking him up from the hike, she'd wondered if he would be resistant to going back to work at Nature Camp, but he'd left for it the next morning without incident or complaint. Even better, yesterday evening he'd hung out with Toby, his old friend from down the block. "Nothing major," as Luke had said—they'd just played foosball and watched some YouTube videos. Still, to Billy it had seemed like a positive sign. And then, when Cal had called her last night from Seattle and said he wanted to take her and Luke out for dinner tonight, Luke had said okay in a way that seemed noncommittal but not, thank God, openly hostile.

After pouring the two glasses of wine, Billy headed out to the back porch, where she found Cal sitting on the top step, throwing a tennis ball for Murphy.

"You know," Billy said, handing him a glass and sitting down next to him, "this used to be a tennis ball–free zone."

"Did it?" Cal asked, amused.

"Yes. It was the only way I could get any reading done out here. And now," she said teasingly, "you're going to completely spoil him."

"That's the idea," he said. "You know that chew toy I brought him? I went into the snootiest pet store in Seattle and said, 'Give me the most overpriced dog toy you have here.'"

Billy laughed. "You know it's only going to take him one morning to get the squeaker out of that thing, right?"

"*A morning?*" Cal objected. "I was going to say *an hour.* I think she's sold you short, Murphy," Cal said as he returned with the tennis ball.

Murphy dropped the ball at Cal's feet and wagged his tail obligingly.

Cal threw the ball for him again, but after Murphy had hurled himself in its direction, Cal turned to Billy, suddenly serious. "That was okay, wasn't it?" he asked. He meant the dinner at the Corner Bar.

"All things considered, I think it was *more* than okay."

"If he has reservations about me, though, I get it," Cal said.

"I think the reservations are more about *me*," Billy said. "Specifically about me . . . dating someone. Add to that his anxiety over meeting his dad, and I think it's a wonder he agreed to go at all tonight."

Cal nodded. "It's a lot for someone his age," he said, putting his wineglass down so he could throw the ball for Murphy again. "He seems like he's handling it really well, though."

"I think so," she said softly. She twirled her wine around in her glass. "I think I'll be relieved, though, when the next few weeks are over. I really want this meeting with Wesley to go well." She'd spoken with him again the previous night to set up a date and time for them to meet in Minneapolis.

"I know," Cal said. "You liked him, though, didn't you? When you talked to him on the phone?"

"I did," Billy said. She stopped twirling her wine. "He sounded nice. Still a little hesitant, of course. But how could he not be? His wife, apparently, is also . . . *surprised*," she added, choosing that word carefully.

"Is she . . . not happy about this?"

"He didn't say that, exactly. But he implied that it's been an adjustment for her." Billy brushed a mosquito away. She didn't want to go inside, though. It was too pretty out here. The sky was a dark purplish black, and the stars were just beginning to come out. Even the fireflies, flickering at the edge of the yard, seemed intent on making the night beautiful.

Murphy came trotting up to them. Cal took the ball out of his mouth and tossed it again. He followed Murphy with his eyes, but he said to Billy, "There's something I wanted to talk to you about." He picked up his wine, and Billy realized with surprise that he was nervous. Had she ever seen him nervous before, even at dinner tonight? She didn't think so.

"Remember I told you about that friend of mine from graduate school, the architect, who I went to see in Minneapolis a couple weeks ago?" Billy nodded. "His name is Steve Landau. We were Skyping while I was in Seattle, and he asked me to work with him on a project starting in September. I said yes."

"Cal, that's wonderful," Billy said, smiling. "Does that mean . . . you'll be staying in Minneapolis this fall?"

"No, it means I'll be moving there. I've been looking at apartments on Zillow."

"You're leaving Seattle?" she clarified.

"I am," he said, watching her carefully. "I feel like my life there somehow got away from me. I need to start over somewhere else, and this time, from the beginning, I need to concentrate on what's important to me. And you're part of that, Billy. I know this is really new, but I want to see where it goes." He smiled at her and, brushing a hair off her face, he kissed her, a lovely, tender, sweet kiss. Well, it wasn't all *sweetness*. There was enough of something else there—lust?—to make her think about that evening and night they'd spent together. It would happen again, she knew, when things settled down a little. Maybe not a whole night, not right away, but she pictured a stolen hour of lovemaking on his twin bed at the cabin. Cal had said the cabin wasn't designed for *that* kind of fun, but obviously, they would prove this idea wrong. Unless . . .

"Cal?" she asked suddenly. "Will you still be using the cabin?"

"I hope so. I haven't told Allie yet. But she said I could use it whenever I want to. And I'm planning on it. Hopefully you and Luke will be coming down to St. Paul, too."

"We will," she said, flushing with pleasure. "We already visit my mom at least once a month. Now, though, between you being there and Luke having a new friend from camp there, I think we'll probably come down more."

"Good," he said, kissing her again. And Billy felt it, the feeling she'd had the evening they'd first made love. It was a clear, sweet, pure happiness. Murphy barked now, a little bark of impatience, standing in front of them, tennis ball at his feet. They both laughed, and as Cal threw it again, Billy sipped her wine. She caught sight then of something out of the corner of her eye. It was the Jane Austen box set sitting on the little table. She must have left it out here overnight. Funny, she'd never done that before. And seeing it made her wonder . . .

"What's wrong?" Cal asked.

"Nothing," Billy said. Had she been frowning? "I just realized something, though. It's going to be complicated, isn't it? Me and you and Luke and Wesley. There won't be any neatly resolved storylines, will there?"

"Storylines?" Cal said, his eyebrows quirking up in amusement. Billy blushed. "No," he admitted. "No neatly resolved storylines. Is that a bad thing?"

Billy chuckled. "I'm a romantic. In novels—not all novels, just my favorite ones—everything has a way of falling effortlessly into place."

He smiled. "Hmm. Well there's definitely going to be some effort involved here. But I'll tell you one thing about this storyline. It won't be boring."

CHAPTER 31

The next evening Cal stretched out on his couch. He had worked all day—probably for the last time—with Jack on the White Pines cottage. He hadn't worked with him since before he'd left for Seattle. He'd gone over to see Jack this morning to tell him about moving to Minneapolis, and he'd ended up helping him put in the new front porch. But despite his tiredness now, when he heard a car pull up outside, he sprang up and opened the door before his guest had even gotten out of the car.

"Oh, it's you," he said, when he saw it was Allie. He leaned in the doorway as she climbed the steps carrying a foil-wrapped casserole dish.

"Yes, it's me," she said, mildly offended. "I brought you leftovers, which I am now seriously considering taking home with me again."

"No, don't do that," Cal said, kissing her on the cheek and relieving her of the dish at the same time.

"Is this what I think it is?" he asked, peeling back a corner of foil.

"Yep. Shepherd's pie," Allie said, of her house-keeper's famous dish. "Lonnie Hagan made it for you," she added, coming into the cabin and closing the door behind her. "And when you told me you were too tired to come over tonight—"

"—you got in the car after dinner and drove it over to me," he finished for her. "Like the amazing sister you are. And I'm going to eat it, too, all of it," he said, setting it on the kitchen counter. "Eventually." He went back and lay down on the couch.

Allie followed him, a quizzical expression on her face. "You're too tired to eat? Jack must be working you hard," she said, sitting down on the end of the couch as he moved his feet up to make room for her.

"No, it's good," Cal said, stretching luxuriantly. "I feel good." And he meant it. It had been this way ever since he'd gotten home from the cottage today; he'd been acutely, but pleasantly, aware of his body's every physical sensation. The ache of his muscles, the heat of the water pulsing over him in the shower, the softness of the flannel shirt and faded jeans against his skin. He wondered how much of this had to do with Billy. Since he'd gotten back from Seattle yesterday, he hadn't had a chance to be alone with her, unless he counted sitting on her back porch last night. It didn't matter, though; he was still hyperaware of all the feelings—physical and otherwise—she called up in him. In fact, the best thing about working with Jack today might have been that it had taken the edge off his need and desire for her. Not in any permanent or meaningful way. Just enough to allow him to think that he could wait a little longer for their relationship to find a balance of its own that would include all three of them—him and Billy and Luke—and perhaps, now, even Wesley. He smiled to think of Billy's concern about all of the convoluted storylines in their future.

Allie, watching him, misunderstood. "You've liked working with Jack, haven't you?" she asked, grabbing the throw off the couch and wrapping it around herself. It had been sunny, but still cool, these last couple of days.

"I *have* liked it," he said. "He's not a trained architect, obviously, but like most builders, *good* builders, he's very intuitive about design. And he's a good worker, too. A fast worker." This was all true, but sometimes Cal thought he valued Jack's camaraderie as much as his work ethic. This had been especially true in the earlier days of the summer, before he left for Minneapolis and Seattle. They hadn't talked a lot as they'd worked, but when they'd finished at the end of the day, they'd often sat on the back porch of the cottage. As the breeze blew in off the lake and the smell of sawdust hung in the air, they'd drunk a couple of the sodas that Jack kept in his cooler. It had reminded Cal, sometimes, of his first construction job, the summer he was sixteen, the summer he worked with one of his dad's crews at the cottage on Cedar Lake. The details were different, of course, but there'd been the same sense of satisfaction at the end of a day, of pride in a job well done.

He told Allie about this now, about how these two

jobs, separated by almost twenty years, still had this in common. She listened, in her slightly proprietorial older sister way. He wanted her to know this, partly because their time together so far this summer had brought them closer together, but partly, too, because he wanted her to understand that what he was going to tell her next hadn't simply come out of nowhere. This summer, in its way, had been a lead-up to it. "Remember when I drove down to Minneapolis last month?" he asked her now. "To see Steve Landau?"

"I do. But you left for Seattle so soon afterward, you never told me how it went."

"It was good. Good enough for him to offer me a job."

"Working for him?" Allie asked, sitting up straighter on the couch.

"Working *with* him," Cal corrected her. "He's looking to expand."

"Cal, are you thinking about moving back here?" she asked, sitting very still. She looked like she didn't quite know if she trusted herself to believe what he was telling her.

"I'm looking at an apartment in St. Paul on Monday," he said.

"Why am I just hearing about this now?" she objected, but when Cal started to explain that he hadn't wanted to get ahead of himself, she waved his words away and instead flung herself down onto the other end of the couch to hug him. "Never mind. I don't care. I just want you to be close by. Or closer than Seattle, anyway."

"I will be," he said, hugging her back. "Can I tell the kids, though?"

"Absolutely. They will be *ecstatic*. They've loved having you here this summer."

"I've loved it, too," he said, thinking especially of two-year-old Brooke, with whom he'd bonded lately. Brooke was going through what Allie referred to as "a Band-Aid phase." The last time Cal had come over, he'd brought her a box of *Finding Dory*–themed Band-Aids and then spent half an hour helping her put all of them on imaginary boo-boos she claimed to have suffered.

When Allie was done hugging him, she said, "You know, this place"—she made a gesture that included the whole cabin—"will always be here when you need it."

He smiled his thanks at her, but she seemed suddenly pensive. "What's wrong?" he asked.

"Nothing," she said. "I'm just glad the mediation between you and Meghan is over. I know it's been hard for you, Cal. I still can't quite believe what Meghan did."

He'd told Allie, the day after he'd told Billy, the reason he and Meghan were divorcing. She'd been shocked at first. And then, once her sisterly instincts had kicked in, she'd been angry. Later, though, once she'd had time to digest it, she'd been more baffled than anything else. Why hadn't Meghan told him the truth about not wanting children in the first place? Cal didn't have an answer to this question, and he'd refused to speculate with Allie about Meghan's motivations. In the end, though, Allie had agreed the important thing was for them to move forward with the divorce.

Now he sighed and rubbed his temples. There was something else he'd been meaning to discuss with Allie: Meghan had not been the only one at fault in their relationship. Yes, she had lied to him, but he, in a sense, had been complicit in the lie. He'd refused to see what was right in front of him. He tried to explain this to Allie now, but she was reluctant to find fault with him.

"No, it's true, Allie. I shouldn't have needed a file folder to tell me what should have been obvious to me from the start: Meghan didn't ever like or want children. She was never interested in other people's children when we went out in public. She never wanted to hold our friends' babies. And once, after we'd left one of my coworkers' apartments—it was a little chaotic because she and her husband had a new baby and a toddler—she said in the elevator on the way down, 'Oh my God. What a nightmare.' And then, of course, there was your family's visit last year. She was *so* tense the entire time because of Brooke and Wyatt. She called Brooke"—he hesitated—"a 'crumb magnet.' I think Meghan thought I'd find it funny, but I didn't." He'd thought Allie would be appalled when he told her this now for the first time, but she only laughed.

"That's not *totally* inaccurate. She does leave a little trail of Pepperidge Farm Goldfish behind her wherever she goes. But seriously, Cal, you shouldn't blame yourself for not seeing that about Meghan. Lots of people aren't interested in children until they have their own. Who's to say Meghan wasn't one of them? And who's to say that you should have known the difference?"

"I don't know," he said. "I was just . . . so lazy."

"You were *never* lazy," Allie objected.

"Or complacent, anyway. I told you I didn't see the things I didn't want to see. But I didn't want to see them because Meghan made everything so . . . so *easy* for me. And I *let* her do that. She took care of everything. I'd come home from work, or home from the session with the personal trainer Meghan had scheduled for me, and I'd reach into the fridge, which was stocked with my favorite coconut water, and then I'd take a shower, which always had the shower gel in it that I liked, and then I'd towel myself off and change into clothes just back from the French laundry Meghan used, and then we'd go out to dinner at the restaurant she'd made us a reservation at—you know, the new restaurant where no one could get a reservation. Except Meghan. Of course Meghan could. And here was the thing: she liked doing all of this. She loved it. If I tried to do any of it, she got annoyed. So I didn't even have to feel guilty about it. She managed all of it: our apartment, our social life, our travel, even my public relations. I mean, my firm had people doing PR, but it turned out Meghan was better at it then they were. Meghan was good at everything she did. Except for being"—he shrugged—"an honest person."

Allie got up and went into the kitchen. Cal heard her opening cupboards and drawers and heating something in the microwave. When she returned, it was with a plate of shepherd's pie, a napkin, and a fork. Cal hadn't realized how hungry he was, but he dug in now. Allie watched him with a gentle amusement.

"Lonnie always tells Wyatt and Brooke that life feels better on a full stomach," she remarked when he'd finished.

"Lonnie's right," Cal said, setting his plate on the coffee table. And because he wanted to focus on something positive, he told her about Billy. She'd known they had "a thing," but he wanted her to understand it was *more* than a thing. He told her about their phone conversations when he was in Seattle, meeting Luke last night, and the three of them beginning, tentatively, to explore a future. He told her about Wesley, too, a piece of information Allie met thoughtfully.

"This is going to be complicated," she said finally.

"You sound like Billy," he said. "You like her, though, don't you?" he asked, already knowing that she did.

"Of course. *Everyone* likes Billy. I just wish things could be simpler, I guess."

He shrugged, thinking that with Meghan, things might have been too simple. Too easy. And look where that had gotten him. "I like a challenge," he said now to Allie. "And besides," he added, thinking of Billy's love of novels, "it's kind of like a good book, right? You don't know what will happen next. You keep reading because you want to find out."

CHAPTER 32

Luke was grinding his skateboard on the library's bottom step that afternoon—his mother *hated* when he did this because it wore down the concrete— when a now-familiar voice said, "Hey, Luke." He looked up. Yep. It was Cal. Cal Cooper. His name, to Luke, sounded like the name of a cowboy in one of the old Westerns Pop-Pop used to watch. But he was okay, Luke supposed. Or at least, he *had been* when Luke and his mom had dinner with him at the Corner Bar. He hadn't asked Luke a lot of questions, which was cool, and he hadn't been all romantic with his mom, which would have been weird. The thing was, he hadn't known then that Cal was going to be staying around. His mom had told him the next day he was moving to Minneapolis and they'd be seeing more of him. *That* worried him a little. How was Cal going to fit into their life? He wasn't sure.

"Hey," Luke said, looking back down at his skateboard. He expected Cal to go into the library, but instead he stopped on the steps.

"What's up?" he asked Luke.

Luke shrugged. He glanced down the block at the drugstore, Butternut Drug, which he'd seen Annabelle go into a little while ago. She'd waved at Luke, a little wave that was barely a wave at all. Since then he'd been wondering if he should go in there, too, or just wait for her to come out again and say something to her.

Cal looked down the street, too. "Anything happening in Butternut?" he asked.

"Not much," Luke said, picking up his skateboard and reaching for the can of Coke he'd placed on the ledge. Not much was happening in his life, either. The earlier rules from this summer were in effect until school started. He could go to Nature Camp, and afterward he could go to the library. The only places he could stop in between were Pearl's and one of the other businesses on Main Street. That was it. Still no cell phone. Still no Van. He wondered, though, what he and J.P. were up to. Wondered whether if he saw them they would even talk to him. Probably not. But he'd been talking, on their home phone, to his new friend Travis from his hiking trip. He was pretty cool, and he liked a lot of the same pro skateboarders Luke did.

The front door to the library opened, and Mr. Niles, the school counselor, came out. Luke instinctively looked back down again.

"Hi, Luke," Mr. Niles said. He sounded friendly, though the last time Mr. Niles had spoken to him, be-

fore he'd gotten suspended, he'd said he was "very disappointed" in Luke.

"Hi, Mr. Niles," Luke said. He took a big sip of his
Coke, and Mr. Niles, thank God, kept walking.

"Who's that?" Cal asked, looking amused.

"That's the school counselor."

"Huh," Cal said. And then he chuckled. "I still have
a very distinct memory of the counselor at my high
school. Mr. Wiggins. He kept a pet gecko in his office.
It was the only good thing about going there."

"Why'd you go there?" Luke asked.

"I got sent there. My first couple of years in high
school, I wasn't doing that well."

"Why not?"

"Mr. Wiggins said I wasn't applying myself. And I
wasn't. But that changed. Or it started to change. The
summer I turned sixteen—the summer between sopho-
more and junior years."

"Why did it change?"

"Um . . . long story," Cal said. "But I liked this girl,
Victoria. And it . . . inspired me to get a job. That's
how I figured out I liked building things. And designing things. I knew after that, if I was serious about doing it for a living, I'd have to do better in school."

Luke swung himself up to sit on the ledge to the
steps and considered Cal with interest. He almost
wanted to ask him more about this girl Victoria, but
then he changed his mind. What he really wanted to
ask Cal about, he decided, was his mom. Because there
was something Luke didn't *totally* understand. According to his mom, Cal had been, like, this big architect in
Seattle. His mom was a librarian in Butternut. Not that

there was anything wrong with that, but . . . And then, Cal was rich, too. Anyone who drove that car had to be rich. Whereas his mom was doing okay—they weren't poor or anything, but, even so. Cal just seemed different, very different, from that guy Ted.

"Why are you dating my mom?" he asked, wishing maybe he could have put it a different way. But Cal seemed surprised for only a second.

"Well," he said, "I like her. She's funny. She's smart. And she's beautiful."

Luke frowned. "That's probably just the moisturizing lotion she uses," he said, thinking about all the little pots on her shelf in the bathroom. "It's pretty expensive."

Cal laughed. "I think it's working, though, don't you?"

"I guess," Luke allowed. He finished off his Coke and then crushed the empty can against the ledge. "You know, I'm going to meet my dad in another week. On August fourteenth," he said, watching Cal. "It's all planned out."

"I know. That's really cool."

"Yeah, it will be," Luke said. But he wondered sometimes if it really *would* be cool. What if his dad didn't like him? Then what would he do?

"If you're nervous about it, though," Cal said to him, "I get it. I mean, who wouldn't be?"

"I'm not *nervous*," Luke said, a little irritated. "Why would I be nervous?"

"I don't know. Maybe because . . . you don't really know what he's like yet, and he doesn't really know what you're like."

"I guess," Luke said. He crushed the can a little more.

"So you'll take some time to get to know each other," Cal said.

Luke nodded, and jumped off the ledge. He looked down the block toward the drugstore. While they'd been talking about his dad, had he missed Annabelle leaving it? He didn't think so. She'd have to walk past the library on her way home. He grabbed his skateboard. Maybe he'd skate by there now. But then what? He didn't really have a plan. He didn't even know if she was still mad at him. And what would he say to her if she was?

"Can I . . . can I ask you something?" he said to Cal, who was still standing there.

"Sure."

This was stupid, Luke thought. He didn't even know why he was asking Cal about it. Finally he shrugged and said, "There's this girl . . ."

Cal smiled. "Luke?"

"Yeah?"

"There's *always* a girl."

CHAPTER 33

The night before they were supposed to meet Wesley, Billy and Luke drove down to St. Paul and spent the night at her mother's house. The next morning, after breakfast, Billy and her mom went for a walk together. Billy's mom, in her eminently sensible way, tried to allay Billy's fears. She pointed out that Wesley was obviously open to the idea of being Luke's father or he wouldn't be meeting with them today. Billy had hugged her, hard, but she was still anxious as she and Luke drove to the airport hotel where Wesley was staying. They got to the hotel coffee shop a half hour early, and they sat in an orange leather booth, Billy drinking water and Luke stirring the ice cubes in his soda, both of them feigning a calmness they didn't feel. Billy was *so* nervous. Partly because Luke was so nervous, and partly because she wanted this meeting to be . . . well, to be whatever it was that *Luke* needed it to be.

When Wesley walked into the coffee shop, Billy recognized him immediately. He was still nice-looking,

Billy saw, and still in possession of that rugged hand-
someness she'd found so appealing when she was eighteen. But the years had worked their changes on him,
too. He had a squint now to his eyes, and a weathering
in his face that suggested how much time he'd spent
on the water. Billy and Luke both stood up and met
him, and there was a moment—an awkward moment—
when Luke and Wesley paused there, neither of them
knowing what to do. And then Wesley solved the problem by grinning, pulling Luke into a hug, and saying,
"Christ, kid, it looks like you got my dad's chin."

Billy watched in amazement as Luke not only came
into his arms but also put his arms around Wesley. And
then her son did something she would never forget. He
closed his eyes. Just for a second. It was such a simple thing, but it spoke volumes of the trust he already
had in Wesley. And it did something else, too. It made
Luke look so young, the way his long, spiky black
eyelashes—Fuller brush eyelashes, her dad had called
them—rested on his suntanned, freckled skin. And
then he opened his eyes and let go of his father, and the
moment was over. Billy and Wesley said hello, and the
three of them sat down at their booth, Wesley setting a
plastic bag down next to him on the seat.

For the first fifteen minutes, Billy, in her need to
fill in the silence, told Wesley about Luke growing up
in Minneapolis and their move to Butternut five years
ago. But when she realized she was the only one speaking, she stopped abruptly. "Sorry I'm doing all the talking," she said, looking sheepishly from Luke to Wesley.
"Nervous habit."

Wesley laughed. "You covered a lot of ground there.

Thirteen years in thirteen minutes," he said, looking at his watch. "Did she leave anything out, Luke?"

"A couple things," Luke said shyly, stirring his soda with the straw. That's when Billy remembered something she'd noticed the first time she'd met Wesley. He had an easy way about him. He was one of those rare people who was comfortable in his own skin, and that made him comfortable to be with. Billy's tension ebbed away after that, and she relaxed. There was something else, too. He was good at drawing people out. So while *he* didn't talk a lot, he got *Luke* to talk a lot, which to Billy was no small feat. He asked Luke about his summer. Luke, who spoke self-consciously at first, gradually became more confident. He touched on his hiking trip, his counselor, Mad Dog, and volunteering at Nature Camp. He even mentioned a few skateboard tricks he was working on. Wesley confessed to Luke that he'd never owned a skateboard. When Luke pressed him about other sports—snowboarding, surfing, BMXing—he said his wife would probably kill him if he even suggested trying any of them. Luke looked momentarily disappointed. But then Wesley said, "Sorry, kid, the only sport that I can lay any claim to is fishing." Luke brightened immediately. He told Wesley about fishing for smallmouth bass with his late grandfather.

While they talked, Billy compared the two of them as discreetly as possible. Funny, she'd always thought Luke had her Black Irish looks. But now she realized he looked a lot like Wesley, too, although it was hard to define their similarities. The shape of their eyes? Their chins? Their foreheads? Oh, well, it didn't matter. It was there, and Billy felt a kind of satisfaction now in seeing it.

Eventually the three of them ordered lunch, and after the waiter had cleared their plates away, Wesley took out his wallet and showed them pictures of his daughters, Eleanor and Hannah. They were both adorable, and Billy was fascinated to see that, once again, there was a resemblance between Luke and the two of them, especially Eleanor, who had an impish quality to her that reminded Billy of a younger Luke. Wesley also told them a little bit about his wife, Erin, who was helping him design a Web site for their charter fishing boat business. He showed them a photograph of her, too. Just like in the photo that Billy had seen of her in the manila envelope, she had an open, friendly face. Billy hoped she would welcome Luke into their world, although she imagined this would not happen overnight.

"Do they know about me?" Luke asked Wesley now about his sisters.

"They do. They sure do. They're already fighting over which one of them gets to talk to you first," Wesley said. Luke's eyes widened, and Billy wondered how this only child would negotiate two sisters who apparently already had a rivalry for Luke's affection.

Later, when Luke left to go to the restroom, Wesley opened the plastic bag he'd brought and extracted a book from it.

"I think this belongs to you," he said, holding it out to her. Billy took it from him, astonished. It was the copy of *Wuthering Heights* she'd left at the fishing lodge in Alaska over fourteen years ago.

"Why . . . ?"

He shrugged. "By the time I realized you'd forgotten it, you and your dad had already left. When *I* left a couple of weeks later, I took it with me. I think I felt guilty about it. I figured you must have really loved it. That night I saw you reading it in the lobby, you were so into it."

Billy smiled. "I'd probably read it at least five times by that point."

"Really? Well, I kept carrying it around with me from place to place. I think I had some idea of mailing it to you, but I didn't have your contact information, and I didn't think the lodge would give it to me. And then I thought maybe I should read it myself since you'd thought it was so good."

"And did you?"

"Eventually."

"What did you think?"

"I didn't like it," he said bluntly. For some reason, this made Billy laugh. "I mean, what the hell?" he said, smiling. "What was Heathcliff's problem? Was he just straight-up crazy or what?"

"He was pretty crazy," Billy agreed cheerfully. "But at eighteen, I found his obsessive love for Catherine very attractive."

Wesley shook his head. "Well, I'm glad I held on to it. I'm not usually a big believer in fate, but in this case . . ." He shrugged. "Maybe I knew I'd see you again."

"Maybe," Billy said, sipping her water.

"Can I tell you something? Honestly?"

"Of course."

"Before today, I wanted . . . I wanted to give you

the benefit of the doubt about Luke. But I also wanted to . . . you know, to be sure he was my son. I was going to ask that we have a paternity test done, but after I saw him . . ." He shook his head again. "He's *definitely* my son. It's a little bit like looking in a mirror. Not that there's an *exact* resemblance. It's the little things . . . and it's not just me he reminds me of, either. It's my family members, too. I mean, Luke's never met my brother, Nick. But he has so many of the same mannerisms. It's strange, but it's strange in a good way."

"I'm glad." Billy smiled.

"He's um . . . he's a nice kid, isn't he?"

"He's an *amazing* kid," Billy said honestly. And at that moment, she caught sight of Luke coming back into the room.

A little while after that, Billy found an excuse to leave them alone together. She ended up browsing in the hotel's little gift shop and buying a few things she didn't really need. She wanted to give them time, though, and when she came back to the coffee shop, she was glad she had. They were talking about fishing again, which, thanks to Pop-Pop, was a subject Luke could hold his own on.

"Hey," Billy said, sliding into the booth, but the two of them, deep in conversation, only nodded. She smiled, sipped her iced tea, and kept an eye on the time. She had to be at work tomorrow morning, and Wesley, she knew, had a flight later tonight. Finally she reminded Luke gently about the four-and-a-half-hour drive ahead of them, and Wesley walked them out to their car to say their good-byes.

They stood beside Billy's car, a little tentative, not

quite sure how to end this. Wesley asked Billy about the drive up north. Billy asked him when he'd get back to Port McNeil. Luke stood there quietly. Billy was wondering how to broach the subject of future communication. Should Wesley and Luke play it by ear? Should they set up a time to talk by phone?

"I'm not sure how this works," Wesley said, obviously thinking the same thing as Billy.

"I'm not sure, either," Billy said with a little laugh.

"What do we do next?" Wesley asked Luke. "Do we talk on the phone? Or Skype?"

"How about both?" Luke said with a smile.

And then Wesley gave Billy a polite kiss on the cheek and Luke a bear hug. "Be good, kiddo," he said before he headed back into the hotel to arrange for a shuttle to the airport.

An hour into the drive home, Billy asked Luke if he was hungry. He'd been quiet, watching the farmland rolling by out the window.

"What did you say?" Luke asked, turning to her.

"I said, are you hungry? We can stop whenever, provided you don't want anything too fancy."

Luke shrugged. "A little," he said.

"What did you think, Luke?" Billy couldn't resist asking now. "Was he different than you thought he would be?"

"Kind of."

"Did you like him?" Billy asked.

"Uh-huh."

"He liked you, too," Billy said.

"You think so?" Luke asked, turning to look at her.

"Definitely. And it sounds like your sisters do, too,

even though they don't know you yet." And then Billy hesitated, wanting to say once again—the same thing she'd been saying, and thinking, ever since she'd told Luke that she'd heard back from Wesley—*We're going to have to take things slowly. See how they go.* But she didn't say it this time.

Luke was the next one who spoke. "Actually, I'm kind of starving," he said with a smile.

CHAPTER 34

uke, *stop*," Annabelle said, laughing. "I can't draw you if you keep doing that."

"You mean doing this?" Luke asked, using his feet to push them off from the ground and move the tire swing in a wide arc.

"*Yes*," Annabelle said. She'd been holding her sketch pad with one hand and her pencil with the other, but now the hand holding the pencil had to hold the tire swing chain, too. "Come on," she said. She tried to be serious, but she was still smiling. "I want to show you what I learned in my figure drawing class this summer. I've really improved since the last time I drew you."

"Okay. We'll stop. Just . . . one more swing, okay?" Luke said, pushing off again. He wanted her to draw him, if that's what she wanted to do, but he wanted to keep swinging, too. When the tire tilted up in the air and then tilted back down again, it made him feel the same way on the outside that he felt on the inside. Which was . . . light. Free. Like he could swing forever.

He felt that way about skateboarding sometimes if he was lucky, and the board was right, and the pavement was right, and his mood was right, but this was different. This was better. Annabelle was here. And when he lifted his feet up and hitched them on the inside of the tire on the upward swing, his knees bumped against her knees. When he leaned toward her on the downward swing, her long, loose hair, which was blowing around her face, touched his face, and that was nice, too.

It was weird how fast things could change. A week ago, he'd thought Annabelle hated him, and now . . . now he knew she didn't. When he'd asked Cal about her on the steps of the library, he'd half expected some big lecture from him about girls. But when Cal had found out Annabelle was at the drugstore, he'd said, "Now? She's there right now? Then why are you standing here talking to me?"

Luke couldn't answer that, so he shrugged and went down the block to the drugstore. When he walked in, Annabelle was still there, standing at the makeup counter, using lipsticks to put these little marks on the back of her hand. Luke had thought a lot about what he'd say to Annabelle the next time he saw her, but what he said to her then was, "Why are you doing that? Putting lipstick on your hand?" And she'd said, "To see what it would look like with my skin tone. They don't let you put it on your lips here."

"Will your parents even let you wear that?" Luke asked because of all the rules they had.

"As long as it looks natural," Annabelle said. "That's why I'm not trying the reds. Just the corals and pinks."

"Oh," Luke said. And then they just started talking.

Not about lipstick, but about other things, like her drawing class, and his hiking trip, and her brother breaking his collarbone, which Luke hadn't even known about. Afterward they'd come back to Luke's house, and Annabelle had wanted to go on the tire swing. Luke thought they were a little old to swing, but once they got on it, he didn't mind. It was actually pretty fun. It was where he'd told her about how he was going to meet his dad in another week, and about his two half sisters. She was really excited, which was good, because it made Luke forget, for a little while, that he was kind of nervous about it. He and Annabelle hadn't been together on the tire swing since that day over a week ago. Partly because he'd been busy with Nature Camp and going to Minneapolis, and she'd been away on a family trip.

He heard the back door open now, heard his mom call out, "Luke? Annabelle?"

He tried to ignore her, but Annabelle used her foot to slow down the swing.

"Yes, Ms. Harper?" Annabelle called back. She was so polite, Luke thought. His mom had told her to call her Billy at least a hundred times over the years, but she still wouldn't call her that. It was a church thing. Her parents said she had to call all the adults in their congregation Mr. or Mrs. or Ms., even if she'd known them all her life. It was just the way they did things, Luke guessed. It seemed old-fashioned, but for some reason it seemed nice, too.

"Are either of you thirsty?" Billy asked, standing on the porch. "I can bring you some lemonade."

"No," Luke said, not looking at her. He was hoping

she wouldn't come over to them. His and Annabelle's knees were almost touching, and he was afraid that if his mom came any closer, Annabelle would move her knees away.

"No, thank you, Ms. Harper," Annabelle said. "I have to go soon, anyway. It's almost dinnertime."

It was? He didn't want her to go. He'd forgotten, though, how early her family ate dinner. That was a church thing, too. Her dad had all these commitments on weeknights, like Bible study groups and things like that.

"All right, then," his mom said, and Luke could tell she was happy that he and Annabelle were hanging out together again. "Let me know if you change your minds." *Please go back inside,* he thought. As if she'd heard him, she said good-bye to Annabelle and did.

"I saw your mom's boyfriend on Main Street today," Annabelle said, starting to draw him again.

Luke nodded. It was weird hearing someone call Cal his mom's boyfriend, but he supposed that's what he was.

"He was parking his Porsche."

"He's selling that. Which is too bad. But he wants something he can drive in the winter. He asked me to look at Jeeps in Duluth with him tomorrow."

"That sounds like fun," Annabelle said.

"Maybe." He shrugged.

Then they were quiet while Annabelle was trying to get something right in her drawing.

"I told my parents about you meeting your dad," she said finally. "Was that okay?"

"I guess," he said.

"My mom said it was like a movie," Annabelle said. "She meant, I think, those made-for-TV movies she watches on the Hallmark Channel."

"I don't think it was like that," Luke said. He was thinking to himself, that if his life were going to be like a movie, he'd prefer *Fast & Furious* to the Hallmark Channel. He'd already told Annabelle yesterday, when he'd briefly run into her, about meeting his dad at the hotel coffee shop. He hadn't told her *everything*. Because he still didn't know how to describe it. He'd thought about it a lot, though, kind of playing it over in his head and remembering little details. He liked his dad, and he could tell his dad liked him, too. But his mom kept saying "You'll just need to take things slowly." It reminded him of Mad Dog saying he needed to be "in the present." Adults had these things they said that were supposed to be so helpful, but they were sometimes just annoying.

"Anyway, my mom is happy for you. And my dad . . ."

"Does he still hate me?"

"No. He said you were a good kid. Basically a good kid."

"*Basically?*" Luke echoed. He wasn't sure if he liked that or not. But Annabelle didn't seem to have a problem with it.

"Yes, and he said you weren't going to be hanging out with Van anymore, either."

"Yeah. I'm not allowed to. In school, though, it might be hard . . ." School was starting soon, and he felt a little nervous. It was his last year of middle school. So much had changed over the summer. What would Van think when he told him his dad didn't live in Alaska, but on Vancouver Island instead?

"You don't know about Van?" Annabelle had stopped drawing and was looking at him a little strangely. The tire swing was still now.

"What?" Luke said. "What about him?"

"He . . . got sent away. I thought you knew. I thought you just didn't want to talk about it."

Luke shook his head, confused. "I haven't seen him since before I went on the hiking trip. What do you mean, 'He got sent away'?"

Annabelle looked upset. She even closed her sketch pad.

"What happened?" he asked.

"Well, my dad said . . . and don't repeat this, okay, Luke? Because a lot of what he hears . . ." She shrugged. "Sometimes he doesn't want it to go any further . . . But Officer Sawyer told him that Van and his friend, that dropout—"

"J.P.," Luke said, and for some reason his heart was beating faster.

"He and J.P.," Annabelle continued, "got caught breaking into the Greys' barn."

"You're kidding," he said. And he meant it. He was shocked. He didn't think they'd really do it. They were always talking about doing stuff that they didn't do.

Annabelle shook her head. "No. They did. And the Greys' handyman called the police. And then he called Mr. Grey."

"Did they get arrested?"

She shook her head. "No, Mr. Grey didn't want to

press charges. But he did want there to be some consequences. So J.P., who'd already been in trouble before,
got sent to some program. I don't know what it was.
Something that's supposed to, you know, get you back
on track. But Van . . . when the police called his parents to come pick him up at the station, nobody came.
And when they went to his house to talk to his parents,
no one was home."

"It's only his dad," Luke said.

"No, I mean, he was gone, too. Van had been living
there all alone. There was supposed to be some aunt or
something that was stopping by to help, but . . ." Annabelle shrugged. "They couldn't find her, either. So he
was just on his own there. He wouldn't really say for
how long. But there were no groceries. And he didn't
have any money."

Luke looked away. He thought about Van on the
riverbank that afternoon the last time he'd seen him,
eating that bag of Cheetos, and all of his ribs showing
through his T-shirt. He was afraid he was going to cry.
"Do you think he was hungry?" he asked Annabelle.

"I . . . I don't know. They found someone, someone
from his mom's side of the family, I think, to take him.
He went to live with them in South Dakota, and . . .
he'll probably be okay. I mean, they're probably nice,
right?"

Luke shook his head. "Not if they're from his mom's
family. I mean, *she* didn't even want him. She just
left him."

Annabelle didn't say anything, but she felt bad. Luke
could see that.

Finally Luke gave the tire swing a push. "He was

my friend," he said, not really to Annabelle. More to himself.

"I know," she said. And for some reason Luke glanced at the charm bracelet on her suntanned wrist. He'd always liked the way it looked there.

"I used to talk to him about my dad," he said. "About finding him."

"Luke, I'm sorry. I have to go. Are you okay?" Annabelle asked, her light brown eyes worried.

"Yeah," Luke said. "It's all right. I would have found out anyway, I guess. Eventually."

"I'll see you tomorrow, okay? We can go to Pearl's."

"Okay," he said.

"Here," she said, opening her notebook and tearing a sheet out of it. "You can have this." She held it out to him and he took it, but before he could look at it, she leaned over and kissed him on the lips, really fast. Then she got off the tire swing and ran toward her back door, calling bye to him over her shoulder.

Luke looked at the picture she'd drawn of him and smiled. It was actually pretty good.

CHAPTER 35

"H ey," Cal said when Luke answered the front door
the next morning. "You ready?"

Cal wondered for a second if Luke had forgotten
about going to Duluth to test-drive a Jeep Cherokee,
but Luke nodded and said, "Almost. Murphy's in the
backyard, though. I just need to put him inside."

"Okay, great. I'll wait here," Cal said.

Luke was back in a minute. "Let's go," he said,
yanking a baseball cap on backward over slightly un-
ruly hair.

"Thanks for doing this, by the way," Cal said as they
walked over to his Porsche, which was parked on the
street in front of the house. "I really appreciate it."

"Huh?" Luke asked, squinting at Cal in the dazzling
morning light.

Cal resisted the urge to smile. If Luke was anything
like he'd been at thirteen, he heard only about twenty-
five percent of what adults said to him, maybe less. "I

said thanks for coming today. Did you . . . get a chance to have some breakfast?"

"Oh, yeah. My mom made some eggs before she left for work. They're one of the things she can do, like, halfway decently," Luke added. "That and hot dogs." Cal nodded but again did not smile, this time out of loyalty to Billy.

He and Luke reached the car and climbed in, Cal waiting until Luke's seat belt was fastened before he turned on the engine. He pulled away from the curb and headed out of town, amused that Luke seemed to be enjoying himself so much. He was adjusting his seat, running his hand over the leather upholstery, and examining the "infotainment touch screen panel" on the dashboard.

"There's wireless Internet if you're interested," Cal offered, looking over at Luke. "Or we can blast some music."

"Really?"

"Sure," Cal said in what he knew was a shameless bid for Luke's approval. "Anything you want, as loud as you want it."

Luke used the touch screen to search SiriusXM, chose an R&B station, and cranked up Drake's "One Dance" loud enough to make the windows vibrate. Cal didn't mind. He liked this song, too.

"The sound is *amazing*," Luke said, swiveling around in his seat. "It's, like, coming from everywhere."

"There are nine speakers," Cal said loudly to make himself heard over the song.

"Are you going to go any faster?" Luke asked hopefully once they were out on the highway. Cal was purposely driving the speed limit.

"Maybe a little bit," Cal said. After checking his rearview mirror, he floored it, just for a second.

"*Whoa*," Luke said. "Keep going."

"Sorry, that's it," Cal said. "I don't think your mom would be too happy if we drove to Duluth like that."

"Probably not," Luke agreed. "Why do you want to sell this car, though?" he asked. "It's *so* cool."

"It's pretty cool," Cal agreed, "but it's not practical anymore. Not up here." And not only that—he also needed a car that could accommodate more than one passenger. Billy *and* Luke were both a part of his life now.

"Maybe it's not practical in the winter," Luke said. "But . . . the rest of the year? Maybe you can have two cars."

Cal smiled. "Maybe, sometime. But not now. This car reminds me of my life in Seattle. I'd kind of like to get something new. You know, start with a clean slate. That kind of thing."

Luke considered this. "Was your life in Seattle that bad?" he asked, turning down the radio.

"No," Cal said. "Not all of it. Parts of it . . . parts were good. But things are different now, and I think it's time for a change."

Luke seemed to accept this. "I was looking at a map last night," he said after a moment. "I wanted to see where Vancouver Island is. It's not that far from Seattle."

"No, it's not. It's only about five hours away by car

and by ferry. I've been there before, a couple of times." Cal had noticed that every time he saw Luke, Luke would slip in a mention of his father. He wondered if he was, consciously or unconsciously, reminding Cal that he already had a dad. Cal was careful to tread lightly. The other day when he was at their house, Billy and Luke had a little skirmish about Luke going to the Nature Museum's picnic on the last day of camp. Luke said it wasn't "mandatory." Billy said she wanted him to "finish strong." They were all in the kitchen, and Cal had quietly excused himself and said he'd take Murphy for a walk. By the time they'd returned, Luke was on the phone with Annabelle, and Billy was humming over the dishes in the kitchen.

"What's Vancouver like?" Luke asked him now.

"It's beautiful," Cal said honestly. "I spent most of my time in Victoria, though. That's the city on the southern tip of the island. But there's a lot more to see than that, obviously. And the fishing . . . I haven't done any there, but I know it's supposed to be amazing." He looked over at Luke.

Luke nodded and then said almost shyly, "I might visit my dad and his family there over spring break. It's still, like, in the planning stages," he added.

"Right." Cal nodded. And then, casually, knowing it had been almost a week since Luke had met his dad, he asked, "Have you talked to him lately?"

"Two nights ago. We're going to Skype every week, for now."

"That's good," Cal said. But he wondered if this was hard on Luke: starting a new relationship with the father he'd never known *and* getting to know the man his mom had just started dating. He wasn't sure how well he would have handled this when he was thirteen.

It was quiet now in the car.

"Your friend Annabelle," Cal asked after a few minutes, "is she in your class?"

Luke nodded. "There's only one class per grade at my school."

"Got it," Cal said. He waited. But there was nothing more about Annabelle, which was probably just as it should be. How forthcoming had he been about girls at Luke's age?

"When do you go back to school?" he asked.

"Um, in a couple weeks," Luke said, lowering his window a few inches. Cal thought he might have heard a little nervousness in Luke's voice. Even sixteen years after graduating from high school, Cal could still remember having a pit in his stomach the weeks before school started every fall. It was part excitement, part fear.

"Where are you going to live in Minneapolis?" Luke asked then.

"I just got an apartment. In Linden Hills. Do you know that area? It's between Lake Harriet and Lake Calhoun."

"I think I know where that is."

"I was thinking," Cal said, "that the next time you and your mom visit your grandmother, you might . . . like to see it?"

"I guess," Luke said. Cal wasn't exactly sure if this was a yes or no. Well, he wouldn't push it.

"Can we open that?" Luke asked, indicating the sunroof.

Cal adjusted the slide-tilt sunroof, and a square of blue sky opened above them. Luke reclined his seat further and, with a sigh of pleasure, crossed his hands behind his head.

"In another two years, I'll be getting my learner's permit," he said to Cal.

Cal smiled. The Porsche would be long gone by then, but a Jeep, he thought, would still be pretty fun to learn to drive in.

CHAPTER 36

Billy pushed open the screen door and let Murphy out onto the back porch. She hesitated for a moment before following him. It was only the fifth of September, but already she could feel the approach of fall in the chilly night air. No matter, she decided, pulling her pale blue woolly cardigan closer around her and cradling her mug of lemon verbena tea. Soon she would have to trade her nightly ritual of reading in her wicker chair for reading in one of the cozy armchairs next to the living room fireplace. But for now, she thought, settling in with her tea, with Murphy lying at her feet, the back porch it was. After all, if you were afraid of a little chill in the air, you probably shouldn't move to northern Minnesota in the first place.

She sipped her tea slowly and listened carefully. The house was quiet. Luke had gone to bed. Tomorrow was his first day of eighth grade, and he'd promised to get a good night's sleep. Billy needed to get one, too. The first week of school was always an incredibly busy time at the library. But she knew she'd end the night talking to Cal. It was how she ended most weeknights now that he was getting settled into his new apartment in St. Paul. And she smiled, thinking about how much she loved his voice over the phone. She would prefer it *in person*, of course, but he'd be coming up to stay at the cabin this weekend. He'd already invited her and Luke to join him and his sister's family for a cookout on Friday night. Amazingly Luke had said yes to this, but only if he could bring Annabelle. Was something going on between them, she wondered, something more than friendship? She didn't know. Not yet.

It had been a month since she, Luke, and Cal all had dinner together at the Corner Bar. And she felt as though the three of them were still learning how . . . how to *be* together. So for now they had the occasional dinner, or boat ride with Allie's family, or trip to the beach to walk Murphy. Cal and Luke had done one thing alone. They'd gone to Duluth to test-drive Jeeps. And when Luke had gotten back, he'd been in a good mood. When she'd asked him about it though, he'd shrugged in a noncommittal way. Billy had suppressed a smile. Luke, she knew, didn't want to make this *too* easy for her.

But though Luke seemed noncommittal about Cal, this was not the case with his dad and his two sisters. He and his dad Skyped once a week. He and his sisters more often. Billy had overheard a recent conversation in which Hannah and Eleanor were squabbling over who had talked to Luke the longest. Then Hannah had asked Luke if he was good at math; she was having trouble with fractions. He'd gallantly offered to help her. Billy noticed that Erin, Wesley's wife, was polite but reserved with Luke. Clearly this was an adjustment process for all of them. What a summer!

She marveled at how much had changed over the course of the last three months. Before June her life had seemed relatively calm, if not downright predictable. There was Luke, the library, Rae, her mom, and Murphy. They were, in many ways, the sum total of her life. Now she had Luke's relationships with Wesley, his sisters, and Cal to consider. And, of course, there was her own relationship with Cal, which continued to deepen. (More than once she'd daydreamed about getting married to Cal and perhaps having a child with him, too.) She couldn't quite imagine how all this would work, and she didn't want to get ahead of herself. But there it was. In any case, her life had not gotten simpler this summer; it had gotten more complicated. That wasn't a bad thing. It was fuller and richer, too. She remembered something Pop-Pop had said to her the night he'd given her the envelope with Wesley's contact information: life *outside* a Jane Austen novel usually was complicated.

Murphy stirred now and looked up at Billy, his liquid brown eyes patient but also plaintive. He was probably pining for his comfy bed in the corner of her room. "I know, Murph," Billy said, petting him. "It's late." She started to gather up her things, but there was only her empty mug to carry inside with her. No Jane Austen tonight. She noticed then that she'd had less time and less need for her ritual lately. Over the years, Austen's novels had offered Billy so many things: comfort, escape, wisdom, truth, beauty, wit, love, and of course, flawlessly happy endings. She would always be grateful to them. But now it was time for Billy to get out there in that big, messy, imperfect world. "What do you say?" she asked Murphy. He wagged his tail obligingly.

EPILOGUE

There's a good turnout this year, isn't there?" Billy commented, standing next to Rae on the front steps of the library. It was the Saturday of Columbus Day weekend, the first of three days of the annual Friends of the Library book sale, and the two of them were watching as several dozen people browsed through the books that volunteers had arranged on folding tables on the sidewalk in front of the library.

"It's the best turnout I've ever seen," Rae said with satisfaction. "And believe me, I've seen *a lot* of these sales. Of course, it helps that it's such a nice day," she added with a little sigh of pleasure.

"Absolutely," Billy agreed. They'd had an early cold snap this fall. When Billy had gone out to walk Murphy that morning, the grass was white with frost and the chilly air smelled of wood smoke. But now it was almost noon, and the sun felt warm on Billy's upturned face. Still, the leaves on the oak trees outside the library were already splashed with gold. By late afternoon, Billy knew, she would be glad of the wool cardigan she'd worn over her cotton dress.

"So, how's Luke doing?" Rae asked.

"He's doing . . . he's doing *really* well," Billy said, knowing that she was not exaggerating when she said this. "I mean, he and Wesley are still adjusting to their new relationship. It's a work in progress."

"Well, it would be, wouldn't it?" Rae said. "I wish there was a video of the two of them seeing each other for the first time, though."

"Honestly, Rae, it never even occurred to me to film it. I was too nervous even to think straight," Billy said.

"Can I see the picture again, though?" Rae asked now.

Billy took her phone out of her dress pocket, scrolled to find the picture, and handed it to Rae. She'd taken it of father and son sitting in the booth at the coffee shop. Luke had it, too. It was his phone's wallpaper now.

"What do you think?" she asked Rae, looking over her shoulder at her phone screen. "Do you see a resemblance?"

"Oh, absolutely," Rae said. "I mean, Luke has your coloring. But the shape of his eyes, his chin, his jawline . . . yeah, it's all there. He's his father's son. And lucky for him, his father's not bad-looking."

"No, he's not," Billy said. But she saw something in the photo that Rae might not have. She saw Luke's shy smile as he sat beside a father who looked bemused to have found himself with a thirteen-year-old son who, a month before, he hadn't known existed.

"And what about his wife? Is she getting comfortable with this?" Rae asked, raising an eyebrow.

"Well, at first, as you know, it was hard for her," Billy admitted. "But with two daughters who are so excited about having an older brother . . . I think that's helped. Luke was Skyping with them last night. He might visit them over his spring break. We're not sure yet."

"Really?"

Billy nodded. "Wesley told Luke they could go to this place called the Great Bear Rainforest. There are Kermode bears there that you can observe—from a safe distance—so Luke is pretty excited about that. We'll see. Fingers crossed." Billy glanced now at her watch. "Oh, Rae. I have to go. It's almost twelve. I'm supposed to meet Luke and Cal at Pearl's for lunch."

Rae shook her head admiringly. "I don't know how you do it, Billy. At the beginning of the summer, Luke had zero fathers, and now he's got two."

"I wouldn't go *that* far." Billy smiled. Cal had told her he was in uncharted territory. He wanted to support her as a parent but didn't want to overstep his boundaries with Luke. Fortunately, Luke seemed to like Cal, though he was still somewhat reserved around him.

"Speaking of Cal, how are things going for you two? Long-distance relationship and all."

Billy smiled, remembering last weekend at Cal's cabin. They'd borrowed a motorboat from his sister and had taken a picnic out on the lake. Later that evening, he cooked a delicious pasta dinner and they cuddled on the couch in front of a roaring fire. (Luke had been away for the weekend visiting his grandma and his new friend, Travis.) The long distance hadn't diminished Billy and Cal's feelings for each other. Far from it.

"Well," Rae broke into her thoughts, "I guess I know the answer to that question by the look on your face. Now get going," she said cheerfully.

As Billy headed down the steps, Mara called out to her. "Hi, Mara," Billy said. "I guess I shouldn't be surprised to see you here," she added, smiling warmly.

"I guess not," Mara said. "I have a question, though. Are these books really for sale?" She held up Billy's box set of Jane Austen novels. She'd put them in the donation bin earlier in the week.

"Yes. They really are. Why do you ask?"

"Because they're so beautiful," Mara said. "Why would anybody want to give them away?"

"Well, to support a good cause," Billy said reasonably. "And to make space for more books at home. And . . . to make time for other things they might want to do," she added gently, not wanting to put a damper on Mara's enthusiasm for the box set.

"Okay," Mara said, apparently satisfied with this answer. "I just wanted to make sure it wasn't a mistake. I mean, they're only ten dollars." She pointed at the price tag a volunteer had stuck on them.

"Ten dollars is still a lot of money for someone your age," Billy said. "Are you sure you can afford them?"

"Uh-huh. I've been saving for this sale all summer."

"I'll bet you have," Billy said. "Have you ever read Jane Austen, Mara?"

Mara shook her head.

"Well, then, you are in for a real treat," Billy said.

"Is there . . . is there love in them?" Mara asked, a little shyly.

Billy resisted the urge to smile. So Mara *did* think

about things other than books. "Oh, yeah. There's love in them. *Big-time love*." She reached for the box set and peeled the price tag off. "For you, Mara, these are free," she said. "There. Now you have ten dollars to spend on other books."

"But . . . can you do that?" Mara asked, looking around furtively.

"I can," Billy assured her. "I can do that for an avid reader like you. I'll tell Ms. Swanson they're on the house," she added of the volunteer in charge of the book sale.

"Thank you," Mara said, pleased. "I'm going to browse a little more."

Billy, surprising them both, gave her a quick hug. Then, realizing she was running late for her lunch with Cal and Luke, she hurried across the leaf-strewn street to Pearl's.

PRAISE FOR
FIRST SEAL

"John Kennedy was right. You have left your mark. The U.S. Navy SEALs will bear your mark as long as they and the freedom they fight for exists."
—U.S. Navy Admiral Whitey Taylor, to Roy Boehm

"Anyone who has wondered how the elite, Herculean U.S. Navy SEALs became so stalwart has only to read this autobiography of the group's founder. . . . A grizzled hell-raiser of a Cold Warrior, Boehm was handpicked to create a Navy commando team in the aftermath of the Bay of Pigs Invasion. If the Boehm presented in this rollicking narrative is genuine . . . then the SEALs had much to live up to. . . . Hair-raisers abound, but the book's best portions involve Boehm's ongoing secret friendship with an enemy Vietcong commander, Minh, with whom Boehm shares a warrior spirit. A short chapter on marital strife . . . is positively hysterical. Unflinchingly patriotic, this memoir of a tough guy with heart will likely be spotted in the clutches of young men at Navy recruiting centers."
—*Publishers Weekly*

"Roy Boehm was a hard-as-nails, throat-slitting, unconventional warrior. He stamped the U.S. Navy SEALs with his personality, which is one reason they are the toughest fighters on earth. *FIRST SEAL* is damned good, as brutal and violent as a knife fight in the dark."
—Stephen Coonts

Books by Charles W. Sasser

First SEAL (coauthored with Roy Boehm)
Smoke Jumpers
Always a Warrior
Homicide!
Last American Heroes (coauthored with Michael Sasser)
The 100 Kill
One Shot—One Kill (coauthored with Craig Roberts)
Shoot to Kill
The Walking Dead (coauthored with Craig Roberts)

Available from POCKET BOOKS